SURRENDERING TO THE SHERIFF

BY
DELORES FOSSEN

Published in Great Britain 2015
by Mills & Boon, an imprint of Harlequin (UK) Limited,
Eton House, 18-24 Paradise Road, Richmond, Surrey, TW9 1SR

ISBN: 978-0-263-25310-8

46-0715

Harlequin (UK) Limited's policy is to use papers that are natural, renewable and recyclable products and made from wood grown in sustainable forests. The logging and manufacturing processes conform to the legal environmental regulations of the country of origin.

Printed and bound in Spain
by CPI, Barcelona

Delores Fossen, a *USA TODAY* bestselling author, has sold over fifty novels with millions of copies of her books in print worldwide. She's received the Booksellers' Best Award and the RT Reviewers' Choice Award, and was a finalist for a prestigious RITA® Award. You can contact the author through her webpage at www.dfossen.net.

Chapter One

Sheriff Aiden Braddock shut the door behind him, tossed his truck keys on the kitchen counter.

And stopped cold.

He didn't hear anything unusual. The whir of the A/C and fridge. The April breeze rattling the oaks outside the window over the sink. All the sounds he should be hearing, but he still got the gut feeling that something wasn't right.

Since that gut feeling had saved his butt a time or two during his time as county sheriff, Aiden listened to it.

He drew his Glock from his holster.

Aiden didn't move yet. He just stood there a few more moments. Listening. And then he heard the thing that didn't belong. A whisper, maybe. Or somebody breathing. Because he lived alone, there darn sure shouldn't be anyone else whispering or breathing in his house.

"Mom?" Aiden called out just to make sure. Though it'd been longer than a blue moon since she came out to his place. Too far in the sticks, she had always complained.

"Laine? Shelby?" Aiden added in case it was one of his sisters. Again, a serious long shot, since they rarely visited, either.

No answer. But he hadn't expected one.

Whatever was going on, this likely wasn't a social visit and could even involve some attempted bodily harm. After all, he was the county sheriff and had riled more than a person or two over the past decade. One of those riled people had perhaps come to settle an old score.

Aiden huffed. He was so not in the mood to bash some heads, but he might have to do just that.

"Let's make this easy for you," Aiden called out. "I'm a damn good shot. Plus, I'm hungry, tired and not feeling up to any idiot who's stupid enough to break into a lawman's house."

"Aiden," someone said in a hoarse whisper.

Even though the person hardly made any sound when she spoke, Aiden thought he recognized the voice.

Kendall.

But that didn't make any sense. This was the last place on earth she'd come.

Especially after...well, just *after*.

Aiden didn't lower his gun, but he inched his way toward the sound of her whisper—in his living room. It was just a few yards away past a half wall, but he kept watch all around him. Kept listening, too. Until he could move into the arched opening that divided the rooms, and he snapped his gun in the direction where he'd pinpointed Kendall's voice.

His heart slammed against his chest.

Because it was Kendall O'Neal all right, but this definitely wasn't a social visit. She was on her knees in the center of the floor, and there was a hulking man on each side of her. The men were wearing black ski masks, and both had automatics pointed right at her head.

"Drop the gun, Sheriff Braddock," the bigger one on the right growled.

Aiden held on to his Glock, trying to figure out what

the devil was going on here. He didn't get many clues from Kendall. She only shook her head. Like an apology or something.

But that was pure fear in her wide eyes.

He didn't see any signs of injury, but then most of her body that he could see was covered with a pale blue shirt, skirt and business jacket—her lawyering clothes. However, her hair was a mess, her blond locks tangled on her shoulders.

So maybe she'd been in a scuffle with these guys after all.

Kendall wasn't the messy-hair type. Nope. All priss and polish for her and never a hair out of place. People didn't call her the ice princess for nothing.

However, that wasn't an ice-princess look she was giving him now.

"What do you want?" Aiden asked the men.

"Your gun on the floor." Again, it was the one on the right who answered. No unusual accent. He was a Texan. And the nondescript dark pants and T-shirt didn't give Aiden any clues, either.

"Do it *now*," the man added, and he jammed his gun against Kendall's head. "Or else she'll pay the price."

The last thing any lawman wanted to do was surrender his weapon, but Aiden was wearing his usual backup gun in a boot holster. Maybe he'd be able to get to it in time if things turned uglier than they already were.

Of course, things were already plenty ugly enough.

Aiden didn't make any fast moves. He eased his gun onto the floor. "Now, what's this about?" he demanded. Thankfully, he still sounded like a sheriff even though it was hard to sound badass and in charge with guns pointed at Kendall.

"You're going to do us a favor," the gunman said. Even

though the ski mask covered most of the gunman's face, Aiden could have sworn the guy was smirking. "And if you don't, then we'll hurt Kendall here. Won't kill her at first. But we'll use her to make sure you cooperate."

The threat was real enough—the *real* guns were proof of that—but Aiden had to shake his head. "You do know that Kendall O'Neal and I aren't exactly on speaking terms, right? Everybody in town knows it. So why use her to get me to do anything for you?"

But his question ground to a halt, and Aiden's gaze snapped back to her.

"This is some kind of sick game, isn't it?" Though he couldn't imagine why Kendall would be playing it with these two armed thugs. "Is this connected to your sister?"

Aiden didn't wait for an answer. His attention went back to her captors. If they were indeed linked to her sister and not paid help trying to trick him into doing something crazier than what they were already doing.

"Just in case you don't know," Aiden told the men, "Kendall's half sister, Jewell, is about to stand trial for murdering my father twenty-three years ago. If this was a real hostage situation, you'd have taken someone that I actually care a rat's you know what about."

Kendall flinched at his stinging remark, but she quickly recovered. The fear, or fake fear, was still in her green cat eyes, and she hiked up her chin in that way that always riled him to the core. She looked darn haughty when she did that.

"There are things you don't know." Her voice cracked on the last word. A nice, theatrical touch.

"Clearly," Aiden said with a boatload of sarcasm. "But let me guess. You're a thousand steps past the desperate stage, and you'd do anything to save your precious, murdering sister. So you want me to try to fix the trial or something."

Aiden rammed his thumb against his chest and had to finish through clenched teeth. "You picked the wrong mark, Kendall. I don't break the law for anybody, especially the likes of you."

And he got another lightbulb moment.

A very bad one. One brought on by the *likes of you* comment. It hadn't been that long ago that he said those very words to her.

Not in the heat of the moment like now.

More like *after* the heat.

Yeah, Kendall and he had had the hots for each other since middle school. Forbidden fruit and all that crap. Aiden had always resisted her because he'd known it would tear his family apart.

Until three months ago.

He'd had to kill a man that day. A domestic disturbance gone wrong. Then he'd had a run-in with his mother. Then another run-in with one of Jewell's smart-mouthed daughters. To make matters worse, he'd dropped by the Bluebonnet for a drink or two. Which had turned into four. All right, five.

And he'd run into Kendall.

Aiden hadn't asked her what kind of bad day she'd been trying to erase with those shots of high-end whiskey she was downing like water. But the drinks had dumbed him down just enough that he'd gone over to talk to her. A mistake.

A big one.

Because the next thing Aiden knew, they were doing more than talking. They'd landed in bed for some drunken sex, and he'd committed one of the worst mistakes he could ever have made.

Did that night play a part in this, too?

Aiden hadn't been very nice to her the next morning what with his hangover and regret. That was where the *likes of you* comment had come into play. Because he'd wanted to leave immediately, find a big rock and hit himself in the head with it. But maybe Kendall thought she was a woman scorned, and paired with her obsession to clear her sister's name, perhaps the desperation had spilled over to this.

"Get out," Aiden ordered them, and he reached down to pick up his gun.

Aiden didn't get far before the shot blasted through the room and sent his ears ringing. The bullet hadn't been aimed at him.

But rather at Kendall.

She screamed out in pain. Not a whimper, but a full-fledged, blood-chilling scream. For a good reason, too. The bullet had gone into her arm, tearing through her jacket sleeve and into her flesh.

Almost immediately, a bright red patch of blood started to spread over the fabric. She struggled, trying to clamp her hand over it, but he realized then that her wrists had been bound behind her back with plastic cuffs.

Aiden's instincts were to rush to her, to make sure she was okay. He would have done that for anyone. But when he started toward her, the guy on the left shifted his gun to Aiden.

"Move and she gets another bullet in the other arm," the man warned him.

Okay. So maybe this wasn't fake after all.

"You've got my attention," Aiden said. "But let's hurry along this little chat so I can get an ambulance out here for Kendall."

The talking guy shook his head. "Her injury isn't serious. Just a flesh wound. That doesn't mean the next one will be, though. We need her alive but not necessarily in one piece."

Aiden's heartbeat hadn't settled down since he first saw Kendall kneeling on the floor, and that didn't do much to slow it to normal.

"What do you want?" Aiden repeated.

"For you to destroy evidence lot BR6847-23." The guy didn't hesitate.

Normally, Aiden wouldn't have known what evidence that was. But he did in this case. It was recently found bone fragments.

His father's bone fragments.

And it was key evidence in the murder case against Jewell.

"So this is about your sister," he said to Kendall. Even though he no longer believed Kendall had orchestrated it. Not after taking that bullet.

She moaned, the sound of raw pain, and clamped her teeth over her bottom lip for a moment. "I don't know who hired these men," Kendall said, her voice shaking. "I was leaving work late, and they grabbed me in the parking lot. They brought me here."

Even though there weren't a lot of details in that, Aiden could almost see it, and it turned his stomach a little. Kendall wasn't a large woman, and these two goons towered over her. She had to have been terrified.

Still was.

No one was that good an actor.

"Jewell's daughters could be behind this," Aiden said just to see what kind of reaction he'd get from them. No one argued. But then, he didn't see anything in their body language that he'd hit a home run, either.

Of course, who else would it be?

Jewell had abandoned her husband and three sons all those years ago when she left town under the cloud of suspicion of murdering Aiden's father. The suspicion had finally been confirmed when the case was reopened, and those bone fragments had been discovered. Jewell was finally where she belonged.

In jail.

And she hadn't exactly mended fences with her own sons and ex-husband.

Still, she had two daughters, a stepson and a now-shot half sister on her side. Once Kendall was safe, Aiden would go to Jewell's spawn and step-spawn and demand answers.

First, though, he had to get Kendall out of this.

"I guess you'll hold her until I destroy the evidence?" Aiden asked.

The talker nodded. "The sooner you do it, the sooner you can have her back."

Not likely.

Except that didn't make sense, either. Jewell's kids knew she loved her much younger half sister. In fact, word was that Jewell thought of Kendall more like a daughter than a half sister.

So why would Jewell's kids have put Kendall at risk like this?

"Why?" Aiden repeated out loud and shook his head. "And that *why* covers a lot of territory. There's plenty about this that doesn't make sense."

Kendall opened her mouth. Closed it. Then swallowed hard. "I thought Laine might have said something."

Aiden shook his head. "My sister? What does she have to do with this?"

"Laine saw me coming out of the doctor's office. I swear, Aiden, I was going to leave town next week. I wasn't going to put any of this on you. I know how you and your family feel about me."

There was a gun trained on him, but Aiden went some steps closer so he could look Kendall straight in the eye. "What the heck are you talking about?"

She made a sound. Sort of a helpless moan that came from deep within her chest. "They took me because I'm pregnant. Because they knew they could use that for leverage."

Kendall's breath shuddered. "Aiden, the baby I'm carrying is yours."

Chapter Two

It was hard to think through the pain, but Kendall braced herself for Aiden's reaction. She expected him to curse or yell. To ask what she'd already asked herself—how could this have happened? But other than a few moments of silence, that was it.

Those moments of silence were his only physical response to the baby.

Unlike her.

She was sweating now. Not because it was hot but because her arm was throbbing. Yes, it was just a flesh wound, but she was bleeding, and she needed the wound cleaned and tended. Later, if there was a later, she'd deal with Aiden's reaction.

Heaven knew what that would be.

"How do you think this is going to work?" Aiden's attention shifted from her to the gunman who'd been doing all the talking.

"You'll leave now. Go to the evidence storage room. You shouldn't have any trouble getting in there, since you're the county sheriff. Tell them you need to look at something else that involves another case. And once you're inside, destroy the evidence."

Aiden shook his head. "It won't be that simple. There are surveillance cameras."

"Then figure out a way around them," the gunman snapped. "After all, your kid's life depends on it."

Now Aiden cursed, but it was under his breath. "And what about Kendall? You shot her. It can't be good for my *kid* to have his or her mother injured like that."

"Don't worry about her. We'll get her to a doctor. The only thing you have to worry about is doing what you've been told." The man took something from his shirt pocket and tossed it to Aiden.

A cell phone.

"It'll take videos," he explained. "Film yourself destroying the evidence and send it to the number already programmed into the phone."

"And then you'll let Kendall go?" Aiden asked with plenty of skepticism in his tone.

"Eventually. In a day or two. We got no reason to keep her, and truth is, she's a pain in the butt. I, for one, will be glad to give her back to you. She bit me," he growled, glancing down at his wrist.

She had indeed resorted to biting and clawing. She'd done everything to try to escape. But when he threatened to hurt the baby, Kendall knew she had no choice but to stop fighting and look for a better way out of this.

So far, she hadn't come up with one.

This definitely didn't qualify as *better.*

"Hate to burst your bubble," Aiden said, "but if you hold Kendall for a day or two, someone will report her missing. And people will look for her. You really want to raise those kinds of red flags, since half of her kin are lawmen?"

Kendall groaned softly. "I've already told my friends, Jewell and the rest of my family that I'd be leaving town tomorrow morning. I said I needed some downtime and for them not to be surprised if they didn't hear from me for a while."

The gunman laughed. "She tied it up in a pretty little bow for us, didn't she?"

Yes, she did, but Kendall intended to shove that proverbial bow down his throat the first chance she got. She wasn't in any position to win a physical fight with him, but sooner or later, he'd let down his guard.

She hoped.

Aiden's gaze came back to her. "I'm figuring you didn't ask to be here, but I know you won't shed any tears over this evidence being destroyed."

"You're wrong," she let him know after she choked back another wave of pain. "I don't want my sister convicted of murder, but I don't want her free like this, either. And neither would Jewell."

The corner of Aiden's mouth lifted in an expression she knew all too well. The Braddock smirk. As an O'Neal and Jewell's sister, she'd been on the receiving end of it a lot since their families were at odds for twenty-three years.

"Time for you to leave," the gunman said to Aiden. "Oh, and don't bother to pull some kind of stunt like pretending to leave so you can double back and rescue her. Kendall will be tucked away someplace safe, where you can't find her."

There was no telling what they'd consider someplace safe, but she seriously doubted these snakes had her safety in mind beyond using her to try to prod Aiden into committing a felony.

Aiden stood there, his glare shifting among them, and he cursed again. "Give me at least two hours, and you'll have your video of me destroying the bone fragments."

Oh, mercy. He was going to do it.

Kendall had thought he'd be able to negotiate his way out of this. Or else fight his way out of it. She figured the last thing on earth Aiden would do was destroy evidence to protect her.

Except it was not just her.

Even though they were enemies, she knew that Aiden was an honorable man. He wouldn't risk an unborn child's life.

Any unborn child.

Still, honor aside, he'd have a heck of a time dealing with the consequences. And worse. Kendall was terrified that destroying the evidence wouldn't even help the baby and her. She hadn't seen either of the men's faces. Had no idea who they were. But they might not let her live anyway.

The thought of it broke her heart.

Not for her own life but for the baby's. This child hadn't been planned. Heck, it hadn't even been on her personal radar. But she'd loved the baby from the moment that she'd known she was carrying it. However, she never expected Aiden would feel the same.

Ever.

"Get her to the doctor," Aiden growled. *"Now."* And he reached for his gun.

"Nope," the man said while Aiden was in mid-reach. "I'm sure you'll have no trouble coming up with another one. We'll keep this one for now."

Kendall's imagination started to run wild. Once Aiden had destroyed the evidence, they wouldn't have a reason to keep her alive. They could use Aiden's gun to kill her and then somehow set him up to take the blame for the crime.

The baby would be motive.

Because an autopsy would reveal the pregnancy, and a DNA test would prove he was the child's father. These men could make it look as if Aiden had completely lost it when he learned of the baby and killed her in cold blood.

"Oh, and, Braddock?" the man said to Aiden. "We'll know if you call your buddies at the county sheriff's office. Or any other law enforcement agency in the area for that matter. Because we've got *ears* in all those places."

That was probably a bluff. Unless, of course, these guys had managed to plant some listening devices.

"Aiden," she said before she could stop herself. Kendall hated to beg for his help, but she would. To save the baby, she'd do anything.

A flash of something went through his eyes, but Kendall had no idea what it meant. Aiden gave the men, and her, one last look before he strolled out.

Kendall tried to tamp down the panic. They wouldn't kill her until they were sure Aiden had destroyed the evidence, and he'd said that would take about two hours. Not much time. But during those two hours, she had to find a way to escape.

One of the men stayed next to her, the gun still pointed at her head, and the other went to the window and peered out. Watching Aiden, no doubt.

Another sound only spiked the panic building inside her.

Aiden's truck engine.

She heard it start, and then he pulled away from the house.

His place wasn't that large by Texas standards, just a couple of acres of pasture for his horses, a barn and the house. From the man's vantage point at the window, he would be able not only to see Aiden leave, but also to see him drive out onto the road.

"He's out of sight," the man said a moment later.

Still, they didn't move. The time seemed to crawl by,

and her throbbing arm and building panic didn't help. Finally, the one who'd been silent latched on to her shoulder and hauled her to her feet.

"Don't do anything stupid," the other one snarled, "or you'll get another bullet."

Kendall was positive that wasn't a bluff, but before this ordeal was over, she would almost certainly have to do something *stupid.* Or at least risky.

As soon as they started moving, she tried to work the plastic cuffs that bound her wrists behind her back. They were loose, but strong for mere plastic, and they seemed to tighten with each tug.

Those tugs also didn't help the jolts of pain going through her arm. And the pain didn't help the dizziness. She'd been light-headed since this whole ordeal started, but it was more than just a light head now.

The gunshot and the fear were no doubt to blame.

Kendall drew in several hard breaths and forced herself to look down at the wound. At the gaping hole in her jacket. It turned her stomach, but she tried to make sure she wasn't bleeding out.

She wasn't.

There was blood all right, but there didn't seem to be much more than when he'd initially shot her. That was something at least. A serious blood loss could cause her to miscarry.

The men finally led her out the front door, the same way they'd brought her in after one of them had jimmied the lock. Aiden had a security system, but it hadn't been on. He probably hadn't felt the need because he was the sheriff.

Too bad.

If the system had been armed, Aiden might have been alerted and could have nipped this in the bud.

They went onto the porch, down the steps and through the yard toward a thick cluster of trees to the right where the men had left the SUV they'd used to kidnap her from the parking lot of her law office. After they'd grabbed her, they'd stopped several miles outside town to change the license plates and to make a call. Kendall hadn't learned a thing from that call, because they'd said only one thing to the person on the other end of the line.

"We have her."

No names used. No hint of the identity of the person they'd called.

So, who had put all this insanity into motion?

Despite Aiden's accusations and suspicions, it wasn't Jewell or her daughters. Not Jewell's stepson, Seth, either. Yes, the three of them loved Jewell, but they wouldn't resort to this. Unfortunately, other than those three children, Kendall and Jewell's lawyer, Robert Joplin, there weren't many people who wanted Jewell to beat this murder charge.

But clearly someone wanted just that.

When they were about ten yards from the SUV, Kendall stumbled just to see how fast the men would react, and she got her answer.

Fast.

Both of them grabbed her, and within a second, she had a gun jammed against her left temple again.

"Keep it up, and you'll be sorry," one of the men growled.

No matter what she did, she could be sorry, but Kendall cooperated.

For now.

She continued toward the SUV and didn't resist when the men practically shoved her inside. As they'd done on the drive there, they buckled her into a seat belt in the middle, and the man who'd spoken only a few words dropped down behind her. The one who'd been doing all the talking walked around the front of the SUV toward the driver's side.

But then he stopped.

That certainly got her attention, but it got his partner's, too. "What's wrong?" the man asked. Unlike the other one, he had some kind of thick accent.

The man still outside raised his finger in a wait-a-second gesture and lifted his head. Listening for something.

Or maybe *someone*.

Kendall hoped and prayed that it was someone who could get her away from these goons.

"Don't move," the guy with the accent said to her, and he stepped out of the SUV. Not far. Just a few inches outside the open door, and he, too, listened. His gaze also darted all around the heavily treed area.

Kendall looked, as well. She tried to pick through the trees and underbrush, but it was spring with everything in full bloom, so she couldn't see anything.

However, she thought that she might have heard something, like a twig snap. The men didn't miss it. With their guns raised, they pivoted in the direction of the sound.

Again, nothing.

For several seconds anyway.

Then the shot zinged through the air. It hadn't been fired by one of her captors but had instead come from the area of that dense underbrush.

It had to be Aiden.

He would have known to cut through the woods and come back after them.

Her captors immediately lifted their guns to return fire, and Kendall sank down into the seat as far as she could. She also looked for something, anything, she could use to cut through the plastic cuffs.

Outside, both men fired, their bullets blasting through the air. She quickly added another prayer that Aiden hadn't been shot.

Both men continued to fire. Kendall continued to struggle, and even though it made the pain in her arm much worse, she managed to move her hand so she could pop the button on the seat belt. It slid off her, and she got to the floor. Not just for protection but so she could look under the seat.

There was a first aid kit.

She fumbled through it as best she could and found a pair of scissors. They were small, the kind used for cutting bandages and not restraints. Still, they would have to do.

It was hard enough just to pick them up with her hands behind her back. Harder still to try to make any cut. But she had to try.

Kendall glanced out. Both men were now at the front of the SUV and they were tearing up the woods with their bullets. Even though Aiden's nearest neighbor was a half mile away, maybe he would hear the noise and report it if Aiden hadn't already called for backup.

The man with the accent looked into the SUV. His gaze connected with hers through the gap between the front seats, and he said something to his partner that she couldn't hear. But the man must have realized she was trying to escape, because he hurried toward the driver's door.

Coming for her.

Her heart was pumping now. The adrenaline, too. Kendall worked even harder at trying to cut through the plastic. She could feel them giving way. Little by little. But the man was practically right on her.

The plastic cuffs gave way, finally.

Just as the man crawled across the seat and grabbed for her.

But Kendall brought up the scissors and stabbed him in the face. Because of the ski mask, she wasn't sure what part of him she hit, but he howled in pain and came at her.

Kendall hit him again with the scissors. This time in his neck.

He made some kind of strangled sound, and she saw the blood. Nothing like her gunshot wound. There was lots of it, and the agonizing sound that he made sent his partner running to him.

Kendall knew she had mere seconds at best. The side door was already open, and she barreled through it. She hadn't realized just how dizzy and weak she was until her feet touched the ground.

Everything started to spin.

And she would no doubt have fallen if someone hadn't caught her by the arm. She could just barely make out Aiden's face.

"Come on," Aiden said.

He turned, fired a shot at the men, and then he and Kendall started running.

Chapter Three

Aiden pulled Kendall behind the nearest tree, shoving her against it so that he could lean out and try to stop these guys from coming after them.

And they were coming all right.

Well, one of them anyway.

The other one had his hand clamped to his neck and was slumped against the SUV. Aiden hoped that whatever the heck his injury was, it would kill him. Harsh, yes, but maybe necessary for Kendall's and his survival. One armed man was enough to deal with, considering that he had an injured, pregnant woman to rescue.

Pregnant.

That one little word came with a boatload of emotions attached and packed a wallop. Especially since Kendall was the one who was pregnant.

With his baby, no less.

That sounded about as unright as something could sound, but he had indeed slept with her. He'd also used protection. However, something had clearly gone wrong other than them just landing in bed together.

Fate had to be laughing its butt off about that. Whitt Braddock's son and Jewell's sister together, making a baby.

The town, and his family, would have a field day with

it. That'd be minor, though, compared to the firestorm going on inside Aiden, but he pushed all those feelings aside for now. It was going to take every bit of his concentration to get them out of this alive.

Aiden had already called for backup. Not using normal channels in case these brainless wonders had indeed managed to plant bugs in his office and others. Instead he'd used his personal cell to phone his deputy Leland Hawks.

With any luck Leland would be here within twenty minutes.

That was way too long for Leland to help save Kendall and him, but Aiden had told the deputy to make a loud approach. Lots of sirens. Hopefully, the noise would send the guys on the run so that Aiden could track them down.

If this fight didn't end with the men's deaths, that is.

Aiden wanted one of them alive, though, if at all possible. Because when this was all said and done, he wanted answers as to who was really behind this.

Another shot smacked into the tree. Though it was hard to hold back, Aiden didn't return fire yet. He didn't have a lot of ammo and didn't want to waste any bullets in case this went on too long. But he did glance out at the pair to check on their latest position. They were in front of the SUV again. Where they were well protected.

Aiden couldn't say the same for Kendall and him.

The tree wasn't that wide, and he figured these two had brought enough firepower with them to tear right through the young oak. Added to that, there weren't any wider, thicker trees nearby for Kendall and him to move behind. Just plenty of underbrush and wildflowers, and none of that would stop bullets.

Kendall looked up at him, her eyes wide. Her breath gusting. Her body trembling. "Thank you for coming back for me."

That riled him. Of course he'd come back for her. It was his job, and there was no way he'd let something personal get in the way of the badge. She probably hadn't meant it as an insult, but it was.

"I found some scissors in the SUV, cut off the plastic cuffs, but then I got so dizzy," she added.

She was still terrified, just as she had been kneeling on the floor of his house. Aiden didn't want to know what kind of effect this was having on her unborn child.

It couldn't be good.

But it was better than the alternative. If those men had gotten Kendall away from his place, they would have killed her. Even if he'd done what they asked, that wouldn't have saved her life.

Then they would have come after him.

"You've lost some blood," he reminded her. "That's why you got dizzy."

No need to mention that it could be shock, but he hoped that wasn't the cause. He might need Kendall's help before this was over, and something like shock could incapacitate her.

"When the smaller one came at me, I stabbed him with the scissors," she said. "Twice."

She looked a little sick about that. Understandable. Most people were never in a position where they were forced to do bodily harm, but Aiden was thankful for the scissors and the stabbing.

"You did what you had to do," he let her know and then cursed himself for sounding so sympathetic.

He didn't want her to suffer. Not over some injury she'd managed to inflict on this homicidal idiot, but each kind word from him, each thought about this pregnancy nipped at barriers that had to stay in place when it came to Kendall.

"Leland's on the way," Aiden whispered when her trembling got worse. "That means we'll have backup soon, and we'll be okay."

Kendall nodded, and he figured she was trying to look a lot stronger than she felt right now.

Another bullet flew at them. Then another. And soon they were coming nonstop. Aiden had hoped it wouldn't come down to this, but the men were no doubt getting desperate, since they knew he probably had help on the way. That meant they had only two choices.

Escape or try to recover their hostage.

They appeared to be going for the latter, though the two had to know they could kill Kendall in the process. Of course, they could be doing cleanup.

Trying to eliminate *all* witnesses.

If so, these next few minutes were going to be bad, because Aiden had no intention of making an elimination easy for them. Nope. He was fighting back along with being fighting mad. How dare these morons pull a stunt like this in his own yard and house!

Now the problem was trying to figure out how to stop them from getting lucky with their elimination attempts.

Aiden knew every inch of his property, and there was a dry narrow gully about ten yards behind Kendall and him. Not as close as he would have liked, but maybe if he could distract these guys long enough, Kendall would be able to crawl to the gully, where she'd be better protected from the bullets.

"I didn't have any part in this," she said. Another look up at him.

Damn. He had enough uncomfortable things running through his mind right now without adding her emotions.

"Yeah. I figured that out." Too bad he had plenty of other things to figure out.

"And I meant what I said about leaving," Kendall added. "I had no intention of ever telling you about the baby."

The woman knew how to rile him. In the middle of a gunfight no less. Aiden didn't have a clue how he felt about this pregnancy, yet, but he darn sure hadn't wanted her to hide it from him. And Kendall had rattled that off as if he'd be pleased about her plan to sneak off.

Well, he wasn't.

Of course, right now he wasn't pleased about much of anything except that Kendall and he were still breathing.

Aiden glanced out at the two men again. They were still in place where he couldn't blow off any of their body parts. Then he glanced at Kendall.

But not at her face.

Too much emotion there for him to deal with, but he needed to see how her arm was holding up. The bleeding had stopped. That was something at least. But that gash was deep, and it had to be throbbing like a bad toothache.

"How does your arm feel?" Aiden asked, and he fired a shot at the men just so they wouldn't try to move closer.

"I'm okay."

A lie, for sure, but Aiden would take it for now. He'd already asked Leland to bring out an ambulance, but the medics wouldn't get close to the place with shots being fired. That was yet another reason for Aiden to put an end to this.

"I need you to get to the ground," Aiden said. "Stay behind me and stay down. Crawl to the gully." He tipped his head in that direction.

Kendall glanced over at the gully. Then at him. "But what about you?"

"I won't be far behind."

Possibly a lie as well, but Kendall had enough fear

running through her without his spelling out that there'd be no one to cover him if he tried to move from the tree to the gully. No, it was best for him to make his stand for as long as he could behind the tree.

She finally gave a shaky nod and inched herself lower to the ground. It wasn't easy. They were plastered against each other—her backside sliding against a part of him that needed no such touching. Especially from her. He got a split-second jolt of the blasted heat that'd always been there between them.

Thankfully, the fresh round of bullets slugged that heat aside.

He pushed Kendall all the way down until she was practically on her belly and then crouched by his side. "Move slowly if you have to." Because of her injured arm and the pregnancy. But Aiden was really hoping that she could do this fast.

Aiden leaned out, took aim at the front of the SUV and fired a shot just as Kendall started crawling.

She stayed down just as he'd ordered, and she moved through the wildflowers and other underbrush. Thankfully, fast. Still, Aiden fired another shot at the gunmen just to keep their attention on him. He breathed a little easier once he saw Kendall slide down and into the gully.

She was safe.

Well, maybe.

He'd parked just on the other side of the gully. Off the road and behind some trees. Aiden hadn't seen any other hired guns lurking around, but that didn't mean there couldn't have been some hiding.

The big talkative guy lifted his head, fired a couple of shots. Not the nonstop barrage like before. And in between the shots, Aiden heard the men talking. Or rather arguing.

Clearly, their plan had gone to Hades in a big ol' hand-basket by losing their hostage and what with one of them being on the business end of Kendall and her scissors. Now they were no doubt trying to figure out a way to salvage this, and it was possible the injured one needed some medical attention, too.

In the distance Aiden heard a welcome sound.

Sirens.

That got the men chattering even more, and Aiden braced himself for whatever they were going to try to throw at him next.

What they *threw* were bullets.

And lots of them.

The men fired into the tree. A volley of gunfire. All of it aimed at Aiden.

He ducked down, trying to shelter his body as best he could, but he was getting pelted with flying pieces of wood from the tree and other debris that the bullets were kicking up from the ground. There was no way he could lean out and try to get off a shot of his own. It'd be suicide, so he stayed put and prayed that he got a break soon.

He got it.

But it wasn't the break he had in mind. The shots slowed to a trickle, but even over the sound of the blasts, he heard another one.

The SUV.

One of them had started up the engine.

No. It was too soon for this to happen. Judging from the sirens, Leland was still a quarter of a mile out. Maybe more. These guys could get away before Leland even arrived.

Aiden moved to the other side of the tree, leaned out 't a fraction and saw the two men already in the SUV. ' one, the injured one on the passenger's side, was firing through the open door, and even though his aim seemed wobbly, he still hit the dang tree.

Aiden had to dive back behind it for cover.

"Stay down!" Kendall yelled.

He wanted to curse when he saw her lift her head. "*You* stay down," Aiden snarled right back at her.

Aiden leaned out again. Took aim at the guy who was firing. And he pulled the trigger.

His bullet smacked right into the man's chest, and just like that, the guy tumbled out of the SUV and onto the ground. If he wasn't dead, he soon would be. But that wasn't Aiden's concern now.

It was the driver.

The chatterbox gunman hit the accelerator and flew out onto the gravel road that fronted Aiden's property. He fishtailed, the tires bobbling over the uneven surface, but that didn't slow him down nearly enough.

Aiden raced out from cover, bracketing his shooting wrist with his left hand, and he kicked the injured gunman's weapon aside. In the same motion, Aiden took aim at the SUV.

The bullet Aiden fired slammed into the back window, shattering the glass into a million little pieces.

But the driver kept going.

Aiden ran after him, took another shot. He missed. Then another. That one hit the SUV. At the right angle to have injured the driver, but Aiden couldn't be certain of that.

Because the SUV sped away.

Chapter Four

Kendall watched while the medic dabbed the wound on her arm with antiseptic and gave her a shot. The throbbing pain quickly turned to fire, but she clamped her teeth over her bottom lip so that Aiden wouldn't hear the groan bubbling up in her throat. He already had enough to handle without adding more concerns about her injury.

Not that Kendall expected him to be overly concerned about her, but at this point, anything and everything would feel like more weight on his shoulders.

The gunman who'd gotten away.

The dead one Aiden had been forced to kill in a shootout.

And then, of course, the bombshell about the pregnancy.

Aiden wasn't dealing with that—yet. He was still on the phone with his deputy who had a team out searching for the man who'd shot her. It was his fifth call since they'd arrived at the Clay Ridge Hospital. She suspected there'd be plenty more before the night was over.

"I'll just do a couple of stitches," the medic said to her while he numbed the area around the wound with another shot. "Then I'll get you to the tech for an ultrasound."

A few stiches didn't sound serious at all, but the second

thing he said captured both Aiden's and her attention. Until his gaze snapped to hers, Kendall hadn't even been sure Aiden was listening to what the medic was saying, but he issued a quick "I'll call you right back" to his deputy and stared at the medic.

"An ultrasound?" Aiden questioned. "Is something wrong?"

The medic shook his head and got busy doing the stitches. "It's just a precaution, something Dr. Kreppner ordered because of the trauma Miss O'Neal's been through."

Kendall's breath rushed out. The emotions, too, and she was no longer able to choke back that groan. Sweet heaven, there had indeed been trauma—both physically and mentally—and the baby could have been hurt.

Aiden shifted his attention from the medic to her, and even though she couldn't fight back the tears, Kendall had no trouble seeing the conflict going on inside him. There was concern in his eyes, and the muscles in his jaw had turned to iron. Maybe because of the possible danger to the baby. Maybe because of her tears.

Or perhaps both.

"Don't borrow trouble," Aiden said to her, his voice a low growl. "You heard what he told you, that it's just a precaution."

Kendall nodded, but she wouldn't breathe easier until she knew that all was well. She was only twelve weeks pregnant, and she wasn't even sure what an ultrasound could tell them exactly. Hopefully, it would be plenty enough to rid her of this overwhelming fear.

Her tears continued, clearly something that didn't please Aiden, because he huffed and handed her some tissues that he grabbed from the examining table.

"Thanks." She blotted her eyes and cheeks, looked up at him. "And for what it's worth, I'm sorry."

That apology covered a multitude of things, including his learning about the baby and this attack that could have gotten them all killed.

Her *I'm sorry* didn't cause his jaw to relax, though. "We'll talk about the baby later. For now, I want to know anything you haven't told me about what those men said to you. And no, I'm not accusing you of being a part of it. I just need to know anything that'll help us find that dirtbag who drove away in the SUV."

Kendall didn't especially want to relive the images of the attack or her kidnapping, but she also didn't want to focus on the pain that the stitches were causing in her arm.

"I don't know either of them," she started. "At least I don't think I do."

Aiden latched right on to that. "You don't *think* you do? Does that mean maybe there's something you recognized?"

"Maybe," she had to concede. "There was possibly something familiar about the one who did most of the talking, but I just don't know what. The other, however... the dead one...he had an accent. Jamaican, perhaps, and he was black, because I saw his hands." She paused. "I'm guessing he didn't have an ID on him?"

"Nothing, but we're running his prints now. Once we know who he is, we might be able to figure out who hired him." Aiden stared at her, apparently waiting for her to suggest who that might have been.

"I don't have a clue who hired them, but it wasn't me or any of Jewell's kids."

"You're sure?" he pressed.

She nodded. Prayed she was right about that. "Rosalie, Rayanne and Seth all love Jewell and want her cleared of the murder charges, but they wouldn't put me at risk to do that."

"They know about the baby?" he snapped.

Kendall shook her head. "Only your sister Laine knows. Like I said, she saw me coming out of the OB clinic. Since she'd also somehow heard rumors about us being together that night at the bar, she put one and one together."

"And she didn't tell me," Aiden grumbled under his breath.

"Don't blame Laine. I begged her not to tell you or anyone else." Much to her surprise, it appeared that Laine had kept her secret.

That comment earned her a glare from Aiden. "She's my sister, and she should have told me."

Kendall was about to ask if he had actually even wanted to know, but the medic eased a bandage on her arm and stood.

"What you heard in this room stays in this room," Aiden warned the medic. "Got that?"

Since Aiden could win an intimidation contest hands down, the guy was smart to nod. "Follow me to the ultrasound room."

As she probably didn't look too steady, Aiden took hold of her arm and helped her stand. Good thing, too, because the dizziness returned with a vengeance, and she had no choice but to lean against him. Judging from the way the muscles in his body stiffened, he wasn't pleased about that. Still, he hooked his arm around her and led her up the hall.

"You were just going to leave town," Aiden said, clearly not pleased about that, either. Of course, she hadn't said anything yet that'd pleased him.

Kendall nodded. "I thought it was for the best."

"Well, it wasn't." He probably said that a lot louder than he'd intended, because the medic glanced back at them. "I had a right to know that I made a baby with you that night," Aiden added in a much lower voice.

He said *that night* as if it were profanity. Which to him it probably had been. Kendall had felt the same way, too, immediately afterward. Yes, Aiden and she had skirted around this attraction for years, but with their families at serious odds, a one-night stand had been a stupid thing to do.

"I won't think of this baby as a mistake," she clarified.

She figured he would disagree with that, but he didn't. Kendall also figured he wouldn't go into the ultrasound room, but once they reached it, Aiden waltzed right in.

"I'm staying," he insisted before she could give him an out.

Again, the medic looked at them, his volleyed glances finally landing on Kendall. "The tech won't be long, but I can wait here if you want." There was concern in both his tone and expression. However, Kendall shook her head to assure him that it was all right for him to go.

"It'll be okay." Well, she'd be safe with Aiden at least, but Kendall could feel a mighty storm coming her way.

About the baby.

About her decision to leave him out of this.

"Okay, then." The medic tipped his head to her arm. "If you need something for the pain, just let the ultrasound tech know, and I'll have the doc write a script."

Kendall thanked him, knowing that she wouldn't be taking any painkillers even if she needed them. They'd be too risky for the baby.

The medic stepped out, finally, and Aiden didn't wait long to get that storm started. "How long have you known you were pregnant?" he asked.

"For about two months." She probably would have figured it out sooner if she hadn't been in complete denial. Denial about a possible pregnancy anyway. The memories of that night had stayed with her.

Big-time.

She'd lusted after Aiden for so many years. Too many. They were both thirty-six now, and the heated looks had started about twenty-three years earlier. The heat clearly had some staying power, because even drunken sex had fulfilled more than a fantasy or two. Sadly, Aiden had lived up to those fantasies in spades. If any part of it had been lacking, she maybe could have finally pushed Aiden out of her head.

So much for that happening now.

Especially since he was right in front of her. And his scowl and bunched-up forehead weren't the lust killers that they should have been. Probably because even with a scowl, Aiden managed to make most men look just plain ordinary.

"Jewell doesn't know?" he asked.

Kendall shook her head. "I figured I'd tell her after the trial."

That deepened his scowl. "A trial that might not happen if the goon in the ski mask gets his way."

She hadn't even thought of that. If whoever was behind this couldn't get Aiden to destroy the evidence, then he or she might just hire someone else to do the job.

"I've had the evidence moved," Aiden said. "It's being couriered to the Ranger Lab in Austin. So Jewell's out of luck when it comes to that."

Maybe out of luck, period. The bone fragments had been identified as belonging to Aiden's father, and that meant Jewell had means, motive and opportunity to have killed the man who was supposedly her lover. It certainly didn't help that Jewell wasn't denying the deed.

And now this.

If this was linked back to Jewell, the DA could tack on some obstruction of justice charges along with other assorted felonies like kidnapping and attempted murder of a county sheriff.

"Even you have to admit that it would be stupid for anyone connected to Jewell to try to destroy evidence," she said.

Aiden made a sound of agreement. "Stupid, yes, but that doesn't mean it didn't happen. I'll be looking at Jewell's daughters and stepson. Joplin, too."

Jewell's lawyer, Robert Joplin. Of all the suspects that Aiden had just listed, he was the one at the top of Kendall's list. Because Joplin was hopelessly in love with Jewell. Had been for years and would do anything to save her. However, that didn't mean Joplin was the only one with motive for this attempted fiasco.

"I hope you'll look at your own family, too," Kendall tossed out there. "Your mother and sister Shelby aren't exactly fans of Jewell, and they might have done something like this to make her look even more guilty."

And while that wasn't as strong of a motive as her family's, Jewell knew that Aiden's family had secrets.

Secrets that even Aiden might not know.

She braced herself for him to jump to their defense. Didn't happen. "I'll be talking to them and anyone else who hated Jewell and my father."

Good. But then, she'd figured all along that Aiden would be thorough. He was loyal to his family. Well, mostly. He didn't exactly have a friendly relationship with his mother, but Aiden would never forget that he was a Braddock.

Never.

Ditto for remembering that she was an O'Neal.

The door eased open, and Aiden automatically reached for his gun. After what'd happened with the gunmen, Kendall didn't blame him, but she was thankful it was a false alarm.

"I'm Becky Lovelle," the young blonde said. "I'll be doing your ultrasound."

Kendall certainly hadn't forgotten about the ultrasound, but her strained discussion with Aiden had pushed the reminder of a possible problem to the fringes of her thoughts. No fringes now, though. Her heart went into overdrive.

"This won't hurt," the woman said.

But Kendall was already tuning her out, her attention nailed to the screen. It was blank now, but soon she'd see her precious baby. Hopefully, unharmed.

Aiden didn't move closer. In fact, he leaned against the wall and watched from there. Even when the tech pushed up Kendall's top and shoved down her skirt to expose her belly and coat it with some goopy gel, he kept watching.

Kendall suddenly felt way too bare with Aiden in the room, but there was no way she'd convince him to leave. There was no way to convince Aiden of a lot of things, and once she had the all-clear with the ultrasound, she'd need to figure out a way to handle him and this situation.

Aiden wasn't going to like it when she insisted she leave.

But she would insist on it.

And maybe Aiden would soon see that it was the right thing for all of them.

The tech put the wand on Kendall's stomach, and when she moved it around, Kendall could see the baby's beating heart. Her breath rushed out.

"The baby's okay?" Kendall immediately asked.

"Appears to be. That's a strong, steady heartbeat." The woman continued to move the wand, and even though it was hard to make out some of the images, Kendall definitely spotted two arms and two legs. All moving.

"Amazing," Kendall said. "So much movement, and I haven't even felt it yet."

"Is that normal?" Aiden snapped.

The tech nodded. "Some women don't experience quickening or movement until week twenty."

That meshed with the maternity books that Kendall had been reading, but obviously this was all new to Aiden. He moved closer to the screen, his focus on the tiny baby.

Their baby.

Kendall saw and heard the moment that it finally sank in for him. Aiden made a hoarse sound that came from deep within his throat, and he mumbled something while his eyes tipped toward the ceiling. Maybe asking for divine help. She'd done that a few times early on, as well.

He dragged in a long breath. "Yeah, you should have told me."

That didn't sound like a man on the verge of rejecting fatherhood. Or even putting this in perspective. The bottom line was his family wasn't going to embrace this child, and hers likely wouldn't, either.

"Is that what I think it is?" Aiden asked.

Because he was looking gobsmacked again, Kendall's gaze rifled back to the monitor, and she tried to brace herself for whatever had put that bleached-out expression on Aiden's face.

"I'm sorry," the tech said, sending Kendall's heart into a tailspin again. "It's usually not that clear this early on, and I should have asked first if you wanted to know the sex of the baby. This is a new machine, and it gives much clearer images than we used to get with the old one."

Oh. Kendall got it then. Nothing was wrong with the baby, but the ultrasound had obviously shown her something she hadn't known before now.

The baby was a boy.

"A son," Aiden said, staggering back a bit.

Kendall had never seen him like this. Aiden was always in control. Always in charge. But this news had shaken him to the core.

"This doesn't change anything," Kendall insisted.

But she had the feeling he would have had the same reaction if it'd been a girl. It was just that seeing the baby on the screen made everything, well, real.

"The doctor will look over these images," the tech said, finishing up. She wiped the goop off Kendall's stomach. "But everything looks fine, right on target for the end of the first trimester."

The moment the woman stepped out of the room, Kendall fixed her clothes. Best not to feel exposed when she had this discussion with Aiden. A discussion he wasn't going to like. It was also a discussion she didn't even get to start because Aiden's phone buzzed, indicating that he had a text message.

"Leland got a hit on the dead guy's prints," Aiden said, reading the info on his phone. "His name was Montel Higgins."

She repeated it, hoping that it would jog some kind of memory. It didn't. "He has a record?"

Aiden nodded. "Both here and in his home country of Jamaica. He's worked as muscle for loan sharks but never anything this serious. Leland's checking to see if he can find a money trail so we can figure out who hired him."

Good. That was a start. "What about the other one? Any sign of him?"

"Not so far, but they'll keep looking."

Kendall didn't want them to stop looking, but she had to be realistic. It'd been several hours since the men kidnapped her, and the one who got away was probably long gone by now.

She stood, straightened her clothes. "You ready to talk?"

His gaze drifted to the ultrasound screen that was now blank. "Not about that. Not yet. But if you're up to it, I need to take your statement about the attack. You might be able to recall some detail that'll help us figure this out."

Kendall definitely wasn't feeling up to reliving the nightmare or giving a statement. She was exhausted and dizzy, and her arm was throbbing. Still, if she didn't do it now, she'd only have to go to Aiden's office tomorrow. Besides, she wasn't exactly looking forward to returning to her house right now. Not with that escaped gunman still at large.

Aiden got her moving out of the ultrasound room and into the hall, but he stopped when they reached the glass doors that led from the ER to the parking lot. He slid his hand over his gun and looked out, his gaze slashing from one side of the lot to the other. Since it was close to 9:00 p.m., there weren't many cars, only those of the workers and the handful of people in the ER itself. But Aiden still took his time, no doubt making sure they weren't about to be attacked.

"Wait here," he said. "I'll get my truck and bring it right to the door."

However, he didn't even make it a step before Kendall spotted movement in the parking lot. Aiden saw it, too, because he pushed her behind him and drew his gun.

But it wasn't the masked attacker coming back for another round.

It was a woman Kendall instantly recognized, and she groaned. It was almost as loud as the one Aiden made.

His mother, Carla, was making a beeline toward them.

Since Carla and she didn't live in the same town and definitely didn't travel in the same circles, it'd been a decade or longer since Kendall had seen the woman. She hadn't changed a bit. Tall and lean and dressed to perfection in a spring-yellow dress. Her dark blond hair was swept up and her makeup flawless. She looked ready for a church social.

Except for that troubled expression.

Aiden grumbled something Kendall didn't catch and maneuvered her back, away from the door.

"Your deputy said you were here," Carla greeted.

"I'm fine. I wasn't hurt."

"Good to hear." She spared him a glance as if it was the last thing she'd intended to ask about. And it probably was, since her attention stayed on her son for only several brief moments before it went to Kendall.

That definitely wasn't a loving look she gave Kendall.

"I figured I'd find you here with my son," Carla complained.

Aiden tapped the badge clipped to his belt. "She's with me because I'm doing my job. Two men kidnapped Kendall, and she was shot."

Again, that didn't appear to be what Carla had come to discuss. "Kendall O'Neal's not only a job to you." Carla's breath shuddered, and tears watered her eyes. "How could you crush me like this, Aiden? How could you let Jewell McKinnon's sister seduce you?"

Oh, no. Not this. Not now.

"It wasn't like that," Aiden insisted, but he might as

well have been talking to the air, because his mother didn't even look at him. She was glaring at Kendall.

"I know what happened between Aiden and you," Carla said to Kendall. "And now we need to figure out what we're going to do about this baby you're carrying."

Chapter Five

Aiden really didn't need his mother in his face right now. His fun meter was at zero, and judging from the start to this particular conversation, everything about it was going to fall into the nonfun category.

He could go two ways with this. Placate Carla with some kind of "we'll discuss this later" and go ahead and take Kendall to his office to get started on the paperwork. Or he could confront his mother as to how she'd learned about a one-night stand that Aiden hadn't mentioned to a soul.

Since he figured the first option had little chance of ending this conversation in a hurry, he went with the second route and maneuvered them to the corner of the room so they could have a semiprivate talk.

"Did Laine tell you?" Kendall asked.

Aiden got his answer to that when Carla's eyes widened. Those eyes then slashed toward Aiden. "You told Laine but not me?" But his mother waved off any answer that he might have given her. "It doesn't matter. Laine and I aren't on speaking terms since she married a McKinnon."

Yeah, and it was something his mom brought up often. Laine had indeed married Tucker McKinnon, Jewell's own son, and they were the parents of adopted twins. Something that had put a permanent rift between Carla and Laine.

Now Aiden was about to give her the same reason for a rift.

"If Laine didn't tell you, how did you find out?" Aiden asked. Not that it was critical for him to know how the proverbial cat had gotten out of the bag, but he wanted to know just who was feeding information about him to his mother.

"I'd rather not say," Carla insisted. "I'd rather focus on how to deal with this baby."

Kendall sighed. "My baby isn't something you need to *deal with*." Her voice was strained, and while her words were crisp, Aiden figured it was better than her telling Carla to mind her own business.

But his mother would see this baby as her business.

"You're wrong," Carla answered. "You're carrying a Braddock. My son's blood. And I can't let my grandbaby be raised by someone whose kin murdered my husband." She pointed to Kendall's stomach. "Your sister murdered that baby's own grandfather."

Oh, yeah. This was definitely not going in a fun direction.

"Someone shot Kendall," Aiden said in case his mother had already forgotten. "The doctor wants her to get some rest." The doc hadn't specifically said that, but Aiden figured rest was much preferred over another dose of stress that his mother was doling out. "You wouldn't want to do anything to cause her to miscarry, would you?"

Aiden hoped the answer to that was no, but his mother didn't budge.

"This won't take long," Carla insisted. Now her gaze came back to his. "Then you and I can have a private discussion tomorrow." The tears threatened again, followed by a whimper. "Why couldn't you just leave Kendall alone?"

Aiden had asked himself that a thousand times and still didn't have an answer. He'd developed an itch for Kendall about the same time he'd started to grow chest hair, and that itch had resulted in a kiss when they were thirteen. Kendall's first. There probably would have been more kisses in their immediate future if just days later they hadn't learned that his father had been murdered, and Kendall had left town with Jewell.

Of course, Kendall had come back to the area a time or two. Just enough to remind him that scratching the itch would feel pretty darn good even if it would also carry a huge price tag. Like now.

Except he didn't want to think of his baby as a *price tag*.

At the moment, he didn't want to think of his baby at all, because it wasn't a good idea for him to be focusing on something that could bring him to his knees when he had a would-be killer gunning for his head.

"You're just like your father," Carla added, giving Aiden another dig. "Unable to resist an O'Neal woman. At least he didn't get Jewell pregnant, though. Now we'll have a baby to raise."

Uh-oh. Definitely not the right thing to say, and Kendall stepped in front of him. "You're not raising my baby." She slid her hand protectively over her stomach. "In fact, you have no say in this whatsoever."

The little glance that Kendall shot him was probably to let him know that he didn't have a say, either. She was wrong about that.

Here came the tears, spilling down his mother's cheeks.

Since this was about to get uglier than it already was, Aiden took hold of Kendall and eased her back away from Carla. "Mom, I need to get Kendall's statement so I can figure out who tried to kill her and the baby."

That got Carla's attention. She'd obviously known about the attack, but it probably hadn't occurred to her yet that anything bad that happened to Kendall also happened to the baby she was carrying. Of course, maybe Carla didn't care about that at all, despite her insistence about raising the child.

"Any idea who kidnapped me and tried to force Aiden to destroy evidence?" Kendall demanded. And it was indeed a demand. There was plenty of anger in her voice and narrowed eyes when they landed on his mother.

"What evidence?" Carla questioned.

"The bone fragments," Aiden supplied.

Carla pressed her hand on her chest as if to steady her head. "Those fragments will convict Jewell of murder. There are only a handful of people who'd want that evidence destroyed. Joplin, Jewell's children and Kendall."

"And you," Kendall added.

Obviously, his mom hadn't seen that coming.

Neither had Aiden.

"You're under psychiatric care," Kendall added a heartbeat later. "Any other secrets you'd like to tell us about?"

Aiden was about to assure Kendall that it wasn't true, but his mother certainly didn't jump to deny it. "How did you know that?" Carla demanded.

Ah, heck.

Apparently, another can of worms had just been opened.

"I'd rather not say," Kendall answered, repeating the words his mother had said earlier.

That put some fire in Carla's eyes. "So what if it's true

that I'm seeing a psychiatrist? That doesn't mean I would try to have evidence destroyed."

"You might if you thought it'd make my sister look bad." Kendall paused. "Or if you thought it'd get rid of me and the Braddock baby I'm carrying."

Aiden mentally repeated his *ah, heck* because he didn't like the sudden look in his mother's eyes. The fire was still there, but he also saw something else.

The hatred.

It'd always been there, of course. But Aiden saw it now in a whole new light. Carla loathed Jewell, and that loathing extended to Kendall, since Jewell had practically raised Kendall after their father died.

Maybe his mother's hatred extended to the baby, too.

Yeah, Carla had demanded to raise the child, but he hoped like the devil that there wasn't something else going on here. Something that had caused her to put Kendall and the baby in danger.

But then he mentally shook his head.

There were plenty of other suspects with a more obvious motive without his reaching, and motive was something he'd take a hard look at soon. Right now he needed to fix this. Kendall was wobbling again, leaning against him, no doubt because she was dizzy. Probably in pain, too. No way did she need to be standing in the ER having words with his mother.

"We're leaving now. Come on," Aiden said to Kendall. "Mom, I'll call you."

And this time he didn't leave any room for argument. He got Kendall out of that corner and left his mother standing there, glaring at them.

Even though he was hurrying, Aiden didn't let his hasty departure make him stupid. He checked out the parking lot again to make sure no one was lurking around ready to attack.

There didn't appear to be.

Rather than leave Kendall there with his mother nearby, he drew his gun and hoped this wasn't a mistake.

"Hurry," he reminded her, though he figured Kendall wouldn't dawdle out in the open where her attacker could have another go at her.

Just in case that was the guy's plan, Aiden kept her close. Right against him to be exact. And even though he didn't break into a run, he got them to his truck as fast as possible. The moment they were inside and had on their seat belts, he drove away and got on the road that led out of town.

"I thought we were going to the sheriff's office," she said, glancing back at Main Street.

"It can wait. You have a security system at your house?"

She nodded but didn't look too certain about this decision. Heck, Aiden wasn't a hundred percent with it, either, but it might get Kendall the rest that she clearly needed.

He took out his phone, and while he kept watch around them, he called Leland. All his other deputies and Leland had their hands full with finding the missing attacker and processing the crime scene at Aiden's place, but Aiden needed some security measures for Kendall. That meant turning to someone he didn't especially want to turn to.

The McKinnons.

All three of Jewell's sons were lawmen. That was the good news. The bad news was they were estranged from their mother, since they blamed Jewell for leaving them after the affair with Aiden's father. An affair that'd led to his father's murder.

And that meant the McKinnon sons were also estranged from Kendall.

Still, he hoped the lawmen would do their jobs, since Kendall's house was in their jurisdiction.

"Call the Sweetwater Springs Sheriff's Office," Aiden told Leland when the deputy answered. "I'll need a protection detail out at Kendall's place."

She was already shaking her head before Aiden finished the request, and if Aiden could have thought of another way to keep her safe, he would have taken it. Leland assured him that he'd get right on that and then gave Aiden a quick update. When he was done, Aiden clicked the end call button so he could argue with Kendall. Not just about this but also the other surprise she'd dropped about his mother.

"Think about the baby," Aiden said. "Yeah, you and the McKinnon boys don't get along, but Cooper, Tucker and Colt will do their jobs. They don't have to like you to protect you."

He let that hang in the air.

"Obviously, that's true. You don't like me, and you're protecting me," she said.

Aiden thought about that a moment, and he decided there was no way to answer that so it wouldn't put him in butt-deep hot water. If he agreed that he didn't like her, it would only make this protective custody arrangement even more uncomfortable than it already was.

Besides, it was a lie.

He did like her. Well, her mouth anyway.

Okay, the rest of her, too.

He was just opposed to putting his mother and his sister Shelby through any more hell because of the choices that brainless part of him made in sleeping partners.

Of course, Kendall was more than just a former sleeping partner. She was the mother of his unborn son.

A reminder that required him to take a deep breath.

The fact they'd slept together didn't automatically mean he had to like her, but again reminding her that they were bad news for each other wouldn't fix anything right now.

"You'd rather I stayed with you than the McKinnons?" he asked, knowing the answer to that.

Now she was on the spot. Similar to him not liking her comment.

"It wouldn't be smart for you to stay with me," she answered.

Finally, they could agree on something, and once he had the McKinnon boys in place, he could get back to figuring out what the heck was going on and stopping any other attacks.

Not that he was positive there'd be another one.

The kidnappers had clearly lost, and with the evidence already moved, the danger might be long gone. Aiden hoped so anyway, but it still wasn't a risk he was willing to take.

He took the turn to Sweetwater Springs and moved onto the next subject. "How'd you know my mother was seeing a shrink? And spare me the answer of you'd rather not say, because that won't work with me."

"It worked when your mother used it so she wouldn't have to tell me how she found out I was pregnant."

"That ship hasn't sailed yet. I'll find out who told her. Now it's your turn to come clean."

She raked her fingers over her eyebrow and shifted in the seat a little. "I've been doing some checking, to try to find anything that might free Jewell."

Of course she had. "And you decided to check out my mother?"

Kendall nodded. "I had a PI follow her, and he reported back to me that she's been visiting a psychiatrist in San Antonio."

"My mother has a history of depression." Though he hadn't known about these visits to a shrink. Did that mean her depression had gotten worse? "It's a stretch, though, to think depression would have caused her to come after you to make Jewell look bad. Especially since I could have gotten hurt."

"But she knew about the baby," Kendall quickly pointed out. "Maybe she was willing to risk hurting you to make sure I'm out of your life for good."

It turned his stomach to think of that, and he wished he could totally dismiss it.

But he couldn't.

The truth was, his mother had been flirting with mental instability for years. All the way back to the time of his father's murder. He'd seen that vacant look in her eyes one time too many. Ditto for the sheer hatred that she just couldn't let go of. So yeah, news of a baby could have tipped her over the edge, and that was why Aiden needed to learn when she'd found out about the pregnancy and who'd been the one to tell her.

"While you were doing this checking and having people followed, did you hear anything else I should know?" he asked.

"Lee Palmer," she said without hesitation. "He also hired a PI to follow your mother."

Yet another hit of news that he hadn't been aware of.

Palmer.

The man's name kept turning up like a bad penny. A nearby rancher and his father's old nemesis. Palmer would love to see Jewell walk on this murder. Heck, Palmer would have loved to do the kill himself. Too bad he had a decent alibi for the time of Whitt's death. The man had been in the hospital recovering from a mild heart attack.

Still, Aiden had to shake his head on this one. "So, why would Palmer have my mother followed?"

"Maybe for the same reason I did." She paused. "He had your younger sister, Shelby, followed, too."

Aiden cursed. "And you didn't think you should come to me with this?"

Kendall lifted her shoulder. "You and I aren't exactly on the same side in this investigation, and technically I'm one of Jewell's attorneys. If anything had come up that was legally pertinent to the investigation, I would have disclosed it as I'm required to do. But a private citizen hiring a PI isn't something I have to disclose."

Hell's bells. She sounded like a lawyer and it set his teeth on edge again. "I'll have a talk with Palmer, and these little following adventures will stop." Aiden gave that some more thought. "Did he have me followed, too?"

"No, not that I know of anyway, but Palmer's digging into your old investigations. Into the McKinnon investigations, too. I think he's looking for anything that'll weaken the case against Jewell."

Yes, and he could try to smear Aiden's name in the process. He followed the law, but there was always a gray area or two when it came to investigations. Palmer better not be looking to throw him to the dogs to save the likes of Jewell.

Palmer also had better not be behind tonight's fiasco.

Apparently, Aiden had yet someone else to question, along with Jewell's attorney, Joplin. Maybe if he poked around enough, he'd find the snake responsible for that bullet Kendall had taken.

"I need some good news," she said, staring out the window into the darkness. "Any good news."

Aiden could possibly help with that. "Leland managed to get the surveillance footage from a camera just up the street from your office. One of the deputies is looking at it now to see if they can find any clues about the attack."

She shivered, rubbing her hands along the sides of her arms. Then she winced when her fingers brushed against the stitches.

Okay, maybe not good news for her after all. Because those images of being grabbed and dragged into an SUV probably didn't qualify as good. Still, if they didn't get anything from the dead gunman's past, then the footage was their best bet.

"How bad is your arm hurting?" he asked.

"It's manageable."

Which meant she was hurting. "I can call the doc and see if there's anything you can take."

But she shook her head. "You've already done enough."

That didn't exactly sound like a big thank-you, but Aiden let it slide. Soon, though, they'd have to talk about the final subject on his to-do list. The final and the biggest one.

The baby.

He took the turn into Sweetwater Springs. Since he'd never been to her place, Aiden followed her terse directions of "that way" and "here." He pulled to a stop in front of a house just one block off Main Street.

A whopping big house at that.

A reminder that Kendall was rich.

Her daddy, Travis, had been a rancher and plenty well-off. Travis had died when Kendall was just a kid, and the money, the ranch and all the other properties had been split between Jewell and her. Jewell had gotten the sprawling Sweetwater Ranch. Kendall, this house. Kendall's folks had divorced years before Travis's death, so her mom hadn't gotten anything, and then her mom, too, died the following year in a car accident, giving Kendall an even larger inheritance.

Aiden's family had money, too, but nothing like this.

"I don't have my remote to open the garage," she said. "The kidnappers took my purse, but I can use the keypad by the front door to unlock the house."

"No butler to let you in?" he mumbled, immediately hating the snark.

"He has the night off," she zinged back. A reminder of one of the things that had always attracted him to Kendall. She was nobody's doormat.

Not even his.

Aiden looked around before they got out, and as he'd done in the parking lot, he quickly got them moving. They reached the front door, where she used the keypad. He hadn't thought there'd be any more surprises tonight, but he got one when he stepped into the foyer. Yeah, it was a mansion all right.

And an empty one.

Kendall pressed in some numbers to disarm the security system and then immediately reset it once they were inside.

"I put everything in storage so I could get the house ready to sell," she said, following his gaze to the rooms off the foyer. Also empty.

"Because you were leaving. Leaving without telling me you were pregnant." And yes, he meant for that to be a zinger.

Unlike her previous gaze dodging, she didn't dodge this time. She met his gaze head-on.

"I'm thirty-six, and I figured even though this baby wasn't planned, it's a good time for me to start a family.

I didn't want to shove my dreams down your throat just because you were the one who got me pregnant."

Ouch. "You're calling me a sperm donor?"

"I'm giving you an out that you'll likely want when you get past the emotional punch of seeing that ultrasound." Kendall didn't give him a chance to challenge that. "Your mother and sister are never going to accept me, and I'm not letting them raise my baby."

He couldn't argue with the last part or the emotional punch, but he could darn sure take issue with the first. "I don't want an out."

But man, it thinned his breath to understand what that meant.

He'd be a father to this baby, no matter who objected. Even if he'd probably suck at it. He hadn't exactly had a good role model, since his father was a cheating, mean old bastard. However, he was a better man than Whitt had been.

He hoped.

Aiden might have convinced Kendall and himself of that if his phone hadn't rung. "Leland," he greeted his deputy when he answered.

"We got a problem, boss. The McKinnons are tied up with an armed robbery at a convenience store just off the interstate. There's a hostage."

Aiden groaned. Not only for the hostage but for what that meant. "Can anybody else do protection detail for Kendall?"

"I'm working on it, but I figure you need to stay there with her."

He didn't miss the slathering of doom and gloom in his deputy's voice. "Why? What happened?"

"There's been a spotting of the SUV that Kendall's attacker used to get away." Leland paused, added some profanity. "Someone's on the way to check it out, but the guy's in Sweetwater Springs." The deputy paused. "Aiden, he was seen less than a mile from Kendall's house."

Chapter Six

Aiden was in her bed again.

Well, in her *bedroom* anyway.

Something that Kendall had sworn would never happen. Of course, their one night together hadn't happened here but rather at the Sweetwater Springs Inn. Because the inn had been walking distance from the bar, and they'd both had too much to drink to drive.

Now he was here, sleeping on the floor next to her bed, because that masked kidnapper might try to come after her again. If most of her furniture hadn't already been put in storage, he might have opted for a guest room. There were six of them in the sprawling house, but since the only bed had been hers, he'd taken the floor.

A wise move.

With tensions running so high between them, the last place she needed Aiden was in bed with her. Even if her body thought that would have been a stellar idea. Of course, her body was always making the wrong call when it came to Aiden.

As it was nearly seven in the morning, Kendall eased out of bed, trying to keep her movements slow and quiet so she wouldn't wake him. However, she wasn't able to muffle the little sound of pain when she flexed her arm.

It hurt. And had done so for most of the night. Still, it was far better than it could have been. The kidnappers could have killed her.

Not exactly a sunshiny thought to start the day.

She'd worn cotton pj's to bed, but she also pulled on a robe before she stood. Since Aiden was right there on the floor, she stepped around him so she could head to the adjoining bathroom. Or at least that was the plan. But one look at him, and her feet automatically stopped moving.

Another wrong call that her body made, but that didn't prevent her from looking at him.

He was a sight all right. No pj's for him. He was still wearing his jeans but had stripped off his shirt, boots and holster, and the stripping had left her with an unobstructed view of his toned chest and abs.

He had a six-pack.

And the hot outlaw looks to go with it.

His dark blond hair was a little too long, but the tousled look suited him and went along with that desperado stubble. Ditto for his gray eyes. She couldn't see them now that he was sleeping, but the color seemed to change. They could be stormy dark or cool as mist depending on his mood.

Most of the time when he was looking at her, Kendall got the stormy version.

"Ogling me?" he asked, and she got a full dose of that gray when he opened his eyes.

"Trying not to step on you," Kendall corrected. And yes, ogling him in the process. She didn't wait around to see if he bought her answer. Kendall headed to the bathroom.

"Stay away from the windows," Aiden called out, something he'd reminded her of a lot since they arrived at her house.

She listened but did take a quick peek outside to make sure that goon wasn't in her yard. No sign of him. She had mixed emotions about that. Kendall wasn't eager to have him anywhere near her again, but if he had been out there, then maybe Aiden could have captured him.

Kendall hurried into the bathroom so she could take a quick shower. And put on some makeup. Fix her hair, too, only to remember that she hadn't brought a change of clothes in with her. That meant putting the robe back on so she could get to the closet in the bedroom. When it came to being around Aiden, the more clothes, the better.

Clearly, he thought so, too, because when she went back in, he was dressed, sitting on her bed and talking on his phone. No more ogling his chest, but sadly, her brain reminded her of how he'd looked lying on her floor. A flash of another memory, too, when Aiden had been naked and in bed with her.

That helped ease the throbbing in her arm, but it didn't help with other parts of her. Nor did the long look that Aiden gave her. His gaze—stormy gray, as expected—slid from her head to her toes, and then he jerked his attention away as if disgusted with himself.

She knew how he felt.

The last time he'd looked at her that way, they had landed in bed, and she'd gotten pregnant.

That brought on another set of images, this time from the ultrasound she'd gotten the night before. Kendall went into the massive closet and slid her hand over her stomach.

A boy.

For weeks she'd wondered about the baby's sex, and now she knew. Ironic that when she was a teenager, she'd fantasized about marrying Aiden and having his son, and here she was carrying that child.

Of course, in her clueless teenage fantasies, Aiden and

she had been perfectly happy. Kendall was still thrilled about the baby, but there wasn't much else that she could slap that happy label on.

She dressed. Not easily, since every little movement of her arm gave her a twinge of pain, and some gave her more than a twinge. But she managed to get on a pale pink dress and sandals. An outfit that Aiden would probably consider too prissy, but she'd already put on some baby weight around her stomach, and most of her other clothes were too tight.

"Anything new on the kidnapper?" she asked when she went back into the bedroom and saw that he'd finished his call.

"Nothing. But Leland had the Rangers do a bug sweep of the office, and it's clean. No listening devices. I also found out from Laine that she wasn't the one who told Carla about you being pregnant."

Good. It was a small thing, but Kendall was glad Laine hadn't gone back on her word to keep it secret. "Then who told Carla?"

"Still working on that." He tipped his head to her bandage. "How's your arm?"

"Fine."

Ah, she got the stormy eyes again. "How's your arm?" he repeated. "And I'll keep asking until I get a truthful answer."

Kendall huffed. "It hurts, and the stitches are pulling. Satisfied?"

"Satisfied that you're in pain? No. Satisfied that we've moved past the polite-answer stage? Then yes. Because I'm thinking we're going to need more than polite responses when we talk about the baby."

She swallowed hard. Kendall had been expecting and

dreading this conversation, of course, but she wasn't sure she was up to what would no doubt turn into a full-blown argument. An argument that would include why she'd planned to leave town and never tell him about their son.

Aiden stood from the bed and walked closer to her. With that holster slung low on his hips, he looked like a Wild West outlaw, ready to draw. "So, why were you at the Bluebonnet Bar three months ago?"

Of all the questions she figured he would ask, that wasn't one of them. Nor was it something Kendall wanted to discuss. "Does it matter?"

He lifted his shoulder. "I'm just wondering if you went there with the idea of finding a sperm donor so you could get pregnant."

She laughed, definitely not from humor but from the absurdity of his suggestion. "You're kidding, right?"

Another shoulder lift. "You said it yourself. You're thirty-six and want a family. Maybe that's why we ended up in bed."

Good grief. The man could irritate every bone in her body with just a few questions.

It was stupid, but she grabbed a handful of his shirt, yanked him closer and kissed him. It took Kendall less than a second to prove her point, because there was a flash fire of heat. She certainly felt it, and judging from the husky groan that Aiden made, he felt it, too. Her body wanted to continue proving the point, but this kind of fire-playing was dangerous.

Kendall stepped back, tried to gather her breath. "That's why we ended up in bed together. Aided and abetted by some Jack Daniel's, of course."

He made a sound of agreement and pursed his mouth a little. A gesture that caused her body to clench. And beg for another round with Aiden. Something it wasn't going to get.

"So, what got you started on the Jack Daniel's?" he pressed.

Kendall hoped the flat look she gave him let him know she wasn't happy about this subject, but like with the arm question, Aiden wouldn't let go until he was satisfied that he'd gotten the truth.

"I'd gone to the jail that day to talk with Jewell." Kendall pointed her index finger at him. "And so help me, you'd better not try to use any of what I'm about to say against her."

That got his attention. And he nodded, eventually.

Kendall gathered her thoughts, tried to put this in the best light. Impossible to do, though. "I asked Jewell to tell me what happened that day your father died. I wanted her to explain how her DNA got on the bedsheets in the cabin."

A cabin where the prosecution was going to say that Jewell and Whitt had carried out their secret affair. An affair that'd ended in violence because Whitt had told Jewell that it was over and that he was reconciling with his wife.

"And?" Aiden prompted when she didn't continue. "Did you think someone had planted her DNA?"

"I'd hoped. But Jewell said it got there because she'd been on the bed. With your father," she added in a mumble.

It'd crushed her to hear that. Jewell had been a mother to her. Someone she loved unconditionally, but Kendall had loved Jewell's husband, Roy, too, and her sister had admitted to what the town had buzzed about for twenty-three years.

That Jewell was sleeping with a married man. Because why else would Jewell have been on that bed?

"So then I came right out and asked Jewell if she'd killed Whitt," Kendall continued. "But she said that was best left for the jury."

Aiden stayed quiet a moment. "You were finally convinced your sister's a killer."

Kendall took her time answering, too. "No, but I think she could be covering for someone."

Roy, maybe. Heck, maybe even Carla if Jewell was somehow rationalizing that she owed the woman because she'd been sleeping with her husband.

"You won't use this against Jewell," Kendall insisted, then paused. "Why were you at the Bluebonnet that night?"

"Looking for the cure to a really bad day." Aiden edged back a little from her. "Topping the list, I'd killed a man in the line of duty."

Kendall had heard about it—a shooting was big news in a small town—but she'd been so focused on her own problems, she hadn't realized what Aiden was going through.

"Running into me at the bar didn't help cure your bad day," she added.

But Aiden didn't answer. He drew his gun and hurried to the windows at the front of the house. Kendall heard the car engine then, but when she went to see who it was, Aiden pulled her behind him.

Then he cursed.

"It's Mr. FBI himself," Aiden grumbled. "Seth Calder."

His arrival was both a blessing and a curse. Seth was Jewell's stepson and therefore Kendall's step-nephew. She loved him like a brother, since they'd practically been raised together, but she was so not in the mood to face yet another surly man today.

Aiden was more than enough.

Kendall headed out of the bedroom and toward the stairs, but as he'd done at the window, Aiden got in front of her. Seth rang the bell, and he didn't wait even a second before he rang it again. Then not even another second passed before he pounded on the door.

"Kendall?" Seth called out.

Yes, definitely surly. He'd no doubt heard about the shooting and probably wanted to know why she hadn't called him. She didn't think he'd buy that the kidnappers took her cell phone.

The pounding continued while Kendall disengaged the security system, and then Aiden threw open the door. And there Seth was. All six feet three inches of him. Imposing. Irritated.

Worried.

Cursing, Seth reached for her and pulled her into his arms. "How bad were you hurt?" he asked in a hoarse whisper.

"Not bad." She stepped back to show him the bandage. Thank goodness there was no pain meter on it, because it was throbbing again.

Seth looked into her eyes, no doubt trying to ferret out the truth, and then his cool blue eyes landed on Aiden again. "What the hell's he doing here?"

"My job," Aiden answered. "What the hell are *you* doing here?"

Since this sounded like the start of a testosterone contest, Kendall shut the door and quickly tried to diffuse it. "Aiden saved my life, and when Cooper and the others couldn't come over to stay with me, Aiden volunteered."

"Well, he can go, because I'm here now," Seth snapped.

Aiden's hands went on his hips. "I don't think that's your call, FBI Agent Calder." He said Seth's title as if it were some kind of scarlet letter. "This is my investigation, and I'm staying close to Kendall until I find out who kidnapped her and put that bullet in her arm."

That would have sounded good if Aiden hadn't added an accusing glare that he aimed right at Seth.

Seth got in his face. "If you're suggesting I had any part in that, then you're a dead man."

Aiden gave Seth the same hard look he'd gotten. "Can you vouch for your sisters, too?"

"Yes. Can you vouch for yours?" Seth fired back.

"Yeah."

"Even the one who's been hounding me?"

"Shelby," Aiden provided on a huff. "My kid sister takes her investigative reporter duties a little over the top. But she sure wouldn't destroy evidence needed to convict Jewell. Shelby's determined to make Jewell pay."

"Then who the devil did this to Kendall?" Seth demanded, tipping his head to the bandage.

"Somebody who wanted evidence destroyed," Aiden readily supplied. "Or else somebody who wanted to make it seem as if Jewell or her kin was into evidence tampering. I'm looking into all the suspects."

Kendall couldn't get a word in edgewise, as Seth just talked right over her.

"There'd better be someone with connections to your family on your suspect list," Seth insisted.

She instantly thought of the conversation they'd had with Carla. Plenty of venom there, maybe enough to want Kendall dead while also making Jewell look even guiltier. Plus, there were things in Carla's past that she was keeping secret from her family. Since Kendall now knew that secret, she probably shouldn't keep it from Aiden. But she wouldn't tell him now, not with Seth ready to latch on to anything he could throw in Aiden's face.

And vice versa.

"There is someone with connections to my family on that list," Aiden admitted. "Lee Palmer. He hated my father enough to want to see Jewell walk for killing him."

"Or maybe Palmer did the killing himself," Seth fired back.

Aiden mimicked the same noncommittal sound that Seth had made earlier. "Palmer had an alibi, remember. And while your stepmother's trial is out of my hands, the attack on Kendall is all mine. I'll find whoever's behind this, and his or her butt is going to jail."

She finally found her opening when they paused. "Once the kidnapper's caught," she added, "and an arrest is made, I'll be okay. There'll be no need for protective custody."

Kendall hoped that would reassure Seth. It didn't. He glanced at Aiden and her, and she could almost see him trying to work things out in that hard head of his.

Seth had known about her attraction to Aiden for years. Since they'd been fifteen, and he'd caught her doodling Aiden's name in her school binder. He hadn't exactly been pleased about that, since the gossip was still hot about Jewell having killed Aiden's father, but Seth had let it pass.

She was betting he wouldn't let it pass this time.

Maybe he sensed something between them. Like that stupid kiss that'd happened upstairs only minutes earlier.

Once the gaze shifting had stopped, Seth's narrowed eyes settled on her. "What exactly is going on here?" He didn't wait for an answer. "And does *he* have anything to do with the reason you're selling this place and leaving?"

Since it wasn't much of a secret any longer, Kendall decided to spill it fast. "I'm pregnant. Aiden is the baby's father."

It got so silent that she could hear her own breath. Her heartbeat, too, after Seth turned an arctic stare on Aiden.

"If you accuse me of taking advantage of her," Aiden grumbled, "you're a dead man."

Seth gave Aiden another long, hard look. One that would have caused most men to take a step back. Simply put, Seth didn't just look dangerous with his black hair and dark blue eyes; he *was* dangerous. Well, he could be when it came to protecting his own, and Seth considered her one of his own.

But Aiden was dangerous in his own right.

"Does he want you to leave town?" Seth asked her.

A million-dollar question, and Kendall didn't know the answer. Maybe Aiden didn't know the answer, either.

"It's my baby," Aiden said.

All right. That wasn't exactly an answer to anything, but it sounded like some kind of declaration of war. Maybe it was. Her quiet exit out of town was already a bust, but any exit now would involve Aiden.

Maybe Aiden demanding to be part of her life.

Although it would create an even bigger rift between their families.

Seth went closer to her, took hold of her hand. "Just say the word, and I'll stay here with you."

It was a generous offer, but he no doubt had work. Plus, he was still looking for anything that would clear Jewell's name despite the fact that her sister wasn't cooperating with any of their efforts.

Kendall shook her head. "I'll be okay."

She hoped. And she also hoped that being okay didn't put Aiden and her on another collision course that would lead them back to the bedroom.

Definitely no more proving-a-point kisses.

"Call me if you need anything," Seth added, giving her hand a gentle squeeze. He shot Aiden another glare before he left.

Kendall rearmed the security system and turned to Aiden to get an explanation as to what his *it's my baby* comment meant, but his phone rang again. She saw Leland's name pop up on the screen. Unlike with the other calls he'd gotten or made throughout the night, Aiden put this one on speaker and went to the sidelight window to watch Seth drive away.

"Jewell's lawyer is in your office, demanding to see you right now," Leland greeted.

Aiden mumbled some profanity. "Tell him I'll be there soon. I'm bringing in Kendall to take her statement about the kidnapping." He was about to hang up, but Leland spoke before he could.

"There's more," the deputy said, and judging from his tone, it wasn't going to be the good news that Kendall was hoping for. "There's been another sighting of the missing kidnapper and his SUV. It was captured on the new traffic camera just off the interstate."

"Please tell me the guy's not headed here," Aiden snapped.

"No, but trust me, boss, you're gonna want to see this."

Chapter Seven

Aiden didn't like this latest turn of events with the missing kidnapper. The idiot had gotten much too close to Kendall again and had gone to a place that only made this mess worse: to the home of one of their suspects.

Lee Palmer.

There wasn't much about the past twenty-four hours that Aiden liked, but the kidnapper's mere presence at Palmer's meant there was a connection that could lead to Palmer's arrest. If Aiden could prove it, that is. He needed to find this kidnapper and get the investigation over and done with so he could settle some personal things with Kendall.

Well, settle one thing with her anyway.

The baby.

Aiden wasn't sure exactly what Kendall was expecting or not expecting him to do, but there was no way he was going to let her leave without some kind of guarantee that he would be part of his son's life.

His son.

And because that was still a little mind-numbing, Aiden pushed it aside so he could deal with the man who had demanded to see Aiden at the sheriff's office.

Robert Joplin.

Joplin was pain in the rear number one. The second pain in the rear was on the way there to Aiden's office, as well. Or at least he darn well better be, since Leland had ordered him to come in.

Palmer himself.

Talking to his dad's old foe wasn't pleasant on any day, but on this particular one, Aiden would have to ask the man some hard questions. It wouldn't be pretty, but if what the camera footage showed was true, then that idiot who'd shot Kendall had driven the SUV directly to Palmer's ranch.

Trust me, boss, you're gonna want to see this, Leland had said to Aiden when he called earlier. Leland had been right. Those images were something that could blow this case right open.

Aiden had another look at that footage that Leland had loaded on the computer in the squad room. Footage taken from a camera that'd been designed to monitor traffic on the interstate. He took his time, examining it frame by frame, despite the fact that Joplin was hollering for him to hurry up so they could talk.

Kendall watched the traffic footage, too, and she pulled in her breath when the SUV took the turn to Palmer's place. It was a grainy image but clear enough to see the license plate. Yes, it was the kidnapper all right.

So, why was he headed there?

And since Palmer's ranch was the only place on that entire road, then the man couldn't claim the hired gun was just paying a visit to someone else.

"Derek and Sarah are heading out to Palmer's place now to see if the SUV's still there," Leland explained.

Derek was the most experienced deputy that Aiden had, and he was glad the night-shift deputy, Sarah, was going with him for backup. Though maybe it wouldn't be needed, and the kidnapper would surrender peacefully.

Aiden could dream anyway.

"Does Palmer know about this footage?" Kendall asked.

Leland shook his head. "I thought it was best not to hear it over the phone. But I did tell him he should probably bring his lawyer."

Which Palmer would do. Since he was always operating just above the law, Palmer kept a team of attorneys to make sure he stayed out of legal hot water.

Leland glanced at the clock on the wall. Nine-thirty. "Palmer should be here soon."

That was Aiden's cue to get moving, and he turned to Kendall. "You want to get started on your statement while I talk to Joplin?"

She gave him a flat look. "Do you really think Joplin is going to leave without seeing me?"

He knew the answer to that—no. Since Kendall had worked with Joplin on Jewell's legal defense, they were allies. Aiden had just wanted to spare Kendall what would no doubt be another confrontation. Not with her. But Joplin sure wouldn't have any nice things to say to Aiden. He never did.

"After you talk with him and give your statement, I'll work on getting you a real protection detail," Aiden said.

"Maybe it won't be necessary if Palmer confesses to everything."

Aiden figured pigs had a better chance of flying before that happened. She'd need protection all right, and she would want anyone but him to guard her. Of course, that wouldn't stop him from doing it, but he did want plenty of backup. That meant a protection detail.

With Kendall right by his side, Aiden went to his office, and the moment they stepped inside, Joplin jumped to his feet and hurried to her. Much as Seth had done earlier, he took her hand.

"Are you all right?" Joplin asked, not waiting for an answer. "I tried to call, but it went straight to voice mail."

"The kidnappers took her phone," Aiden provided. And they'd obviously taken out the tracking device on it, since the Rangers hadn't been able to get a ping on it to find the location.

Joplin didn't even spare Aiden a glance or acknowledge the information. "I tried your home phone, too, and it's been disconnected."

"Because I'm moving." Kendall pulled her hand from his.

"Moving?" Joplin howled. "Why? Because of the attack?"

She shook her head. "Personal reasons."

Joplin's gaze turned to a glare, aimed at Aiden. "You're running her out of town."

Because Seth had already suggested pretty much the same thing, Aiden scowled at the lawyer. "I'm not running anybody out of town, but I do want you to tell me if you know anything about the attack."

Now, that caused Joplin to scowl. Aiden wasn't making many friends today. Not that he wanted Joplin for a friend.

"We just need to find out why those men wanted the bone evidence destroyed," Kendall said, and her tone was a lot nicer than Aiden's. Joplin seemed to respond to that, because his expression softened when he turned to her.

"I don't know." Joplin added a sigh and a head shake. "I talked to Jewell about it this morning, and she's appalled that someone would do this on her behalf. Or appear to do it on her behalf," he tacked on when he looked at Aiden.

"A Braddock's behind this," Joplin insisted.

"And which Braddock would that be?" Aiden asked, none too friendly, either.

"Your sister Shelby, maybe. Perhaps your mother."

That was another of those accusations that Aiden didn't want tossed around. "Nobody in my family wants those bone fragments destroyed, especially not as some kind of reverse psychology to suggest that Jewell is innocent. Because she's not."

But the moment he said that, Aiden got a thought. A bad one. The first he'd had of the sort.

What if Jewell truly was innocent?

Ah, hell.

This was about the kiss in Kendall's bedroom. And the baby. He was softening, and it wasn't a good time for that, since he didn't want the baby or a kiss to deter him from doing his job. Because the job might be the only thing that kept Kendall and the baby safe.

"Did you know the kidnappers?" Joplin asked her.

"No." She glanced at Aiden, who finished for her.

"But we have an identity on the one I killed. Montel Higgins. Ring any bells?" Aiden watched Joplin's face, looking for any kind of reaction.

However, he didn't get one. "No. Should it?"

Well, it would if Joplin had been the one to hire him. "We're checking now to see if he has any connection to our suspects."

Joplin didn't ask if he was a suspect, probably because he knew that he automatically was. Instead he turned back to Kendall. "I heard there were two attackers. Did you know the other one, maybe recognize his voice?"

"Aiden's already asked me that, and the answer's no. At least, I didn't recognize anything specific," she added in a mumble.

"Too bad," Joplin answered. Some emotion went through the man's eyes, and Aiden hoped it wasn't relief.

"Maybe you're behind the attack," Aiden said to Joplin, and he ignored the man's howl of protest and continued. "You're in love with Jewell. Everybody in town knows that, so maybe you made a really bad decision to use Kendall to destroy the bone fragments."

Joplin shook his head. "I didn't."

But then something happened. Joplin's gaze drifted from Aiden to Kendall's stomach. It was just a glimpse, but when Aiden's eyes met his again, it was clear that the lawyer knew something he shouldn't know.

That Kendall was pregnant.

Hell's bells. Did everyone in town know? And if so, how?

Better yet, how had the kidnappers found out? Because they'd certainly known that the baby would be the ultimate bargaining tool to get him to cooperate.

"Who told you?" Aiden came right out and asked Joplin.

Obviously, Kendall hadn't missed the look, either, because she stared at Joplin, waiting for him to answer.

"Carla," Joplin finally said.

That wasn't the answer Aiden had expected. "My mother told you?" he said with a whole boatload of skepticism.

"Carla called me yesterday morning out of the blue," Joplin continued with a nod. "She wanted me to confirm that the baby was indeed a Braddock. I told her I didn't have a clue, that I didn't even know Kendall was pregnant."

Yesterday morning. That would have been enough time for Joplin to throw together a kidnapping scheme so he could get the evidence destroyed. Of course, it would also be enough time for Aiden's mother to do the same. A plan to make the McKinnons or the O'Neals look guilty of obstructing justice.

If Aiden wanted to believe Carla could do something like this, he could buy it happening. But he wasn't ready to believe that just yet.

He hoped there wouldn't be any kind of proof to make him believe it, either.

"Did you tell Jewell about the baby?" Kendall asked, and yes, there was some concern in her voice now.

Joplin dodged her gaze. Not a good sign.

"I didn't tell her, but she guessed," Joplin explained.

Kendall threw her hands up in the air and then winced, no doubt because the motion pulled her stitches. "How?"

Joplin made an *isn't it obvious?* sound. "Jewell started speculating as to why kidnappers would have taken you and not one of Aiden's sisters. You and Aiden have always had a thing for each other, so it wasn't hard for her to figure it out."

A thing? Well, it was a stupid label for this unwanted attraction between Kendall and him. More like an Achilles' heel.

Kendall groaned. "I need to talk to my sister. *In person*," she added to Aiden, knowing that he would suggest a phone call instead of a visit.

Yes. But the timing sucked. "After you're done with your statement, I'll arrange to have you escorted to the jail." Or course, he'd be one of those escorts. He was dead serious about not letting her out of his sight until all this was cleared up.

"And then maybe you'll come stay with me," Joplin said to her.

Both Aiden and Kendall looked at him as if he'd sprouted hooves.

"You can't trust a Braddock," the lawyer added.

"But she can trust you?" Aiden fired back. "A man who'd do anything, and I mean anything, to get your old flame out of jail?"

Joplin certainly didn't deny it. "Jewell's innocent. That's the reason I'd do anything to set her free." And with that declaration he'd made too many times to count, Joplin picked up his briefcase, his attention still on Kendall. "At least consider my offer to stay with me. If not for your own sake, then for the baby's."

Aiden was already operating on a short fuse, and that did it. "Nobody will put as much into protecting the baby as I will, because it's my son."

Judging from the way the whole building suddenly got quiet, everyone inside had just learned that it was his son, too. Not that Aiden had plans to keep it from everyone. But he probably should give his sisters a call so they'd hear the news from him personally. Laine already knew and might not care to hear it repeated. She might not even talk to him, because she was now a McKinnon, and not a Jewell-loving McKinnon, either, since Laine was married to one of Jewell's estranged sons.

But Shelby was a different matter.

Shelby would see this as a slap to her and the family. A betrayal even. She darn sure wouldn't see her brother's attraction to Kendall as a *thing.*

Joplin smiled, likely pleased that he'd fueled Aiden's outburst. Or maybe he was just smiling because he was walking away scot-free after orchestrating an attack on Kendall. But if the man was guilty, he wouldn't be on the streets for long. Aiden would see to that.

"Sorry," Aiden said to her after Joplin left.

Kendall waved him off. "The pregnancy apparently

wasn't much of a secret anyway. Though I'd like to know who told your mother."

So would he, and Aiden took out his phone to do something about getting that info. However, he didn't even get to press his mother's number before he heard yet another voice.

Pain in the butt number two had arrived.

"Where is he?" Palmer's booming voice echoed through the building.

By *he*, Palmer no doubt meant Aiden, so he stepped into the hall. It was Palmer all right, dressed in his starched jeans, white shirt, bolo tie and cream-colored Stetson. Which he didn't remove. Aiden had never seen the man without it, and it was nearly the same color as his hair.

Palmer was in his early sixties now. The same age Aiden's dad would have been if he'd lived. Probably would have had the same build, too, with Palmer's middle going soft and paunchy. Still, Palmer managed to look strong and imposing, rather than a man who was nearly at retirement age.

As Aiden had predicted, Palmer had two lawyers with him. Both dressed in suits, both sporting nervy little expressions that reminded Aiden of twitching rats.

"Go ahead and let Leland take your statement," Aiden said to Kendall. "I'll handle this."

Did she listen?

No, of course not.

Kendall went straight to the computer on Leland's desk and pointed to the screen. "Did you send that goon after me?"

"Well, hello to you, too, Kendall. Long time no see." Palmer gave her a lazy smile that might have been genuine. From all accounts, he actually liked Kendall. Or maybe he just liked the fact that she was butting heads, legally speaking, with the Braddocks.

Kendall certainly didn't smile. "Did you hire two men to kidnap me and try to force Aiden to destroy evidence in my sister's case?"

As if he had all the time in the world, Palmer looked at the screen. At the image of the SUV taking the turn toward his property. If he was concerned one bit about what Kendall was asking, he didn't show it. Instead he smiled at Joplin when the lawyer joined them.

"Aiden's on a witch hunt," Joplin warned Palmer. "Beware."

Kendall shot Joplin a glance that could have frozen the desert a couple of times over. "The man in that SUV tried to kill us."

Her terse glance and comment caused Joplin to step back. "I should be going. I am free to go, right?" he asked Aiden. "Or do you plan to arrest me for something?"

"No plans, yet," Aiden snarled. "But it's early. Give me a few hours, and I'll see what I can come up with."

Joplin got his snarky look back and stormed out. Good. One pain down. Another to go. But Aiden wanted some answers from this one first before he went anywhere.

"Why don't we take this into the interview room," Aiden said to Palmer and his lawyers. Not really a suggestion. He hiked his thumb toward the hall and got them moving in that direction.

Aiden would have preferred that Kendall skip this, and he tried to let her know that with a raised eyebrow, but she just raised one of her own.

"You're just not gonna let go of this bad blood between us, are you?" Palmer grumbled as they filed into the interview room. "That feud with your daddy was a long time ago."

Yeah, it was. In fact, it'd happened twenty-five or so years ago when Palmer basically stole some Braddock land by falsifying old records. Something Aiden had never been able to prove, but he was certain that it'd happened.

"No, I wasn't planning on letting go of it," Aiden grumbled back. "I kind of like hanging on to bad blood."

Kendall's gaze came to his, and Aiden wanted to kick himself. Later, he'd have to let her know that their bad blood was going to have to get a whole lot better because of the baby.

Maybe that was possible.

Maybe.

"Bad blood aside," Aiden said, his attention back on Palmer now, "I'm more interested in why that hired gun in the SUV paid you a visit."

"He didn't visit me." Palmer didn't hesitate. "I wasn't at my ranch last night or this morning."

One of the lawyers extracted a piece of paper from his briefcase. "That's a receipt for Mr. Palmer's hotel room. He stayed in San Antonio on the Riverwalk last night and just got back. We came straight here."

Aiden figured Palmer would try something like this. That bad blood and Palmer's previous scummy dealings always made Aiden think the worst. Including that receipt.

"You got a guilty conscience or something?" Aiden asked the man. "Is that why you brought a receipt with you?"

Palmer shrugged. "I figured if you were calling me in, I'd need an alibi."

"That's not an alibi," Aiden informed him. Best to go with the direct approach and repeat Kendall's question. "It just means you possibly weren't at your ranch when the traffic camera recorded this. Did you hire that guy in the SUV to destroy evidence and then kill Kendall and me?"

Palmer's eyes widened, just slightly and for only a fraction of a second. "Are you okay?" he asked Kendall.

"No," she snapped. "Did you hear that part about somebody trying to kill us? Well, it was the man in the SUV that was on the road leading to your ranch."

Palmer glanced at the other lawyer, and the guy quickly took out a phone. To call the ranch, Aiden realized, because he asked to speak to Leonard Graves, one of Palmer's top dogs who was an overseer at the ranch.

"Did Mr. Palmer get any visitor in a black SUV?" the lawyer asked. A moment later, he ended the call and shook his head. "No visitors."

Maybe Graves was telling the truth, maybe not. Aiden's deputies should already be out at the ranch by now so they could have a look for themselves.

"There are plenty of ranch trails on my property," Palmer reminded Aiden. "As you well know, since you used to play out there as a kid."

Ah, a dig about the land deal. That always seemed to come up. But Palmer was right about the ranch trails. There were plenty of them, and they coiled all around his property.

"That doesn't explain why the kidnapper would go there," Aiden pointed out.

"Maybe because he wanted to make me look guilty." Palmer didn't hesitate.

Again, Aiden couldn't argue with what he was saying.

"Think about it," Palmer continued. "Whoever hired that nut job must have known about the traffic camera. Must have known that it would show the SUV turning onto the road that led to my land. If I'd hired him, then the last place I would have told him to come was my ranch."

"Unless the guy panicked when his partner was shot," Aiden supplied. "Or maybe he was hurt, too. I fired into the SUV, and I might have hit him. Maybe the guy needed a doctor and didn't have any other place to go but to the man who hired him."

That got a rise out of Palmer. His jaw locked. His eyes narrowed. "And I suppose you'll say I wanted him to force you to destroy some evidence to clear Jewell's name?"

"Well, it did cross my mind. Did you?"

Palmer huffed, shook his head. "What evidence?"

"The bone fragments." As he'd done with Joplin, Aiden watched for a response.

He got one.

The corner of Palmer's mouth kicked up into a smile. "Well, I gotta say if I was into evidence tampering, that's the lot I'd like to see destroyed. Without those bone fragments, the jury might not believe a man was even killed. And with Jewell's pretty face and angelic eyes, they might be inclined to let her walk."

In your dreams, Aiden nearly snapped, but then he remembered Kendall was right there next to him.

"If my sister is cleared of these charges," Kendall said, staring at Palmer, "it won't be because of her looks. It'll be because a jury will be convinced that she's not capable of murder."

"We're all capable, sweetheart," Palmer answered, and the *sweetheart* actually sounded like a term of endearment rather than sarcasm. "But I'm betting nobody in the county will want your sister to go to jail for ending the life of a miserable piece of cow dung like Whitt Braddock."

Now, here was the point where most sons would have taken exception to their daddy being called cow dung. But the truth was, Whitt just wasn't a good man. Not a good father, either. Well, not to Laine and him anyway. Shelby had barely been seven when their father was killed, and while he was alive, he'd always treated her like a princess.

That was the reason Shelby was fighting tooth and nail to see Jewell convicted. Aiden was just in it for justice.

Any old justice.

So that he could finally put this behind him.

Maybe then his mother would get her head back on straight, and Laine and he would have some peace.

But justice still wasn't going to change the fact that Palmer was right about this. Plenty of people wanted Whitt dead, and those same people didn't want Jewell punished for doing it. That included somebody who might hire kidnappers and send one out to Palmer's place just to make him look guilty.

Aiden silently cursed, because with that hotel receipt, it meant he didn't have any hard evidence to suggest that Palmer had even caught a glimpse of the idiot in the SUV, much less had contact with him.

Palmer knew that, too, because he stood, the lawyer duo standing at the same time. "If there's anything else, Aiden, just give me a holler."

However, before they could make it to the door, it opened, and Leland stuck his head inside. The deputy lifted a pair of handcuffs and looked at Aiden.

"We got it, boss," Leland said. "We got something we can use to make an arrest." His attention went to their visitor. "Lee Palmer, you have the right to remain silent..."

Chapter Eight

Kendall watched as Leland led Palmer away toward the holding cell. Palmer cooperated, all the while barking out orders for his lawyers to find a judge who'd get him out of there ASAP.

And with Palmer's money and connections, that would probably happen.

However, the evidence against him was pretty clear. First, the SUV driver going out to his ranch. Then the money trail Leland had found that linked a payment from one of Palmer's accounts to the dead kidnapper, Montel Higgins. Strong evidence but still maybe not enough to keep Palmer behind bars.

"I got a bad feeling about this," Aiden said.

So did Kendall.

It seemed, well, too obvious.

Palmer was shady, no doubts about that, but he wasn't stupid. Sure, he wanted Jewell to go free, but if he was truly behind this, why wouldn't he have better hidden his tracks? And Palmer definitely had the money to do that. He could simply have paid the kidnappers in cash, and there would have been no record of it.

"Maybe this is another case of reverse psychology?" Kendall suggested. Yes, she was reaching, but something wasn't right.

Aiden shrugged. "Or maybe one of Palmer's lackeys put this idiotic plan together and forgot to tie up a loose end or two."

Maybe. If so, then perhaps Palmer would call off any other "surprises" he might have planned to get Jewell released.

"Now, about that statement," Aiden added after a long breath.

She shook her head. "I need to see Jewell. I want to explain to her in person about the baby."

"Oh, I think she's already figured it out." But then Aiden huffed. "All right. I'll take you to the county jail, and after that you can do the statement, eat and then rest."

Kendall shouldn't have minded that Aiden gave the same importance to eat and rest as he did a mandatory statement about the kidnapping. It smacked of concern not for her exactly but for her condition. A red flag that Aiden was over his initial shock about the pregnancy and was now on to making plans.

Plans that would no doubt clash with the ones she'd already made.

Of course, she'd made those plans when Aiden didn't know about the baby, when she thought it would be best if she just left him out of things. But there was no way he'd be left out of it.

And that meant she needed to figure out what to do.

Aiden didn't say anything else until Leland had locked up Palmer in the holding cell. The lawyers hurried out of the building as if their tails were on fire, but they were probably just in a rush to find a judge or the DA, with the hopes of swaying one of them to let their boss out.

"Jeb, I need you to follow Miss O'Neal and me to the jail," Aiden said, motioning to the deputy in the corner. The young man practically jumped to attention.

Kendall didn't personally know him, but he looked barely old enough to be wearing a badge. Still, Aiden's pickings were slim, as his other deputies were tied up at Palmer's, and Leland had to man the office.

"This shouldn't take long," Aiden said to Leland.

As Aiden had done earlier before they started the drive to the sheriff's office, he looked out the window, no doubt making sure no one was waiting there. Once he opened the door, he hurried her to his truck. The drive was short, only about five miles and just outside town, but Jeb stayed right behind in a patrol vehicle.

"I'll be with you when you talk to Jewell," Aiden said out of the blue.

"No need. She'll probably be upset."

His glance was more of an *I beg to differ* look. "Sure, Jewell will be upset, and that's why I'll be there. We got in that hotel bed together, and there's no need for you to catch the flak for it on your own."

Kendall opened her mouth to argue that she didn't need Aiden as a crutch, but the truth was, she sort of did. Her nerves were raw, right near the surface, and the scrambled eggs and toast she'd had for breakfast were no longer feeling so great in her stomach. Another argument with Aiden wouldn't help, and besides, Jewell would probably want to see him anyway.

Not to yell at him, though.

Jewell wasn't the yelling type. But there'd likely be plenty of hurt in her eyes when she learned that her little sister had slept with the man trying to convict her of murder.

Aiden parked in his reserved spot right next to the county jail, and he gave his deputy a signal indicating that it was okay for him to return to the office, where Kendall was sure Leland would need some help processing Palmer.

The county jail wasn't a modern facility but rather a converted mental hospital that'd been built back in the 1920s. However, the rough limestone facade was definitely prison gray, and there were coils of razor wire ribboning around the top of the high metal fence.

Even though Aiden was the county sheriff, his deputies didn't staff the jail. The guards and warden were civilians, contracted and paid by the county. Still, Aiden's badge got Kendall and him in quickly through the two sets of security doors.

"We don't have an appointment," Aiden said to the guard at the final checkpoint. As part of protocol, Aiden handed the guard his primary and backup weapons, since only the guards were allowed to be armed beyond this point. "But we need to speak with Jewell McKinnon."

The bulky bald guy grumbled something about that not being a problem and motioned for them to follow him. "I'll get her for you."

The guard then put them in the visitors' room to wait while he brought Jewell out to them. Of course, they'd have to talk to her through the thick Plexiglas panel, but at least they'd be face-to-face.

"I hate that Jewell's here," Kendall said under her breath.

She hadn't exactly planned to say that aloud, but it was something Kendall felt every time she'd visited her sister over the past six months. Everything about the place was depressing from its concrete walls, its gray floors and the lingering smell of disinfectant and sweat.

"The trial's in less than two months," Aiden reminded her.

But that might only be the start of more jail time. And if Jewell was convicted of murder, she'd be moved to a prison much farther away.

They sat in the seats in front of the Plexiglas, but Aiden turned to her. "So, what will you say to your sister when she asks what we're going to do about the baby?"

Twenty-four hours ago, the answer would have been easy. She was leaving town to start a new life. But now her plans would likely have to be amended.

"I still think my leaving is a good idea. For your family's sake," she added when she felt his arm tense beside her.

"Your house in Sweetwater Springs is twenty minutes from Clay Ridge," he reminded her.

Yes, but her law office was in Clay Ridge, where she might run into a Braddock or two. Of course, she'd run into Aiden no matter where she ended up.

"How big a part do you think you want in this baby's life?" she asked.

All right, the wording was terrible. As a lawyer, she probably should have come up with something that wouldn't have lit a new fire in Aiden's eyes. And this time, the fire wasn't from the heat of that stupid morning kiss. She'd riled him again.

Aiden didn't exactly jump to answer. Perhaps because he was mulling over what to sling back at her. But he didn't get a chance to say or sling anything. The fluorescent lights flickered, snapping and crackling above them, before they clicked off.

Since there were no windows, the room instantly went pitch-black.

Kendall reached for Aiden's arm, but he was already reaching for her. "It'll be okay," he assured her. "The generator will kick right in."

There was no one else in the room with them, but Kendall heard one of the guards shout out some kind of code. Probably procedure for emergencies like this.

The seconds crawled by. There were more shouted orders from the guard. She recognized the voice as the same one who'd ushered them into the visiting area. She also heard footsteps scrambling around on the tile floors.

"Hell." Aiden got to his feet. "The power shouldn't be off this long."

Kendall agreed, but she didn't get a chance to voice it, because the alarms started clanging through the room. So loud. Much louder than a home security system, and the pulsing blare seemed to rattle the concrete block walls.

He pulled out his phone, cursed. It took her a moment to realize they had no cell service in this part of the building. The reinforced walls made it a dead zone for phone reception.

Aiden moved between her and the door, and even though she couldn't see him that well, she felt him automatically put his hand over his holster, but the gun wasn't there. He'd had to surrender it to the guard.

Her heart was already in her throat, and that didn't help. Was this some kind of prison break?

As far as she knew, Jewell was the only murder suspect on the women's side of the jail, but this wasn't Club Med, and there were other inmates who'd been charged and in some cases convicted of serious felonies.

They waited for what seemed an eternity and finally heard footsteps headed their way. Kendall pulled in her breath, held it, and the door creaked open. It was the bald guard, and he had a flashlight in his left hand, his gun in his right.

"Follow me," he barked.

But Aiden didn't jump to do that. "Why hasn't the generator kicked in?"

"A malfunction." He glanced back over his shoulder. "Now come on. I need to get you two out of here."

Still, Aiden didn't move. "What was your name again?"

Judging from the huff the guy made, he didn't like that question. Kendall wasn't sure she did, either. She wanted to get out of there, but she also wanted to make sure Jewell was okay. After all, this was the guard who was supposed to be bringing her to them. Did that mean Jewell was outside her cell in the dark where she could be hurt if this was indeed a prison break?

"Who are you?" Aiden repeated.

But he didn't answer.

The guard took aim and fired at them.

AIDEN BARELY HAD time to react.

Just as the shot cracked through the air, he pushed Kendall out of the way, praying that he hadn't hurt her in the process. He wasn't hit, and he launched himself at the guard. It was the best he could do, since he wasn't armed, and Aiden somehow had to stop him from firing again.

Aiden collided with the guy who was a heck of a lot bigger than he was, but it was thankfully enough to offbalance the gorilla, because they both crashed to the floor. The flashlight went flying, but the guard managed to hang on to his gun. It didn't help when the guard slugged him.

Damn, that hurt, and Aiden could have sworn he saw stars.

What the heck was going on here?

Clearly, this was a rogue guard, maybe involved in a prison outbreak. But why had he shot at them? Maybe because Aiden was the county sheriff?

He didn't have much time to dwell on that, because he got another punch to the face. Aiden landed a couple of punches as well, but what he couldn't seem to do was knock that gun out of the guard's hand.

The guard cursed him. Profanity that Aiden gave right

back to him, and the struggle landed outside the visiting room and into the small caged booth where the guards waited during visits. Normally, there were plenty of lights and security cameras, but it was now as dark as the rest of the facility.

Even over the sounds of the struggle and the blare of the alarm, Aiden could hear a voice coming from the communicator clipped to the guard's collar. He didn't hear every word, but Aiden caught enough to realize this guy had some help.

"The plug's been pulled. Get out of there now!" the voice said.

The guard cursed him again and kicked like a mule to get Aiden off him. He scrambled to his feet, turning to fire another shot. Aiden had no choice but to dart out of the way.

And it was just enough for the guard to sprint right out of the booth.

Aiden wanted to go after him, to pulverize the moron for the attack, but he wouldn't dare leave Kendall alone. Especially as she might have been hurt. That gave him another jolt of adrenaline. He scooped up the flashlight and hurried back to the visiting room.

He didn't have to look hard for Kendall. She was right there in the doorway. She'd picked up a chair and was holding it like some kind of weapon. Thank God she hadn't tried to use it on the guard, because he would likely have shot her.

"Let's go," Aiden said. Balancing the flashlight, he managed to get her death grip off the chair.

"Is it safe?" she asked, her voice trembling like the rest of her.

"I'll make it safe."

That was possibly a flat-out lie, but Kendall had already been through enough to hear the truth. A truth that didn't matter, since he didn't have a lot of options here. It definitely wasn't safe for them to stay in a room where they could be trapped—again. Their best shot was to get the heck out of Dodge.

"Stay low and behind me," Aiden ordered.

He turned the flashlight to the floor and got them moving. Slowly. And he tried to pick through all the shadows and sounds to figure out what was going on. He didn't dare call out for the guards because they might be on the bald guy's side. But in addition to looking out for rogue guards, he also needed to make sure Kendall and he weren't attacked by escaping prisoners.

Because the security booth was now empty, Aiden paused there and used the flashlight to locate his weapons and to check the hall to his left. It led to the cells, and if he remembered correctly, there were eight prisoners there in the women's wing. On the men's side, there was triple that number.

While he could hear hurried footsteps, there were no gunshots. That was something at least. Kendall had already dodged enough bullets to last a lifetime.

"This way," Aiden instructed.

He'd take Kendall up the main hall, to the next security checkpoint. After that, it wouldn't be much farther to get her out of the building. However, they'd made it only a few steps when he heard a voice.

"No!" someone shouted.

"Jewell," Kendall immediately said, and she would have bolted in that direction if Aiden hadn't held her back.

"It could be an ambush," he reminded her.

She frantically shook her head. "But she might need our help."

Or she could be the reason Kendall and he needed help in the first place.

Something about that didn't ring true for him, though. If Jewell had planned an escape from jail, she wouldn't have involved Kendall. Not like this. And that guard had fired a shot at them. The guy could have just run off, but he'd come after them. That likely meant this wasn't Jewell's plan.

But then, whose sick plan was it?

"We can't just leave my sister here," Kendall argued. "That guard could go after her."

True. At the moment, though, Aiden wasn't nearly as concerned about that as he was about Kendall's safety. Still, it was clear he wasn't going to get her out of there until he found Jewell.

Cursing the potential *damned if you do, damned if you don't* situation, Aiden reminded Kendall again to stay behind him, and he raced toward the hall where he'd heard Jewell's shouted no.

Thankfully, it didn't take Aiden long to spot her. With her blond hair and pale skin, she looked like a ghost in the shadows. She was cuffed, no guard in sight, and it appeared that she was trying to make her way toward them.

"Kendall!" she said, rushing toward her sister. Kendall did some rushing of her own, and she pulled Jewell into her arms. "The guard's going to try to kill you," Jewell warned them.

"Yeah, we know," Aiden confirmed.

What he wanted to find out, though, was how Jewell knew, but this wasn't exactly the time for questions. Especially since he was going to try to get out of this lethal tinderbox with a cuffed murder suspect and a woman who was already sporting one gunshot wound.

"Follow me," he said to them.

Huddled together, they did just that. Aiden tried to keep watch all around them. Hard to do with the darkness and the rooms that seemed to jut out from every direction.

Every step caused his heart to pound even harder, and that didn't improve when he got to the checkpoint and spotted the guard. Just in case this was the bald guy's partner, Aiden lifted his gun.

"I'm Sheriff Braddock," he announced.

The young guard whirled around and nearly lost his footing. If this was a partner in crime, then he sucked at it, because the kid was shaking more than Kendall was.

"What's going on?" Aiden asked him.

"Somebody tampered with the generator. That new fella, I think, because he just went tearing out of here."

Hell. The guy was getting away, no doubt, and Aiden really didn't want that to happen. Not that he had a lot of choices here.

"Where are the rest of the guards?" Aiden pressed.

"Some are trying to get that generator going and get everything locked down. The rest are in the cell blocks. We got some bad people down there."

Yes, and one of them was right behind him.

"The front door was open," the guard went on. "The new guy left it that way. I just locked it, but you got any idea how many regs it breaks to leave that door open?"

Plenty.

But an open door only meant the rogue and any of his helpers would have an easier time getting to Kendall for round two.

"I'm transporting this prisoner to the sheriff's office for questioning," Aiden let the man know. Not exactly standard procedure, but this was a protocol-bending situation if ever there was one. "Unlock the front door for me."

Aiden didn't wait to get his permission to leave. He

got Jewell and Kendall moving again up the hall and toward the front exit. However, he did spare Jewell a glance.

"If you try to escape, I'll make you pay," Aiden warned her.

Jewell blinked, as if that'd been the last thing on her mind. Maybe it was, but it was best to make that crystal clear.

"Just keep Kendall safe," Jewell said, her voice as thin and ghostly as the rest of her.

That was exactly what he planned to do.

The moment the guard unlocked the door, Aiden lifted his gun and with Jewell and Kendall in tow, he ran toward his truck.

Chapter Nine

The nightmare came again, and Kendall woke with a jolt. And she immediately groaned.

The sharp movement caused the stitches in her arm to pull, and she got an instant reminder of the pain. It wasn't as bad as it had been, but coupled with the images from the nightmare, it was more than she could take.

She looked down at the floor, expecting to see Aiden, knowing that just a glimpse of him would steady her nerves.

But he wasn't there.

Instead of steadied nerves, Kendall got another jolt of fear and adrenaline before she heard the water running in the adjoining bathroom. Aiden was apparently in the shower. Probably for the best. It would give her a moment to regain her composure and try to come to grips with the nightmare.

About her sister.

In the dream, Jewell hadn't made it out of that jail alive. The bald guard had succeeded in killing her. But it was just a nightmare. Jewell was very much alive and temporarily in the jail over in Silver Creek, a town not too far from Sweetwater Springs. Even though the warden had wanted Jewell returned within hours after regaining control of the county jail, Aiden had refused, citing his concern for her sister's safety.

Kendall was thankful beyond words for that.

Yes, Jewell was still in a cell, but Kendall figured she'd be a lot safer there than at the county jail. She knew the Ryland brothers, who were the lawmen in Silver Creek, and they'd protect her sister until other arrangements could be made. Of course, the Silver Creek Jail didn't have the right security level for the county to agree to keep Jewell there for long, but it was better than turning Jewell right back over to the warden before a thorough investigation of the security breach could be carried out.

She hadn't had a chance to talk to Jewell about the baby. Soon, though, Jewell would have to know exactly what had gone on between Aiden and her, and Kendall wanted to be the one to tell her.

When she heard Aiden turn off the shower, she got out of bed and put on her robe. She was wearing her pj's again, but with Aiden around, the more clothes, the better.

Aiden, however, didn't play by the rule of the wearing more clothes.

He came out of the bathroom, toweling his hair. No shirt. No boots. He had on his jeans, but they were only partially zipped. And goodness, he smelled like soap and sex. Her soap at that, but it smelled a heck of a lot better on him than her.

Since she was certain she was just standing there ogling him again, Kendall darted past him and went into the bathroom.

The room smelled like him, too.

She didn't shower. Didn't want to strip down and step into the shower where he'd just been. It might cause her to go running to him and beg him to join her. Instead Kendall washed up, brushed her teeth and forced herself not to put on makeup. Like her more-clothes rule, no makeup might make him take one look at her and decide their lustful past was over.

Or not.

That was certainly not a chaste look she got from him when she went back into the room. He was sitting on the foot of her bed again, still only partially dressed, and now he had his phone sandwiched against his shoulder and appeared to be talking to Leland. However, when he looked up, their gazes met.

And just like that, she was lost.

Good grief.

Since it wasn't a smart idea for her to stay there and risk another kiss, Kendall headed downstairs to the kitchen to take her prenatal vitamin and have a glass of milk. Since she'd gotten pregnant, the taste of coffee made her queasy, but she started a pot for Aiden.

She heard him coming down the stairs, his footsteps echoing in the empty house, and Kendall tried to prepare herself for the sight of him. She would have had an easier time stopping a tornado with a paper fan.

He was now wearing a shirt, thank goodness, one from the clothes he'd had a deputy pick up from his house and bring to him. There was nothing special about the dark gray shirt or his jeans, other than the fact that Aiden was the one wearing them.

"There should be some kind of cure for you," she mumbled.

Obviously, she didn't mumble it softly enough, because he heard, and the corner of his mouth lifted. For a split second anyway. Then he followed the smile with a scowl, no doubt reminding himself that this attraction was only going to get them in more trouble.

And trouble came her way.

Aiden slipped his phone into his pocket and studied her as if trying to figure out what he should do or say about her mumblings.

"Anything wrong at the Silver Creek Jail?" she asked.

He shook his head. "Your sister's fine."

That was it. All the conversation he apparently intended, because Aiden cursed, slipped his hand around the back of her neck and pulled her to him. Before her breasts even landed against his chest, his mouth was on her.

And he tasted so good.

It wasn't fair that with just one little kiss, he could send her body into such a tailspin.

He was fighting it, she could tell. The muscles in his arms were stiff. His hands, too, but he didn't back away. Instead, with his mouth still on hers, he groaned and deepened the kiss.

So not good.

Well, not good for their situation, but Kendall soon forgot all about that. There was no booze involved in this kiss. No quick peck like yesterday to get back at him for his snark. This was all heat.

Kendall hadn't intended to move, but she soon found her lower back pressed against the counter. With Aiden pressed against her. Everything fit, of course. His strong arms around her. Body to body. With his right leg wedged between hers.

His scent coiled around her. Mingling with the heat and the pressure that his leg was creating. The right pressure in the right place.

Which made it incredibly wrong.

The pregnancy was going to be plenty hard enough for their families to handle. They didn't need to add an affair to it.

Thankfully, that was enough to get her to unravel herself from his arms. Her body didn't thank her for it, but it was the right thing to do.

Kendall repeated that to herself.

Her body wasn't quite buying it, though, and with Aiden standing in front of her looking like the hottest of her hot fantasies, it took everything inside her to step away from him.

"My hormones are all out of whack," she said. Of course, they usually were when she was within ten feet of Aiden.

"Hormones," he repeated, sounding skeptical.

With good reason. Pregnancy hormones didn't have anything to do with this, and for a moment Aiden looked as if he might prove that to her with yet another kiss. But hopefully he wouldn't. Because Kendall didn't think she had enough willpower to resist another onslaught from that sizzling mouth of his.

Since the coffee was ready, it seemed like a good time to pour him a cup. "What did Leland have to say? Are there any updates?" Something she should already have asked him along with any other question she could come up with fast.

"I need to apologize for that kiss first," he grumbled.

But Kendall waved him off. "We've been apologizing for kisses for over twenty years now."

And it was the truth.

Twenty-three years. A lifetime to be lusting after Aiden, and the memory of that first kiss came flooding back. The news of his father's disappearance had just hit. No details yet of the blood in the cabin. Only the speculations, gossip and questions as to why Whitt was gone.

In those days the Braddocks had lived close enough to the McKinnons, and Kendall had ridden her horse over there to check on Aiden. He'd said he was fine. But he hadn't been. Even as a young girl, she'd been able to see that, and she had put her arms around him to try to comfort him.

The kiss had happened there in the barn with the smell of the hay and horses. If she'd known that just a couple of days later her sister would be whisking her away, Kendall would have made that kiss last a lot longer.

He stayed quiet a moment. "Yeah." And he gulped down some coffee as if it were the cure for what ailed him. "But we were young and stupid back then. Now we're just stupid."

Kendall couldn't help it, she laughed. Aiden stared at her as if she'd lost it, but then the corner of his mouth lifted. "It was clumsy but effective," he said.

It took her a moment to realize he was talking about that kiss. An apt description for it. Her braces hadn't helped, that was for sure, but that twenty-three-year-old kiss had stayed with her all this time.

A benchmark of sorts.

Too bad no other man had quite lived up to it.

A truly sad thought.

"Palmer's already out of jail on bond," Aiden tossed out there.

Since her mind was still on the kiss, it took her a moment to switch gears. "You knew his lawyers wouldn't let him stay there long." She paused. "But there's something else, isn't there?"

He had another sip of coffee first. "Leland said Palmer went off on him. Yelling and cursing. Leland seems to think if Palmer hasn't already done something crazy, he will."

Yes, that definitely qualified as *something else*. "He could have been the one to orchestrate that attack at the jail."

But why? The attack definitely seemed to have been aimed at Aiden and her, and while Palmer didn't care much for Aiden, he'd never had anything against her.

Unless…

"What if Palmer thinks I can connect the missing kidnapper back to him?" she asked.

Aiden shook his head. "How could you do that?"

"Well, I admitted to Joplin that there was something familiar about the guy. Something I couldn't quite put my finger on. Maybe Palmer doesn't want me to remember the man because it'll connect to him."

"The same can be said for Joplin," Aiden reminded her.

She couldn't argue with that. "When I talk to Jewell about the baby, I also want to tell her our suspicions about Joplin. She might fire him and hire someone else. Of course, that wouldn't be smart with Jewell's trial so close, but if Joplin had anything to do with these attacks, then I don't want him anywhere near my sister. Jewell would feel the same way about me."

Well, maybe.

"Bingo," Aiden said as if reading her mind. "Jewell won't like that I've gotten you pregnant."

Take a number. Plenty of people weren't going to like it.

Aiden stared at her from over the rim of his cup. "I'm not going to walk away from this baby."

"Even if it causes a rift in your family?" she asked.

"Even then," he answered just as quickly.

He sounded so confident, and Kendall immediately got a dose of another fantasy. Aiden and her raising their son together. A little boy who'd look just like his daddy with that sandy-blond hair and those mood-changing gray eyes. Since it was a fantasy she'd had most of her life, it wasn't hard to consider it now.

And dismiss it.

"You're talking about shared custody?" she asked.

Aiden stared at her again. Then nodded.

Okay. Not ideal in the fantasy department. Heck, not even ideal in the real world, because she'd wanted to raise her child herself. She definitely didn't want him to be shuffled from one house to another the way she had been as a child. Her parents had divorced shortly after she was born, and Kendall had often felt pulled between her mom and her dad.

She hadn't wanted that for her baby.

Before Kendall could ask Aiden how he thought such an arrangement would play out, his phone rang, and she saw Leland's name on the screen. She hoped the deputy wasn't calling with bad news about Jewell or some plan that Palmer had to get back at them.

Aiden didn't put the call on speaker, and he actually stepped away from her only seconds after his conversation started with the deputy. Not a good sign. Neither was Aiden's forehead, which bunched up.

"When and where?" Aiden asked.

Kendall moved closer to see if she could hear anything Leland was saying. She couldn't. So she could only stand there and wait.

"What's the COD?" Aiden continued a moment later.

That caused her breath to go thin. COD was cause of death. Oh, God. What had happened now?

By the time Aiden finished the call, Kendall's heart was in her throat. "It's not Jewell," she managed to say.

"No." He put away his phone, reached out and touched her arm. "It's the bald guard. His name is Deacon Lynch, and his body was found in a wooded area just off the interstate. He died from gunshot wounds to the head."

Her breath rushed out. Pure relief. Jewell was okay.

But it didn't take long for the obvious question to come to her. "Who killed him?"

Aiden shook his head. "No sign of anyone but the dead body. He was shot at point-blank range."

Even though she wasn't a criminal trial attorney, Kendall was familiar enough with police investigations to know what that meant. "Lynch probably knew his killer."

"Yeah, and his killer is likely the person who hired him. Maybe to silence him so he wouldn't talk."

Of course. The guard had botched the attack and was on the run. His boss wouldn't have wanted him trying to work out a plea deal with the cops. Too bad. Because a plea deal could have given them information so they could put an end to the danger and lock up the monster behind these attacks.

"It's not over," Kendall heard herself mumble, heading out of the kitchen. "I should get dressed so I can visit Jewell."

And then the blasted tears threatened.

She'd already cried way too much, and it only made things worse because it put an even more troubled look in Aiden's eyes. He was worried enough about the safety of the baby and their situation, and now he had to be concerned about how this stress was affecting the pregnancy.

Aiden caught up with her in the foyer. As he'd done earlier, he cursed. Then reached out for her. No kiss this time, but he tugged her away from the door and the two sidelight windows. He didn't stop there. Aiden pulled her into his arms and tucked her head beneath his chin.

"You don't seem to have a lot of faith in my abilities as a sheriff," he said.

Maybe that was meant to lighten the mood. She did have faith in him, because Aiden was a good cop, but someone wanted them dead. And the worst part? Kendall wasn't even sure why.

He brushed a kiss on the top of her head. And the heat came again. Not that it'd ever completely gone away, but it gave her another slam of a reminder she didn't need.

"I should change," she said, but she didn't move. Her feet were anchored to the floor.

Aiden made a sound of agreement, but he didn't move, either.

Heck, she had to do something. "If you kiss me again, you know where it will lead."

Straight to the bedroom.

Another sound of agreement from him, and he leaned his head back. Enough to make eye contact with her. Brief eye contact. Then wham.

Another kiss.

Oh, mercy. This wasn't going to stop.

Well, not stop with just a kiss anyway. Kendall definitely felt the difference between this one and the other. Both were scalding hot, but this one had some urgency to it, and even though Aiden was trying to be gentle, he seemed to be losing that battle, too.

It was a battle she just might have let him win.

If she hadn't heard the sound.

Aiden heard it as well, and he whipped toward the door, shoving her behind him in the same motion.

It didn't take long for Kendall to see the source of the sound. There, on the front porch peering through the sidelight window, she spotted their visitor.

Aiden's mother.

And it was clear from Carla's glare that she'd seen exactly what Kendall and Aiden had been doing.

"Open up," Carla shouted. "We need to talk *now*."

Chapter Ten

Aiden groaned. He definitely didn't need his mother's visit this morning. Neither did Kendall, but she stepped away from him, disengaged the security system and opened the door so his mother could come in.

From just the sound of her voice, Aiden had already known that Carla was in a snit, but without the glass between them, he could see every bit of that fury in her eyes.

"You were kissing her," Carla snapped.

"Yes," Aiden admitted. "Last I heard, that wasn't a crime."

Though he knew Carla would put it on the same level as a felony. Ditto for some members of Kendall's family, too.

"We just got upsetting news," Kendall explained, obviously trying to make this better.

But there was nothing she could say to do that, and that was why Aiden stepped between them. He closed the door, too, just in case whoever had killed the prison guard was waiting out there with a high-powered rifle.

"And kissing my son makes bad news better?" Carla fired back.

"Yes," Kendall said after a long pause. "As a matter of fact, it did help."

Aiden nearly laughed. Kendall had some backbone

all right, but it wasn't a trait that Carla was going to appreciate right now.

Every muscle in Carla's jaw turned to iron, and she aimed the next glare at him. "So, now you're staying here with her?"

He nodded. "Someone's tried to kill Kendall twice. She's pregnant with my baby, and I want to be able to make sure she's safe."

Of course, so far he was doing a lousy job of that, but Aiden swore to himself that he'd do better.

"One of your deputies could have stayed with her," Carla argued. "Or one of Jewell's sons."

Aiden put his hand on Kendall's stomach. "This is my baby," he clarified, knowing he sounded smart-mouthed in the process. "I've got more at stake here than my deputies or the McKinnons."

"Well, I don't like it." Carla's glare got worse.

No surprise there. Aiden didn't like a lot of things about this—her visit included.

"Why are you here, Mother?" he asked.

Even with the direct question, she still didn't take those glaring eyes off Kendall and him. She finally reached into her enormous purse, pulled out a padded envelope and handed it to him.

"I have some evidence against Robert Joplin," Carla said. "It should be enough for you to arrest him for these attacks."

You could have knocked Aiden over with a feather, and judging from the slight gasp Kendall made, she was equally shocked.

"What kind of evidence?" Aiden wanted to know. As the envelope wasn't sealed, he looked inside and saw a cell phone.

"There's a recording of Joplin meeting with a hired

gun." For having just delivered a bombshell, Carla stayed pretty calm. "If you dig around, I think you can link it to the man who kidnapped Kendall."

Okay. That would be nice if that truly happened, but Aiden had his doubts. "How'd you get this?"

Now she dodged his gaze. "I hired a PI to follow Joplin, and he managed to record it."

Aiden gave her a flat look. "Did this PI you hired break any laws to get it?"

Carla lifted her shoulder, managed to look a little indignant. "What does it matter? It's practically a confession."

"It matters. If the PI obtained it illegally like with a wiretap, then I can't use it to arrest Joplin." However, it would be proof of the lawyer's guilt, so maybe it would give Aiden a jumping-off point to launch an investigation.

He looked at Kendall to see how she was handling this, but she shook her head. "If Joplin's guilty, I want him to fry."

So did Aiden.

Since the phone had already been compromised for prints while in his mother's purse and heaven knew where else, Aiden took it out and clicked the button to hear the recording. The quality was far from ideal, but he had no trouble hearing the voices of two men.

"You'll get half the money now and half when the job's done," Joplin said.

"You want it done at her place?" the second man asked.

"It doesn't matter," Joplin answered. "Just get it done."

And that was it.

While it wasn't exactly a confession of guilt, it certainly sounded suspicious. Still, there was a big problem. "Joplin could say he was talking to his gardener or any other employee that he was sending to somebody's house to do work."

His mother handed him a piece of paper she took from her purse. "That's the name of the man on the recording. Barry McNease. If you check, you'll find he has a long criminal record."

Aiden would check all right, but he had some other things to settle first. "I'll need the name of the PI who did the recording," he said to Carla.

She hesitated and finally extracted a business card from her purse. "I don't know why you just can't see this recording as a gift to get a guilty man off the streets."

"I'd rather be sure that this *gift* isn't just some trumped-up nonsense designed to send the wrong man to jail. Arresting the wrong person won't keep Kendall safe."

Aiden paused and went on to the next matter he needed clarified. "I had a chat with Joplin yesterday, and he said you're the one who told him Kendall was pregnant."

Carla pulled back her shoulders as if she might launch into a denial. Then she shrugged. "I told him because I thought maybe Jewell and he could talk some sense into Kendall."

"Excuse me?" Kendall didn't stay behind him. She came out to face his mother head-on. "What's your definition of talking some sense into me?"

Carla's gaze darted around for a few uncomfortable seconds. "You shouldn't be raising a child. Your sister's a killer, and your blood is the same as hers."

"Alleged killer," Aiden corrected. He was glad Kendall wasn't the hitting, hair-pulling type, because his mother had just crossed a very big line. "That's why we have courts of law and such."

"And you think you'd be a better person to raise my baby?" Kendall asked Carla, but she didn't wait for an answer. "Because you're not. You're a bitter woman, and you have no say whatsoever in my life or this child's."

Aiden hoped like the devil that the *no say* didn't apply to him, too. But it was clear this visit was not making things better. Well, maybe with the exception of the recording, but there were so many possible snags that went along with it that it would likely turn out to be nothing. Still, before he ushered his mother out, he had one more question for her.

"How did you even know Kendall was pregnant?" Aiden demanded. "And this time I want the truth."

Carla looked him straight in the eye. "Your sister told me."

"Laine," Kendall said on a huff.

"No. Shelby," Carla corrected. Her chin came up. "That horrible Lee Palmer hired PIs to follow all of us around so he could get some dirt to help out Jewell. Shelby found out about it and started following one of the PIs. She saw you two leave the Bluebonnet together three months ago."

"Wait a minute. The PI that Palmer hired was following me?" Kendall asked.

"Or maybe Aiden. Shelby wasn't sure, so she stuck close to him and then followed you to the hotel. We'd both hoped the one-night stand would be the end of it between you two. We were obviously wrong."

Yep. They'd been wrong. But now Aiden knew how the word had gotten around about Kendall and him at the bar. Either his sister had blabbed it. Or maybe the PI. Maybe even Carla once she got the info from Shelby.

"That doesn't explain how you knew I was pregnant," Kendall said to his mother.

"I'm not sure how Shelby found out, but she's the one who told me." With that, Carla turned to leave, and like a child who'd just gotten scolded, she slammed the door behind her.

"I think it's time I had a little chat with Shelby," Aiden said.

He put the phone with the recording on the stairs and took out his own cell. He also motioned for Kendall to lock the door and reset the alarm.

"I can put the call on speaker," he said to Kendall. "But it's highly probable that my sister will say some things you won't like."

"I already know what people are saying. Please put the call on speaker."

Aiden did, but he hoped he didn't regret it. Especially as Kendall had already had enough ill will thrown at her this morning.

"What?" Shelby snapped when she answered the call. Obviously, he'd woken her, but Aiden didn't care. His sister had some serious explaining to do.

"So you followed Kendall and me?" Aiden demanded.

Shelby made a sleepy, irritated sound. "Just Kendall. Well, actually I followed a PI who was following Kendall, but since you were with her, let's just say you got caught up in the net."

Thankfully, Kendall didn't snap about that being a violation of her privacy, because if Shelby knew she was listening, she might not be so willing to answer his questions. But if she didn't supply those answers now, she *would* give them to him. One way or another.

"So you followed Kendall, you found out that we'd spent the night together in the hotel and you spilled it to Laine and then Mom," Aiden recapped.

"They told you that?"

"Mom did. I just had a *friendly* chat with her about it. You might have given me a heads-up, Shelby."

"I hadn't meant to tell her. It just sort of slipped out. But while we're doing the finger-pointing, you should have told me that you were messing around with the likes of Kendall O'Neal."

Kendall gave a heavy sigh, stepped away and would have headed to the sidelight window, no doubt to look out to make sure his mother was gone. But Aiden didn't want her in any potential gunman's line of sight, so he held her back.

"Aiden, I can't believe you slept with her," Shelby added.

He reminded himself that he loved his sister. Not right at the moment. But in a big picture kind of way, he loved her. "It happened. Now Kendall's pregnant and in danger. What do you know about that?"

Silence. For a very long time. "When you talked to Mom, did she seem, well, okay?"

That definitely wasn't a question that Aiden had expected. "No. But then she never seems okay. She's been in a bad mood for twenty-three years." And seeing a shrink. "Why? Does she seem okay to you?"

More silence. "I'm not sure. Something was off."

"I can say the same thing about you," Aiden countered. "Why exactly did you follow the PI?"

"Because I want to make sure Jewell's convicted, that's why," Shelby answered.

Aiden's huff matched Kendall's. "There's a boatload of evidence against Jewell," he reminded his sister. "Lots of Dad's blood in the cabin. Jewell's DNA on the sheets. Those bone fragments found just a stone's throw away from the cabin. Sounds like a slam dunk to me."

Well, with the exception of a confession.

And the niggling feeling Aiden was getting that this

particular slam dunk seemed to be tied up into a too-neat package.

But maybe that was the fault of the pregnancy. And the kissing session. Or just being around Kendall.

"I don't want any questions in the jury's mind of Jewell's guilt," Shelby continued. "Jewell weighs a hundred and ten pounds soaking wet, and Daddy was a big man. I figure she must have had help moving the body from the cabin to the creek."

That had come up plenty of times, and most folks thought Jewell's husband, Roy, had helped. But an eyewitness had recently cleared Roy.

"So you're looking at possible accessories to a murder?" Aiden concluded.

"Yes. Joplin and Palmer are tops on my list. From everything I've learned, Joplin was in love with Jewell even back then. And we both know how much Palmer hated Daddy."

Aiden made a sound of agreement. "Am I on your list? I was big enough to have helped move a body, and Dad and I weren't exactly on friendly terms, either."

Shelby made a garbled sound of outrage and shock. "What the heck does that mean?"

"It means that not everything about this case is black-and-white." And he waited, figuring that would prompt an argument or maybe Shelby would bring up that he was going soft because of the baby.

But his sister stayed quiet. Quiet enough for Aiden so that the niggling feeling became even worse.

"Mom gave me the recording with Joplin and an alleged scumbag who might have been hired to kidnap Kendall," Aiden explained, hoping to squish that feeling. "She said she got it from a PI she hired, but I'm assuming you gave it to her."

"Well, you're assuming wrong." Shelby paused again. "What's on this recording?"

"Maybe nothing. I need to talk to Joplin about it." And Aiden figured the lawyer would try to explain it away just as Palmer had tried to do with the traffic camera footage.

"Joplin has plenty of motive to want those bone fragments destroyed," Shelby insisted.

So did others. But that brought Aiden to something he wanted to make crystal clear. "Shelby, you need to back off from this investigation."

"What—"

Aiden talked right over her howling protest. "Here's the deal. What you're doing could be construed as interfering with a murder investigation and possibly even the judicial process. Do you really want to give Joplin a reason to file a motion to have the case against Jewell thrown out?"

"He'd have no grounds for that," she fired back.

"And don't give him any. Back off, Shelby, and that's not brotherly advice, that's a warning from the county sheriff."

Aiden braced himself for an argument, something that Shelby was darn good at, but more of that unsettling silence followed.

"Are you and Kendall okay?" Shelby finally asked. "I heard about the attack at the jail. It sounds as if you two could have been hurt."

Her concern for Kendall was a little surprising. And welcome. "We could have been killed. I don't guess in all your digging around that anything came up about a scumbag prison guard on the take?"

Oh, man.

It was suddenly quiet enough to hear a pin drop.

"All right, what the heck is wrong?" Aiden demanded.

"Maybe nothing," Shelby said almost in a whisper.

That got Aiden groaning because it not only confirmed that something was indeed wrong but that it was something Shelby didn't like.

"It's about Mom," Shelby finally said.

Kendall pulled in her breath, moved closer to the phone. Aiden held his breath, too, because he was a hundred percent certain this was something he wasn't going to like.

"I think we can agree that Mom's been acting a little erratic lately," Shelby continued. "She's upset about the baby."

Heck, no. He did *not* like the direction this was going.

"What the hell did she do?" Aiden growled.

Shelby cleared her throat. "When I was at the house last night, I saw a bank statement on her personal computer. Not for her regular bank. This was one I didn't know about."

Strange, since Shelby managed the family's finances and Carla's trust fund.

"I told Mom about the baby four days ago," Shelby went on, "and twenty-four hours later, she withdrew a large sum of money from this account that I didn't even know she had."

That put a tight knot in his stomach. "How much?"

"Fifty thousand," Shelby admitted after yet another pause. "I hoped maybe she was planning a big trip or something, so after dinner I asked her about it. She claimed she didn't know what I was talking about. When I went back to her office to show her, the account had been deleted, and there was no trace of it. I can't think of a good reason why Mom would do something like that, can you?"

No, but he could think of a bad one.

Apparently, Kendall could, too.

"Oh, God," Kendall whispered, and she pressed her fingers to her mouth.

And Aiden knew why. Fifty thousand dollars was plenty enough to pay for the attacks on Kendall.

"I have to go," Aiden said to Shelby. "I need to talk to our mother now."

He pushed the end call button, but before Aiden could scroll through for Carla's number, his phone rang. At first he thought it was Shelby calling back to tell him to go easy on their mom.

But unknown caller was on the screen.

That knot in his gut tightened.

"Sheriff Braddock," Aiden answered. He didn't put the call on speaker, but Kendall moved so close that she'd likely hear anyway.

There was a lot of static on the line, and it took several seconds before the caller said anything. "This is Harry Yost."

Aiden looked at Kendall to see if she knew who that was, but she only shook her head.

"Who are you and what do you want?" Aiden asked the man. He didn't bother to sound friendly, either, because there were rarely good reasons why someone didn't want their number viewed.

"I'm the person who kidnapped Kendall O'Neal and took her to your place," the man volunteered. "If you want to find out why I did that, then come and see me so we can talk."

Chapter Eleven

Kendall didn't have to ask the caller if he was lying about who he was. He wasn't. She recognized his voice. It was indeed one of the men who'd kidnapped her.

And the very one who'd shot her.

He had also tried to kill Aiden and her before getting away in the SUV. Because he'd been missing for two days, she'd thought that maybe they'd seen the last of him. Apparently not.

"I'm listening," Aiden said, pressing the speaker button so she could hear better. Probably because she was right against him, and he needed to take out a small notepad and pen from his pocket.

"Don't bother trying to trace the call," Yost said. "I'm using a burner, and I'll toss it as soon as we're done talking."

Maybe they'd get some answers before that happened. "Why me?" Kendall asked.

"Can't answer that. I got orders to take you and use you to get the sheriff to destroy that evidence."

"Who gave you those orders?" Aiden demanded.

It sounded as if the guy chuckled. "Not gonna get into that over the phone. I'm looking for some help here, and I figure the only way I'll get that help is to have something I can use to barter."

Kendall hung on every word. Processing it and mentally repeating it. "I know you," she said.

Yost, if that was truly his name, didn't jump to verify that. "Our paths have crossed. When you were at the pharmacy waiting for your prescription to be filled, I started chatting to you about headache meds."

It took her a moment, but it all came back. A big guy, dark hair with a military cut. "You followed me there."

"I did." No trouble admitting it, and that fact caused Aiden to mumble some profanity. "My partner and I were supposed to take you from the parking lot, but somebody was following you. Thought it was wise for us to back off and take you from your office instead."

The someone following her had probably been the PI Palmer had hired. Or maybe it was the one working for Aiden's mother. There were an awful lot of PIs lurking around, and it turned her stomach to think that she hadn't noticed them. Of course, with the pregnancy and Jewell's trial, she'd had a lot on her mind.

That misstep had turned out to be dangerous.

"I thought you might have remembered my voice," Yost confirmed a moment later. "And that you maybe could have picked me out of a photo lineup."

"I could have. Is that why you tried to have me killed at the jail?" she asked.

"I had no part in that one, but I got caught up in the flak."

"How?" Aiden snapped. "And did you have something to do with the dead guard from the county jail?"

Silence. For a long time. "That's something for a face-to-face conversation, something I want to have with Miss O'Neal and you."

Aiden was shaking his head before Yost even finished. "I'm not letting Kendall get anywhere near you."

"You will if she wants to know who's trying to kill her. I'm at the football field at the high school in Clay Ridge. It's early, but there are plenty of kids already here for track practice. Some cheerleaders, too."

"Don't you hurt those kids," Aiden growled.

"Wouldn't dream of it. I just figured you'd be more inclined to visit with me if I made it in an *interesting* location."

His smugness made her want to reach through the phone and slap him. How dare he play with people's lives like this? And apparently he'd done it all for money, as Yost said someone had hired him.

"How do you think a meeting between us would play out?" she asked.

Aiden glared at her, letting her know with those narrowed eyes that such a meeting wasn't going to happen. Still, she wanted to know what this dirtbag expected of her.

"I'm thinking you'll show up here in a half hour," Yost went on. "Since you're probably still at your house over in Sweetwater Springs, that should give you enough time if you don't dawdle. Or if the sheriff doesn't take the time to drop you off somewhere."

Which was exactly what Aiden would do. No way would he let her go near this guy again after what he'd done to her the last time. Kendall could still hear the gunshot. Still feel the pain in her arm. And while she wanted to know the truth, she couldn't put her baby at risk.

Couldn't put Aiden at risk, either.

However, Kendall seriously doubted she'd be able to stop him from going to this meeting.

"Then what?" Aiden pressed. "You expect to tell me whatever it is you think I want to know and then just walk away?"

"No. I expect protective custody. The real kind where I'm, you know, actually protected and not shot or beat to death while I'm in a holding cell."

"You need protecting?" Aiden didn't sound any more convinced of that than she was. This guy was a killer. That said, the jail guard was dead, and it was likely that his killer wanted to do the same to Yost.

But why?

Why set this monster into motion and then kill him?

Maybe because she could identify him and somehow link him back to the person who hired him.

She glanced up at Aiden, their gazes meeting, and even though he didn't say anything to her, she figured he was on the same wavelength. Now Kendall needed to make the connection. And fast.

"Of course I need protecting," Yost finally said. "My partner, Montel Higgins, is dead. Don't want to end up like him… I gotta go," he quickly added. "I see somebody." No more smugness. Judging from his tone, he was scared. Or else he was pretending to be.

"Who do you see?" Aiden asked.

"Gotta go," Yost repeated. "Just get here fast, because in thirty minutes, I'm outta here." And with that, he hung up.

Kendall didn't waste a second. She headed straight for the stairs. "I'll get dressed."

"This doesn't mean you're coming with me," he called up to her, and she heard him start on some phone calls. Hopefully, arranging backup for himself so he wouldn't have to face Yost alone.

Kendall dressed as fast as she could, throwing on a pair of jeans and a top. When she made it back downstairs, Aiden was still on the phone, so she disengaged the security system. As he'd done other times, he looked around outside, finished his call and got her moving to his truck.

"I'll drop you off with Leland and Sarah at the sheriff's office," Aiden explained. "Jeb will go with me."

Jeb, the most inexperienced deputy in the department. That didn't help steady her nerves.

"Yost said you wouldn't have time to do that," she reminded him.

He gave her a determined glance. "You're staying with the deputies."

She wished that Aiden could do the same, stay tucked away safely with her, but Kendall knew she had zero chance of talking him out of this. After all, he was the sheriff, and he'd want to talk to Yost to see what he could learn.

And they had plenty to learn.

"What are you going to do about your mother?" she risked asking.

No look this time. Not at her anyway. Aiden kept watch around them. Still, she had no trouble seeing the muscles at war in his jaw. "I'll treat her like any other suspect."

From some people, that might have been lip service. It wasn't from Aiden. "Can you think of a reason why your mother would withdraw that money?"

A reason that didn't involve kidnapping her to force Aiden to destroy evidence.

A reason that didn't involve the baby, either.

"You know that my mother is seeing a shrink," he finally said. "Well, she needs it. I told you about her depression, but she's also been battling extreme mood swings since Dad was killed."

Another reminder of how many lives had been affected from that one tragic day.

"Did she have mental problems before?" Kendall asked, causing Aiden to give her a questioning glance.

Even though it'd been a simple question, apparently he knew that it hadn't come out of the blue.

"Before what? Did you find out something about my mother?" he asked.

That required a deep breath. "Maybe." And another deep breath. "Like Shelby, I've been doing plenty of research, and I came across an elderly woman who used to work for a psychiatrist. She said she thought your mother had been his patient a long time ago."

The surprise went through his eyes. "How long ago?"

"Before she married your father. But I don't have any other details," she added. "In fact, I'm not even sure it's true. The woman's almost eighty years old, and her memory might not be that good."

Kendall was clinging to that. Even if Carla had spent time there, she could see why the woman wouldn't want to share something like that with her kids. Still, if Carla had had issues for that long, then maybe those *issues* had resurfaced with news of the baby.

"Carla never mentioned it?" Kendall asked.

Aiden shook his head, and he sat there, stiff and silent as stone.

Kendall waited a few moments. Not nearly enough time for him to process all this, but they were just scratching at the surface and didn't have a lot of time to work this out.

"Of course, I now have to wonder about the money that Shelby saw in the account," Kendall added.

More silence, and he seemed to be trying to tamp down his nerves. "Carla might be hoping to use it as some kind of payoff to you. Maybe to get you to give up the baby."

Kendall's mouth fell open. "I'd never give up this baby. *Never.* Not for any amount of money—"

"I know that, but my mother's desperate, so she might be willing to do desperate things."

"How desperate?" she pressed when Aiden didn't continue.

He swallowed hard. "Desperate enough to try to get you out of the picture."

That caused her heart to slam against her chest. Of course, Kendall had already considered it after everything she'd learned, but it was another thing to hear it said aloud. From the woman's own son, no less.

"I'll handle it," Aiden went on. "I'll bring her in, question her. If she's behind this, I'll get the truth."

A truth that could shake him to the core. Yes, Aiden's relationship with his mother was rocky, but she was still his mother. And if she'd truly been behind the kidnapping, then that also meant she was responsible for the attempts to kill them.

Good God, had Carla tried to have her own son killed? Or was he just possible collateral damage, because Kendall would have been Carla's real target?

"I'm sorry." Kendall slipped her hand over his. More tight muscles. But he didn't pull away. "And it might not even be her. After all, we have two other suspects. Palmer and Joplin."

Aiden didn't answer, but she figured he was hoping that it was anybody but Carla.

His phone rang, and when he fished it from his pocket, she saw Leland's name on the screen again.

"We got a problem," Leland said the moment that Aiden answered. "There's been a report of gunshots near the high school."

Aiden cursed. "I'm still five minutes out."

"Sarah and I are on the way there now. I know that only leaves Jeb in the office to watch Kendall, so I called Seth Calder. He was at the jail going over what happened, and he'll be at the office by the time you get there."

Aiden groaned slightly but thanked Leland. His phone also beeped, indicating that he had another call coming in. One look at the screen, and Aiden cursed again when he saw it was from an unknown caller.

Yost, no doubt.

"I'll call you back," Aiden said to his deputy and then switched over to Yost. "What the hell's going on?"

"Well, it's not going as planned, that's for sure. Somebody's shooting at me, and I had to return fire." Yost sounded out of breath, as if he was running. And there was a loud bang. Probably the sound of another shot.

Oh, God. The students could be hurt.

"Who's shooting at you?" Aiden demanded.

"Don't know. Yet. But obviously there's been a change of plans. Don't come here. I'll call you when I'm out of this mess."

"My deputies are on the way to you now," Aiden told the man, but he was talking to the air, since Yost had already hung up.

Aiden sped up even more, but he continued to keep watch around them, and when he reached the sheriff's office, he didn't go into the parking lot. He literally drove onto the sidewalk so he could stop his truck directly in front of the entrance. Seth was already there, stepping out of his vehicle, and he hurried toward her.

"Tell Jeb to lock down the place," Aiden told Seth. "And thanks."

Seth grumbled a terse "you're welcome" and he got her inside. He didn't have to tell Jeb to do a lockdown, because the deputy started it right away.

Kendall looked out the reinforced window, praying that Aiden would be all right, but as soon as he put his truck in gear to drive away, she heard a sound that she didn't want to hear.

A gunshot.

And this wasn't coming from the school a mile away. It was close. So close that Seth pushed her behind him, drew his gun and looked out the window, as well. Kendall came up on her toes so she could look over his shoulder, but there was nothing to see. Not at first anyway.

There was another thick blast.

Followed by the sound of Aiden's truck door.

And a moment later, she saw Aiden peering around the edge of the building, his attention on the park behind the sheriff's office.

"The shooter's out there," she whispered, her voice already shaking. She wasn't worried for herself but for Aiden.

"Aiden's deputies are coming," Seth reminded her, no doubt sensing the bad scenarios going through her head. "He'll have backup soon."

But maybe soon wouldn't be soon enough.

There was another shot.

Mercy, who was doing this? Yost? Or was this the person he'd mentioned seeing at the school? She figured whoever that person was, he didn't have friendly intentions, because Yost had ended the call darn fast.

"Stay down." Seth looked back at her with a warning glance. "The glass is bullet-resistant, but a cop-killer bullet can get through. Sorry," he added in a mumble when she gasped.

Cop-killer. A coated bullet that could penetrate walls. And kill cops like Aiden.

"I just don't want you hurt," Seth said to her. "And neither does Aiden."

That was true, but that still didn't level her breathing. Why was this happening again?

"I'm Sheriff Braddock," Aiden called out to the shooter. "Drop your weapon."

That didn't happen. There was a fourth shot. Thankfully, it didn't seem to come Aiden's way, but he was out there and could be gunned down.

"There," Seth said. He used his gun to motion toward a cluster of trees that were about thirty yards from the building.

At first Kendall didn't see anything, but then there was a blur of motion. Someone running from one tree to the other. However, she couldn't tell if it was Yost. Maybe it was an innocent bystander just trying to get out of the way of those bullets.

Kendall pulled in her breath. Waiting and praying. The seconds crawled by, turning into one very long minute. No more shots. No more blurs of motion.

"The deputies are here," Seth told her.

But when Kendall tried to see, he blocked her way again.

"They're just up the street," he added.

Good. Hopefully, just their arrival would cause the shooter or Yost to back off. If Yost was indeed the one doing the shooting, that is.

Just as that thought crossed her mind, someone fired. The shot seemed even louder than the others. Judging from the way Seth's shoulders tensed, the bullet had come closer to the building.

It was the same for the next shot.

But that bullet sounded different. It took Kendall a

moment to realize why. It was the sound of a shot hitting someone.

"Aiden?" she called out and would have bolted to the door if Seth hadn't caught on to her.

"You can't go out there," he insisted.

Yes, she knew that. She couldn't put the baby in danger that way, but she had to make sure Aiden was all right.

"It's not Aiden," Seth warned her.

Because she was trying to fight through the panic, it took her a moment to realize what he meant. Then she spotted the movement in the trees again. Not a blur this time. Someone pushed through the low-hanging branches and staggered out into the parking lot.

Yost.

Even from the distance she could tell it was the same man who'd spoken to her in the pharmacy. He wasn't wearing a ski mask as he had been when he kidnapped her, but he did have a gun in his hand.

"Drop your weapon!" Aiden shouted to him. He came out farther from the building, his own gun aimed right at the man.

Kendall braced herself for a shoot-out. Yost had already tried to kill them at least once, and he likely wouldn't hesitate to try again.

But Yost didn't lift his weapon. It stayed by his side while he clutched his chest with his left hand.

That was when Kendall saw the blood.

The man had been shot.

"He can't die," she blurted out. "He has to tell us who hired him."

"Call an ambulance," Seth ordered the deputy. "He's alive," he added, glancing back at her. "Wait here, and I'll see what I can do to keep him that way."

Chapter Twelve

Dead.

That was not how Aiden had wanted this to play out.

He'd wanted Yost alive and talking. Especially talking. But the two gunshots to the man's chest had prevented him from saying anything, along with killing him within a matter of seconds.

Hard, though, to feel any sympathy for the man who'd kidnapped Kendall and then shot her.

Within minutes of Yost's collapsing in the parking lot, Aiden had gone after the shooter. So had two of his deputies while Seth and Jeb had stayed behind in the office to protect Kendall in case this had been some kind of diversion. But after a half-hour search of the area and no trace of Yost's killer, Aiden and the others had given up.

Yeah, definitely not how Aiden wanted this to go.

The look on Kendall's face sure wasn't helping, either. Aiden already felt as if he'd failed her and the baby, again, but now her face was even more bleached out than before, and while she was trying to put up a strong front, she was doing it by leaning on Seth.

Literally.

Aiden tried not to feel jealous about that.

After all, it was Seth who had stayed with her during

the attack, and he'd continued to stay with her after Aiden returned to the office and started the flurry of calls to arrange a full-scale search for the killer. But even after Aiden finished those calls, Kendall had stayed by Seth, his arm around her while she continued to look more and more upset.

Since Aiden had plenty to do, he ignored the arm position, tried to ignore the rest of her reactions and got back to work.

"Anything yet on the recording that I got from my mother?" he asked Jeb. The one that might implicate Joplin in all this.

The young deputy shook his head. "The Ranger Lab hasn't finished with it yet. I'm still trying to get in touch with Joplin so I can ask him about it, but he's not answering his phone. The calls are going straight to voice mail."

Not a good sign.

Well, maybe not.

The lawyer could just be tied up with another case, and if Joplin was as guilty as sin, then maybe he was already on the run. Headed far away from Kendall. And if he was indeed in flight mode, maybe he'd get caught. Aiden needed something to break in this case soon.

Also something to break that armlock Seth had on Kendall.

Yep, it was bugging him, and it was bugging him even more that he couldn't seem to stop thinking about it.

He checked out the window to see how things were progressing in the parking lot. The ME was there as Yost's body was being loaded into the van. A pair of CSIs were processing the area for evidence.

They might get lucky and find one of the spent shell casings from the killer, which would really come in handy, as the bullets that'd killed Yost had gone clean through.

If they could get their hands on just one slug or casing, they'd be able to determine the type of gun. Might even be able to get a match if the gun had been used in some other crime.

"We got the surveillance footage of the high school," Leland announced when he finished his latest call. "It's loading on my computer now, and I'll go over it frame by frame."

Good. Because all this had started near the high school, so maybe Yost's attacker had been caught on the footage.

The one good thing in all this was that no shots had been fired near the kids. That was something at least. And they'd also gotten lucky that none of the stray bullets had hit anyone in the park.

Or Kendall.

She'd been in the building during the attack, but that didn't mean she couldn't have been hurt. Her being in danger was becoming a pattern that Aiden didn't like one bit.

Of course, there were a lot of things he didn't like about their situation.

"I'm okay," Kendall said out of the blue, and that was when Aiden realized he was scowling at her. Actually, he was scowling at Seth, but she probably figured she was in on that facial expression, as well.

"Are you really?" Aiden asked. "Because the stress isn't good for you. Or the baby."

A sigh left her mouth, and she finally moved out of Seth's arms when he got a call and stepped away from her to take it. "It's not good for you, either."

She went to Aiden, sliding right into his arms as if she belonged there. "You could have been killed." Her voice was strained, barely a whisper, but he heard the emotions loud and clear.

Uh-oh.

That wasn't ordinary concern for a fellow human being. Nope. That was concern for her baby's daddy. Maybe even for him.

Aiden pulled back, looked in her eyes.

Yeah, it was concern for him all right.

After his reaction to Seth's embrace, that should have felt darn good. But it only added another layer of complications to their already complicated situation.

Kendall was pregnant with his baby. They were a Texas version of Romeo and Juliet. Star-crossed lovers. And because that story hadn't had a happy ending, this extra layer only made him worry more.

Did that make him move away from her?

Nope.

He'd clearly developed a fondness for complicated layers. Apparently, a fondness for having Kendall in his arms, too.

"I'm sorry," he whispered.

Now she looked up at him. "For what?"

"Everything" seemed like a really good answer.

Kendall stared at him, those eyes so green that they looked like spring itself. Spring with heat, of course. Even now, the heat was there. No doubt in his own eyes, too, so Aiden added another "I'm sorry" for it.

She blinked. Then the corner of her mouth lifted just a fraction.

"Next thing, you'll be apologizing for the weather." Kendall took his hand, pressed it against her stomach. "The baby and I are both fine, and you're the reason for that."

Another uh-oh.

That was playing with fire in its purest form. Her gratitude. Touching her stomach. Touching her anywhere for that matter.

Seth noticed, of course.

And Aiden didn't think it was his imagination that Mr. FBI hurried to finish his call so that he could come back to his step-aunt's aid. However, Kendall stayed put, right against Aiden, even though he did move his hand from her stomach to her shoulder.

"That was Sawyer Ryland, the agent who's investigating the attack at the jail," Seth informed them.

That got Aiden's attention. Kendall's, too. "Did he find out anything?" she asked.

"It's all preliminary stuff, but obviously plenty went wrong yesterday. Ryland thinks that a few of the male prisoners were paid off to cause a commotion to get the guards to the cell block after the power went off."

That would explain why there was only one guard at the checkpoint. "Have any of the inmates talked?"

Seth nodded. "One said money was deposited into his online account. Not much, just a couple of hundred dollars, but he's claiming the only person he dealt with is the dead guard, Deacon Lynch."

That was likely true. Because the person who'd hired Lynch and Yost probably wouldn't have wanted to have his identity revealed to inmates.

"How the heck did Lynch even become a jail guard?" Aiden asked.

Seth gave a frustrated huff. "Because he doesn't have a record as an adult. He had a juvie one, but it was sealed, of course. But what he did have was debt and plenty of it. Two ex-wives, five kids, and he was way behind in his child support payments. At least he was until a couple of days ago when he gave one of his exes the five grand he owed her."

Those debts should have been a red flag to the county agency who handled employment records for the guards, and Aiden would do some checking to see who'd dropped the ball.

But there were other things that needed checking, too.

At least five grand to Lynch alone. Probably that and maybe more to Yost and his dead co-kidnapper. The SUV, the weapons and ammo. The bill for this fiasco was adding up, and that meant a money trail.

One that Aiden had possibly already found.

"Any indication if there were other guards working with Lynch?" Kendall asked Seth before Aiden could say anything.

"None right now, but there were definitely some breaches of protocol and security during the attack. There'll be some heads rolling."

And Aiden would make sure it happened. Even though he wasn't in charge of the jail, it was right there, practically under his nose, and he didn't want anything like this happening again.

"What about the generator?" Aiden asked. "Anything back on why it failed to kick in when the power was cut?"

"Someone tampered with it," Seth answered. "But the person also disabled the camera out there."

That likely had been Lynch's doing, too. He could have managed to tamper with it hours or even days before the attack. And that led Aiden to another question he had about all this.

How had Lynch known that Kendall would be at the jail that day?

Aiden already knew that Kendall visited Jewell two to three times a week, so maybe Lynch just figured she'd be there eventually.

Or maybe it was more than that.

Maybe Lynch knew Kendall would be arriving soon to tell Jewell about the pregnancy.

Of course, that led to yet another set of questions. One in particular that Aiden needed answered.

"Sarah," Aiden said to his deputy, "could you take over looking at those surveillance films for Leland? I need to borrow him for a while."

She nodded and went to Leland's desk, not even asking why the shift in duties. Good thing, too. Aiden really didn't want to explain this to a lot of people. Seth included. But Seth latched on to it like a dog with a juicy bone.

"What's wrong?" Seth asked.

This seemed like a good time to take this conversation into Aiden's office, and he motioned for them to head there. Seth followed, of course, and Aiden wanted to come up with a reason to exclude him. One that didn't sound petty, since Seth had no doubt noticed Aiden's reaction to the arm contact with Kendall.

But the truth was, Seth might be able to help.

"For starters," Aiden said when the four of them were in his office. He aimed the intro at Seth. "You're not to go off running with what I'm about to tell you. We just need some information right now, and if it pans out, then the running can start. Got that?"

"What kind of information?" There was plenty of suspicion in Seth's voice. He didn't answer Aiden's *got that*, either.

"Money trails. I figure you can use your FBI channels to find a trail faster than I can." Aiden waited until Seth nodded. "This whole operation would have taken some money. We need to look at Joplin and Palmer to see if they've recently moved around this kind of cash."

Aiden stopped and looked at Kendall. Unlike Seth, she wasn't glaring at him. There was a healthy dose of sympathy in her eyes. It was sad, but he actually needed it. Because he was about to throw Carla under the bus.

"You'll also need to look at my mother," Aiden said to Seth.

Clearly, neither Seth nor Leland had seen that coming, so Aiden spelled it out for them. "It's possible that Carla withdrew fifty thousand from an account that she's kept hidden from the family. At best, the timing is suspicious."

Aiden didn't fill in the *at worst* part. Judging from Seth's profanity, he'd already figured it out.

"Your mother came after Kendall because of the baby?" Seth didn't wait for an answer. He cursed, turned, groaned and then turned back around.

Aiden figured Seth wanted to punch his lights out. With reason. And it wouldn't help if he told Seth that he hadn't seen it coming. A massive understatement. He hadn't wanted to believe his mother was capable of such things.

Still didn't.

"You might have to dig deep to find this account," Aiden added. "She's already aware that someone could be onto her." Best to leave his sister Shelby out of this for now. "So Carla could have closed the account."

"If it existed, I'll find it," Seth snarled.

It sounded like a threat. Which in this case was good. Because if it came down to an *at worst* conclusion, then Aiden wanted his mother behind bars. No way could he ever forgive her for trying to hurt Kendall and the baby.

Now, with that painful chore done, Aiden looked at Leland. "I want you to call my mother and tell her she's coming in for questioning. You'll need to ask her about Kendall's kidnapping, the attack at the jail. And the two murders," he added. It wasn't easy, but he got out the words.

Leland stared at him a moment and looked mighty uncomfortable. "You're sure?"

Aiden nodded. “It’s got to be done. I want it official, on record. Tell her to bring her lawyer with her.”

Leland stared at him, belted out some profanity. “Well, that oughta be fun,” he grumbled.

“Sorry, I’d do it myself…”

“But it’d be a big-time conflict of interest,” Leland finished for him. “I understand.”

Aiden figured his mother wouldn’t be so generous with the understanding. She’d pitch a fit, cry and disown him.

“I’m sorry,” Kendall whispered to him.

That didn’t make things peachy, but it did help.

More than it should have.

“I’ll get started on this,” Seth said, taking out his phone. He stepped out into the hall, but he’d barely gotten started when Aiden heard the footsteps.

Because every nerve in his body was on edge, Aiden automatically moved Kendall behind him. But it wasn’t a threat. It was Sarah.

“I think I found something, boss,” she said, her voice high-pitched and edgy. “You need to see this.”

Oh, man. He had no idea what Sarah wanted to show them, but her body language said they were in for yet another round of bad news.

Sarah led him to the computer where the footage from the high school had been loaded, and the moment Aiden’s attention landed on the screen, he spotted Yost.

Alive and waiting beneath a shade tree.

Yost wasn’t exactly in camera range, but Sarah had blown up the shot. The result was a grainy image but enough for Aiden to tell that the man was almost certainly carrying a concealed weapon beneath his windbreaker.

“He’s talking on the phone to someone here,” Sarah said, scrolling through the images.

"Probably to Aiden," Kendall provided. "He called twice."

Sarah nodded. "That makes sense, because here he is again on the phone." She moved to that shot.

"Did he call anyone else?" Aiden asked the deputy.

"No. At least not while he was in camera range. Now, here's what I want you to see."

Aiden watched as Yost was on the phone, and suddenly the man's gaze rifled to the area to his right. Not in camera range.

I gotta go, Yost had said. *I see somebody.*

Whoever or whatever it was the man had seen, it'd spooked him. Yost took off running, and it didn't take long for the camera to lose him.

"Just wait," Sarah said, advancing through more of the frames.

Aiden moved closer to the screen, waiting. Hoping this wasn't something that would feel like a punch to the gut. And it didn't take long for the camera to pick up more movement.

A person, more blur than image, on the far side of the screen.

"I enhanced it," Sarah continued.

When the next image popped up, Kendall gasped and landed in Aiden's arms again. Not his mother as he'd braced himself for. But definitely one of their suspects.

Joplin was there, and he was holding a gun.

Chapter Thirteen

"You need to eat," Aiden reminded her again.

Kendall knew he was right, but she also knew her stomach was protesting the ham-and-cheese sandwich and three small containers of milk that Aiden had ordered for her from the café up the street. Apparently, Aiden had remembered that pregnant women should drink milk.

And rest.

Because he was making sure she did that, too.

He had her sitting at his desk while he munched on his own sandwich and pored over the preliminary financial info that Seth had managed to gather. Considering that it'd been only several hours since Aiden told him about Carla's withdrawal, Kendall's step-nephew had managed to come up with a lot.

Including a bank account in Carla's name that had been closed within the past twenty-four hours.

Judging from the bits and pieces of the conversation Kendall had overheard, Seth hadn't been able to find out what had been in the account, but he was still working on it.

Just as Aiden was working on making sure his mother came in for questioning.

Because Leland had initially been the one to call Carla,

Kendall hadn't heard any of that conversation, but Leland had relayed to Aiden that Carla refused, saying she didn't feel well enough to be questioned. Aiden had intervened then with yet another call that Kendall hadn't heard. However, at the end of the call, Aiden had assured Leland that Carla would be coming in at two o'clock and would be bringing her lawyer with her.

That was only an hour from now.

"Are you okay?" she asked Aiden.

He looked up from the computer screen, practically doing a double take when he saw her. It instantly made her aware of just how thrown together and frazzled she must look.

"Despite how bad I look, I feel fine," Kendall volunteered. She didn't want Aiden to worry about anything else. He already had enough.

"You don't look bad," he said, and tore his gaze from her and went back to the computer screen.

That shouldn't have made her feel even marginally better, but it did. Because for just a second, she'd seen the attraction that had gotten them where they were now.

"Seth said you used to come up with baby names," Aiden remarked, still not making eye contact with her.

That stopped Kendall in mid-sip of her milk. "He said what? When?"

"Right before he left, he pulled me aside and told me he once saw you doodling baby names. *Our* babies' names." A muscle flickered in his jaw.

That brought her to her feet. "Seth told you that?" He was a dead man, or at least a hurting one. "I was a teenager, barely thirteen, and had very romantic notions about that first kiss we'd shared."

"Yeah," Aiden agreed several snail-crawling moments

later. "Since it was my first real kiss, I had a few notions about it, too. None involved baby names, though."

"Because you're a guy." She hoped that was all there was to it anyway, and that the kiss for him had been fueled only by teenage lust.

Of course, maybe that was all it'd been, period.

And this was getting her mind off the question she really needed to ask.

"Why the devil would Seth tell you that?" she snapped.

"It was tacked onto a threat," Aiden admitted. "He said if I hurt you he'll pound me to dust."

Oh.

"Seth shouldn't have said that." She could feel the heat rise in her cheeks and sank back down into the chair.

"So, do you remember what names you doodled?" Aiden asked. "They might come in handy."

Of course she remembered. When you doodled something a hundred or more times, it was glued in your memory. "Matthew Landon."

He made a small sound. Maybe surprise, maybe not. "Matthew, my middle name."

"Landon is Roy's middle name," she provided in a mumble.

Definitely not something Aiden would want to hear. Her, merging the Braddock and McKinnon family names. Heck, there were plenty of things she was saying, plenty of things she'd done that Aiden wouldn't want her to repeat.

"I'll bet you wish your first real kiss had been with someone else," Kendall said. "So that you'd actually want to remember it."

Aiden's eyes were already dark, and they stayed that way. "If I had a do-over on that first kiss, it'd still be with you. The only thing I'd change is that there would have been a second kiss."

Had her heart actually skipped a beat? It certainly felt like it.

The silence came. The air was suddenly so still, it felt as if everything was holding its breath. Waiting. But it wasn't Aiden or her who broke that silence, it was a knock at the door. A moment later, Leland stuck his head in.

"Joplin's here," Leland said. "He wants to know what we're planning to *discuss* with him."

That got Aiden and her standing again. Well, this was a surprise, since Joplin had been ignoring Leland's calls for hours.

Aiden, Leland and she went back into the squad room, but Joplin was already making his way to them. "Your deputy here left five messages for me. Five! Before I get a sixth, you need to tell me what's going on."

"Are you armed?" Aiden asked, not budging.

Joplin made a sound of outrage. "Yes. I have a permit to carry a concealed weapon."

"So do thousands of people, but you're not going into the room with Kendall until you've surrendered your weapon. You're a murder suspect, Joplin."

No sound of outrage this time, but the lawyer did go pale. Kendall wanted to feel sorry for him, but if he'd truly done these horrible attacks, then she wanted him behind bars for the rest of his life.

Joplin took his gun from a shoulder holster that his jacket had hidden and handed it to Aiden. Aiden tipped his head to Leland. "Frisk him."

If looks could have killed, Joplin would have done just that with the glare he shot Aiden, but he submitted to the search. Once Leland gave them the all-clear, Aiden handed his deputy Joplin's gun and then escorted the lawyer not to his office but to an interview room.

"Bring me the recording," Aiden added to Leland.

"What recording?" Joplin asked.

But Aiden didn't answer. After they were seated and Leland delivered the phone with the message, Aiden hit the play button.

"You'll get half the money now and half when the job's done," Joplin said on the recording.

"You want it done at her place?" the second man asked.

"It doesn't matter," Joplin answered. *"Just get it done."*

Joplin was cursing before the recording even finished. "How the hell did you get that?"

"It doesn't matter. What I want to know—is it true? Did you hire those men to kidnap Kendall?"

"No!" Joplin yelled, and he repeated the word several times. He looked at her, the glare gone. "I wouldn't hurt you, Kendall. You know that."

She wanted to believe it. "I'm not sure of a lot of things right now."

That brought on more profanity. "You did this," he accused Aiden. "You turned her against me."

"Unless you can explain that tape, Kendall won't need anyone to turn her against you." Aiden leaned in and got right in Joplin's face. "Did you hire those thugs?"

"No." This time when Joplin answered, it wasn't a shout, but it was just as intense, and his eyes had narrowed to slits. "The man on that recording with me is Barry McNease. He does occasional legwork for me during investigations."

"What kind of legwork?" Aiden pressed.

Joplin stayed quiet for several seconds. "It's no secret that I believe Jewell is innocent, so I've been looking at other possible suspects. Something that the cops and DA didn't do."

"Oh, they looked," Aiden argued. "But everything pointed to Jewell. Sorry," he added, glancing at Kendall.

She waved him off because he was right. Everything did indeed point to Jewell.

"Was this McNease helping you look for suspects?" Kendall asked.

Joplin nodded. "I wanted surveillance cameras set up so I could keep tabs on Meredith Bellows. She was someone else who was rumored to have had an affair with Whitt shortly before he was murdered."

It wasn't the first time Meredith's name had come up, but the woman had been dismissed as a suspect. There hadn't even been any solid corroboration of her affair with Whitt. Just rumors and gossip.

"Meredith had an alibi," Kendall reminded him.

"She did, but her husband's alibi was thin at best. I think he could have killed Whitt, and he's big enough to have disposed of the body himself."

Aiden dragged in a long, weary breath. "Did you ask Sheriff McKinnon to question Mr. Bellows?"

"Yes, and he did, but Bellows denied everything, of course. I thought maybe if I watched them, the Bellowses would do something that I could use to get the charges dismissed against Jewell."

Kendall went back over every word of the recording. Yes, it was possible that that's what Joplin was doing, but he was acting pretty suspicious for an innocent man.

"Let me guess," Aiden said, "these cameras weren't going in a public place. And you had no authorization for them."

Bingo. That would explain the guilty look.

Maybe.

"Since you're a lawyer," Aiden went on, "I don't have to tell you that anything you obtained from those cameras couldn't have been used in a court of law."

"It's the same for that recording," Joplin fired back.

"But I wasn't looking to use the footage to convict Meredith or her husband. I was looking for anything that I could turn into an investigation to help Jewell."

That was really grasping at straws, but then again the trial wasn't that far off, and everyone on both sides was feeling anxious and desperate.

Kendall included.

Aiden got in Joplin's face again. "Now tell me why you're on a surveillance video near the high school shortly before a man was shot and killed."

For just a moment, Joplin's eyes widened in surprise, and then he frantically shook his head. "No, you're not going to try to pin that on me—"

"Why were you there?" Aiden demanded, talking right over Joplin.

"Because I got a call from one of the PIs I'd hired, and he asked me to meet him there."

Kendall stared at him. "Really?"

"Really!" Joplin snapped. "I didn't speak to the PI himself but rather someone from his office. When I arrived, he wasn't there, and I saw that suspicious-looking guy hanging around, so I drew my gun."

She wanted to groan. It was so unlikely that it made it likely. And while he looked guilty, Joplin could indeed have been set up.

"I'm trying to clear Jewell," Joplin restated. "I don't need to kill anyone to do that."

Aiden did groan. Obviously, this was as frustrating for him as it was for her. "If you're so innocent, then why did you ignore the five calls from my deputy?" Aiden continued.

Kendall was interested in hearing the answer to that as well, but before Joplin could respond, the door flew open.

One look at Leland's face, and Kendall knew something was wrong, again.

Apparently, so did Aiden, because he cursed. "What happened now?"

"Palmer and your mother got into an argument outside city hall." Leland swallowed hard. "Carla's holding him at gunpoint."

THIS DAY JUST kept going downhill.

Aiden had hoped Leland was wrong, that Carla truly wasn't involved in a mess that she shouldn't be involved in. Yet there she was, standing on the sidewalk outside the courthouse.

And yeah, she had her .38 revolver aimed right at Palmer.

"Oh, God." Kendall's gaze went to the fiasco about fifteen yards ahead of them.

Some divine intervention might help right now, but Aiden figured he'd be the one to handle this.

"Stay down," Aiden warned her for the umpteenth time. "And wait with Kendall," he ordered Leland.

That put a frustrated look on Leland's face, probably because he wanted to be out there with Aiden, but the deputy was staying put with Kendall. There'd be no arguments about that. It'd been bad enough that he'd had to bring her here, but Aiden hadn't wanted to leave her in the building with Joplin.

Of course, he also didn't want Kendall anywhere near gunfire, either, so that was why he'd come in a squad car. Aiden fully intended to disarm his mother immediately, but just in case somebody else started shooting, he wanted Kendall protected as much as possible.

"Be careful," Kendall said when he opened the cruiser door to get out. Her expression was similar to Leland's but a lot more intense.

"It's my mother," Aiden reminded her. "She won't shoot me."

He hoped.

But since that didn't lessen the worried look on Kendall's face, he brushed a kiss on her cheek. Then her mouth.

Oh, man.

He was in a lot of trouble, and it didn't have anything to do with what he was about to face. Soon, very soon, Kendall and he were going to have to sit down and talk about what the heck was going on between them. And also start making plans for the baby. Plans that would have to wait until he put out yet another fire.

Kendall added a second "be careful" as Aiden got out and started toward Palmer and his mother. They'd drawn a crowd, at least a dozen people who were thankfully hovered behind the building and nearby cars.

"Stay back," Aiden warned everyone. "And put down that gun!" He added some volume and grit to his voice for that last order to Carla.

His mother spared him a glance but didn't lower her weapon. Though she was licensed to carry the gun, he wasn't even sure if she could shoot straight with it. And Aiden didn't want to find out.

Everything about Carla's body was wired and stiff. Unlike Palmer. His hands were raised in the air, but there wasn't much concern on his face. This was like a joke to him, but Aiden sure wasn't laughing.

"Aiden," the man greeted as if this were a friendly meeting. "Glad you got here so fast. Your mother's clearly lost her mind."

"I've found it," Carla snapped. "And I know Palmer's the one who's trying to set me up."

"Set you up?" Aiden asked, going closer. He didn't

want to lunge for the gun, since it might accidentally go off, but he had to get it out of her hands.

"For Kendall's kidnapping." Carla sucked in her breath, making a hiccuping sound. And there were tears on her cheeks.

A gun and tears were never a good combination.

"Just why would I set you up?" Palmer asked. Butter wouldn't melt in that mouth.

Aiden could think of a reason or two for a setup, but his mother voiced it first. "Because you hate me and my family. Because you'd like to see Whitt's killer walk. Because you're on the side of the McKinnons."

Palmer shrugged. "That doesn't mean I'd obstruct justice to get those things."

Yes, it did, but there wasn't any proof of it—yet—and even if there had been, the more immediate concern was disarming Carla.

"Hand me the gun, Mom," Aiden demanded.

Carla's hand started to shake. More tears came. But she lowered the gun, then gave it to him.

The safety was on, Aiden noticed right off. Maybe that meant she hadn't planned on doing bodily harm after all.

"The rest of you can clear out," Aiden said to the bystanders. "The three of us are talking," he added to Palmer and Carla.

Normally, Aiden would already have taken this chat back to his office, but he really didn't want to cram Palmer and his mother into the cruiser with Kendall. Of course, they'd eventually have to be brought in to make a statement and in his mother's case, an arrest, so he motioned for Leland. When his deputy stepped out of the cruiser, Aiden instructed him to call Sarah to come to the scene so she could escort Carla to the station.

His mother wiped at the tears that just kept coming.

Aiden fished out his handkerchief, handed it to her and looked at Palmer, hoping the man would get started with an explanation about this that would make some sense.

"Your mother accused me of setting up some kind of bank account in her name," Palmer said. "An account that supposedly someone used to hire those men who kidnapped Kendall."

Interesting. "Did you?" he asked Palmer.

"Of course not. Why would I?"

"For all those reasons Carla just mentioned," Aiden pointed out.

Palmer cocked his head to the side. "Really? If I'd wanted to get back at Carla, I could think of a better way."

Since that sounded like a threat, Aiden mimicked his cocky head tilt. "What way?"

"One that wouldn't involve hurting Kendall," Palmer said.

"Yet you think I'd do something to hurt my own son?" Carla snarled.

Palmer shrugged again. "Maybe that wasn't your plan. Maybe you thought you could get Kendall arrested and jailed for a long time for setting up her own kidnapping and destroying evidence. Then you could raise the Braddock baby she's carrying. All without putting your son in danger."

Too bad it was indeed the kind of plan a sick mind could come up with. A mind filled with hate and the need for revenge.

Like his mother's.

But Palmer's mind was equally sick.

From the corner of his eye, Aiden saw Sarah pull up in a patrol car, so he motioned for Carla and Palmer to follow him. Leland got out of the cruiser. So did Kendall.

"I know Palmer set up that account," Carla mumbled.

"You have proof?" Aiden asked.

"No," she admitted after several long moments.

"Because there is no proof," Palmer argued. "If I'd wanted to set her up, I wouldn't have used a bank account. It leaves too many trails. I would have just hired some lowlifes and told them they were working for Carla. Then I would have arranged for them to go to the cops with that news."

True. Bank accounts were messy. And there had indeed been such an account, as Shelby had seen it. So why would his mother risk that?

"I'm betting Carla probably didn't think a bank account leaves all kinds of telltale signs, even when it's erased. Follow the money trail," Palmer insisted, pointing his finger at Aiden. "It'll lead to your mother."

Carla spun around and would have launched herself at Palmer if Aiden hadn't grabbed her. Palmer laughed. And Kendall got there in time to step between Aiden and the idiot that Aiden wanted to punch. He wouldn't have done it, of course, but he sure wanted to wipe that smirk off Palmer's face.

"I told you Carla was crazy," Palmer went on. "She needs to be locked away in the loony bin *again*."

Aiden froze. So did Carla. And Palmer got that gleam in his eye.

"You didn't know." Palmer didn't laugh, but it was close enough. "Tell him, Carla, or I will."

Oh, man.

Aiden was a thousand percent sure he wasn't going to like this.

He especially didn't like it when Palmer's gaze shifted to Kendall. "Or maybe it'd be better if Aiden heard it from you."

Kendall didn't answer, though Aiden was certain she knew what Palmer was talking about.

"I was in an institution," Carla muttered. "It happened a long time ago, before I even married your father."

Judging from the way Kendall dodged Aiden's gaze, she knew something more about this than she'd already told him.

"Does this have anything to do with the elderly woman you were telling me about?" Aiden asked her.

She nodded, eventually. "After I pressed Jewell for anything I could use to help her, she gave me the name of the psychiatrist that Carla saw all those years ago. He's long been dead, but I tracked down the nurse who worked for him." Kendall's voice was as ragged as his mother's. "But I didn't know that your mother had actually been in the institution."

Kendall's comment put some flames in Carla's eyes. "Whitt must have told Jewell about the psychiatrist," Carla said.

"Why were you in an institution?" Aiden demanded.

More flames popped into her eyes, directed at both Palmer and Kendall. She aimed something considerably worse at Aiden.

"I'm not saying another word until I speak to my lawyer," Carla snapped. And she stormed off toward Sarah, getting into the cruiser with the deputy.

Even though Aiden wanted answers, he didn't go after her. He also didn't leave Kendall standing out in the open any longer. He hurried her back to the car with Leland, but the moment they were inside, Aiden snapped toward her.

"Start talking," he demanded. "And, Leland, get us back to the office."

Leland pulled away from the building, but Kendall sure didn't start talking. It seemed to take her several moments just to gather her breath. Or maybe she was trying to figure out the best spin she could put on this. However, there was no good spin to something she'd obviously kept from him.

"I wasn't even sure it was true," she finally started. "Whitt told Jewell that Carla had needed psychiatric help when she was a teenager."

Not exactly ideal pillow talk, spilling secrets about your wife to your lover. "Why was Carla there? And why am I just now hearing about this after all these years?"

Kendall shook her head. "There are no records of it. I know because I looked for them."

Yes, so that Kendall could try to pin his father's murder on anyone but her precious sister. Aiden tried not to be riled to the core about that, but it was hard to do.

"Tell me everything that Whitt told Jewell," he demanded. "And everything the nurse told you."

Another nod, followed by another long pause. "I didn't get much of anything from the nurse, just a confirmation that the doctor she worked for had treated your mother. No details."

Aiden studied her expression. "But Jewell got some details from Whitt, didn't she?"

"Details that Jewell wasn't even sure were true," Kendall added.

He stared at her. "Details that I want to hear right now."

Kendall swallowed hard. Nodded. "According to what Whitt told Jewell, your mother tried to murder someone."

Chapter Fourteen

Aiden was pacing across his office while he talked on the phone, something he'd been doing for at least an hour since they had arrived back at the station.

For this latest call, he hadn't put the phone on speaker, so Kendall could only guess what was going on. Of course, she didn't need to hear the other half of the conversation to know that things weren't going well. Aiden was scowling. The muscles in his face were tight. And he had a crushing grip on the phone.

Kendall knew he was talking yet again to his sister Shelby, but she had no idea how much longer this particular call would go on. Probably until Aiden got the information he wanted.

Information he hadn't gotten from Carla.

His mother was sitting in an interview room, waiting for her lawyer to show up, and she'd made it crystal clear that she wasn't talking to her son or his deputy. Of course, she hadn't talked to Kendall, either, though she had glared at her every chance she got. Kendall tried not to glare back, but it was hard. After all, Carla might be responsible for the kidnapping and the attacks, and if so, that meant Aiden's mom had put the baby in serious danger.

If Carla had truly done that, Kendall would never forgive her.

However, the jury was still out on the woman's guilt.

It would take time to prove if she had any involvement with the kidnappers. She would be charged for the altercation with Palmer, of course, and endangering the public, but as there'd been no shots fired, Kendall was betting the woman would be released on bail.

"What else haven't you told me?" Aiden growled to his sister. A question he would no doubt repeat to Kendall once he had the chance.

Again, she couldn't hear Shelby's answer, but despite his obvious anger, Aiden motioned for Kendall to eat. It was yet another meal he'd had delivered from the café. This time a pasta salad and more milk. Because she didn't want to add to his misery, Kendall nibbled at it.

Aiden's conversation went on with his sister for at least another minute before he snarled, "Don't you dare withhold anything else." And he jabbed the end call button with far more force than necessary.

Before turning to her.

He didn't glare at her, not exactly. But it was close enough. Then he groaned and cursed.

Kendall decided it was best if she just got this out in the open.

"I didn't know your mother had actually been in an institution. I swear. Jewell never said. Heck, she probably doesn't even know. We only knew that Carla had seen a psychiatrist." Kendall paused. "But Shelby knew?"

He nodded, eventually. Cursed some more.

"How did she find out?" Kendall asked. "Because I tried, and every call, email and question was nothing but a roadblock."

"Shelby's a little too good at getting past roadblocks," he mumbled.

Probably because she was an investigative reporter

and had plenty of connections. Or maybe Carla had even told her.

"My mother wasn't raised around here," Aiden said, dropping down in the chair across from her. "That's why no one knew. Well, no one except for my father and her folks, who've now passed away. As you said, the records no longer exist, but Shelby managed to track down some employees who worked at the facility."

Kendall didn't press with another question. She just waited until Aiden was ready to continue.

"When she was eighteen, Carla apparently met Lee Palmer," Aiden finally went on. "He was twenty, a broke rodeo rider, and he was engaged to a very wealthy woman. Carla's family had money, too, so they ran in the same social circles as Palmer's fiancée. Depending on whose side you believe, Carla had an affair with Palmer. Or else she became obsessed with him and wanted him to break off the engagement. When he didn't do that, she tried to run him over with her car."

"Sweet heaven." Kendall was glad she was sitting down. "But why hasn't Palmer said anything about it? This would have been the perfect information to get the DA and cops to look at someone other than Jewell for your father's murder.

"Sorry," she added. That was probably something Aiden didn't need to hear her say.

Though he no doubt had already thought about it.

He waved off her apology and had a long sip of water, probably wishing it was something a lot stronger. "Shelby only has bits and pieces, but apparently Palmer agreed to drop the charges against Carla for a sealed settlement and the agreement that she'd go to the institution for help."

It all became clear. For his silence, Palmer no doubt got a boatload of money from Carla's wealthy family, and if he'd indeed had an affair with her, then the sealed settlement might have prevented his fiancée from finding out about his cheating. Also, Carla's family could have a nondisclosure clause for Palmer himself. That way, if Palmer had indeed discussed it with anybody, he could have lost the settlement money.

And that brought Kendall to consider something else.

"If Carla and Palmer had this bad history, how did they end up living so close to each other?" she asked.

"The Braddocks have lived around here for six generations. Palmer moved here not long after my parents got married."

Good grief. Palmer had no doubt used the settlement money to start his own cattle empire. Right under Carla's nose. And the bad blood had just continued with Palmer's constant presence stirring the pot.

"I'll have to tell the DA all this," Aiden grumbled.

Yes, and while it might end up helping Jewell's case, Kendall knew that Jewell wouldn't want to be helped at the expense of someone else. Not even Carla.

This was tearing Aiden apart. She could see it. Feel it. So she stood and went to him. He got up as well, and his expression had a *back off* vibe to it. Kendall ignored it and put her arms around him. Too bad her stitches brushed against his shirtsleeve, causing her to wince.

And causing Aiden to curse.

He pulled her back, lifted the bandage and had a look. There was still no relief on his face, though. "You didn't pop a stitch, but you need to be more careful."

True. So, when she reached for him a second time, she put only her unstitched right arm around him.

Their gazes met. For some very long moments. Before his gaze dropped to her mouth, a place it usually went when they were within a half mile of each other. Kendall knew, because she was looking at his mouth, too.

"You need to be more careful," he repeated.

Since they were no longer talking about stitches, Kendall eked out a smile. And kissed him. Like their other kisses, this one had all the fire, and it slid right through her. But also like with all the others, the guilt came.

Especially now.

With this news about his mother, it almost felt as if they were on different sides again. Of course, with the baby and the attraction pulling them right back together, it seemed as if they could overcome even this latest wrinkle.

Almost.

"We can't keep skirting around this," he said.

That rid her of any trace of a smile. Because he also slid his hand between them and put it over her stomach. Definitely no smiling matter.

"You want shared custody." Kendall moved away from him. "But for that to work, we'd need to live fairly close to each other. Especially when he's still a baby. That means one of us living in a place where we won't exactly be comfortable."

She was fairly sure that Aiden would want her to be that *one of us*. After all, he was grounded in place as the county sheriff, and she could live anywhere in the state. However, that was why Kendall had made plans to move—so that she wouldn't be in the middle of his family feud.

"In addition to a move *for one of us*, you'd also need a nanny," she went on. "And you'd have to make sure that your family doesn't despise the baby so much that it could be traumatic for him."

Aiden stayed quiet a moment. "You've given this some thought."

"Plenty."

"And you don't think it can work," he concluded.

Kendall huffed. "I hadn't thought it would work from the beginning. That's why I was planning to leave." Now she paused. "I guess my feelings have changed a little about that, though."

"Because we keep kissing."

Aiden certainly had a way of cutting right to the heart of the matter. Of course it was because of those kisses. Even now, it was because her body was still humming from having been in his arms.

"Nobody in my family will despise this child," he said with absolute authority. "And if they do, they won't be in my life for long."

It was the right thing to say to make her feel better. But the wrong thing to muddle her mind even more. Kendall still had no idea how they were going to fix this.

"Come on," Aiden said, taking her by the hand. "Even when my mother's lawyer shows up, I shouldn't be the one who does the interview. I'll take you back to your place so you can get some rest. Sarah can follow us."

Kendall didn't say no to that. They'd been at the sheriff's office most of the day, and it wouldn't be long before it was dark. Now that both her attackers were dead, the prison guard, too, she could breathe a little easier, but there'd be no relaxing until the person who'd hired them was behind bars.

And maybe that would soon happen.

But it probably wouldn't happen tonight unless they got a confession from Carla or one of their other suspects.

When they stepped out of Aiden's office, Kendall spotted Carla seated at one of the interview tables. Her back was board straight. Her eyes, focused on the drab gray wall.

"Leland will be doing your interview when your lawyer arrives," Aiden told his mother.

Carla's mouth tightened, though she still didn't look directly at them. Nor did she speak. Which might have been for the best. There wasn't much she could have said that would make this situation better.

Aiden got Kendall outside and in his truck, and with Sarah in a cruiser right behind them, they headed to Kendall's house in Sweetwater Springs. The place had been her home for a long time, but since the attacks, it felt more like a holding cell.

"You're probably sick of sleeping on the floor," she said. Then she winced. It sounded like an invitation for him to share the bed with her.

He smiled that half smile. The one that had no doubt seduced many women. Of course, Aiden didn't have to smile to seduce her. He did that just by breathing.

"I'm not leaving until we're sure the danger has passed," he insisted. "The floor's optional." He paused a heartbeat. Then cursed. "Except we both know that's a bad idea."

Yes, they did. Sleeping together again would just cloud their minds and get in the way of working out a custody decision. Of course, it might ease some of this tension between them.

Kendall mentally repeated that rationalization and groaned.

Oh, yes. She had a bad case of Aiden Braddock all right.

"Twenty minutes," he said when he pulled into her driveway. He checked the time on the dashboard clock. "If I move to the east side of Clay Ridge, I'd still be close enough to work, and I'd be close enough to you and the baby." He dropped a quick, unexpected kiss on her mouth. "Just give it some thought."

Kendall would. Especially since he'd included her in that and not just the baby. That kiss helped, too.

The fantasy wheel started again. Of her, Aiden and the baby being a family. Definitely not something she should have on her mind, since she'd be sharing a bedroom with Aiden again.

Sarah got out of the cruiser, waiting for them to go in, so Aiden and she hurried to the porch. Kendall unlocked the door, and she immediately turned to the keypad on the interior wall so she could disarm the security system.

But it wasn't armed.

There was no beeping sound, and the lights were off on the keypad.

"Something's wrong," Kendall whispered.

And then she heard the footsteps.

EVERYTHING SEEMED TO happen at once. The porch light blinked off, and Aiden drew his gun when he saw a blur of motion to his left.

Right behind Kendall.

She made a muffled sound of surprise, and it took Aiden a split second to realize that it was muffled because someone had grabbed her from behind and had slapped his hand over her mouth.

That someone put a gun to her head.

From what Aiden could see, it appeared to be a man wearing a ski mask, similar to the ones that the other kidnappers had used.

Hell.

This was another thug coming after Kendall again.

"What's wrong?" Sarah called out, and from the corner of his eye, Aiden saw the deputy making her way to the house.

"Tell her to stay back," the masked guy warned Aiden.

He took his hand from Kendall's mouth so he could hook his arm around her neck. "And put down your gun."

Aiden did the first, motioning for Sarah to stay put. He didn't want this moron shooting her. Didn't want him hurting Kendall, either, so that meant he had to figure out how to diffuse the situation.

Fast.

"How'd you get in here?" Kendall demanded, sounding more defiant than strong. Maybe because like Aiden, she was fed up with these attacks.

"Hacked into your security system," he said, and in the same breath he tipped his head to Aiden's gun. "I said drop it."

The last time Aiden had refused to do that, Kendall had been shot in the arm. Still, if he didn't have a weapon, there was nothing to stop this guy from just shooting him and taking off with Kendall.

"What do you want?" Aiden snapped.

"To take her out of this house. Soon, someone will contact you about what you need to do to get her back."

So this was indeed another kidnapping attempt. Probably another attempt at getting him to obstruct justice or destroy evidence.

Or to make it look that way.

"Just do as you're told," the man added, "and Miss O'Neal will be okay."

Kendall shook her head a little, obviously not believing him. Aiden wasn't buying it, either. But there was something about this situation that told him loads. If the guy had wanted to shoot Aiden, he could have already done it. He could have pulled the trigger the moment that Aiden stepped inside.

So why hadn't he?

Why hadn't this guy taken out the biggest threat—the

county sheriff? That was an unsettling thought because it led him back to his mother.

Aiden pushed that aside, since it wouldn't help him now, and he tried to figure out the best way to approach this. The guy had the gun to Kendall's head, but Aiden had to believe the kidnapper had been told to bring her in alive. That meant he didn't want to kill her.

Well, not now anyway.

"Come on," the guy said to Kendall. He dropped his left arm to her waist and started dragging her out of the entry.

Unlike the other kidnapping thugs, this guy was a little shaky. And he'd apparently given up on his demand to disarm Aiden. That could be both good and bad. Good because a nervous kidnapper would be more likely to make a mistake. Bad because a mistake could lead to Kendall getting hurt.

Aiden motioned for Sarah to come closer, and he waited for the guy to glance behind him to see where he was about to step.

That was the best chance Aiden figured he'd get.

Aiden tossed his gun aside, figuring he'd need both hands for this half-thought-out plan. He did. Aiden pushed Kendall to the side, praying that she wouldn't fall, and in the same motion, he went after the goon. He put his old football skills to work and tackled the guy.

They both went to the floor.

His shoulder hit, hard. So hard that the pain shot through him. Aiden hoped he hadn't dislocated it, because the guy tried to wallop him upside the head with his gun. Aiden grabbed hold of the guy's shooting wrist to stop him from doing that and from getting off a shot.

Kendall scrambled out of the way, thank God. At least Aiden thought that was what she was doing, but she didn't run out of the house and toward Sarah. She scooped up his gun and tried to take aim at the would-be kidnapper.

"Run!" Aiden managed to shout to her.

She didn't listen. Worse, she didn't get behind Sarah when the deputy made it into the house. Sarah, too, took aim. Not that she had any more of a clean shot than Kendall did. Aiden and the masked idiot were punching each other's lights out, too close to each other for Sarah or Kendall to try to take out the kidnapper.

Using as much force as he could, Aiden bashed the guy's shooting hand against the marble floor. It didn't work. The guy held on. So Aiden did it again.

And again.

Aiden could have sworn that he heard fingers breaking, and finally the idiot let go. The gun dropped from his hand. But before Aiden could even knock it out of the way, the guy scooped it up again and took aim.

At Kendall.

The blast was deafening, and it echoed through the nearly empty house. Echoed through Aiden, too, and even though he couldn't actually hear, he yelled out Kendall's name. He turned, praying that she hadn't been shot again. But she was standing there.

Aiden said a quick prayer of thanks for that.

But she still had his gun in her hand. A gun that was still aimed at the kidnapper. Unlike Kendall and Sarah, the man wasn't standing. He'd flopped back onto the floor, his breath rattling in his throat.

"I shot him," Kendall said, and sounded as if she was about to fall on the floor, too. Not from an injury but from the shock of what'd just happened.

She had indeed shot the man.

"Call an ambulance," Aiden told Sarah.

He scrambled across the floor, tore off the man's mask.

A stranger. A stranger who was about to bleed out. No way would he last long enough for the medics to get there.

"Who hired you?" Aiden demanded. "Tell me!"

But the man didn't speak. His eyelids drifted down, and there was another gravelly breath.

His last one.

Kendall made a sound, too. One that let Aiden know that she was within seconds of falling apart. He made it to her in one step and pulled her into his arms.

Chapter Fifteen

Kendall was afraid if she stopped moving, she would collapse. First, she'd paced while waiting for the ME and Jeb, the young deputy, to arrive. Of course, Aiden had tried to get her to sit down, but she couldn't. She had to keep moving. It was the only thing that seemed to be keeping the horrible images at bay.

She could still feel the gun in her hand even though Aiden had long since taken it from her. She could also still hear the sound of the blast. Could still see the glimpses of the kidnapper falling to the floor. The pacing pushed them aside, for several seconds anyway, but it was that brief reprieve that was keeping her from falling apart.

"You ready?" Aiden asked Sarah, and the deputy nodded. "Let's go," he said then to Kendall.

He led her out of the house, past the group of CSIs and lawmen who'd come to investigate the shooting, and they headed to his truck. Sarah was right behind them and got into one of the cruisers.

By Kendall's calculations, it'd been nearly an hour since the shooting, and a death almost certainly meant Aiden and Sarah had plenty of work to do. But he didn't drive toward his office.

"Are we going to your place?" she asked.

"Yeah." He glanced around, no doubt to make sure there wasn't another attacker lurking around. "Sorry that it'll have some bad memories for you, but it was either there or a hotel. At least my house has a security system. And this time, I'll use it."

That brought on the images again, and even though she didn't say a word, Aiden reached over, took her hand and brushed a kiss on her knuckles.

"This wasn't your fault," he said, his voice strained but yet soothing at the same time. "You did what you had to do."

"I didn't intend to kill him. I only wanted to stop him from shooting. Now he can't say who hired him to come after us."

"You," Aiden corrected. "Not us."

Because her head was a mess, it took Kendall a moment to realize what he meant. The kidnapper had definitely come after her, and he'd been trying to get her out of her house and to heaven knew where when he was dragging her out of the foyer. And then there was what he'd said to Aiden.

Soon, someone will contact you about what you need to do to get her back.

"Someone still wants to use me to get you to destroy evidence," Kendall concluded.

"Or maybe that someone wants it to appear that way." He drew in a long, weary breath. "Whoever hired this latest thug could just want you dead. Maybe because he or she believes Yost said something in the pharmacy that could blow his boss's identity."

"But Yost didn't say anything that could have done that."

Had he?

Like now, she'd certainly had a lot on her mind, so Yost could have accidentally revealed something.

But what?

"If there's anything to remember about what he said, it'll come to you," Aiden added.

Maybe. But if she did remember, would it be in time to stop them from being attacked again?

"I need to press all three suspects once more," Aiden went on. "Well, at least the two who might talk. My mother's lawyer told her to remain silent."

Something normally reserved for the guilty. But there probably wasn't much that Carla could say that would make her look innocent. Not about the fifty grand or her stay in the institution. A past stay in an institution wasn't proof of guilt, but the DA could argue that she had a history of violent behavior. Of course, the DA would need more than just a history to file charges against her for these kidnapping attempts and attacks.

"Anything on Palmer's and Joplin's financials?" she asked.

Kendall wasn't even sure she wanted to have this conversation, but it was better than just sitting there and staring out at the darkness. Plus, her hands had started to tremble again. And Aiden noticed all right, because he was still holding on to one of them.

"Nothing so far," he answered, "but that doesn't mean we won't find something. Eventually, this person has to make a mistake."

Yes, but that didn't mean he or she couldn't keep hiring gunmen.

Aiden took the turn to his small ranch, and when he reached the house, he stopped the truck directly in front of the porch. Definitely some bad memories here, since it was where she'd been shot and one of the kidnappers had died.

Of course, her own house was loaded with plenty of bad memories now, too. Along with the jail and the sheriff's office. She was running out of places where she felt safe.

They waited until Sarah had parked, and Aiden hurried them inside. This time, he set the security system and had Sarah and her stay in the entry while he did a thorough search of the house. No doubt to make sure someone hadn't broken in and was lurking inside, waiting to attack.

There was no sign that it'd been a crime scene just forty-eight hours earlier. Someone had even cleaned up the blood on the floor. Kendall was especially thankful for that.

"There's the guest bedroom and a bath next to it," Aiden said to Sarah, pointing to a room just off the hall. "Help yourself to whatever's in the fridge. I'll have Kendall upstairs with me."

Upstairs, in his bedroom.

Despite the fact that it meant another night in close quarters with Aiden, at least the second floor would be a little more secure, since an attacker would have to get past Sarah and then up the stairs. Plus, with the security system, they should have enough warning.

She hoped.

"I'll have someone pick you up clothes and such in the morning," he told her while he shucked off his holster.

When they got to his room, he dropped the holster on the nightstand and was about to sit down on the bed when he looked at her, then at the floor. Aiden didn't groan, not out loud anyway, but she could see the dread of spending another night on the floor.

Kendall was dreading it, too.

For a different reason.

She was still trembling, her mind and body a basket case, but Kendall knew there was a fix for that. A temporary one anyway.

And the fix was Aiden.

"Yes, I'm sure of this," she said because she knew the question would come up fast.

Heck, it still might come up, but Kendall did something about that, too. She slipped her arm around Aiden's neck, pulled him to her and kissed him.

AIDEN KNEW THIS was a mistake, but he just didn't care.

He was tired of fending off this fire. Tired of wanting and not having. And especially tired of not having Kendall in his arms.

Well, he had her there now.

A sane man would have just kissed her a time or two and put her to bed. *Alone.* So that she could get the sleep she needed. But because he'd been forced to kill a man a time or two and knew what was going on in her head, there wouldn't be much sleep for her tonight.

Kendall made a soft sound, part relief, part pleasure. Aiden was right there with her on that. Yeah, kissing her amped up every part of his body. Made him burn. But there was also the buzz beneath the fire. The feeling that this should already have happened again.

Multiple times.

He pulled her closer, mindful of the stitches in her arm, but if they were bothering her in the least, she didn't show it. However, what she did show was that she was just as eager to keep up the kisses as he was. So Aiden moved his mouth to her neck, dropping some more kisses along the way.

Kendall responded with another of those silky sounds.

Not much relief in it this time, though. The heat was taking over and making them both crazier than they already were.

Somehow in all that craziness, Aiden remembered to lock the door just in case Sarah came up to check on them. He also killed the lights and kept Kendall away from the window. Once he had those things taken care of, he went back to kissing her the way he wanted.

All over her body.

From her neck, he went to her breasts, shoving up her top so there'd be no clothes in the way. He wanted his mouth on her bare skin, and that was exactly what he got.

She tasted like everything good that he'd ever wanted or needed.

Probably not a good thing, but he was past the point of reason here. Past the point of anything that didn't involve getting Kendall on that bed.

Kendall wasn't exactly fighting the idea, either. She was already battling with his shirt, trying to get the buttons undone while she surrendered to the kisses that'd made their way down to her belly. Going with his no-clothes rule, Aiden rid her of her jeans. Then her panties.

And he kissed her in another spot that he'd wanted to kiss since this insanity started.

Oh, yes. This was definitely leading straight to the bed.

Kendall got them moving in that direction all on her own. While she yanked at his clothes. While she cursed him, too, but Aiden was pretty sure it was the good kind of cursing brought on by the need for immediate relief of this fire inside them. He knew exactly how she felt.

They landed on the bed, Aiden adjusting her at the last second so that her arm wouldn't be pressed against him or the mattress. But her stitches seemed to be the last thing on Kendall's mind.

Ditto for the pregnancy.

That stopped him for a moment because he darn sure should have considered it before now.

"Is this okay?" Aiden glanced down at her stomach.

"Of course." And she hauled him right back to her, along with ridding him of the rest of his clothes.

Aiden accepted her *of course*. Obviously, at this point he would have accepted almost anything as long as he could have her.

His bare skin against hers only revved up the heat. And soon, very soon, Aiden knew that foreplay was about to go right out the window. Later, if there was a later that involved kisses and such, maybe he could make it up to her. For now, though, he just took everything Kendall offered him.

Everything.

He adjusted their positions again, moving on top of her, and eased into her. He immediately felt that punch of need explode in his head. It was something he would have liked to have savored for a while, but Aiden knew that wasn't going to happen.

That need dictated everything. The speed and intensity. And it wasn't just for him but for Kendall, too.

"Let's finish this," she said in that satin voice that he couldn't have resisted even if she hadn't been looking up at him.

Aiden kissed her. Because it was his way of holding on to this. With the taste of her on his mouth. The heat of her skin on his.

With everything falling right into place, Aiden finished this.

Chapter Sixteen

Kendall nearly jumped when she opened her eyes. It was dark, everything unfamiliar around her. Well, everything except for the man next to her.

Aiden.

She was in his bed, in his house, and hours earlier they'd had incredible sex. This time without having been the least bit drunk. He'd regret it, of course. Heck, she might, too, but for now she just settled down and enjoyed the moment and the view.

And what a view it was.

Aiden was on his stomach. Completely naked. And the moonlight was streaming in through the window, spilling like a spotlight over his perfect body. He'd always been hot, even when they were teenagers, and now he was many steps past the hot stage.

Of course, looking at him only reminded her of how much she wanted him all over again. And how much that want for him complicated their lives. A custody arrangement would be difficult enough without them lusting after each other, and she figured this attraction wasn't going to end just because it made things harder.

She slid her hand over her stomach and let her mind wander. Would the baby look like Aiden?

Probably.

And her imagination was good enough for her to see the sandy-haired toddler trailing along after his father. Aiden had said he would protect their baby from his family, and he no doubt would. But while her son might have a near-perfect father, he'd be born into a very imperfect situation.

"You should be resting," Aiden said without even opening his eyes.

She wasn't sure how he even knew she was awake, but he reached for her and eased her back down next to him. Kendall lost the great view of his body, but the snuggling wasn't a bad consolation prize.

"We'll work this all out," he added. "For now, just rest."

Kendall was certain that wouldn't happen, but it didn't take long for her muscles to go slack. She could probably thank the amazing sex for that. And the fatigue that was gnawing away at her. However, she'd barely had time to close her eyes when she felt something she didn't want to feel.

The muscles in Aiden's arm tensed.

He didn't jackknife to a sitting position, but he did ease away from her, lifting his head. Obviously listening for something.

But what?

She hadn't heard anything, but Kendall certainly listened now. There were no sounds of Sarah moving around downstairs. Nothing outside, either, even though there was a breeze stirring the oaks just outside the bedroom windows.

"What's wrong?" she whispered, her heart already in her throat.

Aiden listened some more and finally shook his head. "I thought I heard the horses."

Kendall hadn't heard them at all through the night, but then the barn, corral and pasture were a good twenty yards from the house.

Aiden eased his head back onto the pillow just as Kendall heard a sound. He heard it, too, because it got him not just off the pillow but out of bed.

It was indeed one of the horses, maybe more, making a whinnying sound.

Aiden pulled on his jeans as he made his way to the window. Kendall got up as well, but he motioned for her to stay back. She did, but when Aiden stood there for several long seconds, she decided to get dressed.

Just in case.

Sadly, their *just in case* could turn out to be something bad.

"Do you see anyone?" she asked.

Another wait before he shook his head, but he kept his attention pinned to whatever was going on outside the window. "Something spooked the horses."

Because she'd spent a lot of time on a ranch, Kendall knew there were plenty of things that could do that. The area had coyotes who sometimes ventured closer to the animals, but with the awful things that had happened to Aiden and her, Kendall automatically thought the worst.

Another kidnapper could be out there, ready to come for her.

She finished putting on her clothes, and even though she stayed back, Kendall went closer to see if she could get a glimpse of anything. The moon was full and bright, casting shadows on the ground.

One of those shadows moved, causing her heart to slam against her chest.

She made a strangled sound and stepped back just as Aiden cursed and grabbed his shirt.

"It could be a kid pulling a prank," he said. But Aiden didn't sound as if he believed that any more than she did.

He threw on his clothes, grabbed his gun and headed for the door. Kendall hadn't thought her anxiety could go any higher, but that did it.

"You're not going out there," she insisted.

Aiden dropped a kiss on her mouth as if that were the cure for everything, and he opened the bedroom door. "You're waiting inside with Sarah."

So he was indeed going out there. Alone. And with the moving shadow that could be an armed thug.

Kendall hurried down the stairs behind him, but before Aiden could even knock on Sarah's door, the deputy had already opened it. "I heard your footsteps on the stairs," Sarah said. She was already dressed. Armed, too. But maybe she'd slept that way.

"Keep an eye on Kendall," he said, giving Kendall another kiss. Probably because he figured it would stop her from arguing with him.

It didn't.

"You should wait until you call for backup," Kendall suggested.

But she was talking to herself, because Aiden was already heading for the front door so he could disengage the security system.

"Reset this when I'm out," Aiden said to Sarah. He grabbed a flashlight from a table in the entry. "The security code's one-eight-six-three. And call Leland to let him know I might have a problem."

Sarah nodded, and as soon as Aiden was outside, the deputy punched in the code to reset it. She also motioned for Kendall to follow her back into the hall and took out her phone. To call Leland, no doubt.

Kendall wished they could at least go into the living

room so she might be able to catch a glimpse of Aiden outside the window, but before she could suggest that to Sarah, the deputy mumbled, "What the heck?"

"What's wrong?" Kendall asked.

"My cell phone's not working." She hurried to the kitchen and picked up the landline that was mounted on the wall. Kendall knew from the way the deputy's face dropped that it wasn't good news. "It's not working, either."

Oh, mercy.

That couldn't be good, and Kendall doubted that it was a coincidence. Someone had likely jammed the lines, and that someone was out there.

With Aiden.

"We have to tell Aiden," Kendall insisted. "He could be attacked."

Sarah nodded, then glanced around as if trying to figure out what to do. "If I open the living room window to shout out to him, the security alarm will go off. So I'll have you disarm it just long enough for me to tell him what's going on."

Now it was Kendall's turn to nod, and she hurried to the keypad on the wall next to the front door. Thankfully, unlike in her own house, there were no sidelight windows, and the door was solid wood.

"Now," Sarah said, reaching for the window.

However, reaching for it was as far as she got. Because before Kendall had even touched the keypad, she heard the beeps. Sounds coming from the security system.

"What happened?" Sarah asked. "I haven't opened the window yet."

The entry was dark, and it was hard to see, but Kendall pulled down the flap on the keypad and saw the lights. Indications of where the sensors had been armed on all the doors and windows. They were green.

Except for one.

It was red and blinking, causing the sound that was pulsing through the house.

"Someone's breaking in," Sarah said on a rise of breath.

Yes, and according to the red light, that someone was coming in through the back door.

THE HORSES WERE definitely spooked. Aiden had three mares, two fillies and a stallion in the corrals and pasture, and all were prancing and snorting. Someone had invaded their territory.

But who, and where the heck was the intruder?

Aiden had seen that shadow from his bedroom window, but he darn sure didn't see anything now. Once Leland got out here, they could divide up the area and have a look around, but not now. He didn't want to leave Kendall and Sarah alone until he was sure they weren't about to be attacked again.

He turned, intending to head back to the house, but something on the ground caught his eye.

Footprints.

He fanned the flashlight over them. They looked fresh. Too fresh, since this was a spot where the horses usually went back and forth to the water trough.

Somebody had been out here.

Aiden turned, hurrying back to the house and trying to keep watch at the same time. He still didn't see anyone, but he heard something.

The beeps from the security system.

Someone had tripped it. Maybe Sarah hadn't reset it properly after he left. Maybe.

But that seemed way too much to hope for.

He was almost back to the front porch when he heard something else. No more beeps. The security system started to blare. His gun was already drawn, and he wasn't exactly strolling, but that got him moving even faster.

The front door was still locked, and he wasn't sure if that was a good sign or not. "Open up," he called out to Sarah.

Nothing.

Not only didn't she answer, but he also didn't hear anyone coming to open the door. Definitely not good. While he kept watch around him, Aiden fished out his keys, unlocked the door and cautiously stepped inside. He spotted Sarah and Kendall almost immediately in the hall.

Thank God.

They were all right, though Sarah was standing in front of Kendall. The deputy, too, had pulled her gun, and she motioned toward the kitchen. Aiden didn't see anyone in that general direction, but he didn't have a full view of the kitchen, either. Someone could be in there. Someone responsible for tripping the security system.

While he kept watch, Aiden punched in the code to turn off the blaring alarm so he could listen for anyone inside the house. Hard to hear, though, over the sound of his own heartbeat crashing in his ears.

This couldn't be happening again. Kendall and the baby couldn't be in danger. Maybe this was literally a false alarm.

But Aiden had to ditch that hope fast.

The front door was open just a fraction. Enough for him to hear a strange sound out in the front yard. Since this could be some kind of diversion, he motioned for Sarah to keep watch of the kitchen, and he glanced behind him. The sound turned to more of a crackle, and while he watched, both his truck and Sarah's cruiser burst into flames.

Hell.

Not just little fires, either. These were full light-ups. As he didn't smell any accelerants, that meant someone had likely put some kind of incendiary devices on them. It also meant Aiden couldn't use the vehicles to get Sarah and Kendall out of there.

Time to do something other than just stand around and wait for something bad to happen, because the *bad* had already started.

"I'm Sheriff Braddock," he called out to whoever might be in the house. He eased the front door shut so that he wouldn't be ambushed from behind. "If you have a weapon, put it down and come out so I can see you."

He didn't expect that order to work. And it didn't.

Certainly no one surrendered a weapon or stepped out. But he did hear someone moving around in the direction of the back door. Aiden figured that with the break-in and the fires, the intruder wasn't leaving.

Aiden hurried across the entry, fully expecting someone to fire a shot at him. He thanked his lucky stars that it didn't happen, and he joined Sarah and Kendall in the narrow hall. Both were unharmed as far as he could tell, but Kendall had her hand over her stomach and was looking many steps past the terrified stage.

"He set the vehicles on fire?" Kendall asked in a whisper.

Aiden nodded.

"And I tried to call for backup, but the phone lines are jammed," Sarah added. "I can't get in touch with Leland."

That was *not* what Aiden wanted to hear. It wasn't hard to jam lines, but along with the fires, it meant whoever was behind this was serious about kidnapping Kendall again. If the person had simply wanted them dead, he could have set fire to the house and then shot them when they ran outside. Heck, he could have gunned down Aiden, too, when he went to check on the horses.

But he hadn't.

Why?

If the goal was just to get Kendall or kill them all, then why hadn't this idiot already struck?

"Are you waiting for your boss to arrive?" Aiden called out.

Yeah, taunting this guy probably wasn't smart, but he wanted to hear something, anything, to pinpoint his location.

And to make sure he wasn't outside setting fire to the house.

Again, there was no answer. Well, no verbal one anyway, but again Aiden heard somebody moving around in there.

"Take Kendall into the bathroom," Aiden whispered to the deputy. "I'll see what this guy is up to."

Kendall frantically shook her head. "You don't have backup."

True, and he might not get it. But at least he had Sarah to protect Kendall. Now he needed to eliminate any possible danger so he could get Kendall the heck out of there and to a safe house.

Aiden was about to insist that Sarah and she get going to the bathroom. Not ideal, but the tiles would better protect them if bullets started flying. However, the moment he opened his mouth, he heard something else. And this time it wasn't coming from the kitchen.

But rather the guest room. The same area where he'd been about to send Kendall and Sarah.

It sounded as if someone was coming through the window.

"Change of plans," Aiden whispered. "The three of us are getting out of here now."

The question was—which way? There were fires in the front of the house. Someone was in the kitchen by the back door. Someone else was about to come at them from the hall. That didn't exactly leave many options, and none of them was a sure thing when it came to keeping Kendall out of harm's way.

He looked around, his attention landing on the side window. Away from the fires, away from the back door. And that probably meant the brains behind this had already figured out that it was the escape route Aiden would take.

In other words, a trap.

Even though he hated to do this, Aiden figured their best chance of survival was eliminating the threats one by one. And to do that, it meant taking Kendall with him and Sarah into the lion's den.

"Come on," he whispered to them.

Aiden headed toward the kitchen, knowing that he was about to face down yet another hired gun.

Chapter Seventeen

With each step that they took toward the kitchen, Kendall's heart raced even harder.

Her thoughts were racing, too. This could turn deadly fast, and with the vehicles now on fire, it meant they would have to escape on foot. As it was still dark outside, there could be even more hired guns waiting to attack.

First, though, they had to deal with the two thugs who might already be inside the house. That pair would be more than enough to finish what had already been set in motion.

Aiden was ahead of her. Sarah behind. Both were armed, but Kendall wished she had a gun. It was too late for her to try to grab one, so maybe they could get out of this without shots being fired.

Of course, they hadn't managed to avoid violence with the other attacks, and because of it, four men were now dead. Too bad that body count hadn't stopped their boss from hiring yet another crew to do the job where the others had failed.

Kendall kept her hands over her stomach. Not that her hands would do much if someone did start shooting at them. But she had to do something to protect the baby, and this was all she had.

Aiden inched them across the living room, past the very spot where days earlier the other two gunmen had held her captive, waiting for Aiden to come home. Kendall had no idea how long she'd been forced to kneel on that floor. It'd felt like hours before Aiden finally arrived.

Despite the gunshot wound, he'd managed to rescue her, and while she hated relying on anyone to do that for her again, if she needed a rescuer, she preferred it to be Aiden. Other than her, no one else would fight harder to keep their baby safe.

Their baby.

Not a good time for the image of that ultrasound to skip through her mind. It only revved up her heartbeat and breathing even more. She didn't need that. She needed to focus in case there was some way she could help Sarah and Aiden.

They walked past the sofa, and Aiden focused his attention ahead while Sarah kept watch behind them. There was no one in the living room. No sounds to indicate the intruders were still in the house, but she doubted they'd just leave without getting what they had come there to get.

And what they no doubt intended to get was her.

But why?

Why did this keep happening?

Too bad she might finally know the answer when it was too late to do anything about it, but she figured it had something to do with the evidence against Jewell. Or maybe the person behind this wanted to silence her for good.

Aiden stopped just short of the entry into the kitchen and glanced around. There were half walls that divided the living room from the kitchen, but toward the back door was also a pantry and laundry room. Someone could be lurking there.

"Hell," Aiden cursed.

Kendall's heart went to her knees. So did she, because Aiden pushed her down and took cover behind the wall. He also aimed his gun at something or somebody toward the back door.

"Come out with your hands up," Aiden snarled.

Kendall didn't hear any indication the person was doing that.

Sarah stayed on her feet, hovering over Kendall while she continued to keep watch all around them. Kendall looked, too, and listened.

Did she hear someone breathing?

If the intruder was there, then why hadn't he just fired at them?

"Behind you, Sarah!" Aiden shouted.

Even though Sarah had been keeping watch in that direction, she obviously hadn't seen the intruder in the shadows. She snapped toward the living room, already aiming her gun.

"Wouldn't pull that trigger if I were you," the man said.

Like all the other attackers, he was wearing a ski mask, and he had a gun pointed right at them.

Or rather right at Kendall.

"We can do this the easy way," the man continued, "and Miss O'Neal can come with us."

"That's not gonna happen," Aiden snapped. "But you can make this easy on yourself by surrendering."

Kendall couldn't be certain, but she thought the guy might have chuckled. Probably because surrendering was the last thing on his mind, but he had to have known that Aiden wasn't just going to let her walk out of there with a kidnapper.

"You don't have a way out of this," someone else said.

Yet another man, and this was the one in the kitchen.

Kendall couldn't see him, but she figured he was on the other side of the fridge. Behind cover. So even if Aiden shot the one in the living room, this one would be there to continue the attack.

"You're not taking Kendall," Aiden growled.

"Oh, no?" That came from the guy in the living room. "You'll want to rethink that."

Before Kendall could even consider what to do or say, Aiden shoved her to the side of a chair and turned, pointing his gun at the guy in the kitchen. Sarah took aim at the one in the living room.

"Don't shoot!" someone called out.

Not the voice of the thugs. This was a woman, and Kendall immediately recognized who it was.

Carla.

Aiden and Sarah both froze, and because Kendall didn't want to distract Aiden by leaving cover, she just pulled in her breath and held it. Waiting and praying.

God, no.

Of course, she'd known all along that Carla could be the one behind this, but it was another thing to have it confirmed. Aiden had to be falling apart inside, but he kept his gun and aim steady.

"What are you doing here?" he asked his mother.

Carla made a rough sobbing sound. "Please, just put down your gun. If not, they'll kill you."

Now Aiden reacted. His nostrils flared, and his teeth came together. "You'd really have them kill your own son?" he snapped.

Silence. For what seemed an eternity.

Sarah volleyed glances between the living room, Aiden and the kitchen. She was clearly waiting for Aiden to tell her what to do, but Aiden stayed silent as well, glaring at his mother.

But then he flinched.

Aiden's grimace changed, and a single word of profanity slipped from his mouth. Even Sarah turned to the kitchen to gape and stare.

"I'm sorry," Carla said, her voice barely audible. "But if you shoot, they'll kill me, then you."

Kendall didn't get up, but she did lift her head slightly so she could take a quick look over the half wall. She wanted to see what had grabbed Aiden's and Sarah's attention.

And she soon saw what.

Carla was there all right, partly hidden in the shadows of the dark kitchen. Her face was stark white, and she appeared to be trembling. She wasn't armed.

But the person standing behind her was.

That person had a gun aimed right at Carla's head.

AIDEN HADN'T THOUGHT this night could get any worse, but obviously he'd been dead wrong about that.

"Hell." And because Aiden didn't know what else to say, he repeated it.

When Aiden had first seen his mother in the kitchen, he thought for certain that she was in on this latest kidnapping plan. After all, she had motive, means and opportunity. Well, motive if he counted her wanting to get back at Jewell and her family by making them look guilty as sin of trying to destroy evidence. However, with the missing money and news of her being in a mental hospital, Carla had gone to the top of his suspect list.

She didn't look so much like a suspect now.

Unless she was faking all this so she could clear her name. Anything was possible, including that.

"Are you in on this?" Aiden asked her.

No sound of outrage or drama from his mother. She just shook her head as tears trickled down her cheeks. It was hard to push those tears aside, but Aiden still wasn't convinced she was innocent.

"I'm going to fire a shot at that jerk behind you," Aiden said to Carla. "And since he's already said he'll fire back, now would be a good time for you to come clean of any of your own wrongdoing."

Carla shook her head. "Please don't shoot. He'll kill you."

"Yeah, I will," the guy verified. "I'll kill her, too. Saving her isn't part of the plan. In fact, the only one I'm supposed to save for sure is the pregnant woman."

If Aiden could have believed this guy, it would have made him feel a little better to know that Kendall could be spared. But the idiot was a hired gun, and even if killing her wasn't in the plan, that didn't mean it wouldn't happen.

Kendall touched her fingers to her mouth, both her hands and lips trembling. Yes, she was afraid. So was Aiden. But he also saw the fire in her eyes. She wasn't giving up without a fight.

That was both bad and good.

Good because he might need her help in the next couple of minutes. Help that might include her running for cover somewhere else in the house. But he didn't want the fire in her eyes spurring her to get in the middle of this fight.

"I want you to think of the baby first," he whispered to Kendall.

Oh, that didn't sit well with her, but he could see that it sank in. Good. She'd run if it came down to it, and Aiden was afraid that it would. Now he only hoped Sarah could eliminate the thug in the living room. While he was hoping, Aiden didn't want there to be any other hired guns waiting outside.

These two along with his mother were plenty enough.

"This is a little bit of déjà vu for me." Aiden motioned around the living room. "The last time two clowns tried to kidnap Kendall, that didn't work out so well for them. So, is that your plan, to die tonight like they did?"

"I've got your mother," the one in the kitchen growled. "You'll cooperate."

Carla's mouth tightened. "Clearly, you don't know the strained relationship between me and my son. He's not going to put protecting me over his unborn child. And he shouldn't."

If she meant that, it was a sentiment that Aiden had never expected to hear coming from her, and later, he'd thank her for it. For now, though, that was still a big *if.*

"I'm a good shot," Aiden said to the man. "And since you're a head taller than my mother, it won't be hard taking you out. Even if you try to scrunch down." He hiked his thumb to Sarah. "My deputy's a good shot, too. You want to test that, or do you two just want to put down your guns right now?"

The guy in the kitchen laughed. "He said you had a smart mouth, and he was right."

Aiden picked right up on that. *"He?"*

"He," the guy verified without clarifying it. "Now, here's the way this is really going to work. If the O'Neal woman doesn't come with us, then we start shooting. First, your mother. Then you and the deputy."

So the three of them were expendable, making him wonder who they'd nab to destroy evidence. If that was still what they wanted to do, that is. Maybe there were new rules now.

"Your plan sucks," Aiden insisted. "How soon do you

think I'll leave you alive once you've pulled the trigger? You'll have a bullet in your head before my mother hits the floor."

Aiden knew it sounded cold and uncaring. He had to be right now. Because if he showed any fear or any indication that he would back down, then it'd start a gunfight. Not only would his mother be killed, maybe Sarah, too, but a stray bullet could hit Kendall.

"Who's behind this?" Aiden asked his mother. "And if it's you, I want to know now."

"It's not me." Carla's voice cracked on the last word.

Aiden hoped he didn't regret it later, but he believed her, and that meant if she hadn't hired these men, somebody else had. Somebody with plenty of money and enough hatred for him and his family that he didn't mind seeing them die.

"I can't say anything else," his mother added in a mumble.

The gunman behind her touched his finger to the communicator that was in his ear and then cursed. "Time to put an end to this now!"

He no longer sounded cocky, just nervous that this wasn't going down as planned. Well, Aiden wasn't too easy about it, either, but he was damned if he did and damned if he didn't. He couldn't shoot without risking Kendall's, Sarah's and his mother's lives, and he couldn't let these goons take Kendall.

"No," Aiden said, and he didn't mumble it, either. "If you want to try to take Kendall, you have to come through me."

That didn't please the masked guy because his profanity went up a notch, and it took Aiden a moment before he realized the hired gun wasn't the only one talking.

He heard another voice. This one coming from his back porch.

"Hell, kill them all," the man said. "Burn the place to the ground so I can finish this."

And Aiden recognized the voice of the man who'd just ordered their murders.

Chapter Eighteen

Lee Palmer.

Kendall knew she shouldn't have been surprised to hear Palmer's voice. After all, he was a suspect. But it was the first time she'd heard him speak with such venom toward her.

Kill them all.

Kendall lifted her head, staring at him, and she knew this wasn't a bluff. Palmer wanted them all dead, including her precious baby.

That realization got Kendall standing so she could face him down. By God, if he was going to try to kill them, she wanted to know why. She also wanted to know if Carla was in on this. One look at Aiden's mom, though, and Kendall was thinking no. The woman seemed just as terrified as Kendall.

"Why are you doing this?" Kendall demanded, staring at Palmer.

Some of that venom faded from Palmer's expression, and he even made a weary sigh. "Killing you wasn't part of the plan, Kendall. Sorry that you got caught up in this mess."

The apology didn't help matters at all, and the anger rippled through her. Apparently through Aiden, too, because he looked ready to tear Palmer limb from limb. Kendall wouldn't have minded that happening, but she didn't want Aiden hurt in the process. And he would be hurt, since Palmer and his thugs had their guns aimed at him.

Three guns against Aiden's and Sarah's two were not good odds. Heck, there were no good odds when it came to her baby and these killers.

"Why?" Kendall repeated to Palmer.

Aiden inched closer to her, no doubt so he could be in a better position to protect her when the attack finally happened.

"This all got out of hand," Palmer finally said. "Yost and his partner weren't supposed to shoot you. They were only supposed to make Aiden destroy those bone fragments so your sister could get out of that jail cell."

Kendall desperately wanted Jewell free but not like this. "Jewell wouldn't want that evidence destroyed."

Palmer lifted his shoulder. "Well, I was helping her out, wasn't I? She always was a little too goody-goody for me, but hey, any woman who sliced up Whitt Braddock and left his body to rot is a friend of mine. I figured I owed her a favor or two."

This had to be hard for Aiden to take, but he didn't respond to Palmer. He only moved closer to her. Maybe that meant Aiden had a plan to try to get them out of this.

"Like I said," Palmer went on, "I'm sorry you got caught up in this. If Yost hadn't told you that I'd hired him, we wouldn't be here right now."

Kendall froze. Shook her head. "He didn't tell me."

Palmer studied her as if trying to decide if she was telling the truth, then he cursed. "Well, he said he did, and I believed him. I couldn't take that chance, could I? Especially since Yost was stupid enough to drive out to my place and get it all captured on that traffic camera. Coming to my place wasn't part of the plan."

"But he panicked," Aiden filled in, "when I killed his partner."

"Like I said, he was stupid," Palmer added. "Couldn't risk him being out there. It was the same for that moron of a prison guard. He botched that big-time."

And now both Yost and the guard were dead. She hoped that caused the two hired guns in the house to have second thoughts about doing this, because if Palmer would kill the guard and Yost, then anyone connected to this plan would likely be eliminated.

"You set up Joplin and my mother?" Aiden asked, though she wasn't sure how he could speak with his jaw that stiff.

Palmer scowled. "*Set up* is such an ugly phrase. All I did was fix it so Joplin would show up at that meeting with Yost. It took some of the spotlight off me and put it on him."

"You set him up," Aiden confirmed. "So, Joplin didn't fire those shots at Yost. One of your hired guns no doubt did that. And I'm also betting you did that disappearing act with the money from Carla's bogus account."

No denial there, either. Heaven knew how long Palmer had been planning this, but Kendall still wasn't convinced of his reasons for doing it.

"Helping my sister seems a little extreme," Kendall said to Palmer. "Especially since we didn't ask for your help."

"He didn't do this for Jewell. He did it because Palmer hates me," Carla volunteered. "Yes, I had an affair with him. If you can call what a teenager does an affair. I was stupid, and I paid dearly for that stupidity." She paused. "In addition to the settlement money he got for my car rage *incident*, he extorted money from my family. That's how Palmer got so rich."

Kendall glanced at Aiden to see if he knew that. He apparently didn't. "Palmer was the one who was engaged at the time, not you," Aiden reminded her. "So, how could he have extorted more money?"

Palmer smiled. "Tell him, Carla. I'm sure your son will want to hear all about this."

And Kendall was equally certain that he wouldn't. Still, it sounded as if this was all at the heart of what was going on now.

Carla took a deep breath. "Palmer made sex tapes of us. I didn't know," she added. "But when he broke things off with me, he told my father he'd mail copies of the tapes to all our friends and family if we didn't pay up. So we paid him a hundred thousand dollars."

Definitely not petty cash, especially forty years ago.

"Palmer gave us the tapes," Carla continued. "We destroyed them, and I thought that was the last of it. Then, when I married Whitt, Palmer came around demanding more money. He had copies of the tapes."

Palmer didn't deny any of that, but the smile did vanish from his face. "What Carla left out was that Whitt hired some muscle to break into my house. They beat me within an inch of my life until I told them where I'd hidden the tapes, and then they stole them."

It took Kendall a moment to process all that. Aiden was obviously a few seconds ahead of her, because he cursed.

"This is why you have a vendetta against my family?" Aiden snapped.

Again, Palmer didn't deny it, but it was clear that was the reason. "Hey, I'm not the only one with a vendetta. Remember, your daddy was always trying to butt heads with me over any little thing. I kept besting him, and it riled him. That, and his getting my *leftovers*."

With that, Palmer aimed a smug glance at Carla. A glance that nobody, including Carla, missed.

A sound of raw anger came from Aiden's throat, and Kendall was afraid he would just launch himself at Palmer. Kendall had never cared much for Palmer, but she could see now the true monster that he was.

Carla had almost certainly already seen the monster a time or two, and the sound that Aiden made was nothing compared to her shriek of outrage.

"Yeah, leftovers," Palmer repeated.

Kendall could have bet it was a bad idea to throw that in Carla's face. And it was. Maybe a bad idea for all of them.

Because Carla turned and launched herself at Palmer.

"STOP!" AIDEN YELLED to his mother.

But he was already too late to try to diffuse this. Carla rammed right into Palmer, and despite the fact that the man outweighed her by a good fifty pounds, it was enough to off-balance him.

Both his mother and Palmer fell to the floor, where they started a wrestling match.

That was only the beginning of the chaos.

The hired gun in the kitchen ducked out of the way so he wouldn't get knocked down on the floor, too, but as soon as he recovered, he whipped around and aimed his weapon at Aiden.

"Get down," Aiden told Kendall, not waiting for her to do that. He pushed her to the floor and tried to move in front of her as best he could.

Right before the blast echoed through the room.

The idiot in the living room had fired at him, and if

Aiden had been just a split second slower, he wouldn't have gotten Kendall out of the way in time. That riled him to the core, but he was more than just riled.

He was scared that he wouldn't be able to get them out of this alive.

Sarah fired at the shooter in the living room, all of them scrambling to take cover. Kendall and he landed next to the chair. Sarah behind the sofa. Aiden lost sight of the guy in the kitchen, but the one who'd fired darted out into the entry.

Just out of range for Aiden to blast him to smithereens. How dare this moron try to kill Kendall and the baby?

Another bullet came barreling past him.

Not from the guy in the entry this time. It'd come from the kitchen, and the bullet landed just a fraction away from Sarah. Thankfully, his deputy hurried to the other end of the sofa, and she came up ready to fire.

So did Aiden.

There was no way his mother could hold off Palmer for long, and like his hired guns, Palmer was armed. Considering that he'd called Carla his "leftovers," Aiden doubted that the man would spare her life.

Or anyone else's for that matter.

No, Palmer probably had plans to kill all of them, including these two that he'd hired.

"Stay down," Aiden whispered to Kendall.

Even though the seconds were ticking away, Aiden took a moment to glance at her and make sure she was okay. She wasn't. Kendall wasn't hurt, thank God, but she was shaking and clearly terrified.

"Do you have a backup weapon I can use?" she asked.

Okay, maybe not as terrified as he thought. Aiden didn't like the idea of putting a gun in her hands, because it might make the hired pair zoom in on her as a target. But like him and the others, Kendall was already a target, and it was best if she had a way to protect herself.

"I still want you to stay down," he insisted, but he removed the small gun from his boot holster and handed it to her. Aiden added a firm glance, hoping that Kendall would listen.

The gunman in the kitchen fired another shot at Sarah, and since he was focusing on the deputy, that meant he probably figured his boss could take care of a middle-aged woman like Carla. But his mother was holding her own. She rammed her knee into Palmer's groin and had the man howling in pain.

That distraction wouldn't last, either.

After all, Palmer still had hold of his gun, and he was trying to aim it at Carla so he could shoot her.

Aiden had to do something, fast, and that something started with getting rid of the shooter in the kitchen. The guy had Sarah pinned down. Plus, the one in the entry could get in on this at any second.

"Watch behind me," he said to Kendall because he had no other choice. He needed to get in a better position, and he couldn't risk doing that if the guy was going to shoot him in the back. If that happened, Kendall's chance of survival would go down significantly.

Kendall shifted her position, still staying down, but she aimed in the direction of the entry. Aiden aimed at the kitchen. He leaned out but immediately had to duck back when the shooter sent another bullet his way.

From the corner of Aiden's eye, he saw Sarah maneuvering herself for a better shot as well, but Aiden waved her off and instead motioned toward the entry. He wanted Kendall and Sarah to focus on that, since there were two guns in the kitchen.

His mother screamed, a bloodcurdling sound that

knifed right through Aiden. No, Carla hadn't exactly been mother of the year, but it sounded as if Palmer was killing her.

Aiden moved out of cover again, taking aim at the hired gun.

The hired gun did the same to him.

But Aiden pulled the trigger first.

The bullet smacked into the guy's chest, and because the shooter was still lifting his gun toward the living room, Aiden was forced to fire a second shot at him. That one sent the guy to the floor.

"Stay back," Aiden warned Kendall one last time.

He raced into the kitchen, and the first thing he saw was the blood on his mother's face. Palmer had obviously hit her, but she was still fighting, and she had a tight grip on his right wrist.

But not tight enough.

Before Aiden could even get to her, Palmer turned the gun and pulled the trigger. The shot didn't go into his mother, but it came right at Aiden. He had to dive to the floor.

And it wasn't the only shot.

Behind him, Sarah shouted, "Watch out!"

Aiden scrambled to the side of the kitchen, only to realize that Sarah wasn't yelling at him.

But rather at Kendall.

Aiden's heart slammed so hard in his chest that it felt as if his ribs had cracked. The shooter had his gun aimed right at Kendall, and even though she was hunched down, he had a direct shot to kill her.

"No!" Aiden called out, hoping to get the guy's attention off Kendall.

It didn't work.

The shot tore through the room.

Chapter Nineteen

The shot was so deafening that it drowned out everything else. Aiden was shouting something to her, but exactly what Kendall didn't know.

From the corner of her eye, she could see Aiden hurrying toward her. Sarah, too. But they stopped, their attention rifling to the gunman in the entry. At least, he'd been in the entry just seconds earlier.

Now he was tumbling to the living room floor.

Because Kendall had shot him.

Oh, God. Not another one. That was the only thing that registered in her mind when she saw that the man was still moving. And not just moving. Even though there was blood on the front of his shirt, he was trying to aim his gun at her again.

Aiden fixed that.

He tore across the room, kicking the gun out of the man's hand, and pointed his gun at him. "Move and you die," Aiden said, and there was nothing in his voice to indicate he was bluffing.

The guy stopped, groaned and rolled onto his back, clutching his chest. Kendall could see that he was bleeding, but it didn't look as life-threatening as she'd originally thought. The bullet appeared to have caught him in the shoulder.

"Watch him," Aiden told Sarah, and he hurried to Kendall. "Are you all right?"

She planned on lying, telling him that she was fine. She wasn't, not by a long shot. But the sound coming from the kitchen stopped her from saying anything.

"No!" Carla said. Not a shout, but Kendall could hear the heavy emotion in the woman's voice.

Kendall turned, dreading what she might see. It seemed a horrible thought to wish a person dead, but she was hoping she would see Palmer lying next to the gunman whom Aiden had killed.

But he wasn't.

Palmer was on his feet, but he'd still somehow managed to keep hold of his gun. A gun that he now had pointed at Carla's head.

"Let go of her," Aiden insisted.

Palmer chuckled. "I'm thinking the answer to that is no."

He sounded cocky again despite the fact he looked as if he'd lost that fight with Carla. The woman had clawed at his face and left streaks of blood on his cheeks. He must have been in pain, but he certainly didn't show it.

Unlike Carla.

Aiden's mother had her teeth clamped over her bottom lip, and she was wincing. Probably because Palmer had managed to hit her multiple times. There were bruises already forming on her face.

"It's over," Aiden said. He kept his left hand braced on his shooting wrist and inched closer to Carla and Palmer. "There's no way you can get out of this."

Palmer's smile said differently. "Are you forgetting I have a hostage?"

"Are you forgetting that every cop in the state will be looking for you?" Aiden countered.

"Maybe not," Palmer mumbled.

And that answer chilled Kendall to the bone.

Because it didn't sound as if he was worried at all about being caught. Probably because he'd already arranged to kill them all.

Aiden must have realized that, too, because he glanced back at the injured man. "Sarah, ask him if there are any firebombs set in the house or if there are other gunmen waiting outside. If he doesn't answer, beat him until he tells you."

Yes, it was harsh, but they had to know. Kendall wanted nothing more than to get out of there with Aiden, Sarah and Carla, but that wasn't going to happen unless they got that gun away from Palmer and they made sure it was safe. After all, Palmer had already hired plenty of men to come after them, so he could have planted others to make sure he carried out his plan.

"I'm leaving with your mother," Palmer insisted.

Sarah grabbed the injured gunman, dragged him onto the sofa and snapped him right to her face. "What's out there? What did your boss do?"

"And remember, Palmer's not saying a thing about taking you with him," Aiden added when the guy attempted a smile.

"Come on." Palmer grabbed hold of Carla and started backing out the door with her in tow. He no longer wore that cocky smile, which meant he was perhaps worried about what his hired gun was going to tell them.

"You're leaving me here?" the guy shouted.

But Palmer ignored him and kept moving.

The gunman spat out some profanity and came off the sofa to face his boss. "There's one more guy waiting on a ranch trail about a quarter of a mile from here. He's in an SUV, and it's the getaway car."

"What about explosives?" Aiden pressed.

"None. And I would have been the one to set them." He added some more profanity, aimed at Palmer.

If Palmer even heard him, he didn't react. Not at first anyway. Then, without warning, he took aim at the man and shot him. Just as quickly, Palmer put the gun back against Carla's head.

"Can't have anybody talking," Palmer threatened. "Now, can I?"

Yes, he was definitely planning on killing them all. But how? Had the dead man been wrong about more firebombs?

Palmer moved his grip from Carla's arm to her hair and pulled her out onto the porch with him. Kendall didn't know where this ranch trail was exactly, but if Palmer somehow managed to clear the barn, there were plenty of trees back there that he could use to hide and escape.

"This one's dead," Sarah said, touching her fingers to the gunman's neck.

Again, no reaction from Palmer. Not that Kendall expected one. He'd just shot a man in cold blood.

Aiden used the appliances and cabinets for cover, following Palmer inch for inch until he reached the back porch. When Kendall tried to follow, Aiden motioned for Sarah to get in front of her, and the deputy did.

Protecting Kendall, again.

She hated that she had to put someone else's life in danger, but she also had to think of her baby.

There were flagstone steps leading to the unfenced backyard, and that was exactly where Palmer headed. Sarah stopped in the doorway, and Aiden made his way out to the porch. Kendall had her attention focused just on them, and that was why she nearly missed the slight snapping sound behind her.

She whirled around.

And the man was there. Another gunman wearing a ski mask. He put his gun not to her head but to her stomach.

"I thought you might need help," the man called out to Palmer.

Aiden pivoted around, the color blanching from his face. No doubt because he saw the new threat. The gun pointed at her.

"Get out on the porch with the sheriff," the newcomer told Sarah.

Sarah volleyed some glances between Aiden and the gunman, and Aiden finally nodded. She didn't hurry to join him, but when she made her way there, she turned her gun toward the new attacker.

While Palmer continued to drag Carla across the yard.

It was still dark and it was hard to think or see with her pulse racing a mile a minute, but Kendall knew they didn't have much time. Once Palmer cleared the yard, this monster would kill Aiden, Sarah and her. Palmer would take care of Carla. If Palmer did manage to destroy all the evidence, then he could get off scot-free.

"I'm not going to let you kill my son and that baby," Carla spat out.

Without warning, she dropped to the ground. Palmer fired, but Kendall didn't see where the bullet went. That's because the goon behind Kendall grabbed her. No doubt ready to shoot her. And he would have done just that.

If Aiden hadn't come right at him.

There was a rage in Aiden's eyes. All aimed at the scum holding her.

Kendall managed to get out of the way, barely, and Aiden rammed his full weight into the guy. There was another shot. Not from this goon, Kendall realized. It'd come from the yard.

"Help my mother," Aiden said to Sarah, and he stripped the gun from the man's hand and body-slammed the gunman against the wall.

Hard.

So hard that it rattled the porch.

The guy made a guttural gasping sound. Clearly Aiden had knocked the breath out of him, and he also slammed his fist into the man's face. Not once but three times. Before Aiden latched on to him and dragged him into the yard.

Carla was sprawled on the ground, and Sarah was struggling with Palmer, trying to disarm the man. However, Aiden pulled her off him and grabbed Palmer as he'd done with the gunman.

Kendall's breath was already thin, and that robbed her of what little she had. For a moment, she thought Aiden might kill Palmer right then, right there.

But he didn't.

"You're under arrest," Aiden said, reaching for Palmer's gun.

An oily smile bent Palmer's mouth, and there was a loud blast.

Oh, God.

A gunshot.

"Aiden!" Kendall shouted, hurrying down the porch.

A thousand things went through her head. None good. Palmer had managed to shoot Aiden, and now he'd die without knowing how she felt about him. Without ever having seen his son.

"I'm okay," Aiden managed to say when she flung herself into his arms.

And he was.

However, she couldn't say the same for Palmer. With that sick smile still on his face, he crumpled to the ground, the gun falling out of his hand.

The gun Palmer had used to kill himself.

"Sarah, call an ambulance," Aiden said, and she felt the muscles in his arm go stiff. He also moved away from her.

That's when Kendall saw the blood.

Carla had been shot.

Chapter Twenty

Aiden felt as if he'd been through a war. A war that wasn't over yet.

Yes, Palmer was dead, most of his hired guns, too, and Kendall and the baby were no longer in danger. But that danger had ended with a high price tag.

His mother was unconscious in a hospital bed after having had surgery, and Kendall looked as if she might faint at any moment. That's why Aiden had tried multiple times to make her sit down, but she'd insisted on waiting in the hall outside his mother's room.

Maybe because Kendall felt that Carla wouldn't want her in there.

Or maybe because Kendall wanted some distance from his mother and him.

Aiden couldn't blame her. He'd always thought of himself as a damn good lawman, but here he hadn't been able to stop four attacks on Kendall. Any one of which could have left her dead.

Just the thought of it twisted his stomach into a hard knot.

It probably wasn't doing much for Kendall's stomach, either. Or the baby. Thank God his son wouldn't remember any of this, but it would stay with Kendall, his mother and him for a lifetime.

"Your sister Shelby is on the way," Leland said, sticking his head in the door of the hospital room. "She was in Houston, and she'll get here as fast as she can."

Good. His other sister, Laine, was already there in the waiting room, and once Carla woke up, it would probably help to see her kids.

Probably.

There was a good chance that Carla would want to wash her hands of him. A good chance that he'd want to wash his hands of her, too, if she didn't have a change of heart about Kendall and the baby.

With that thought, Aiden moved away from his mother's hospital bed and stepped out into the hall. Kendall's back was against the wall there, and she was chewing on her bottom lip.

"Is she awake?" Kendall asked.

Aiden shook his head, and because she looked as if she could use another hug, he pulled her into his arms. Something he'd been doing most of the night, and like the other times, Kendall stayed there a couple of seconds and then maneuvered away.

"I'm okay." Another repeat of what she'd already told him. "You should be with your mother."

He stared at her, wishing he had a translation for that. Even though he had two sisters, Aiden knew he didn't always interpret the signals right. And Kendall definitely seemed to be sending out some kind of signal here.

"I should be with my mother," he admitted. "But I'd like to be with you, too."

Oh, man. That sounded pretty lame, and it was a massive understatement. "I *need* to be with you," he tried again.

And that need encompassed a lot. He not only wanted her in the room with him, but he also wanted her in his arms.

"When I hold you," he said, "it makes the worst of the images disappear."

She blinked.

Aiden groaned. He was making a mess of this. "I want you in my arms for other reasons, but that's one of them."

Kendall nodded, slipped back into his embrace.

It definitely helped. Well, it helped him anyway, but he wasn't so sure Kendall was getting anything out of this.

"What can I do to make things better for you?" he asked.

She didn't move away this time, but Kendall did look up at him. "You can kiss me. When you kiss me, the worst of the images disappear."

All right. Aiden preferred a kiss to a hug anyway, so that's what he did. He kissed Kendall, probably not for all the right reasons, either. Of course, he wanted to get those nightmarish images out of her head, but kissing her was also the purest form of pleasure for him.

Like always, the heat slid right through him. Head to toe. And it helped a whole heck of a lot to push his nightmares aside, too. Nightmares of the attack anyway. But there were plenty of other things about their situation that would give him some sleepless nights.

"I could have lost both you and the baby," he said.

"But you didn't."

She kissed him again, a nice reminder that both she and the baby were okay. Aiden hadn't taken her word for that, though. Kendall had had a checkup and another ultrasound while his mother was in surgery. Thank God this latest attack and stress hadn't caused any physical harm.

His mother was a different story.

She'd come out of the surgery to remove a bullet from her chest. A bullet that Palmer had put there. If the man weren't dead, Aiden would have gone after him and made him pay. He and his mother didn't have a perfect relationship, nowhere near it, but she didn't deserve this.

Aiden heard the footsteps, and because the adrenaline was still fueling his body, he turned, ready to draw his gun. But it was just Leland, making his way down the hall toward them. Aiden hoped the deputy wasn't there to deliver bad news, because Aiden had met his quota for a lifetime or two.

Kendall started to step away, probably so that she wouldn't be in his arms while he talked to Leland, but Aiden held on. He wasn't ready to let go of her yet. Maybe not ever.

He mentally repeated that.

And then took out the *maybe*.

He had no intention of letting Kendall go, but the problem was—how did he make that happen?

"You two okay?" Leland asked, eyeing them. Maybe because of the snug embrace but also because they'd been put through the wringer and back.

Aiden nodded. "Did you get Palmer's hired gun to the jail?"

"Yeah. And he's talking. Neither of our other suspects was involved in this." Leland's gaze drifted to Carla. "And we're gathering the money trail to prove that it was all Palmer's doing."

Kendall gave a heavy sigh. "Palmer did all this because of bad blood. For revenge. And what did he get out of it? Nothing. He's dead, and we're all left to deal with the aftermath of this mess he created."

Yes, that was the problem with bad blood. It stayed bad and festered unless someone did something about it.

And that's what Aiden intended to do.

"I want us to put this bad blood aside," he said to Kendall. "If our families don't do the same, then that's on them, but I don't want this between us any longer."

She looked up at him. Smiled. Okay, it wasn't a big smile, but man, it lit up her whole face.

"And I want you to marry me," he added.

Aiden wasn't sure who was more surprised that he'd just blurted that out: Kendall, Leland or himself.

"Uh, I think I got something else to do," Leland said, making a vague motion toward the exit. "I'll call you if there are any updates."

Aiden mumbled something about that being fine, but he kept his attention on Kendall. She wasn't exactly jumping for joy over his proposal.

Of course, it'd been a lousy proposal.

"I know," he explained. "That was bad. I should have gotten down on one knee. Should have had a ring. Probably should have waited until we were in a place that didn't smell like antiseptic."

Kendall stared at him, obviously waiting for something, so he kissed her again. At first, she stayed a little stiff, but by degrees, she softened until she melted right into his arms.

Just a few days ago, Aiden had never thought of himself as the marrying kind. Not the fathering kind, either. But he was looking forward to both. At least he was if he could convince Kendall to say yes. The kiss had helped plenty, but Aiden wasn't sure he wanted her saying yes simply because they were good at kissing and falling into bed.

Though those things did help.

This time, he was the one to break the kiss so he could put his mouth to use, hopefully convincing her that marriage was the right thing to do. But he didn't get a chance to say anything, because he heard a soft moaning sound. His gaze flew to the hospital bed, and he saw that his mother was opening her eyes.

"Aiden," Carla said, her voice as weak as her hand that reached out for him.

Kendall didn't just let go of him, she nudged him in Carla's direction, and Aiden went to his mother's bedside so he could give her hand a gentle squeeze. "How are you, Mom?"

Her eyes fluttered open, and she managed a smile. She also looked past him, her attention landing on Kendall. Kendall started to back out of the doorway, but Carla motioned for her to come closer.

"I'm so sorry," Carla said.

Aiden could count on one hand how many times he'd heard his mother apologize over the years. Maybe it was the painkillers or the ordeal, but the apology was aimed at Kendall.

"This wasn't your fault," Kendall assured her. "Palmer was a sick man, and he put a very sick plan into motion." That was generous of Kendall, considering that his mother hadn't exactly been kind to her.

"A plan that Palmer wouldn't have come up with if he hadn't hated me so much." Carla groaned softly and closed her eyes.

"I'll get the doctor," Aiden insisted, but Carla caught on to his hand to stop him.

"You can do that later. For now, let's just talk for a couple of minutes." Again, her attention went to Kendall. "I don't want you to push Aiden out of your life because of the things I said." She gave Kendall's stomach a soft pat.

"If you can find it in your heart to forgive me, then I want to be a part of this baby's life."

Kendall swallowed hard, and for a moment Aiden thought she might tell Carla to take a hike. She certainly had a right to do that. But Kendall nodded.

"You're his grandmother, and I don't want this baby to experience any more fallout from bad blood."

It was a bighearted concession, and Aiden was darn thankful for it.

"You mean that?" Carla asked.

Another nod from Kendall. "No matter what happens with my sister's trial, you'll be part of this baby's life. Aiden's sisters, too. If they want to be part of his life, that is."

Tears sprang to his mother's eyes. To Kendall's, too, and while this was a moment that went a long way toward mending some fences, there was something missing.

Something huge.

Because while Kendall had agreed to include his family, she hadn't exactly extended that invitation to him. And she hadn't said a word about his marriage proposal.

"Go ahead," his mother said as if sensing he had something on his mind. "I need to rest." As if to prove her point, she closed her eyes again.

Aiden didn't intend to go far from the room, but he did want to have that talk with Kendall. He led her back into the hall, got the attention of one of the nurses and let her know that his mother had regained consciousness. While the nurse went into the room to check on Carla, Aiden took Kendall several yards away.

"Thank you for that," he started. Except the start was as far as he got. He paused, waiting to see what the verdict was on his proposal.

No verdict. Kendall stared at him. Then she huffed.

"So, you should have proposed somewhere else and gotten down on one knee. Is there anything else you should have changed?"

And with that, she kissed him again. Hard. Unlike the others, this one had a bite of anger in it.

That's when Aiden got it.

Even a semi-angry kiss with Kendall was still enjoyable, but Aiden broke away because he knew where this conversation had to go.

To the L-word.

In case he was wrong about that, Kendall quickly clarified it. "I won't marry you just because I'm pregnant with your baby."

Yep, that was confirmation, so Aiden did a turnabout and kissed her. A real kiss. No anger involved. But he made it long and hot. It went on for so long that one of the nurses cleared her throat.

Aiden ignored her. He ignored everything but Kendall.

"Would you marry me if you were in love with me?" he asked. "Let me rephrase that. Are you in love with me, Kendall?"

Her left eye narrowed a little as if she was suspicious. "Yes. I am. And I'm surprised you even had to ask."

That was mighty good to hear. "What can I say? I'm a little thick when it comes to such things."

But she loved him.

Kendall loved him!

And that made him grin like an idiot.

"I don't know why you're smiling," she said. "Yes, I'm in love with you, but that doesn't mean I'll marry you." Kendall looked him straight in the eye. "The only way I'll marry you is if you're in love with me, too."

Problem solved. "Well, heck. I guess that kiss wasn't good enough after all."

"It was plenty good enough, but you have to say it."

Judging from the look she was giving him, Kendall probably thought he would choke on the words. But this was the easiest thing he'd ever done.

"I'm in love with you, Kendall. Have been since I kissed you over two decades ago. And I'm still in love with you now." He slid his hand over her stomach. "This baby is just the icing on the cake."

The best kind of icing.

"So, what do you say about marrying—"

"Yes," Kendall answered before he even finished. And she gave him one of those delicious kisses. "Because I've been in love with you, too, since that first kiss."

More than two decades seemed like an awfully long time before they came to their senses, but he had plenty of sense now. Aiden pulled Kendall into his arms and held on, something he planned to do a lot of for the rest of their lives together.

* * * * *

Find out the truth behind Whitt Braddock's murder when USA TODAY *bestselling author Delores Fossen's* SWEETWATER RANCH *miniseries comes to a gripping conclusion next month.*

Look for A LAWMAN'S JUSTICE!

"Sorry. I didn't expect anyone to be here."

Brodey's gaze traveled over her cashmere sweater, worn jeans and loafers, then came back up, lingering on her face, making her cheeks fire. *My goodness, the man has a way.* Had she known she'd be seeing anyone, particularly the intriguing detective, she'd have dressed more appropriately. But at 4:00 a.m., that thought hadn't crossed her mind.

"I couldn't sleep," she said. "The colours for the kitchen were driving me mad. Where's your sling?"

"You're here by yourself?"

"Of course."

"Anyone ever tell you it's dangerous for a woman to be driving around a city alone in the middle of the night?"

Prior to her panic a minute ago, she hadn't even questioned it. Maybe she should have. But that was the trusting part of her. The part that didn't include the male species and wanted to see pretty things instead of danger. She wasn't a complete lunatic and understood the world to be a dangerous place, but when it came to her creative process, certain things, like possible danger, couldn't get in her way. "I live ten minutes from here."

"A lot can happen in ten minutes."

THE DETECTIVE

BY

ADRIENNE GIORDANO

Published in Great Britain 2015
by Mills & Boon, an imprint of Harlequin (UK) Limited,
Eton House, 18-24 Paradise Road, Richmond, Surrey, TW9 1SR

ISBN: 978-0-263-25310-8

46-0715

Harlequin (UK) Limited's policy is to use papers that are natural, renewable and recyclable products and made from wood grown in sustainable forests. The logging and manufacturing processes conform to the legal environmental regulations of the country of origin.

Printed and bound in Spain
by CPI, Barcelona

Adrienne Giordano, a *USA TODAY* bestselling author, writes romantic suspense and mystery. She is a Jersey girl at heart, but now lives in the Midwest with her workaholic husband, sports obsessed son and Buddy the wheaten terrorist (terrier). For more information on Adrienne's books, please visit www.adriennegiordano.com or download the Adrienne Giordano app. For information on Adrienne's street team, go to facebook.com/groups/dangerousdarlings.

Chapter One

Lexi Vanderbilt's mother taught her two very important lessons. One, always wear coordinating lipstick, and two, recognize an opportunity when it presented itself.

Standing in the ballroom of the newly renovated Gold Coast Country Club, Lexi planned on employing those lessons.

All around her workers prepared for the throng of club members who would descend in—she checked her watch—ninety-three minutes. As the interior designer about to unveil her latest masterpiece, she would spend those ninety-three minutes tending to everything from flowers to linens to centerpieces. A waiter toting a tray of sparkling champagne glasses cruised by. She took in the not-so-perfect cut of his tux and groaned. The staff's attire wasn't her jurisdiction. Still, small details never escaped her. At times, like now, it was maddening.

Oh, and just wait one second. "Excuse me," she said to a woman carrying a stack of tablecloths. "The sailboat ice sculpture belongs on the dessert table by the window. The Willis Tower goes by the champagne fountain."

The woman hefted the pile of linens, a not-so-subtle hint that the sculptures weren't her problem. "Does it matter?"

If it didn't, I wouldn't ask. Lexi sighed. "It matters. Unless you'd like to tell your boss, who specifically requested the placement of the sculptures, that it doesn't."

For added effect, Lexi grinned and the woman rolled her eyes. "I'll get the busboys to move it."

"Thank you."

One minicrisis averted. And maybe she could have let that one slide given that the club's manager had to be 110 years old and most likely wouldn't remember which sculpture went where, but why take a chance on something easily fixed?

Besides, tonight everything had to be perfect.

Functions attended by the richest of the rich were a breeding ground for opportunities. Opportunities Lexi craved for her fledgling design company. At twenty-nine, she'd already been profiled by the *Banner-Herald* and all the major broadcast stations in the city. She was quickly gaining ground on becoming Chicago's "it" designer, and that meant dethroning Jerome Laddis, the current "it" designer. He may have had more experience, but Lexi had youth, energy and fresh ideas on her side. A few more insanely wealthy clients touting Lexi's work and *look out, Jerome.*

Then she'd hire an assistant, rehab her disaster of a garage into an office and get some sleep.

Lots of it.

Right now, as she glanced around, took in the exquisite silk drapes, the hundred-thousand-dollar chandelier and hand-scraped floor she'd had flown in from Brazil, no questions on the tiny details would haunt her. She'd make sure of it. Even if stress-induced hospitalization loomed in her near future.

The upshot? She'd lost five pounds in the past two weeks. Always a silver lining.

"Alexis?"

Lexi turned, her long gown swishing against the floor and snagging on her shoe. She smiled at Pamela Hennings while casually adjusting her dress. *Darned floor-length gowns.* "Mrs. Hennings, how nice to see you."

Mrs. Hennings air-kissed and stepped back. On her petite frame she wore a fitted gown in her signature sky blue that matched her eyes. The gown draped softly at the neckline, displaying minimal cleavage. As usual, a perfect choice.

"I love what you've done in here," Mrs. Hennings said. "Amazing job."

Being a club board member, she had no doubt shown up early to make sure the unveiling of the new room would be nothing short of remarkable. "Thank you. I enjoyed it. Just a few last-minute details and we'll be ready."

"Everything is lovely. Even the damned ice sculptures Raymond couldn't live without. Waste of money if you ask me, but some battles aren't worth fighting."

So true.

A loud bang from the corner of the room assaulted Lexi's ears. *Please let that be silverware.* She shifted her gaze left and spotted the waiter who'd passed her earlier scooping utensils onto a tray. *Thank you.*

Mrs. Hennings touched Lexi's arm. "By the bye, I think I have Gerald convinced his study needs an update. All that dark wood is depressing."

Now, *that* would be a thrill. If Lexi landed the job and nailed it, the top 10 percent of Chicago's executives would know it. And competition ran hot with this social set. Before long, they'd be lined up outside her office for a crack at outdoing Pamela and Gerald Hennings.

"I think," Lexi said, "for him we could leave touches

of the dark woods. Macassar ebony would be fabulous on the floor."

"Ooh, yes. Do you have time this week? Maybe you could come by and work up some sketches?"

"Of course." Lexi whipped her phone from her purse and scrolled to her calendar. "How about early next week? Tomorrow I'm starting a new project that might eat up the rest of my week."

"I'll make sure I'm available. What's this new project? Can you share?"

Rich folks. Always wanting the inside scoop. "Actually, it's quite fascinating. Remember the murdered broker?"

"The one from Cartright? How could I not? The entire neighborhood went into a panic."

The residents of Cartright, the North Side's closest thing to a gated community without the gates, employed private security to help patrol the six city blocks that made up their self-titled haven. That extra money spent on security kept the crime rate nearly nonexistent in those six city blocks.

Except for the offing of one crooked stockbroker.

"That's the one," Lexi said. "I've been hired to stage the house. The real-estate agent suggested it to the broker's widow and she hired me."

"I heard they couldn't sell. The market is destroying her. That poor woman. He left her with a mountain of trouble. He paid top dollar and if she lowers the price again, she won't make enough to clear his debts. Add to that any retribution owed to the clients he *borrowed* funds from without their knowledge."

As expected, Pamela Hennings was up to speed on the latest gossip. Gossip that Lexi would not share. Being told this information about a client was one thing.

Sharing it? Not happening. "I'm looking forward to the project. It's an incredible house."

Being an interior designer didn't always give Lexi the chance to change someone's life. Her work allowed people to see the beauty in color and texture and shape and made their homes more than just a place to live, but she didn't often get the opportunity to alter an emotionally devastating situation. Now she had the chance. Getting this house sold would free the broker's widow from debt and give her children a comfortable life.

And Lexi wanted to see that happen.

Plus, if she got the thing sold in forty-five days, she'd make a whopping 20 percent bonus. The bonus alone would pay for an assistant and give her a life back.

Nap, here I come.

Mrs. Hennings made a tsk-tsk noise. "They never did find the murderer, did they?"

"No. Which I think is part of the problem. I may do a little of my feng shui magic in there. Clear all the negativity out. When I'm finished, that house will be beautiful and bright and homey."

"The debt, the children and now the police can't find the murderer. And it's been what, two years? No woman deserves to be left with that."

Again, Lexi remained quiet. *Don't get sucked in.* But, yes, it had been two years, and from what Lexi knew, the police were no closer to finding the man's killer. Such a tragedy. "The case has gone cold."

Sucked in. She smacked her lips together.

"You know," Mrs. Hennings said, "my husband's firm recently did some work with a pro bono cold case. I wonder if the investigator who worked on that wouldn't mind taking a look at this. I'd love to see the man's family given some relief. And, let's face it, it would certainly be good PR for the firm."

It certainly would.

Investigative help wouldn't hurt the real-estate agent's chances—or Lexi's—of getting the house sold in forty-five days. "Do you think they'd be interested?"

"Oh, I'm sure it can be arranged."

Gerald Hennings, aka the Dapper Defense Lawyer, pushed through the oversize ballroom doors, spotted the two women and unleashed a smile. Even in his sixties, he had charm to spare. Salt-and-pepper hair and the carved cheekbones of a man who'd once been devastatingly handsome—all combined with his intelligence—added up to someone who ruled a courtroom.

"Gerald," Mrs. Hennings said, "perfect timing. The board meeting will be upstairs. Believe it or not, we're the first ones here."

The Dapper DL eyed his wife with a hint of mischief, smiling in a rueful way that probably slayed jurors. "Shocking." Then he turned his charm loose on Lexi. "Alexis Vanderbilt, how are you?"

"I'm fine, Mr. Hennings. Thank you. And yourself?"

"I was quite well until fifteen seconds ago when my wife announced my timing was perfect. That means I'll either be writing you a healthy check or she's volunteered me for something. Either way, I'm sure it will be painful."

BRODEY HAYWARD BLEW out a breath as he watched his sister saunter into the Hennings & Solomon reception area. Finally she'd stopped wearing her blouses unbuttoned to her belly button. He never needed to see that much of Jenna's skin and said a silent thanks to whichever saint covered brothers in distress.

Jenna stopped in front of him and gave him a half hug so she didn't bump his sling and the wrecked arm inside of it.

"Nice shirt," he said.

She waved him off. "Don't start."

Hey, he couldn't help it if he had opinions. "Just commenting is all."

"How's the elbow?"

"It works."

"So, it's killing you."

He didn't bother answering. What good would it do? Six weeks ago he'd blown out his elbow changing a damned tire. The guys at the precinct tore that one up. *Hey, Hayward, helluva way to go out on disability. Hey, Hayward, you'd better make up a better story. Hey, Hayward, real detectives don't get hurt changing a tire.* Each day a slew of texts came in from his squad mates, and it didn't look as if the taunting would end soon because the surgery on his elbow left him with a raging infection that earned him a second surgery and another six weeks of leave. Leave that was slowly, deliberately, driving him insane. Torture was the only way to describe the abundance of nothingness that filled his days. As a homicide detective, he could tolerate a lot of things.

Boredom was not one of them.

Hell, he'd even taken to driving to his parents' house each day for cop talk with his retired detective father. A week into that, his mother had booted him and told him to get a life.

Thanks, Mom.

Jenna motioned him down the long corridor. "Thanks for coming in first thing. We're meeting in the conference room. You sure you're okay with this?"

"Yeah. I'm not getting paid. All I'm doing is giving you my opinion, right?"

"Right."

"Then I'm not violating any rules."

Jenna—a private investigator for Hennings & Solomon—had called him the night before asking if he'd assist on a cold case that somehow landed in her lap. Why not? He could kill time—no pun intended—and keep his mind sharp for his eventual return to the job. Plus, there'd be no emotional involvement with this case. Technically, it wasn't his, so he could walk away without running himself through a meat grinder over it.

"Good. I've looked over all the files, but I'm missing something."

Brodey followed Jenna while eyeing the art lining the walls. Some would call it modern. He'd call it weird with all those slashes of color, but whatever. Art meant a real picture of something. A woman in a park, a kid flying a kite, something he could look at and recognize. This hoity-toity stuff, he didn't get.

They reached the conference room, where a huge whiteboard smothered with notes and charts covered one wall. His sister had been busy. She'd also done a fine job of organizing her evidence.

She gestured to the wall. "I have it all laid out for you. Just the way Dad taught us."

He wandered to the board and glanced at Jenna's notes. Victim's name, Jonathan Williams. Scene of the crime, brownstone on the cushy North Side. Cause of death, gunshot to the head.

"Crime-scene photos?"

"No. I was hoping you or Dad could help with that."

Not if he wanted to stay under the radar he couldn't. "I'll talk to Dad. Tell me again how you got this case."

"It's kind of convoluted."

"It always is, Jenna."

"Remember how I worked on Brent's mom's murder case a few months back?"

How could a guy forget Brent, the giant deputy US marshal who had stolen his sister's heart *and* managed to convince her she didn't need to walk around half-naked for people to notice her? Brent had enough baggage to fill a 747 jet and Jenna had still fallen in love with him. If nothing else, it showed a boy could overcome a rotten childhood and grow into an honorable man.

"So this has to do with Brent?"

"No. Mrs. Hennings. She was the one who convinced my boss to take on Brent's case. She's at it again with this one."

Did someone say *convoluted*? *"Oooookay."*

"Mrs. Hennings attended a social function and ran into a decorator she knows."

Brodey gawked. A *decorator*? This should be good.

Jenna held her hand up before he could crack wise. "The decorator was hired by a real-estate agency to stage the house of the murder victim. The house has been on the market for two years and they're about to drop the price. Before they did that, the victim's estranged wife—they were separated, but not yet divorced—wanted to try redecorating it. I suppose when a house is worth close to two million hiring a decorator isn't an issue."

Brodey let out a low whistle. "I'll say. Why am I here?"

"The decorator told Mrs. Hennings about the house, and here we are."

"What do you get out of it?"

"My boss's undying gratitude for keeping him out of trouble with his wife."

Brodey laughed. One thing about Jenna, she knew how to stay on a man's good side. He pointed to the board. "Whatcha got?"

"You may remember this case. He was a stockbroker living the good life until the market crashed. For years he'd basically been running a Ponzi scheme with his clients' money. His marriage fell apart and he was drowning in debt. The FBI eventually caught up to him and he was under investigation."

"He was murdered before the Feds charged him, right? Is that the guy?"

"Yes. On the day his body was found, he didn't show up for a meeting with his biggest client. That was unusual so his firm called his wife. Apparently he hadn't updated his emergency contact at the office so her cell phone was the only number they had."

"Ah, damn. Don't tell me the ex found him."

Jenna nodded. "In the laundry room."

Poor woman. Brodey still hadn't gotten used to viewing murder victims' bodies, inhaling that nasty metallic odor of blood and trying to remain unaffected. Forget about a loved one. That? No way.

Refusing to give in to his thoughts, Brodey stood, arms folded, studying the board. "I think I remember this. Looked like a robbery gone bad, right?"

"Yes. In the two years since the murder, the widow has spent most of the insurance money settling their debts, but she's not in the clear yet. It's a mess. With the divorce pending, the finances hadn't been worked out. The house was paid off, but she can't unload it and needs the cash."

"Enter our illustrious decorator."

Jenna gave him a snarky grin. "You're so smart."

Whatever, wisenheimer. "The house is empty?"

"Yes. Why?"

He waved at the board. "No photos. I don't know what you want me to do without seeing the crime scene."

His sister should have known he'd need photos or some kind of visual. Or maybe that was just the way *his* mind worked. Needing to see how the crime occurred, run the scenarios, figure the timing and options. All of it helped him work a case.

"I wasn't sure how involved you wanted to be."

Outside of being bored out of his skull, he *didn't* want to be involved. He'd made detective only a year ago and wasn't about to aggravate his boss by poking around in another guy's case. This case wasn't even his jurisdiction. This belonged to the North Side guys, while he worked Area Central.

"Yeah, but I can't help you if I don't know what I'm dealing with. Take me to the house. I'll walk through it and then study what you have here. Then I'll tell you what I think, and I'm out."

Tops, he was looking at two days of research. Two days of not being bored. Two days of getting closer to the end of his disability leave.

All he had to do was pony up an opinion and send his little sister on her way.

Piece of cake.

Chapter Two

Lexi stood in the expansive living room of the Williamses' brownstone studying carpet that made her think of dirty snow. Such an abomination. What were they thinking putting that disgusting carpet in this house? Given the budget constraints, she'd have to keep it simple, but she could, without a doubt, restore the house to its classic elegance. Flooring she'd splurge on because the situation begged for hardwood. Everywhere else she'd do subtle but warm paint colors and effective accents with doorknobs, handrails and fixtures.

"Every inch of this carpet has to come up," she said to Nate, the contractor she'd chosen for this job. "I'm betting there's hardwood underneath."

And, if it could be salvaged, it would help her budget.

Nate made notes on his clipboard as they wandered through the house. She liked Nate. They'd worked together on several projects, and although he was closing in on fifty, he had the mind of a thirty-year-old. When he did a renovation, he saw youth and exuberance, and his attention to detail and superior craftsmanship made him her go-to guy on important projects.

She moved through the kitchen—again with the dirty snow? This time it was on the walls. She had nothing against light beige. Neutrals with the right texture and undertones—wisps of green, yellow or orange—gave a room dimension. *Depth.* This beige?

Awful.

"We'll be repainting in here."

"Just tell me what colors."

"Let's do that soft gray we did in the Wileys' kitchen. We'll add color splashes to brighten it up. It'll be fabulous with the natural light."

"Got it."

The laundry room off the kitchen came next, and she hesitated at the doorway. Did Nate know a man had been murdered in here? The real-estate agent had assured Lexi the scene had been sanitized, but what made her nervous, made that little twitch in her cheek fire, was what had seeped *beneath* the tile. When they tore up that floor, would they find dried blood?

Lexi reached in and groped along the wall for the light switch. *Where are you? Got it.* The room, roughly ten by ten, lit up, its glossy white walls glowing. A built-in closet with shelves and coat hooks and storage bins lined one wall. The opposite wall housed the washer and dryer.

How odd that the only room not needing updating was the one room she'd been directed to completely redesign.

Then again, a dead body tended to destroy positive energy. She glanced at the floor, imagined Jonathan Williams sprawled across the slate-look porcelain and closed her eyes, hoping to clear that nasty image. A dead body definitely killed creativity. *Ditch the body.* She opened her eyes again. "I'd like to know what's under the tile. It's a shame they want this redone. With all the traffic that comes through here, porcelain is perfect." She waggled her fingers. "Give me your hammer. Please."

The tile had to come up anyway and, well, she didn't want to stress about what had seeped under there. She'd find out now. Face it head-on, as she did any other issue.

Nate pulled the hammer from his tool belt and handed it over. She squatted, ready to administer that first whack, when the front door chime sounded. Someone coming in.

"You expecting someone?" Nate asked.

"No. Hello?" she hollered.

No response. A few seconds later a man appeared—and what a man he was with all that lush dark hair. He wore a sling on his right arm, flat-front khakis and a white button-down shirt under a leather jacket. The arm in the sling was tucked under the jacket, his sleeve hanging loose. His lace-up oxfords were just the right touch. Not too formal, not too casual. His dark emerald eyes zoomed in on the hammer and his jaw—really nice, strong jaw—locked. Modern-day Indiana Jones here.

He stepped forward. "What the hell do you think you're doing?"

"Excuse me?"

Grabbing the hammer with his free hand, he gave it back to Nate. "You can't do that."

"I most certainly can. Who're you?"

"Who're *you*? Wait. Don't tell me. You're the *decorator*."

Oh, and the way he said it. All sarcastic and snippy as if she was some dope. Some airhead incapable of forming a sentence. She breathed in, counted to three and stood tall. "I'm the *interior designer*. Alexis Vanderbilt. Hired by the owner of this home to do my magic. That includes tearing up this tile. Something I'd rather not do, but when a client makes a request, I generally respond."

"Brodey?" A woman called from the front of the house.

Brodey. Had Brenda Williams mentioned a Brodey? Lexi ticked names off in her mind. No Brodey.

"Back here," Brodey Whoever said. "I just met the decorator."

"Well, technically, we haven't *met*. All you've done is come in here and make unreasonable demands."

That made Brodey Whoever smile, and it wasn't just one of those run-of-the-mill, see-it-every-day smiles. *This* smile developed slowly, like a growing—and sometimes devastating—wave. *Hello, smile.*

"You're right," he said. "My apologies. I'm Brodey Hayward. I'd shake your hand, but..."

He gestured to his sling just as a stunning brunette stepped behind him. When the brunette spotted Nate and Lexi, her head jerked back. "Oh, hello."

Now might be as good a time as any for Lexi to take up meditation. "Excuse me, but who are you people?"

The brunette angled around Brodey and stuck her hand out. "I'm Jenna Hayward from Hennings & Solomon. I'm a private investigator assisting on Mr. Williams's case. I believe you're aware we'd be helping. This is my brother Brodey. He's a—"

"I'm helping," Brodey interrupted, clearly not wanting his sister to explain.

How very interesting. Mental note: do an internet search on Brodey Hayward.

The investigators. *Got it.* Lexi shook Jenna's hand. "Right. I'm sorry. Mrs. Williams hadn't mentioned you were coming by today. We should be done in the next hour or so. Feel free to ignore us. Now, if you'll step back, I need to see what's under this tile." She flopped her hand out to Nate. "Hammer, please?"

"I don't think so," Brodey said.

"Pardon?"

"An unsolved murder occurred in this room. Could be potential evidence under there." He jerked his thumb to the kitchen. "How about working around this area until I can look at it?"

Again, Lexi breathed deep. Channeled her inner calm. "Mr. Hayward—"

"Brodey is fine."

"Brodey. Great. Thank you. Now, I'm sure the Chicago Police Department has been through here." She waggled her hands. "They have all their crime-scene people and whatnot. After all, this house has been empty for two years."

Two years without an offer because potential buyers were spooked about the murder in a supposed high-security community.

Imitating her gesture, Brodey waggled his hand. "If it's been empty all that time, another hour won't hurt." He stepped aside. "If you'll excuse us, we have work to do."

The inner warrior in Lexi didn't just yell, she roared. Frustration railed, turning her vision a starker white than the glossy walls. She didn't care what kind of an investigator Brodey Hayward was. Treating them like rodents would not do. *Relax. This is not a problem until you make it one.* Lexi swung to Nate. "Would you give us a minute, please?"

He nodded. "Sure thing."

Jenna, the beautiful brunette, stepped aside, smiling at Nate as he gave her more—much more—than a brief once-over. She smiled, but averted her eyes, letting

Nate know in expert fashion he should forget about her and keep on moving. Nice move on her part. But right now, Lexi needed to strike a deal. Figure out how long they needed to be here and when she could start tearing the place apart. Compromise. That was what she'd do.

"Brodey, I'm trying to get this house redesigned and sold in forty-five days. Do you have any idea what an undertaking that is?"

He smiled at her, a slow, cocky grin that would surely lead to a sarcastic remark. "I'm sure you're being well compensated."

Bingo. Everyone liked to rip on the *decorator*. How she hated that word. As if her bachelor's in interior design coupled with her master's in business didn't qualify her for the Intelligent Club. "Okay, well, just so you know, it's a *huge* undertaking. But I'll get it done. I'm a woman with the promised land in sight and I *want* the promised land. Tell me how long you need to be in here and I'll see if I can make that happen."

"So, all you care about is selling this house? Doesn't matter that a guy bled out in here?"

Of course it mattered. That was the point. "That's not what I meant, and you know it. This place has been a financial drain on Mrs. Williams. And, simply put, I like her and she deserves a break. If we get the house sold, she can put her children's lives back together. If that's even possible."

Behind Brodey, his sister was all big blue eyes taking in not just every word, but every vowel, and Lexi didn't like an audience. She sighed, grasped the sleeve of Brodey's jacket and drew him into the kitchen away from Jenna.

Once in the far corner, Lexi let go of him and folded her arms. "We've definitely gotten off to a bad start here. I want to help you. I do. And it's not about my compensation."

Not entirely.

Brodey, quite handsome in his khaki pants and button-down shirt, studied her. Typically, she didn't go for non-corporate guys. And it had nothing to do with her being a snob. Not one bit. Her world revolved around the ultra-wealthy, and with that came an acceptance of spending ridiculous amounts of cash on items most people couldn't afford to spend ridiculous amounts of cash on. Regular Joes tended to scoff at twenty-thousand-dollar sofas. For up-and-coming executives, it was the norm.

And they didn't think her frivolous for it.

But something about Brodey Hayward's dark green eyes made her think of fresh air, lazy days and picnics by the lake. Something she hadn't allowed herself in a long—very long—time. Her business had taken priority in her life. Yes, she dated, had even thought she'd fallen in love once. At least until she found her up-and-coming executive across his desk exploring his intern's anatomy. Such a cliché.

Brodey cocked his head and grinned. "You were saying?"

She held up one finger. "Right. Yes. I was *saying* that each day this house sits on the market, Mrs. Williams is one step closer to financial ruin. I can help change that, but it won't happen overnight. I need to tear up floors and repaint. I need to dismantle part of the house."

"And destroy possible evidence."

She gritted her teeth. "Which is not my intention. Are you always this way?"

"What way?"

"Contrary."

He shrugged. "I'm a cop."

Lexi dipped her head forward. "You're a cop? I thought you were a private investigator?"

"No. Jenna is the PI. I'm a homicide detective. Chicago PD."

"Oh."

"But, I'm not on this case in an official capacity. I'm giving my sister an opinion. That's all. I'm here to look at the scene and then I'm gone."

"You could have said that. I mean, we went through this whole thing and you're here for a quick visit?"

"There might still be evidence somewhere. Particularly in that laundry room."

She'd say one thing about Brodey Hayward—the man had a spine. And the way he stood there, shoulders back, so confident and, well, *commanding*, even in a sling, she didn't think for one second he'd let her take a hammer to that tile.

This might take a while. Lexi turned back and peered at the laundry room doorway, where Jenna put her thumbs to work on her phone. "Well, maybe I could work around that room. For now. How much time do you need?"

"I'm not sure."

"Now you're just being annoying."

Brodey laughed. "Maybe. But it's partially true. Give me an hour and we'll see what's what. Is that a deal?"

"One hour?"

"Yes."

"Deal."

Chapter Three

An hour turned into two and Brodey wasn't done. He squatted in the laundry room, ran his free hand over a chipped edge of grout. Without the actual case file outlining the details of the crime scene, he couldn't form any solid opinions.

He was flying blind. In the dark. Although, if he was flying blind, it would already be dark.

And, hell no, he would not get sucked into this. He'd give an opinion. That was it. Unfortunately, giving an opinion required a basic understanding of the case.

"I need the case file," he said to Jenna.

His sister stood in the doorway, leaning against the door frame. "I don't have that."

"I still need it."

Maybe he could cash in on a couple of favors. Or his father could. Being a retired detective, the old man had more contacts in the department. And it would keep Brodey off the radar.

Alexis strode into the kitchen, her sky-high heels clicking on the tile. "How's it going?"

Even on those heels, he looked down at her. Judging by his six-foot-one size, he'd put her at around five-four. Five-five if he wanted to be generous.

Alexis Vanderbilt.

Vanderbilt.

Her name stank of money. Seriously, how many women walked around in five-inch heels, a pair of tight-fitting black pants that made a man's mind go wild and a blazer over—get this—a leather halter-top-looking thing. Who did that?

Nobody Brodey knew. That was for sure.

But he kinda liked it. From a purely male point of view.

"It's not going," he said.

"Excuse me?"

"I need to talk to your client."

Jenna stepped farther into the room to make way for Alexis. "I could have Mr. Hennings contact her."

Alexis dragged her phone from her jacket pocket. "I'll call her."

Maybe the sexy decorator wasn't so bad after all. Brodey grinned. "Thank you."

She gave him a sarcastic, bunchy-cheeks grin. "It has nothing to do with your enormous charm. It'll be faster if I call her. By the time Jenna tracks down her boss and he calls my client, you could be on your way over there. I'm all for efficiency."

That made two of them. And when efficiency looked like Alexis Vanderbilt, preferably a naked Alexis Vanderbilt because yeah, he was wondering what that looked like, he'd welcome it any day, any time without a doubt. Professionalism aside, he was still a guy who liked action. Plenty of it.

"Brenda?" Alexis said into her phone. "Hi. It's Lexi Vanderbilt…yes…I'm fine."

Lexi. He liked that. It fit with her sassy attitude. She bobbed her head while going through the pleasantries with her client and Brodey surmised that, like him, she had issues being idle. For any length of time.

"Yes," she said. "I'm at the house now. There are two investigators here from Hennings & Solomon."

Technically, Brodey wasn't from Hennings & Solomon, but he'd let that go. Not worth the hassle.

"They got here a couple of hours ago," Lexi continued, "and they have questions for you. Would you be able to speak with them?"

Three seconds passed. Then she handed Brodey the phone. He immediately looked at his sister, waggling the phone at her to make sure she didn't want to take the lead. She shook her head.

Excellent answer. Not that he would have minded her taking the call, but when the phone hit his hand he got that familiar push of adrenaline, that spark that came with a fresh case and the possibility of leads. At the age of thirty-two, he hadn't been a detective long enough to turn jaded. The older guys on the squad liked to call him Greenhorn. Being the youngest—and newest—detective to join his squad, he still viewed every case as an opportunity to make a difference while the old guys hoped to retire with their sanity. Twenty years of working homicides on the streets of Chicago would emotionally annihilate even the toughest of the tough. Brodey hoped to retire long before annihilation occurred and already had a start on a healthy nest egg.

He held the phone to his ear. "Mrs. Williams, this is Brodey Hayward. Thank you for taking my call."

There was a short pause and Brodey checked the screen to make sure the call hadn't dropped. Nope. Still there. "Hello?"

"Yes," she said. "I'm here. I needed to step into the

other room. My youngest is playing and I didn't want her to hear."

The youngest, according to Jenna, had been three when her father died. So, she'd be five now and Brodey tried to imagine that, tried to imagine growing up without his own father, without the memories of ball games and amusement parks and beach visits. All of it a dead loss. Poor kids. A squeeze in his chest ambushed him and he held his breath a second, waited for the pressure to ease before exhaling and clearing his throat.

Stay focused. Forget the kids. That was what he needed to do. "No problem. Are you able to answer some questions for me? I could drop by."

Because really, what he wanted to see was her. Study her body language and responses. Call him cynical, even as a rookie detective, but the spouse—particularly an estranged one—always got a solid look.

"Now?"

"Yes, ma'am. If it's convenient."

"I need to pick up my son from school and then take him to basketball practice at four-thirty. Lexi is coming by at four with samples. I can't imagine that will take long. I could meet with you then, also. Would that work?"

He wasn't sure how Lexi would feel about that, but in his mind, murder trumped decorating, so he'd make an executive decision. "I'll make it work, ma'am. Thank you."

Brodey disconnected and handed Lexi the phone. "We're riding shotgun on your four o'clock."

"Say again?"

"She said you were meeting with her at four and we could meet with her then, too. She's busy running kids around. We need to maximize our time."

"She only gave me thirty minutes."

"She's now splitting that thirty minutes between us. You'll need to shorten your list."

SHORTEN HER LIST? Brodey Hayward had a serious superiority complex if he thought she'd let him dictate how to do her job. First he horned in on her meeting and now he was trying to take over?

"Uh, Brodey?" Jenna said from her spot against the wall. "I can't meet with her at four. I have another meeting."

Thank you. At least now Lexi would still get her measly thirty minutes for what could evolve into a two-hour discussion.

Brodey turned to his sister, his posture stiff and unyielding. He held his uninjured arm out. "What do you want to do, then?"

"Hey," Jenna shot, "don't get snippy with me. You're the one who booked a meeting without checking my schedule. If you want to meet with her on your own, go to it. All I'm saying is I can't be there."

"I'm not getting snippy."

"Yes, you are."

And now the two of them were going to argue. Terrific. Lexi held her hand up. "Can you two fight about this later?"

"We're not fighting," Brodey said.

Patience. Lexi squeezed her eyes shut, begging her beloved and departed grandmother to channel some of her legendary patience. Just a bit. Lexi had inherited her gram's artistic ability, as evidenced by the stack of patchwork quilts she kept in her closet, but she'd be selfish now and ask for patience, too. Just a little. She breathed in and opened her eyes.

"For the record," Brodey said, "if we were fighting, there'd be yelling."

Jenna nodded. "And I might throw something."

"That's true. She gave me a black eye with a hockey puck once. And somehow, I got in trouble. Figure that one out." He stepped over to her, lifted his arm, the one in the sling, and winced. "Ow. Forgot about the bum arm."

"Ha!" Jenna said. "That's what you get for thinking you'd give me a noogie."

"I wasn't."

"Liar. I know you. And now that you're injured, you're a lame duck. Lame, I tell you."

He and Jenna both laughed. And just that fast—*boom*—the tension flew from the room.

Being the only child of an artist and a musician, both of whom enjoyed their alone time, Lexi hadn't experienced sibling rivalry. She wasn't sure she wanted to, but this? This was different. This was about love and family and history. As much as she wanted to be irritated with these two, watching them snark at each other and then laugh about it tickled something down deep.

But she wouldn't show them that. Instead, she rolled her eyes. "Okay, you're not fighting. Glad we cleared that up. What are we doing about this meeting at four?"

"I'll do it alone." Brodey turned back to Jenna. "You sure you're okay with that? It's your case."

"It's fine. Just make sure she knows you're only helping. I don't want her upset when you disappear."

"I will." He faced Lexi and pulled a pocket notepad from his jacket. "I guess it's you and me. Where am I meeting you?"

Chapter Four

Brenda Williams's two-story house butted up against the neighboring homes and looked like any other on the block. Weathered brick, a few steps leading to the small porch that barely spanned the front door, a single large window facing the street on the first floor, all of it as ordinary and indistinguishable as every other structure on the block.

Without a doubt, a long way from the pristine five-thousand-square-foot, multimillion-dollar greystone she'd shared with her husband. That house screamed vintage details on the outside but modern upgrades on the inside. To say the least, Brenda Williams had downsized. Apparently not by choice.

A wicked January wind whipped under Brodey's open jacket to the blasted sling. Leave it to him to screw up his arm in the dead of winter. Despite the doc's cautions, Brodey had been ditching the sling for an hour or two each day to give himself some freedom. That hour happened earlier when his shoulder cramped up. Now he was stuck in the sling for the remainder of the day. Unless he wanted his doctor to rail on him. *What he doesn't know won't hurt him.*

He stepped to the side of the concrete walkway

leading to the porch and waved Lexi forward. "Do the honors."

She climbed the stairs, her long coat covering her amazing rear, and on any day he'd call that one of the great tragedies of his lifetime. And that was saying something for a Chicago PD homicide detective.

Twisted perhaps, but hey, the little things kept a guy like him sane.

Lexi rapped on the door, then turned back. "Did you say something?"

Could be. While working a case he talked to himself. A lot. "Probably."

She wrinkled her nose. "I'm sorry?"

"I talk to myself. I work crime scenes by talking my way through them, trying to figure out what happened. Half the time I don't know I'm doing it." *Like now.* "What did I say?"

Because given his lack of focus on anything but her delectable rear, he could easily be accused of lascivious thoughts. Thoughts he'd never deny when it came to a woman who looked like Lexi Vanderbilt.

"You were mumbling something about tragedies."

Phew. Easy one. "Ah. I was thinking about this house versus the one we left. The whole situation is tragic."

"That it is."

The front door eased open and a petite brunette wearing jeans, boots and a long gray sweater greeted them. She wore her shoulder-length hair tucked behind her ears, and minimal eye makeup accented her brown eyes. Beautiful eyes. Big and round and probably at one time alluring to any man. All he saw now was sadness.

"Hi, Lexi."

"Hi, Brenda. We're a little early. I hope that's all right."

"It's fine. But I just got home, so I'll need a minute. Come in."

Brodey followed Lexi into the foyer, where a blast of warm air thawed him. Directly in front of them a staircase with an oak rail and cool twisted spindles led to the second floor. To his left, through a set of glossy white French doors, was the living room.

Children's voices carried from the end of the hallway. Kitchen probably. Most of these row houses were built with the same basic layout. Living room, small dining room, kitchen on the first floor. Three bedrooms upstairs. He'd lay money on it.

Lexi spun back to him. "Brodey Hayward, this is Brenda Williams."

"Hello, ma'am. I'd shake your hand, but…" He pointed to his bad arm.

"That must be horrible in this cold. Aren't you freezing?"

"It's not bad."

No sense in complaining about it. In the grand scheme, he could count his problems in three seconds or less, and that alone was enough to be thankful for.

Brenda led them down the long hallway to the back of the house where the kitchen—*called it*—conjoined with a small sitting area. Didn't call *that* one, but he was close enough. That particular room must have been a modification to the original floor plan. That was what he'd go with.

An older boy of about eleven sat with two girls at the round kitchen table. Table for four. The boy met Brodey's eyes, and nothing in his gaze conveyed anything he should see in a preteen boy's expression. No mischief, no relaxed demeanor, no lightness. All he saw there was suspicion. A shame, that.

The girl with long blond hair kept her gaze focused on her notebook. Not even a glance at him. The other girl, the one with her brown hair in a ponytail, gave him a cursory once-over and managed a whisper of a smile. Cripes, these kids were locked up tight. Of the three, he guessed the order of ages would be the boy, blonde girl and then ponytail rounding out the pack.

"Sam," Mrs. Williams said, "please take the kids upstairs to play for a few minutes while I speak with Miss Lexi and Mr. Brodey. We need to leave in half an hour, so make sure you have everything."

The boy glanced up, his big eyes drooping and, well… miserable. Suppressed. "Okay," he said. "C'mon, guys. Let's go."

The kids left, shuffling out of the room like obedient soldiers, and to Brodey, none of it seemed right. When he was a kid, all they did was yell and run around and get hollered at. They were kids. Kids did stuff like that. This? He didn't know what this was. Check that. He did know.

This was decimation.

Mrs. Williams watched them go, her gaze glued to them. "It's a sad day when the eleven-year-old becomes the man of the house."

"That it is."

She slid into the chair her son had vacated. "Please, have a seat. I thought we'd work in here so we could spread Lexi's samples out."

Would it be rude if he groaned? Probably. But he was a damned homicide detective. What did he know about decorating? He dragged a chair out for Lexi. "You first?"

With any luck, she'd disagree, which was what he really wanted, but since he'd already crashed her meeting he might as well at least try to be accommodating. Even if he hoped it went the other way.

She shook her head. “No. You go first.”

The decorator is growing on me. He gave her chair a gentle push and walked to the other side of the table next to Mrs. Williams.

“What can I help you with, Mr. Hayward?”

From across the table, Lexi handed him the legal pad he’d asked her to stow in her briefcase. Using his usual pocket notepad was impossible with one arm in the sling. Another reason he needed to deep-six the thing. He angled the pad on his lap so he could write on it without disrupting the elbow too much. “It’s Brodey. I have questions. Basic timeline stuff. I’m sure it’s in the case file, but Hennings & Solomon doesn’t have access to those files.”

“Of course. Whatever you need.”

“You separated from your husband a few months before his death. Is that right?”

“Yes. Two months. Things in the marriage had been off. For a while. We tried therapy, but he was so distracted with work, it was a wasted effort. Toward the end, I couldn’t stand his moodiness and the children were miserable. I knew we had to get out.” She waved her hands around the room. “We found this place and moved in.”

Brodey jotted notes, taking a few seconds to get his thoughts in order. Distracted husband. Any number of things could cause that. Money, job in jeopardy, gambling, drugs, an affair. “Were his work distractions typical?”

“Yes and no. He’d always been obsessed with his job, but that last year was worse. When I asked about it, he continually put me off. I knew something was wrong. I just didn't know what. After he died, I found out he was stealing from his clients, basically using their money to fuel our lifestyle."

And, hello, fraud investigation. "How?"

"Every time he signed a new client, he'd take money from their account. He'd keep part of it and then pay dividends to existing clients with the rest." She squeezed her eyes closed and shook her head. "My husband ran a Ponzi scheme." She opened her eyes, stared right into Brodey's. "We lived on stolen money."

Beside him, Lexi shifted, played with her fingers, staring down at them as if fascinated. She needed a poker face. But, in her defense, the average citizen should be uncomfortable with this conversation. Not Brodey. To him, this was nothing. "Do you know if he'd received any threats prior to his death?"

"I don't know. The police asked me, but I was such an idiot—completely in the dark. I know we had a plan. At least I did. I wanted that happily-ever-after. Only, my husband turned out to be a liar and a thief. I'm not the one who committed a crime, but I'm left with the fall-out and the paralyzing debt. I guess you could say my plan blew up."

Sure did.

She shrugged. "I'm trying to make it right. As much as I can anyway. My kids don't deserve this, and I'm not sure how much to tell them. Sam is old enough to have suspicions, but he's never asked specific questions and I don't have it in me to tell him. Does that make me a strong parent or a weak one?"

Brodey wasn't sure she really wanted an answer and it probably wasn't his place to give one, but being naive didn't make her a criminal.

Unless, of course, she murdered her husband.

"I'd say it makes you human," he said. "You'll figure out what to tell them when the time is right."

She met his gaze and her eyebrows lifted a millimeter. Classic body language for surprise. Excellent. If he'd scored points, great, but in this situation, he was damned certain his answer was the right one for different reasons. Reasons that involved three kids who'd lost their father.

Williams was a schmuck, but he was their schmuck.

Brenda glanced at the oversize clock on the wall. "I'm sorry. We'll need to leave in a few minutes and I know Lexi had some samples for me."

"Of course," Brodey said. "Is it all right if I follow up with you in a day or so?"

"Certainly. And thank you. If we can, I'd like to know what happened to him. He wasn't a great husband, but I loved him. Whatever his sins, I loved him."

AT SIX-OH-FIVE Brodey hustled through his parents' front door and got the shock of his life.

Jenna and Brent, his sister's massive US marshal of a boyfriend, had beat him there. What the hell? On any normal day, he arrived early and they were late. Tonight, he needed them to be later than he was because one thing was for sure. If dinner was ready and you weren't there, they didn't wait.

No. Sir.

"Well, hell. The one time I'm late and you two can't throw me a bone and be even later than I am?"

Brent scooped a mountain of mashed potatoes onto his plate, then passed the bowl to Brodey's youngest brother, Evan. "My fault," he said. "Problem with my witness got squared away faster than I thought."

"Anything good?" Dad asked.

"Eh, death threat. Not on my shift, though. Shift before mine. I got him to a new location and headed back before the Eisenhower went schizo."

Brodey slid into his normal chair next to his mother just as the meat loaf hit his spot. But damn, he loved his mother's meat loaf.

"I swear," Mom said, "we cannot get through a meal in this house without some form of law-enforcement talk."

"Sorry, ma'am," Brent said.

"It's certainly not *your* fault."

Across from him, Jenna snatched a roll from the basket of bread and handed it over. "How'd you do today, Brodey? With the widow?"

Pretzel rolls. Mom had gone all the way tonight. He took two rolls and sent the basket to his father. "I need the case file. She says she didn't know anything until after he bit it. I think I believe her. Not sure. Dad, can you get me any notes on this thing?"

Before his father could answer, Jenna held her hand up. "What happened to you getting in and out quick?"

"Still goes. I'll look at the file, tell you what I think, then I'm gone. I'm still holding to my two days of research."

"She got to you."

"Stop it."

"Or maybe it was the kids."

He breathed in, sent his sister a glare. "Stop. It."

She elbowed Brent. "Told you this would happen. He's cooked. He must have seen those kids and his heart melted. I know my brother."

Dad snorted. "That you do, my angel."

Whatever. "Maybe I'm curious. I'm a detective doing

my due diligence. The widow was cleared, but she's definitely angry."

Dad swallowed a mouthful of food and waved his fork. "You like the widow for this?"

"I don't see her taking this guy out, but she should get another look. See what's what."

Dad did his quasi head tilt/nod. "After dinner I'll make a couple of calls. See who can get a copy of a report or two. You never know."

Exactly what he'd walked in here needing. His father always came through. Always. "Thanks, Dad." He looked across to his sister, who eyed him like a tiger on prey. "I'm not denying I saw those kids and all I could think was they got screwed out of ball games and fishing trips with their father." He poked himself in the chest. "I got that. They didn't. Doesn't seem fair."

"It's not fair," Jenna said. "That's why I knew you couldn't walk away from this. Family is too important to you."

What the hell did that mean? "You played me?"

She grinned. "Only a little."

His little sister, the conniver. And a damned good investigator. "At least you admit it. After today, we're in this together. You, me and decorator Lexi."

Chapter Five

Dawn broke just as Lexi finished sketching the Williamses' kitchen. She stood at the center island, random sheets of discarded sketches strewn around her. Half the night she'd stewed over the color of the kitchen walls until finally, unable to visualize the finished product—something that rarely happened anymore—she'd dragged herself out of bed, grabbed her sketching tools and drove to the house.

Here she'd be able to create a sketch and add the color variations until she found the perfect combination. When all else failed, her artistic ability, her skill in re-creating a room by hand drawing it, always came through. Unfortunately for her, this time it happened at 4:00 a.m. when she'd had next to no sleep. But if sleep wouldn't come, she'd do what she always did and work.

And with the lost time due to the Hennings & Solomon people—Brodey Hayward specifically—she needed to get moving on this project or risk blowing that forty-five-day deadline.

She glanced at the window above the sink, where morning sun peeped through the wooden blinds. Streaks of burnt orange splashed across the countertop in neat little rows, their perfection beautiful and uniform. Using pencils and charcoal, she shaded the area around the window, then added a touch of tangerine. Instantly the drawing came to life. Excitement bloomed in the pit of her stomach and launched upward as her fingers flew across the sketch, then switching colors, shading, switching colors again and filling in accents. All of it combining to create a visual of a room that would be homey, bright and warm.

Finally, after an hour of discarding sketches, she'd hit on it and now, with the sun rising, she moved faster, trying to capture every nuance, every shadow, every angle, before the light changed.

The long, shrill tone of the alarm sounded—door opening—and Lexi shot upright, pencil still in hand. Someone was here. She'd locked the door, hadn't she? Sometimes she forgot that little task, but even she wouldn't be foolish enough to walk into a strange house at four in the morning and not lock the door.

The buhm-buhm of her heart kicked up, a slow-moving panic spreading through her body. Had she locked that damned door?

A second later Brodey stepped into the doorway, his head snapping back at the sight of her. He wore black track pants and a heavy sweatshirt. No jacket in this cold? The man was insane. His sling was gone and he held a manila envelope in his left hand.

Lexi blew out a hard breath and tossed her pencil on the counter. "Goodness' sake, Brodey. You scared me."

"Sorry. I didn't expect anyone to be here."

His gaze traveled over her cashmere sweater, worn jeans and loafers, then came back up, lingering on her face, making her cheeks fire. My goodness, the man had a way. Had she known she'd be seeing anyone, particularly the intriguing detective, she'd have dressed more appropriately. But at 4:00 a.m. that thought hadn't crossed her mind.

"I couldn't sleep," she said. "The colors for the kitchen were driving me mad. Where's your sling?"

"You're here by *yourself*?"

"Of course."

"Anyone ever tell you it's dangerous for a woman to be driving around a city alone in the middle of the night?"

Prior to her panic a minute ago, she hadn't even questioned it. Maybe she should have. But that was the trusting part of her. The part that didn't include the male species and wanted to see pretty things instead of danger. She wasn't a complete lunatic and understood the world to be a dangerous place, but when it came to her creative process, certain things, like possible danger, couldn't get in her way. "I live ten minutes from here."

"A lot can happen in ten minutes."

Time to get back to work. Arguing with stubborn people never accomplished much. This, she knew. She resumed drawing a roman shade on the kitchen window. Tangerine would work beautifully.

Brodey wandered to the island, where her discarded sketches smothered the top. Immediately, she snatched them up, but he set his hand on one, tilted his head one way, then the other. "You drew these?"

"Yes, but they're my discards."

"They're pretty good to be discards."

"That's nice of you to say, but trust me, they're discards."

He pointed at the almost-complete sketch on her pad. "That one looks great."

"Thank you. I was stuck on which colors to use. Sometimes when I put it on paper it helps me work it out. When the sun lit this room—" she swooped one hand "—it was spectacular. I think I need bursts of tangerine in here."

"Uh, okay."

Lexi laughed. "You didn't tell me where your sling was."

"Home. It annoys me. I've been trying to do a few hours each day without it."

"Maybe you should check with your doctor about that?"

"Nah."

As suspected. "Don't tell me you're one of those know-it-all stubborn males."

He gave her one of his cocky grins where one side of his mouth quirked, and she immediately wanted to draw it. "Don't call me stubborn."

Once again, that smile, a little devilish, a little charming and a whole lot irresistible, turned her liquid. It had been months since she'd had even a remote interest in a man. Finding your so-called soul mate sprawled across his desk with another woman tended to do that to a girl. Made her a little less inclined to trust males in general and a whole lot more inclined to demand absolute honesty. No secrets. At all.

And now, tough guy Brodey Hayward had released her smothered sexual desire. On the bright side, at least she wasn't a dead loss and still felt *something*. Even if it was only lust. "What are you doing here so early?"

He held up the envelope. "My dad got me copies of crime-scene notes. I wasn't sure if you worked on Saturdays, but figured I'd get here early and get out of your way. Who knew you'd be here at the crack of dawn?"

"You rolled out of bed this early so you didn't mess up my schedule?"

He shrugged. “You compromised with me yesterday. I owed you one.”

All that female desire inside her whipped into a frenzy and she damn near needed a cold shower. “Please tell me you’re single because I could kiss you smack on the lips.”

“I am most definitely single.”

She snorted, then waved him off. So much for her hoping to make him blush. Huh. How she loved a man participating in a little verbal swordplay. “Brodey Hayward, I think I like you.” She gestured to the laundry room. “I don’t need to be in there yet, so help yourself. I can work around you for an hour or so.”

He held up the file. “Thanks. I read the detective’s notes, but I need to see the room. Something isn’t right.”

“Why?”

“I don’t have the photos yet. Can’t picture the scene. If I set it up, it’ll make sense. Want to be my dead body?”

Ew. “Are you kidding?”

“Actually, I’m not. I brought tape, but it’ll help if I could see an actual body. All I need is for you to lie on the floor."

She glanced at the sketch desperately waiting for her attention.

He held up his hand. “It’ll take five minutes. Promise.”

“Five minutes?”

“That’s all. I need a visual.”

A visual. Considering her early-dawn sketching, she could relate. “Fine. But only because I understand about visuals.”

“And, uh, after you play the dead guy, I’ll take your place on the floor and maybe you could sketch it for me?”

A frustrated laugh burst free. This man. "What happened to five minutes?"

He grinned. "That's just for lying on the floor. The sketching is separate. Look at it this way. The faster I know what the scene looked like, the sooner I form opinions and hand this thing over to my sister. Then I'm out of here and you're free to do your thing."

Now this boy was talking. And good for him for being intellectually competent enough to figure out how to motivate her.

"If I sketch and lie on the floor, you'll let me get to work in there? Including tearing up that tile?"

"Assuming we don't discover evidence that needs to be collected, yes."

Lexi sighed.

"Hey, I know," he said. "But I won't promise that until I know what I'm dealing with. At the very least, it'd be irresponsible."

For that, she'd give him credit. Some men would lie simply to get their way. Like her cheating ex. *Not going there.* Thinking about him only aggravated her.

She tore her sketch off the pad, set it aside and grabbed her chalk and a pencil. "I have a house to dismantle. Let's get to work."

BRODEY WATCHED OVER Lexi's shoulder as she finished her sketch, and the faint smell of her shampoo, something minty, he thought, like spearmint but not really, worked its way into his system and—look out now—relaxed him. He liked it.

Maybe too much.

She angled back, looking up with those greenish-brown eyes, and something in his brain snapped. Something being the male side of him that hadn't seen any action from a female in a couple of months. Sure there were women he could call, but with the damned arm in a sling, everything—sex included—was way too much work. And it scared the hell out of him because how many men didn't want sex? None that he knew.

Whatever. Mind snap.

"Are you paying attention?" Lexi asked.

More than you know...

"Yeah. I'm thinking." He brought one arm around her so he could point at the sketch and brushed her shoulder along the way. Immediately, he regretted it. Even that meaningless interaction brought his body—very male body—into the red zone. Only thing to do here would be to put his growing erection out of his mind. Maybe today would be the one time that trick worked, but not likely. Considering it had never worked before. "The body needs to be closer to the door."

"Well, Brodey, this is not to scale. You have to allow for some wiggle room."

"I know. It still needs to be closer."

She flipped her pencil to the eraser side and scrubbed it across the paper. A minute later, she'd busted off the outline of the body in the exact place he wanted. "Perfect," he said. "You know, you're really good at this. You should work for the PD."

"No. Thank you, though. What was he wearing that night?"

"Black pants."

She filled in some shading to reflect the slacks the victim wore. "That's better."

"Why not?"

She glanced over her shoulder at him, her perfect lips slightly puckered, her eyes zeroed in as if she'd read his every X-rated thought. Only the hum from the furnace below could be heard in the quiet house, and Brodey's pulse knocked harder. All he had to do was bend down a few inches and those perfect lush lips would be his.

"Wow," he said.

She stepped away, putting distance between them. "It wouldn't work for me. I generally don't sketch people. I do furniture. Furniture is easy. Even if I had the level of skill it requires, I'm not sure I could handle that type of work. I have a friend whose mom was a sketch artist, and it's emotionally draining. What you do—a homicide detective—is a gift. Whether you realize it or not, the average citizen couldn't face the horrors you see every day. I'm one of those people. I like serenity and homey environments. It's what I'm good at."

Good observation since he was already counting down the years—fourteen and a half—until he reached retirement. Not that he didn't have a passion for the job, a passion for righting a wrong, a passion for justice. That justice was what got him out of bed every morning, but studying mangled bodies for thirty years, like some of the guys on the job, didn't seem like a banner way to stay sane. Twenty years would be plenty. Like his dad.

After shading the body, Lexi scratched her cheek, leaving a dark smudge trailing down her face, and he itched to run his fingers across the spot, over the delicate curve of her jaw, and wipe it away. Just to put his hands on her.

She held the sketch out. "What do you think?"

I'd like to tell you what I think. Back to business here. He took the sketch. "It's good. Let's put it on the floor so I can look at."

"Okay. You're all set, then? You don't need me?"

And, hell, if she wasn't the cutest damn thing with that smudge on her cheek. "I'm all set. Except…" Against his better judgment—considering his partial erection might go full-blown—he gently ran the pad of his thumb where the remnants of her sketching marred her creamy skin. Major mistake because now his body went haywire, every nerve snapping.

More.

That was what he wanted. More of her skin under his hands.

She didn't flinch, but locked her gaze on his, and the message was clear. She knew what he wanted. And she wasn't running.

"Smudge?"

"Yep."

"I do that all the time. You'd think I'd learn by now. Thanks for telling me. I'd have been walking around like that."

"No problem," he said. "If touching a beautiful woman's face is the worst thing I do today, I'd say I hit the jackpot."

For a good twenty seconds, she stood in silence, clearly deciding whether to take the bait. *Come on, Lexi, let's play.* But, nope. She broke eye contact and headed to the kitchen, where she'd left her sketches. She turned back to him, casually leaning against the island, but her folded arms and fingers digging into the sleeves of her sweater screamed confusion.

"You know," she said, "you're quite charming when you want to be. I like that about you."

Charming. He'd take it. There were a lot of things he liked about her, too—her confidence, her skill, her ability to shut down an uncomfortable conversation without making a big deal about it. The woman had a way about her.

"I do try."

She nodded toward the laundry room. “How long until you’re finished?”

“I don’t know yet. I’ll read the ME’s report and the crime-scene notes again. The angle of the body is weird.” He shifted in the doorway. “Unless he was standing like this, facing the wall. Or maybe the killer moved the body. I don’t know. I need to study it.”

“So, what you’re telling me is I won’t be able to get into this room again today?”

Here we go again. All that light banter from twenty seconds ago? Gone. Vanished. Vamoosed. “Lexi, I don’t know. Trust me, I’d love to tell you it’ll be today. It might be. I need to study these notes more. Sorry if it’s ripping into your forty-five days, but the guy is dead.”

“Oh, don’t even go there. Do *not* try to make me feel like I’m being unreasonable for wanting to get this project done. I have been nothing but cooperative. I want to give this woman peace as much as anyone. Part of that will come from unloading this house before she’s forced into bankruptcy. So, spare me your lecture.” She scooped up her pad and shoved the loose sketches into it. “Call me when you’re through holding up my work.”

Great. Mad. How the hell had this become his fault? He moved to the island, where she’d already left skid marks on her way to the front door, and held his arms wide. For once, the elbow didn’t holler, but the gesture was useless since she couldn’t see him. Well, fine. His whole point of getting here early was to work alone. All she did was distract him. Between her looks and the way she smelled, his body responded to her. Couple that with her insistence that he rush through his investigation, and Alexis Vanderbilt snatched his energy. Just sucked him dry.

The front door slammed and he shook his head,

pondering whether or not to chase after her. *Let her go.* He'd get more done without her.

Even if she smelled good.

LEXI TROMPED DOWN the Williamses' walkway, sketch pad in hand, coat flapping and the wrath of a winter day descending on anyone fool enough to venture outside. Mere breathing brought the wind—frigid, bone-shattering wind—burning down her throat.

"I need to be a snowbird," she muttered.

"Morning."

She halted a second before slamming into a man walking his Yorkie. "Oh, I'm sorry. I wasn't paying attention."

"I see that."

The man wore a long wool coat over a suit. His close-cropped, graying hair gave him an edge of sophistication that topped off the whole "I have money" vibe. By the looks of him and the adorable dog, he was a neighbor. He held a mug in one hand, and the aroma of hazelnut reminded Lexi she hadn't put anything into her system in nearly twelve hours. On the way home, she'd stop at the coffee shop and load up on caffeine and sugar. A chocolate croissant might do the trick. The man eyed her, then glanced back at the house. "Are you the real-estate agent?"

On the surface, the question seemed harmless, but Lexi had worked with enough gossipmongers to know her words could storm this community. "No. Not the real-estate agent."

"Ah. The designer, then." Mug in hand, he gestured down the block. "Phillips. We live two doors down. We heard Brenda hired someone to stage the house. It's a rotten situation."

The gossip trail. How she despised it. "It is indeed."

But wait. He was a neighbor, presumably questioned by the police. Perhaps he saw or heard something that could help Brodey's investigation along.

And get her back on schedule.

"Mr. Phillips, were you home the night Mr. Williams died?"

The tiny Yorkie nudged the leash and Phillips took three steps closer to the tree. "I was. The police talked to my wife and me."

"Did you see anyone?"

"No. Didn't hear anything, either. With the increased security, we're usually aware of problems, but it was quiet that night. Perplexing."

Perplexing. Interesting word choice. And the cadence, so direct, pegged him as a lawyer or maybe an executive with a lot of authority.

"I see. Thank you."

"Of course. When your work is complete, do you mind if my wife and I take a look? She wants to redo the kitchen."

Lexi smiled. Crabby and dressed like a coed but somehow she might gain a client from this. "That would be up to Mrs. Williams, but I'd be happy to ask her if you'd like."

"I'd appreciate that. Thanks."

Once tucked into her car, Lexi jotted Mr. Phillips's address and a note to herself to ask Brenda about him. Maybe she'd even be nice and share her conversation with Brodey. *Maybe.* For now, she needed food and a shower before her appointment in Lincoln Park. A quasi-appointment. Her college roommate, thanks to her new job as an on-air anchor for a local cable news station, had finally taken the plunge and bought a house. If it could be called a house. Sucked from the clutches of foreclosure, the three-story monstrosity needed loads of work.

Candace had recruited Lexi to help.

Ninety minutes later, Lexi knocked on Candace's front door, where the knocker promptly fell off in her hand.

The door swung open. "Hi, doll." Candace spotted the detached door knocker and plucked it from Lexi's hand. "I forgot to warn you about that. I have a new one. I just don't know how to install it."

"I can do it. Do you have a drill?"

"You're kidding, right?"

Lexi laughed. "About me installing it or the drill?"

"The drill. You can do anything. Everyone knows that."

"I love when you suck up."

She swept her arm in a huge semicircle. "Welcome to paradise."

Lexi glanced around the foyer, where fist-size holes marred the walls. Someone had done a number on the place. "If this is paradise, I want out."

"I know. The old owners ripped every light fixture out. They even took the copper pipes. The place is an eyesore, but your very own Nate said it's structurally sound. Don't worry. All the mold has been removed."

Mold. Dear God. "Excellent."

"Thank you for squeezing me in."

"It's fine. I'm working on another project that suddenly has a delay. A delay by way of a hunky detective."

Being a single and clock-ticking female, Candace pursed her lips. "Hunky detectives?"

"One hunky detective. Not plural."

Candace rolled her bottom lip in disappointment and

Lexi raised her hands. "Don't stress. The way things are going, he and I don't exactly agree, so he might be yours by default."

"What happened?"

"It's the Williams project. Brodey is on short-term disability leave—elbow surgery—from the police department. He's a homicide detective."

"Ew."

"Exactly. Anyway, his sister, Jenna, is a private investigator Mrs. Williams hired to look into her husband's murder. Jenna recruited him to help. The man is bored and has thrown himself into this. At this moment, he's coming up with all the reasons I can't demolish the laundry room."

Candace folded her arms and leaned against a railing that looked barely stable enough to support its own weight, never mind hers. "And that's killing your forty-five-day timeline."

"Yes. Thank you! The hunky detective doesn't seem to understand that I need to get this house sold. I want that bonus. The bonus gets me my assistant, a solid seven hours of sleep every night and time to clean out my garage so I can make it an office. I'm ready to collapse."

"I can't believe you haven't cleaned that mess out. Hire someone to do it, for God's sake."

"No. There's a ton of stuff in there from the old owner. There might be lost treasures I can use."

Candace waved her to the kitchen. "I have a fresh pot on. You need to decompress for a few minutes before we get into this."

That sounded heavenly. Decompression. With a pal. Realization hit that she'd spent the past months virtually ignoring her friends. "I'm sorry."

"For what?"

"For being a bad friend."

"Honey, you're helping me with this pit and not charging me. You're a great friend."

"That's not what I mean. I've been busy and haven't made time for the people I care about. That's not right."

"So, you help sell the Williams place and hire an assistant. You're fixing it. Don't be hard on yourself because you're ambitious. Now, back to more important matters. What's up with this hunk? Has he discovered anything on the murder?"

They entered the kitchen, and the aroma of freshly brewed coffee taunted Lexi's senses. The surprisingly clean maple cabinets glowed, but the peeling linoleum counters had to go. The cabinets could probably stay, but not the linoleum. Candace filled two mugs and set one down next to the cream and sugar so Lexi could destroy a perfect cup of black coffee. Her friends knew her so well.

"He just started. Heck, I'm even helping him. On the way out of the house this morning I met one of the neighbors walking his dog. He stopped me. Being nosy, I guess. Anyway, I asked him if he saw anything the night of the murder."

"And?"

She dumped two teaspoons of sugar into her coffee, poured milk in and took a gulp. "Nada. Of course, I don't know what I expected. I just want this thing wrapped up so I can get to work."

Candace set her cup on the island and leaned on her elbows. "I've been following this story for work. It's amazing that in such a tight community they have no leads. Someone had to have seen something."

"You'd think. Maybe talking to the police scares them."

"What does your hunky detective think?"

"He thinks there's evidence in the laundry room and won't let me rip it up. We had a blowout about it this morning."

Candace tilted her head and narrowed her eyes in that determined-reporter way of hers. "You like this guy."

Unfortunately, yes. "You haven't seen him. There's plenty to like. Setting aside that whole pushy-alpha-male thing. Honestly, he's a little annoying."

"And, yet, you like him. Which, correct me if I'm wrong, is a big step for you. You haven't been interested in a man since—"

Lexi's arms shot up. "Whoa, girlfriend. I know exactly how long it's been. We don't need to discuss it."

Candace waved her off. "What are you doing about this blowout with the detective? Come on, Lex, I can tell you like this guy. It sounds like he's just trying to do his job—even if it is a volunteer assignment." She leaned in, gave Lexi a wicked smile. "How often do hunky detectives come into your life?"

Not very often. In fact, there hadn't been an onslaught of hunky men in her life at all lately. But the stubborn part of her didn't want to give in and admit she was wrong.

Coffee sloshed in her stomach, letting her know that maybe the chocolate croissant hadn't settled so well. Since she'd walked out on Brodey, she'd felt like this. Nauseated. Uneasy. Off-kilter. And she hadn't felt any of those things in a very long time.

She shook her head. "I'm not wrong for wanting to do my job."

"I didn't say you were. I think this is one of those situations where you're both right and simply can't agree.

All I'm saying is maybe you need to look at it from his side, too."

Candace came around the island, dropped her arm over Lexi's shoulder and gave her a squeeze. "Honey, I think it's time you let yourself like men again. And this detective sounds like he might be a great start."

Chapter Six

By 3:00 p.m. Brodey made his second trip of the day to the Williams place. Bit by bit, more information streamed in from detectives who owed his old man favors. The latest was a detailed evidence list, including descriptions of a slug that had been pulled from the wall in the laundry room. Apparently, one shot missed its target. By now the wall would have been repaired, but he might as well satisfy his curiosity and have a look.

Crime-scene photos would help. They'd show the blood spatter that often told the story of who was standing where when life got ugly.

Biting wind ripped into him and he dipped his head lower, huddling into his jacket. Even with his hatred of winter coats, he wouldn't tackle a three-block walk in these temps without one. So far today he'd managed four hours without the sling. After his blowout with Lexi that morning, he'd gone home and sacked out for two hours. Between sleep and the afternoon back in the sling, he was good to go again.

At the corner of the Williamses' block, he hooked a right and—hello—found his sister and one extremely hot blonde, otherwise known as Lexi, standing in front of a tree. What were they up to?

Lexi handed a piece of paper to Jenna, who held it up to the tree, ramming it home with a staple gun. "Ladies," he called, "what the hell are you doing?"

After one last staple, they both turned. "Hey," Jenna said. "What are you doing here?"

Still approaching, he held up his suddenly ever-present file. "Dad got me an evidence list. Getting a look at the wall where they pulled a slug."

"Nice," she said. "We're almost done here and I'll join you."

He stopped in front of the tree and studied the paper. The one with a photo of their vic and a phone number to call with information. Silently, he read off the number, but didn't recognize it.

"Brodey," his sister said, "don't even try it. It's a good idea. And it certainly can't hurt."

"You want to crack a cold case by posting flyers?"

"Yes," Lexi said. "She does."

Great. Now they were a team. "Lexi," he said, "how'd you get involved in this?"

"I was heading to the house to try out samples and spotted Jenna posting the flyers." She grinned. "I'm the helper."

Jenna waved the staple gun at him. "And before you start in, I called Brenda this morning and talked to her about it. Her only concern was the kids seeing them, but since she doesn't bring the kids here anymore she said it's okay."

"And, frankly," Lexi said, "this case is stalled. Someone around here must have seen something. Maybe the police accidentally missed something. Who knows?"

Jenna went back to stapling. "You know people talk to me, Brodey. It'll be fine."

No doubt they would talk to her. One thing about his

baby sister, men saw her coming and a different part of their anatomy took over. She knew that. Had used it to her advantage many times, but this? This was insanity. "Jenna, why don't you just write your number on a prison wall? Do you have any idea how dangerous this is?"

That got him an eye roll. "Relax, it's a disposable phone. When we're done, I'll get rid of it. You know, it wouldn't kill you to give me a little credit. Between my law-enforcement father and my US marshal boyfriend, I've learned a few things."

"Yeah, well, how about putting what you've learned to use and not setting yourself up to be attacked?"

Jenna poked the staple gun at him. "You're out of line."

Brodey flapped his hand at her. "Quit waving that thing around. I don't like you two wandering around handing out flyers. Anyway, in this neighborhood there's probably an ordinance prohibiting posting them."

"Got that covered, big brother. Brenda called the security people and cleared it."

"Right," Lexi snarked. "One of their residents is dead. They want this solved as much as we do. Leave her alone. She knows what she's doing."

Like his sister, Lexi had an answer for everything. His chances of coming out on top here were zip. A smart man knew when to run like hell, and his mama never accused him of being stupid. He'd try a different approach. The scary-as-hell one. "You two do whatever you want, but I'd appreciate it if you tried not to get killed." He angled around them and headed for the house. "I'll be inside. Call me if you need me."

A few seconds later, a solo Jenna ran up beside him, her heels clicking against the concrete. For probably the thousandth time, he marveled over how women ran in high-heeled boots. "Where's Lexi?"

"Back at her car grabbing carpet samples."

He stopped, shifted sideways and spotted her popping the trunk on a vehicle not half a block away.

"Brodey, she'll be fine. I have never met such a worrywart."

"It never hurts to be cautious."

"Cautious is one thing, paranoid is another."

"I'm not paranoid." *Yeah, I am.* "Maybe I'm a little paranoid, but with what I do for a living, I think that's normal."

Jenna snorted. "You're funny."

Leaving him on the sidewalk, she dug out the key to the Williams home and unlocked the front door. Once again, he glanced back, making sure Lexi was squared away. Still down the block, she shut her trunk, checked that it had latched and hefted a bag over her shoulder.

That bag looked pretty damned heavy. He started back down the block toward her. "Sit tight. I'll help you."

"I've got it!"

Of course. He liked independent women, but could they accept some help every now and again? "You sure?"

"Yes." Four cars down she hesitated, stared down at the few samples in her hands. "Shoot. I forgot one in the car. I'll meet you inside."

He stood for a minute, waiting. Another few minutes wouldn't matter. Once she got back, they'd go inside together.

"Brodey," Jenna said from the open doorway, "she's fine. Can we do this? Mr. Hennings called me an hour ago with a lead on a case that's *not* pro bono, and I need to get moving on it."

For another few seconds, he watched Lexi head back

to her car, pop the trunk and mess around in there. "You good?" he hollered.

She slammed the trunk and held up her hand.

"I'm going in," Jenna said. "Hurry up and stop obsessing."

Ha. He'd never stop obsessing and she knew it. Doing what he did for a living, he saw things that horrified and shocked him on a daily basis. Maintaining his sanity meant locking up the bad guys and reducing the depravity.

Lexi might be only half a block away, but a lot could happen in that half a block. Rape, abduction, wayward bullet. None of it would surprise him. He glanced up and down the block, saw nothing suspicious, then checked on Lexi finally making her way back to him. In another minute she'd be walking into the house. "Go inside!" she hollered. "I'm fine. I'll be right there."

"Okay," he muttered. She had only a short distance to go. Plus, his sister was in a rush and he didn't want to hear her griping. He turned and marched up the steps. "Let's see if we can find this bullet hole."

LEXI HEFTED THE bag of carpet samples and hoped she hadn't forgotten anything else because it was darned cold and her toes were blocks of ice. She beelined for the warmth of the house, determined to get this thing staged and sold by her deadline. Even if it destroyed her.

With Brodey traipsing around, it just might. The man created all sorts of interruptions. Before he stormed into her life, she hadn't missed the simplicity of a physical connection. Now, between fantasizing about him touching her, his overprotectiveness and his pain-in-the-butt way of trying to control every situation, she wasn't sure if she wanted to kill him or curl into a warm bed with him. Although, either choice might work. For a fling. At this point, she had no interest in falling in love, but maybe Candace was right and she needed to lighten up. At least a little. If only she could unsee that pig of an ex stretched across his desk with the twenty-year-old.

Crash. Her shoulder connected with something—definitely bigger—and she wobbled sideways. A man caught her arm and kept her from going over, but her bag of samples tumbled to the ground.

How many times would she plow into strange men before she started paying attention? She bolted upright, attempting to balance herself as he gripped her arm. "I'm so sorry," she said.

"No. My fault. I wasn't paying attention. Are you hurt?"

His voice had a rawness to it, a weird rasp that made her think of singed vocal cords. "Oh, heavens no. I'm fine."

She shrugged free of his too-tight grasp and adjusted her coat sleeves. He wore a down jacket with a ripped left sleeve and a pair of ratty, faded jeans. The shredded hems must have been dragged across pavement as he walked. She raised her head and took in his face—day-old beard, crisp blue eyes and untrimmed hair that dipped well below his earlobes. His cheekbones cut severely into a slope to his pointy chin, giving him a cartoonish appearance. Distinctive features.

His nearness kicked up a dull throb in her stomach. The man looked harmless, if a bit messy, but that stomach thing didn't happen often and she'd take it as a message to move on.

She stepped back, reached for her sample bag and glanced at the Williams home, where Brodey no longer stood on the sidewalk. "Thank you for keeping me upright."

"I've seen you in the neighborhood," the man said.

She backed up another step. *Come on, Brodey. Come back outside.*

When she didn't respond, he gestured with his chin to the opposite end of the block. "I live down the street. You're doing work on the Williams place, right?"

The pinnacle of rudeness would be to simply walk away. That she wouldn't do. With her luck, he'd be an eccentric billionaire hunting for a designer and he'd tell every one of his rich friends she blew him off.

No blowing him off.

Faking it the whole way, she smiled and pointed to the home. "I'm the interior designer. I'm sorry, though, I have people waiting for me."

Letting him know she wasn't alone couldn't hurt.

"Sure," he said. "But if I'm in the market for a designer, how should I get hold of you?"

Normally, she'd whip out a business card, but not this time. Compared with meeting the man with the Yorkie earlier, something about this encounter didn't fit. She patted her pockets, then riffled through her purse. Her hand landed on her wallet, where she stored her business cards in the outer pocket, but she continued feeling around. "Well, shoot. I forgot my cards, but I'll be working here for a while. If you'd like, leave a note on the door with your phone number and I'll call you."

He tilted his head one way, then the other, those icy blue eyes on her in a way that wasn't quite sexual, but definitely wasn't innocent, either. Lexi's stomach twisted. An absolute clue to leave if there ever was one. "Thank you again."

She moved away, pulling out her phone as she marched down the street. She glanced behind her. The man continued to watch her and she picked up her pace, tripping on a raised edge of sidewalk. Ouch! Toe throbbing, she stumbled three steps and almost, once again, hit the ground. Finally, she caught her balance and checked behind her. The man turned in the opposite direction, the direction he said he lived, and hunched into the wind, walking away from her.

Probably a false alarm. Or Brodey's paranoia rubbing off. She grunted and hurried up the steps. Inside the house, she set her bag on the dirty-snow carpet, squatted and began organizing her samples. She'd love to do a hand-scraped walnut in here. If the budget didn't allow it, she'd find something cheaper, but the room begged for hardwood.

Something poked her shoulder and she flinched, the movement knocking her off balance enough that she toppled to her rear. After the first two saves so far today, this time she couldn't keep herself upright. *So elegant.*

"Whoa," Brodey said. "You okay? What took you so long?"

He held out both hands and she grasped them, letting him boost her up. In contrast to those of the man outside, Brodey's hands were warm and gentle and steady and nothing, not one thing, about them made her uneasy. Exactly how it should be. "I'm…fine."

"You don't sound fine."

"Brodey, I'm fine. I need to go through these samples, though."

"Who was that guy you were talking to?"

He'd seen. *Grrr...*

"I don't know. He said he was a neighbor. I wasn't paying attention and bumped into him."

He tilted his head, studied her face. "Did he say something?"

"No. Why?"

"Because before you talked to him you were smarting off and relaxed. Now you're like a trip wire. What did he say?"

Damned perceptive man. Considering his job, she shouldn't have expected any different.

Squatting again, she lined up two more samples. "It wasn't what he said so much."

"What, then?"

She shrugged. "He knew I was working here. And his clothes. This morning I met a neighbor and—" she circled one hand "—well, he *fit*. Everything about him screamed affluence. The guy just now, not so much. Ripped jacket, torn jeans and an overall messy look. But I could be wrong."

He grabbed her notepad and pen from her briefcase and shoved them at her. "Lex, do not minimize what you are feeling here. That's your first mistake. Sketch him. Before you lose the details."

"Brodey—"

"I want the details before you forget. Please. Humor me?"

And oh, that look in his eyes. Soft and pleading and so darned beautiful. Totally playing her and she didn't care. So what? A little caution couldn't hurt. She dug in her purse for a pencil. "I can't use a pen."

Dropping to a sitting position on the carpet, she roughed out a sketch—the sloping cheekbones, the pointy chin and messy hair. "His eyes were a weird blue. Icy blue."

"What's up?" Jenna asked from the hallway leading to the kitchen.

"Shh."

Brodey remained quiet as the minutes ticked by and Lexi finished her sketch. Not perfect, but enough.

"That's good. Did he say where he lives?"

"Not specifically. He said down the street. South end of the block."

He nodded, tore her sketch from the pad and hopped to his feet. "Wait here. I'll be right back. Do *not* leave this house. Either of you."

Jenna sighed. "Where are you going?"

He held up the sketch. "To find this guy."

BRODEY KNOCKED ON the neighbor's door, automatically reaching for his badge that wasn't there. Another thing he hated about disability leave. Giving up his gun and creds. He'd work around it. The door opened and a middle-aged woman, smartly dressed in gray slacks, a black turtleneck and a string of pearls, greeted him. If this was her hanging-around-the-house look, she needed to ease up.

"Can I help you?"

"Yes, ma'am. I'm Detective Brodey Hayward. I'm looking into the Williams murder."

Probably, he shouldn't have added *detective* to his name. Call it habit, call it adrenaline zapping his good sense, call it whatever, but he was in it now and if this woman was smart, she'd question his lack of badge, shut the door and call the PD to verify what he'd told her. If it got back to his boss, he'd be cooked. But he couldn't worry about it now after every alarm bell—the skittering pulse, the tickle at the base of his neck, the sweating on a blistering-cold day—went off.

"I see," she said. "I hope they find who did it soon. It's completely unnerving."

"Yes, ma'am." He held out the sketch. "Would you mind taking a look at this? Do you recognize this man?"

Shivering against the wind, she glanced down and puckered her lips. Her eyebrows squeezed in and the no-clue look told him everything he needed to know. She didn't know him. And with a neighborhood this tight, she'd know him.

"I can't say that I recognize him. Should I? Is he a suspect?"

"We're looking into several persons of interest."

She shrugged and handed him the sketch back. "I'm sorry. I don't recognize him."

"Thank you. I appreciate it."

Next house. In fact, he'd hit every house on the block until he found this guy. Even as a beat cop he never minded canvassing a neighborhood. He got off on the lure of detective work, questioning people, searching for that one element that might crack a case.

Canvassing on a fall or summer day was a whole lot more fun, but he'd keep moving and get body heat going. He zipped his jacket, stepped off the porch and trekked on.

Three houses later, no one recognized the sketch. Which meant Lexi had either heard something incorrectly and the guy didn't live on this block or he'd lied. Lexi, with her attention to detail, wouldn't screw something like this up, and with the guy's banged-up appearance, it was more likely he'd lied. Brodey pulled out his phone and scrolled to the number Lexi had given him before their meeting with Brenda the day before.

"Hi," she said. "Where are you?"

"Canvassing. Are you sure he said he lived on this block?"

"Yes."

"You're sure?"

"Positive. He said he lived 'down the street.' Those were his exact words. I took that to mean he lived on the block. Why?"

Okay, he'd buy that. "Because I've been to three houses and no one recognizes him. In a neighborhood like this, they know who lives on their street. I'll finish the rest of the block and if I can't find him, I'm going to security. They'll know everyone here. If they don't, then we need to figure out who this is and why he knew you were working at the Williams place."

Brodey ended the call and continued the search. After hitting every house on the block and visiting the security guard cruising the block in an SUV, he returned to the house, where Jenna tore out of the kitchen mumbling various swearwords. Apparently, he'd made her late. But, hell, they were investigating a damned murder.

She stuffed her arms into her coat and buttoned it with the speed of a sprinter. "Did you find him?"

"No."

Behind her, heels clicked against tile in rapid-fire tap-tap-taps and Lexi swung into the hallway. He watched and let his gaze move up her legs, and immediately his temperature shot up. "Security doesn't know him and no one I talked to does, either. I'd say your assessment that he doesn't fit here is correct."

For a few seconds, she stood stock-still, only her throat moving as she swallowed once, then a second time. "Could he have been a thief casing the neighborhood?"

Brodey clucked his tongue. "Maybe. But if he is, he's

one of the worst ever. Why would he approach you and ask if you were working here? No thief does that."

"Okay, kids," Jenna said. "I'm sorry, but I have a lead to chase before my boss gets mad at me. Can you guys handle this?"

"You're dumping this on us? After you brought me in on it?"

Jenna tugged his sleeve and planted a kiss on his cheek. "I know. I'm sorry. This other case is a real heater, though, and you know that means Gerald Hennings will be all over the news. Likely with information I've provided, so I'd better get to it and be right about whatever I tell him. I'll call you later. Let me know what I can do to help you find this guy."

"I will. Be careful. And, as much as the pair of you call me paranoid, he probably saw two beautiful women posting flyers and was either up to no good or hitting on you. If he was hitting on you, his technique stinks."

Lexi sighed. Too bad. She'd have to endure it because that guy tripped every one of Brodey's alerts.

Jenna waved both arms at him. "I'm leaving before I throw something at you. Call me later."

She flew out the door, once again leaving Brodey alone with Lexi. Not altogether a horrible situation.

"So," Lexi said, "you think he intended to attack one of us?"

"That or he saw you two posting flyers and wanted to pump you for information about the case. Maybe he knows something. *Maybe* he's involved."

"Oh no."

Using her right hand, she grabbed the index finger of her left hand, fiddling with it, pressing on her nail, then slowly moving to the next one. Nervous habit. When she spotted him watching, she dropped her hands, let her arms hang at her sides.

"Precisely why I reamed you two for the flyer stunt. Not only does the guy know you're working here, sometimes alone—which has to stop—but now he has my sister's phone number. Lexi, seriously, you cannot be here alone. This guy might have nothing to do with the Williams murder, but whoever he is, he shouldn't have been here. At the very least, he's probably a thief. And we don't want to consider what he could be at his worst."

She propped her hands on her hips and blew out a breath. At any second, she would, as his sister always did, accuse him of being paranoid or cynical. Cynical until a murderer carved someone to pieces and shoved the body into a trunk. "Whatever argument you're planning, forget it. It won't work. I'm dug in."

"I wasn't going to argue."

Sure she wasn't. He snorted.

She touched his arm, gently pressing her fingers against his sleeve. Not hard, but enough to get his attention. "I was thinking about how having someone here with me constantly would slow me down."

"Better slow than dead."

"I get it, Brodey. Relax."

He'd never relax. That was half his problem. Always watching—and waiting—for what could go wrong. Where Lexi saw possibilities, he saw problems. How many times had he gotten in trouble with dates because he couldn't sit through a meal at a restaurant without constantly scanning the place? The force of that, the final acceptance that his quest to keep people safe had turned into a daily pummeling over the world being a hideous place, set him back a step, literally pushing him.

"What's wrong?"

He scrubbed his good hand over his face, focused on his pounding heart and breathed in. "I don't know. No. That's a lie. I do know. My job is important. I know I make a difference. But I see the world from a cop's eyes. Every damned day, I'm scanning, searching for what might go wrong. Maybe I am paranoid."

She moved closer, close enough that the energy around him charged his already amped system and…yeah…he needed to blow off some steam.

In ways he couldn't admit right now.

"You're overly cautious," she said. "It's not a bad thing. With what you do for a living, I'd think it's natural. But give yourself a break." She tugged on his shirt, inched just a little closer and grinned. "Enjoy the fact that you were right. I don't intend on letting that happen a lot."

Holy hell, all that crackling energy fried him. Parts of the southern end of his body went rock hard.

"Lex?"

Her gaze moved to his lips. "Yes?"

"You might want to step back."

"I might." She looked up, locked eyes with him. "Or I might not."

That right there would be what his boss called a go sign. A giant one. He dipped his head lower, testing, anticipating her reaction. In response, she tilted hers up.

Definite go sign.

Before he analyzed this thing too much, he slid his good arm around her waist, sunk his fingers into the warm, soft flesh under her blouse. He needed this woman. No doubt. He kissed her. At first gently—and man oh man—better than he thought. She boosted up on her toes, slipped her arms around his neck, pressing her body dead against him, and if he didn't have this damned sling on, he'd have mauled her. Just clamped his fingers over her rear, dragged her even closer and feasted on her.

Possibly reading his mind, she drove her tongue into his mouth and—*thank you, thank you*—it appeared a man didn't have to die to get the express train to heaven. He pulled her hips closer, let her feel just how much his body craved her, and a small noise came from her throat.

Yeah, honey, that's what you do to me.

He was coming apart and losing his damned mind.

Here he was, standing in the foyer of a murder victim's house, sucking the hell out of the decorator. What was wrong with him? The fact that he hadn't gotten any action in a few months might be a clue.

Another noise filled the empty house. A clanging and it wasn't his imagination.

Lexi pulled back. "Just shoot me."

"Not on your life. What's that banging?"

"The alarm on my phone."

"Why?"

"I have an appointment in fifteen minutes."

Come on. Really? Now?

She backed up two more steps, as if to level the death blow, the seriously hurtful this-is-not-happening one.

"I'm sorry," she said. "Can we pick this up later?"

No. *Forget the appointment.* Not fair. Not for one second. But then he imagined the roles being reversed, imagined he'd caught a case. Her job might not include getting called to a crime scene, but she had responsibilities. To her clients and to herself.

Which blew things for him.

He ran the back of his hand along her cheek, the heat there not escaping him. "Sure," he said. "Later is good."

Hopefully, really good.

AFTER HER APPOINTMENT, a consultation with a doctor and his wife who lived in a Gold Coast high-rise, Lexi treated herself to Thai. Strong buying signals from the doctor's wife deserved a celebration. If she landed that job, there were plenty of other residents in the building who undoubtedly, based on their location, could afford to hire her.

Yes, sirree, that assistant was in striking range. After dinner, she'd go through the growing stack of résumés she'd received and see if there were more possible candidates. So far, she'd interviewed a handful of applicants and had narrowed it to two possibilities. One being an art and design student from Columbia College. Attending school so close to Lexi's client base was a plus and hopefully, she could grow into being more than an assistant and take on clients of her own. Expansion. What a lovely word.

Continuing on her good-luck streak, Lexi claimed a parking spot half a block from her Bucktown cottage. The short distance allowed for her to make only one trip from the car. If Brodey were here he'd tell her that with her hands full like that, she'd be a prime target for a mugger. Even with Bucktown considered a moderately safe neighborhood, she glanced around, checking behind her and across the street. Total darkness.

Still, she'd made the effort.

Originally named because Polish immigrants raised male goats—aka bucks—there, Bucktown had grown into a community loaded with musicians and artists. While house hunting, she was intrigued by the artsy vibe. She loved this neighborhood. Then she'd seen her cottage and vowed to have it. She'd bought the barely nine-hundred-square-foot cottage from a man whose father had passed. The son lived out West and, given the state of disrepair, couldn't tend to the cottage. Lexi offered to take it off his hands—well below the asking price—and rehab it herself. With the spectacular price came a detached garage.

Full of junk.

At the time, it seemed like a steal. Now, almost two years later, she'd yet to find time to gut the garage and turn it into her dream office.

Turning onto her walkway, she spotted the silhouette of someone—most definitely male—on her bench by the front door, and Brodey's lecturing voice filled her head. She loosened her fingers on her briefcase and bag of Thai, preparing to fling them and run. A cold, relentless pounding in her chest stole her breath, kept it trapped in the center of her throat, paralyzing her.

Run.

"It's me," the man said. "Brodey."

Air came in a whoosh, flooding her oxygen-deprived brain, and she dropped her briefcase and dinner, bent at the waist and breathed. Heaven help her if she passed out.

"Brodey! You scared the daylights out of me."

He stood, barely a shadow moving in the blackness. Typically, the Jansens had their porch lit, but not tonight. Of all nights for the light to be off. That little fact was sure to earn her another lecture from King Paranoid.

"Sorry. But you know—"

She picked up the briefcase. "Save it. I know I should have a light on. Usually the Jansens—my neighbors—have the block lit up."

"At the very least, a motion detector."

In the darkness, she grinned. The man took obsessive to new heights. But after this little episode, that motion detector might not be a bad idea.

She set her briefcase and dinner on the small bench Brodey had just risen from. "It's freezing out here. Let me dig out my key and we'll go inside. And don't nag me about how I should have had the key out. My hands were full and I forgot to grab it before I loaded up. I know I shouldn't have had my hands full."

Good grief. Everything she did around this man was wrong.

"It's for your own good."

She sighed. "This protective streak is nice, but let's not get carried away. How'd you know where I live?"

He gave her a droll look.

"Never mind. Dumb question to ask a homicide detective. Why are you here anyway?"

"I…uh…wanted to apologize if I was hard on you earlier."

She unlocked the door, pushed it open and flipped on the light before waving him in. *Apologize.* Maybe she wasn't *always* wrong. "When?"

He grabbed her dinner and briefcase off the bench and carried it in for her. "When you told me about the neighbor who's not a neighbor."

Ah. That. "Jenna told you to call, didn't she?"

"No."

"I don't believe you."

He smiled, lightning fast and devastating. "Well, maybe she suggested it."

"What did she really say?"

"She said I can be an overbearing ape and I probably owed you an apology."

"Wow."

"Yeah. We don't pull punches in my family."

"I guess not." She took the bag and waved him in. "Dump that briefcase by the door and have a seat."

Doing as he was told, he set the briefcase down, shoved his hands into his pockets and studied the room. He did that a lot. Studied things. Must be the investigator in him.

"This place is something," he said. "Guessing you decorated it."

There was that word again. "Yes, I *designed* it."

Every inch of the mint walls, the camel-colored leather chairs and pops of red on the side tables had been her creation. She breathed in. "This place launched my career."

Brodey dropped onto the sofa and rested his head back. "Oh, man. I want this."

You should, big fella. Considering the twenty-thousand-dollar price tag, he'd better keep his feet off it.

"Amazing, isn't it? I didn't even have to pay for it."

"No kidding?"

"Nope. That was part of my career launch, too. I entered a contest in *Home Design Magazine*. I was in the Small Spaces category and took second place. I still think I got robbed, but whatever. Anyway, I talked Fireside Furniture into sponsoring me and they gave me the sofa. When I made it to the finals, they got great PR out of it and I had a flood of clients from all over the city calling me. It was the proverbial win-win. I love this place."

He cocked his head and met her gaze. "That's… impressive."

"Not bad for a *decorator*, huh?"

He held up his hands. "All right, I've got it. No more decorator cracks."

The kitchen was an extension of the living room, and she placed the Thai on the breakfast bar separating the two areas. "Thank you. The only thing left to do is the garage. As soon as I have time, I'll get it cleaned out and make an office out of it."

Then I'll have a life again.

"There's a garage?"

"Out back by the alley. Have you eaten? I bought Thai."

"Not yet. You go ahead, though."

"I have plenty. I always buy extra for leftovers." She batted her eyes. "I'll share."

He pushed out of the sofa and moved to the kitchen, his eyes still on her and, well, unnerving her way more than she'd like. "Why are you staring at me?"

He jerked one shoulder. "I like to look at you." He pointed to the bag. "Can I help?"

That was his answer? He liked to look at her? As if it was no big deal. As if they hadn't shared that amazing kiss earlier, and now the staring, and what? She wasn't supposed to jump him? Really? A man who looked liked this said something like that and she was supposed to act as if her hormones weren't in a twist. She spun away from him, breaking the eye contact. Otherwise, she'd break something else when she pounced on him. "Park yourself and I'll get dishes. I'm having water to drink. Would you like something else?"

"Water is good. Thanks."

She grabbed two water bottles from the fridge and a couple of glasses from the drying rack and poured. "How did you do with the wall?"

"The slug? Not good. There's nothing there. They replaced the drywall. I don't know what I was looking for anyway."

"Is there something bugging you?"

"I don't know. Probably."

She laughed. Men. Such funny creatures. "From what

I know of the case, the original detectives thought it was an intruder who shot Mr. Williams."

"Yeah. They thought someone came in through the laundry room window because it was open."

"You don't believe that?"

"I don't *not* believe it. By the way, the sketch you did for me is almost dead-on to the actual crime scene. You have amazing instincts. Which I guess is why you're so good at what you do. The only thing we missed was the broken glass on the floor. That was in the detective's notes, but you didn't know that."

She smiled. "Instincts help, but I think for me it's more about details. I see things people don't usually see."

He eyed her, his gaze fixed and steady. Thinking. About what, who knew?

"What is it?"

"The glass on the floor."

"What about it? Food is ready."

She set the bowls down, but Brodey sat back in the high-backed stool and stared at the ceiling. "Crime-scene photos showed the open window the intruder came through. The outside entry door was to the left of the window." He gestured sideways with his hands. "The broken glass on the floor."

"Okay. But shouldn't Jenna be doing this? I mean, it is her case."

"Technically, yeah. But she called before and she's knee-deep in this other case. The *paying* client. I told her I'd run with this. See what I came up with."

"You're a good brother."

That got a smile out of him. All crooked and wicked and enough to chip away at the wall of stone around her heart. "I do try. Even when she drives me insane."

Lexi scooted around the counter and took the stool

next to him. He could theorize all he wanted, but she hadn't eaten since breakfast and needed fuel.

"The broken glass," he said.

"What about it?"

He reached for one of the glasses. "Stand up."

There goes dinner. Before moving, she shoved a forkful of noodles into her mouth—how incredibly elegant—and took the glass.

"You be the victim," he said. "I'll be the bad guy. Don't put that glass down yet." He walked to the front door. "Let's say this is the entry and I come in." He stepped outside. A few seconds later, the door flew open and—*whap*—hit the wall with a bang, the noise loud enough to make Lexi flinch and send water sloshing.

"Brodey!" She slammed the glass down and shook water off her hand. "A little warning would have helped."

How many times would he scare the daylights out of her tonight?

"Exactly," he said.

Grabbing napkins from the counter, she patted her hand dry. "So you meant to give me a bath in my living room?"

"Where's the glass?"

She rolled her eyes and wiped the floor. What a mess. "I put it down."

"That's the point. You put the glass down. If Williams heard an intruder in the laundry room, late at night, would he be carrying a glass?"

"I don't know. Maybe he was in the kitchen getting water."

"Maybe. But he'd still put the glass down. Think about it. Can't fight a guy with a glass in your hand. Unless he was gonna throw it at him. But let's say he didn't do that and he carried it into the laundry room with him."

"Okay."

"What does that indicate?"

Something told her this would take a while. Might as well eat while he did his detective thing. She sat again, grabbed her dish and swung back to him. "I have no idea."

"How about he didn't feel threatened? He wasn't surprised by whoever was in there."

"What if he knew the person?"

Brodey rolled one hand. "Right. And according to autopsy reports, the time of death was after eleven o'clock. Who would be coming to his house in the middle of the night? Think about it."

A lover. Or… Oh no.

"Come on, Lex, I know you have it."

"Okay, but if a family member—"

"Maybe his wife."

Narrowing her eyes, she waved a finger at him. "If a *family* member did it, why didn't the original detectives figure that out?"

Brodey returned to his seat, gave her a light, backhanded pat on her leg and dug into his food. Second time he'd done that patting thing. Affectionate man. Something to get used to, considering she'd never been overly affectionate in the physical sense. Growing up, her parents didn't subscribe to touchy-feely and the pig of a cheating ex-fiancé—God, she refused to even say his name—wasn't much into PDA. Unless, of course, it included his intern.

And his desk.

But now, sitting with Brodey, suddenly touchy-feely seemed…nice.

"We detectives have theories," he said. "Particularly the old-timers. Once they get a scent of something, tunnel vision can set in. They latch on to something and lose their open mind. I could see them liking the intruder-through-the-open-window theory and—*bam*—case solved."

Remind her never to get murdered, because the idea of detectives incorrectly latching on to a theory terrified her. Appetite destroyed, she tossed her fork into the bowl. "That's not comforting."

He shrugged. "It happens. No one does it to hurt a case. Usually."

This just kept getting better and better. She swiveled sideways and faced him. "What now?"

"That's easy. Now I pay a visit to his wife and any close friends and see who came over to the house a lot." He stood, dropped a quick kiss on her lips. "I gotta go. Thanks for dinner."

"You barely touched it."

"I know. Duty calls. I'll call you if I find anything."

Chapter Seven

First thing Monday morning, Lexi stood in the hallway outside the Williamses' master bedroom watching Nate rip up more dirty-snow carpet. This family loved beige. And not even a decent one at that.

But thankfully, dirty-beige carpeting was the only thing she needed to think about this morning. Considering she'd tossed and turned two nights straight obsessing over Brodey's kiss. She couldn't even blame her restlessness on lust. Hardly so. Calling his kiss chaste would be an overstatement. The ease with which that kiss was delivered, that casual peck, as if he kissed her that way every night and should be used to it, had thrown her. Thrown her enough that she'd kept her distance from him the day before by using work as an excuse. Not a complete lie, but not altogether the truth, either.

In her mind, men were lying pigs who couldn't be trusted. Getting used to anything with a man, falling into a casual routine and becoming too complacent, had been the catalyst to her not sensing her beloved spent his lunches *interfacing* with his intern.

"Whoops," Nate said.

Whoops what? Lexi hated *whoops*. Just as she stepped into the room, he pressed two fingers along the baseboard.

"Loose baseboard. I'll replace it."

With that, he tore off six inches of board and tossed it into the pile of scraps behind him.

"Now, that's weird," Lexi said. "Why would only that small piece be loose?"

She squatted to check the rest of the board between the closet and the bathroom. "Someone definitely cut this in half."

If the baseboard needed replacing, why not replace the entire section? Why just this small piece? In a house of this quality, she'd expect the owner to spring for the thirty dollars it would take to replace the entire board. Unless there was a reason. Couple that with someone being murdered in this house and her curiosity exploded. At this point, everything was questionable. She glanced at her winter-white slacks—*need to risk it*—and dropped to her stomach, laying her cheek against the carpet. If she soiled her clothes, she'd go home and change. Simple as that.

She peeked into the opening. Too dark. "Got a flashlight?"

Nate shined his penlight into the opening. Behind the cobwebs she spotted a small notebook similar to the little black books men used to joke about. Mystery solved. "There's something in there."

"What?"

"Looks like an address book."

She reached in, hesitated for half a second because somewhere down deep a flicker of warning hit her system. *Don't touch it.* But with the amount of cobwebs, who knew how long it had been there. It was probably nothing.

But she'd never know unless she looked. Shoving her hand farther in, she felt the gauzy slide of cobwebs close over her hand—ugh. Definitely washing up after this. She dragged the book from its hiding spot and brushed dust from the faux-leather cover.

Only a few pages had handwritten entries. Not someone's everyday calendar. Unless the person led a seriously boring life.

But, *hmm*. She flipped to December, the month of the murder, and thumbed through each page. On December 16, someone—presumably Jonathan Williams—wrote *CLEANER* across the top of the page along with a Chicago phone number. Had she just found evidence? If so, her fingerprints were now all over it.

Again the flutter of panic—the warning she'd ignored thirty seconds ago—came to life. What she probably—no *probably* about it—should have done was call Brodey.

Too late for that.

"What is it?" Nate asked.

"An appointment book."

"Hidden in the wall?" He peeked over her shoulder. "I bet he didn't want his wife to see it. Why else would it be in the wall?"

"They were separated?"

"Not for that long. He probably stuck it in there when they were still together."

Typical male response. "You don't think his wife would have noticed that loose baseboard?"

Nate shrugged. "You didn't and you look for stuff like that. Plus, how do we know there wasn't a chair or dresser in front of it?"

Men just had an answer for everything. She held up the open book. "What do you think *CLEANER* means? Housekeeper?"

"No idea. Call the number. I guarantee a woman will answer. I'm telling you, he hid this from his wife."

Okay, smart guy. For no other reason than to prove him wrong, she'd do it. She dug her cell phone from her jacket pocket. "Read me the number. I'll bet you lunch you're wrong."

Nate read off the number and Lexi punched the speaker button. Three rings later someone picked up. "Yeah?"

Male voice.

Distinctive. Rough. As if nails had scraped his vocal cords, leaving them damaged and raw.

I know that voice.

"Who is this?" the man said.

Definitely him. The creep who'd talked to her on the sidewalk yesterday. The creep she'd drawn the sketch of. The creep Brodey couldn't find.

Panic, swift and obliterating, shot straight up Lexi's neck. *Hang up, hang up, hang up.* She poked at the screen, pounding it with her index finger until the call disconnected.

"A man," Nate said. "Now, *that's* interesting. I guess I owe you lunch."

She glanced up at Nate and sickness poured into her stomach, flip-flopping her morning coffee.

Nate cocked his head. Studied her for a second. "You okay? You look a little sick."

I am sick. And she needed to get out of this house before The Creep realized it was her calling his number and came looking for her. "I'm fine. I…uh…need to make calls. Will you take care of this?"

"Sure. I'll let you know when we're wrapped up here."

She charged down the steps, teetering on her high heels and praying she didn't land on her face along the way. At the moment, she wasn't sure what would be worse, the face-plant or Brodey's reaction to her calling that number. Either way, it would be trouble.

At the base of the stairs she stopped, stared at the front door and gasped. What if that creep was out there somewhere? Watching her. Brodey had warned he could be keeping an eye on the place. And she'd be walking to her car alone.

Can't do it.

She'd have to stay here—inside with Nate upstairs. At least she wasn't alone.

And when Brodey heard this news, he'd go crazy. The lecture he'd level on her would turn her to stone. Her own fault for not thinking through her actions, for not calling him when she saw that notebook and for not listening to her instincts when they told her not to touch it.

The latch on the front door thunked. *Him.* But how would he know it was she who had called?

"Nate!"

She backed up a step, her heel catching on the stair as she kept her gaze glued to the bottom of the front door when it opened. A man's boot hit the threshold. She brought her gaze up along the jean-clad leg to the worn leather jacket—she knew that jacket—and the arm tucked in a sling under it. Her breath caught.

"Brodey?"

He popped his head in. "Hi."

Gushing blood pounded at her temples and she pressed her palms against her head. *I'm not alone.* Slowly, focusing on Brodey, she inhaled, held it a second and exhaled until the pounding eased.

"What's up?" Nate called from the landing above.

She tilted her head up. "Nothing. False alarm."

"You are wigging out on me today."

Nate disappeared and she turned back to Brodey. "I'm so happy to see you right now."

He grinned. "I like that greeting. But you look like hell."

She rushed down the stairs, careful not to move too fast and tumble down. A trip to the hospital would be the capper. "You're going to be really upset with me and I'm sorry. I didn't… Ugh."

"Oh, boy. What'd you do?"

She held the appointment book in her hand, contemplated the lecture she'd get and shoved it at him.

Slowly, he shifted his gaze to her hand. "What's this?"

"I found it. Upstairs. Behind a piece of loose baseboard. I touched it. I'm sorry."

He puckered, but didn't take the book. Instead, he slid his free hand into the messenger bag slung over his shoulder and retrieved a pair of latex gloves.

The silence alone, from a man who took great pride in offering his opinions, made her stomach bunch. "Um, there's an entry on December 16."

"Uh-huh."

"With a phone number."

He snapped on the gloves and went back to the book, his fingers riffling through the pages.

Time to fess up. Now or never. "I called the number."

"Somehow," he said, his voice low and calm, "I knew you'd say that."

She hated that voice. From him she wanted sarcasm and lecturing—maybe even yelling. This calm? It terrified her. "I'm sorry. I got carried away. Nate and I were debating why the book was hidden and he figured Jonathan hid it from his wife because it had phone numbers for women in it."

"Okay, well, that's a leap."

"I thought so, too, and to prove my point, dialed the number. I didn't think it through."

"An issue, for sure. After the guy from yesterday, anything you find in this house could be evidence."

The lecturing voice again. Good. That she could deal with. "I got caught up."

And if he thought he was irritated by her handling the book, wait'll he heard who answered.

He held up a gloved hand. "Let's argue about it later. You said you called the number."

"Yes."

"Did a woman answer?"

"No. A man. And I recognized the voice."

SHE RECOGNIZED THE VOICE. Of all the things Brodey thought she might say, that one knocked him sideways. Whether or not she actually recognized the voice or simply thought she recognized the voice had yet to be determined. At times, witnesses were sure what they saw.

Until they weren't.

Lexi stood on the first step, eye to eye with him, her greenish-brown eyes lacking that Lexi spunk. Nope. What he saw here was stone-cold fear. "You're fine. Okay? Don't panic. Who do you think it was?"

"I don't think—I know. It was that creepy guy from yesterday."

Damn it. Forget not panicking because it was definitely time to panic. He wouldn't tell her that, though. He nudged her to a sitting position on the step and settled in next to her. "How do you know?"

"He has a distinctive voice. Really raw."

"Uh-huh."

"It was him. I know it was."

Brodey opened the book to December 16, where

CLEANER had been written across the top. That could mean anything. Cleaning lady, a trip to the dry cleaner's, carpet cleaning.

An assassin.

But if it was the number for an assassin and Williams wanted to hire him—for what reason Brodey didn't know—why would Williams be the one dead? He needed to find this guy. Fast.

Not only did Brodey want the 411 on him, the guy now had Lexi's cell number. Brodey ran his fingers over his forehead and squeezed. With that cell number, any halfway resourceful person, particularly a criminal with connections, could easily find her address. Assuming she'd used her phone and not Nate's to place that call.

He let out a long breath. "You called on your cell? Or Nate's?"

"Mine."

"Of course you did."

"Sorry."

"You're making me crazy." He waved the address book. "You've got to stop and think about what you're doing."

"I know."

Did she? He wasn't sure because she continued to do things that put her in danger. "It doesn't feel like you do. You need to consider ramifications. Now, whoever this guy is, if he tried, he'd figure out where you live."

She closed her eyes. "I shouldn't have called that number. Part of me knew it and then I blew that part off. I'm so sorry."

"Hey, it's done now. We'll deal with it. Anything in this house could be evidence, though. Treat it as such. Don't touch it until you call me. Got it?"

She nodded. "Got it."

"Good. I'll run the phone number and see what we find."

"Shouldn't we give this information to the police?"

"Maybe. We don't know what we have yet. The guy on the other end of that call could have been a poker buddy of our victim."

She considered that, then held her hands out. "You're not even supposed to be working on this case. How will you trace that number?"

Carefully, that was how. He boosted off the step, grabbed his messenger bag with his laptop and headed for the kitchen. "The wonders of the internet. Amazing what a credit card and online research will get you. Even if I strike out on who the number belongs to, I should be able to find out if it's a cell number. Guessing it is. If so, let's hope it's a carrier I have a contact with."

"And then?"

"And then I get a name, run him through the system and see if our boy here has a rap sheet. If he's ever been accused of murder, I'd say we have a suspect."

In the kitchen, Brodey swung his messenger bag onto the island, used his free hand to drag his laptop out and booted it up. The night before, with his sister AWOL on another case and Brodey unable to sleep after striking out on contacting Mrs. Williams regarding her husband's friends, he'd downloaded and scanned all the reports he'd obtained on this case. If his hard copies suddenly went missing, he now had a backup. Yeah, he always planned for the worst. Couldn't help it.

Thanks to the hot spot from his phone, he clicked on the icon for his browser. Lexi stood next to him, not too close, but close enough that she once again upset the energy around him. From the second he'd put eyes on her, she upset his energy.

Massively.

"Read me the number again."

He entered the digits into the search engine, and a list of options for obtaining information on phone numbers popped up. He didn't recognize any of the sites. Probably bogus. The truly easy thing to do right here would be to call one of his buddies at the station and have him run the number, but seeing as he shouldn't be working on this, he couldn't risk anyone in a jackpot with him.

But his sister had gotten him into this in the first place. Blame it on her.

"Time-out." He grabbed his phone off the counter and scrolled to Jenna's number. "My sister can get us this info."

Voice mail. He left her the phone number, told her what he needed, hung up and sent her a text. "Give her ten minutes. Guaranteed."

"That fast?"

"She's an animal."

Six minutes later, his phone rang. Jenna. "Called it." He hit the button. "Hey. Whatcha got?"

As usual, she dispatched with the pleasantries. "That number belongs to one Ed Long. He lives on the West Side. Who is he?"

"Don't know. Lexi found an appointment book at Williamses' house. The number was written in on December 16."

"Stop it! That's the day he died."

"Sure is. I'm gonna run this guy down, see if he's in the system."

"I thought you were worried about getting caught."

"I am. Which is why I'm gonna ask Dad to call in a

favor or two. Text me Long's address. While Dad's doing his thing, Lexi and I will pay a visit and see if he's the guy in her sketch."

As much as she wanted an assistant, Lexi didn't think chasing down a suspected murderer would get it for her. After all, what good would the assistant do her if she were dead? "We're going to his *house*?"

"Bet your life," Brodey said. "I want to know if he's the guy you saw. And if the address is valid." He went back to his laptop. "Let's do an internet search on him."

"You're *searching for* him?"

"Is there a reason you keep repeating my statements?"

"Uh, shock maybe?"

He smiled and pounded the enter key. "You're cute."

"Better cute than dead, handsome. Know what I mean?"

"This is not a big deal. You'll stay in the car." He turned away from the computer, leaned one hip against the island and ran the roughened tips of his fingers along her jawline, a slow, tender sensation that made the girl who never much liked PDA want to reconsider her stance.

"Brodey—"

"I wouldn't let anything happen to you. You know that, don't you?"

Yes. She did. Absolutely. He had that protective—not to mention stubborn—streak in him. Her own modern-day Hercules this one. Plus, if he didn't stop stroking her jaw… "I know that. It makes me nervous is all. Like he knows me, but I don't know him."

"Which is why we're tracking him." He dropped his hand, waggled his eyebrows and went back to his laptop.

"I always do a search on a suspect. You find all kinds of stuff on the internet. Even if it isn't rocket science, why not use every tool available? Whoa. Lots of Ed Longs. Okay. Let's narrow this down." He went back to the search bar and typed in *Ed Long Chicago Illinois* with his free hand. "Let's see what we get now."

"We could go back to you rubbing my face. That was a whole lot nicer than the thought of coming face-to-face with Creep Man."

Again, he turned to her, slid one hand under her blazer, and suddenly she wanted that sling gone, wanted both of his hands on her as he patted her hip. "I promise you, this'll be okay. For all we know, he probably teaches kindergarten. Don't worry about it until there's something to worry about."

She stepped a tiny bit closer, her body craving the heat and security that came with Brodey Hayward. Security. Something she'd never wanted or needed from a man. At this moment the independent career girl in her, the one who'd marched out of her loser fiancé's office swearing she'd never allow herself to need a man, the one who constantly reminded her that men were dishonest, rutting animals, didn't have much to say. Now the career girl went on hiatus? She squeezed her eyes closed. *So confused.*

"Lex?"

Subject change. That was what they needed right now. And given this whole mess, she had plenty of choices. "I could have destroyed evidence with that damned book."

"We'll work around it. The book might not even be his. Maybe it's the previous owner's."

She gave him a baleful look. "Nice try."

Then something changed. His smile—that flashing quickness that, when unleashed, could do a girl in—

faded, and she locked her jaw. Where he focused so intently, his gaze on hers, his mouth soft, no tightness, could do a girl in worse than the smile. *I'm a mess.* She forced herself to stay quiet. With that look, who knew what went on in his brain? In addition to being rutting animals, men had tendencies to say the exact opposite of what a woman wanted to hear. Maybe he'd lecture her again on being more careful and less spontaneous. Maybe he wouldn't. All she knew was, on a purely phys ical level, she wanted whatever Brodey Hayward had in mind.

He inched closer, tipped his head sideways. "I hope you're aware that I'm extremely attracted to you."

"In fact, I wasn't. Not really. Well, it sort of felt like—"

"Stop."

"What?"

"Talking. We don't need to analyze. A yes-or-no answer would have done it."

"Yes. Now I'm aware. For sure."

He grinned. "Close enough. Thank you."

"You're welcome."

"So, Lexi."

"So, Brodey."

"If I were to ask you to dinner, what would you say?"

"I'd say maybe. After I get this project done."

"Ouch."

She stepped closer, the collar of his jacket barely two inches from her lips and the clean scent of his soap lingering on him. She inhaled, loving the closeness. If she looked up, she'd be useless. All her nights spent alone paraded in her brain, reminding her how much of a life she didn't have. "Please don't be offended. My life is a nightmare. I'm interviewing assistants, which I won't be able to afford unless I get this house sold. I'm averaging four hours of sleep a night because I'm building a business and refuse to turn clients away. A couple of more big clients and I'm on my way. That's what I want. To be self-sufficient. To have a safety net."

No rutting animals.

"I get that. But you have to eat."

"I eat while I'm working."

He went back to his laptop. "No problem. Tonight, I'll call you and find out where you're working and I'll bring you dinner. I like that idea."

"Brodey—"

"Yes or no, Lex. That's all this requires."

Rutting animal or not, that hand on her hip, combined with the chin stroking from a minute ago, did amazing things to her libido.

"Come on, Lexi, live a little." He leaned in, got right next to her ear. "I promise I'll behave."

That tore it. If they didn't get back to the task at hand, she might do something really stupid and tilt her head sideways, just that small hint that—yes indeed—she would like to revisit kissing him. Yes indeed. "Yes. To…uh…dinner."

Smooth, Lexi.

He backed away. "Excellent. Now, let's get back to work before I convince you to let me do things to you on this island."

And just that fast, he went back to his laptop. "Yow. Check. It. Out. Hello, Ed Long."

"You found him. Is there a photo?"

He clicked on a link that led to a local newspaper article from six years ago. "No photo. If this is our Ed Long, he was arrested on robbery charges." He whistled. "Did three years."

"Oh my."

"Don't panic. He's not a murderer. Nothing here indicates violence. Money motivates him, not blood."

Brodey dug a notepad from his messenger bag and, sling and all, jotted notes. "Let's check the address we have. If it's still good and you recognize him, I'll go see his lawyer. The lawyer won't tell me much, but it never hurts."

Did she need an assistant enough to risk visiting a potential murderer?

No.

Not unless she intended to have a life again. If she went and was able to identify Ed Long, it might move this investigation along. In turn, allowing her to complete the renovations and get the house sold.

Debating the assistant-versus-no-assistant dilemma, she tilted her head one way, then the other. Sleep. That was what she needed. Sleep would happen when she hired an assistant.

"Okay," she said.

"Good. Let's do this." He squeezed her arm. "This'll be good. Trust me. I'll take care of it."

She believed that. She believed when Brodey Hayward put his mind to something, nothing stopped him. Why she felt that way, she wasn't quite sure, but the way he entered a room, that commanding presence, his ability to take charge of a situation—no matter what that situation—she imagined he always took care of it.

"I know you will. I don't know how I know, but I do. And I like that. It doesn't happen very often."

"You? Really? I thought you were the trusting one."

"I am, but this is different. I trust people until I *don't* trust them. I'm not stupid and I won't hand a stranger my life's savings. But you? I might give you my life's savings, and I'm not sure I'm happy about it."

In truth, it terrified her.

Above her, something crashed. She glanced up at the ceiling, hoping a sink didn't plummet through.

"It's fine!" Nate yelled from upstairs.

"Thank you!" She went back to Brodey. "All I need is him putting a hole in the ceiling."

"Can I ask you something?"

"Sure."

"How old are you?"

"Twenty-nine."

He pulled a face. "Wow."

"What does 'wow' mean?"

After closing the laptop, he slid it into his messenger bag. "It's good. You're twenty-nine and managing contractors who've probably been in this business longer than that, if I'm any good at guessing Nate's age. You're fearless. I don't know many women like you. Well, except my sister, but she's twisted that way. She grew up surrounded by cops. That fearlessness scares the hell out of me, but it's impressive. You're impressive. Makes me wonder why you don't like trusting me. Then again, maybe that's why you haven't let a man snag you."

Rutting animals. "I almost did. We were engaged. Last year."

"Uh-oh."

"One day I walked past a jewelry store downtown and saw a wedding ring that I loved. I was a few blocks from my so-called beloved's office so I swung by there to tell him about my find." She smiled a little, let that feeling of happiness come back to her. Occasionally, she liked to think about those moments, the joy and excitement as she raced the three blocks to tell him the great news. "I was so happy. Probably the happiest I'd ever been."

"What'd he say?"

The memory, as it always did, faded to that second when her world broke apart. "I never got a chance to tell him. I opened the door to his office and found him on top of his twenty-year-old intern."

"Come on! That is *harsh*."

"And incredibly cliché, don't you think?"

"Oh, man."

"I was so humiliated." She flapped her arms. "I mean, how does that happen? He's the one doing a college student—never mind his employee—on his desk, and I'm humiliated?"

Again, he reached up, ran one of his big, giant and incredibly warm hands down the side of her head. "What'd you do?"

She shrugged. "I walked out. Left the door open so everyone could see, and I walked out. I was dead inside, but I wasn't about to let his entire office see me come apart. I saved that for when I got home. Had a good cry over it, then I got mad. I packed every bit of his stuff up and told him the box would be on my doorstep at eight o'clock. Then I deleted him from my contacts."

Brodey laughed. "Damn, I love that. He deserved it."

"You know it. I'll forgive, but I don't forget. He hurt me and no matter how many times he begged, I didn't see myself ever having faith in him again."

"And you think that was unfair? After he betrayed you?"

She shrugged. "I don't know."

"He was messing around. You think he wouldn't have done that after the wedding? No. He got what he deserved. If he was smart, he learned from it. Seriously, I don't get guys like that. I mean, I'm no saint, I like sex as much as the next guy, but if you're gonna make that commitment, stick to it. If you wanna be off-leash, then don't make the commitment. What's the big deal?"

"Exactly!"

"Guys are stupid sometimes. What can I say?"

Lexi laughed. "You know, Brodey Hayward, you might be part woman underneath all this machismo."

His face distorted, his lips peeling back into a look that indicated she might be next in line for the electric chair. "What does that mean?"

"You're just…reasonable. You get it. A lot of men don't. And I also think I may wind up sleeping with you."

"Uh, pardon me," Nate said.

She spun back, heat not just creeping but sizzling up her neck. Nate was not blind, nor was he stupid, but being a good man, seeing Lexi's embarrassment, he turned his attention to the molding above the doorway, running his hand over it. "We may need to replace this."

Sure they did.

The inferno raging in Lexi's cheeks cooled. She just might get out of this disaster. "Everything okay?"

Behind her, Brodey brushed his hand along her lower back, distracting her, reminding her that for the past year, the majority of her life had been spent alone, without simple touches of affection. Even for a woman who disliked PDA, she craved the basic comfort of human touch.

"Yeah," Nate said. "I…uh…need to run and check on another job site. It'll take about an hour. Will you be okay here?"

Earlier, she'd told him about her experience with the supposed neighbor who wasn't a neighbor and, not surprisingly, he'd agreed with Brodey about her not being alone in the house.

"She's good," Brodey said.

Oh. She was, was she? One soul-baring conversation and suddenly he was in charge? She shot him a look.

"I'm not bossing you around. We just said you'd go with me to check this guy out. See if he matched the sketch. That's all."

She hesitated, ticked back the conversation. "You're right. I'm sorry."

"So, we're squared away here?" Nate asked.

"Yes, thank you. Apparently I'm going on a suspect hunt."

BRODEY DROVE PAST the broken-down duplex that matched the address Jenna had given him for Ed Long. The rental sign stuck into the front lawn, if that small patch of dirt mixed with splotches of dormant grass could be considered a lawn, didn't look promising. Could be for the adjoining unit.

Otherwise, Ed Long was in the wind.

In the passenger seat, Lexi fiddled with her phone—probably checking emails. Or ignoring him after she'd announced that maybe she'd give him a shot in the sack. An announcement he couldn't drop-kick from his mind. Yep, when he got her alone again, he'd make up for lost time. For now, she could ignore him all she wanted.

"Hey," she said, "what are you smiling about?"

"You, actually."

"Me?"

"Yep. Thinking about getting you alone again makes me a happy boy."

He'd heard silence before, brutal silence that made him twitch, but this went beyond that. Beautiful Lexi Vanderbilt sat beside him, her eyes wide and focused and her breaths coming in short, uneven bursts. Total panic attack. He patted her leg. "Relax."

"I…don't have a lot of free time. I can't drop everything. And thinking about squeezing…uh… Wow…bad word choice." She winced. "I don't have room for a lot in my insane life. And I don't want you mad at me."

"Who says I'll be mad at you? We had a conversation. It doesn't equal a lifetime commitment."

"You're okay with that?"

"I'm thirty-two years old and have never come close to considering marriage. I'd say, yeah, I'm okay with that." Her head snapped back—whoops—a little sensitivity might have been in order there. *Way to go, Brodey.* "That sounded bad. Probably should have worded it differently."

"I'd rather have the truth. I'm a lunatic about it. No secrets or lies. It's vital to me, so I appreciate you being so up-front. You're looking for fun. I get it."

Was he? A few months ago, definitely. After grueling twelve-hour days, a hot woman, a warm bed and no attachments worked fine. Just fine. Now, being on disability, bored out of his skull in his empty apartment, drove him crazy enough to realize the definite lack of a relationship wasn't so great.

And then his mother cracked that joke about him needing to find a wife so he'd stop coming over and disrupting her schedule. *Thanks, Mom.*

Even his mother had dumped him.

Half a block from the busted-up duplex, he snagged a parking spot. "Okay," he said. "Wait here. I'm gonna knock on the door. See if he answers."

"Wait. What if he recognizes you? If he's been watching the Williamses' place, he'll have seen you coming and going."

Before getting into the car, he'd ditched his sling and now slowly reached into the backseat. He grabbed a skullcap, shoved it on his head along with his sunglasses. Instant disguise. "If he's seen me, he's never gotten close enough to recognize me with the hat and glasses. Sit tight. Lock the doors."

He slid his ASP expandable baton from under the seat, shoved it into his back pocket and started the trek. Hunched against the wind, he shoved his hands into his pockets to retain any heat possible. Damned frigid weather. To distract himself, he counted down the addresses. Next unit on the left was Long's, and not for the first time Brodey wished he'd had his badge and sidearm. At least he had the ASP. No self-respecting cop walked into a situation like this without a weapon. If necessary, he could snap a bone with that baton.

If necessary.

He opened the aluminum screen door and winced at the squeak. Catching the door with his foot, he wedged between it and hammered on the inside door.

Nothing.

In another few seconds, he'd bang on it again. Harder. The door to the adjoining unit opened, revealing a more-than-middle-aged guy in a stained white T-shirt and flannel pants. His thinning gray hair stuck up on one side and grid lines dented his left cheek. *Late sleeper.* Considering it was almost lunchtime.

"You here about the rental?" he croaked. "Give me a second. I'll get the key."

Now, on a normal visit like this, Brodey would badge the guy and identify himself. Not today. This visit, he'd be a lowlife looking for another lowlife.

"Nah." He gestured to the door in front of him. "Lookin' for Ed. You seen him?"

The man's face pinched. "That no-good bum? He burned me on a month's rent. Haven't seen the SOB."

Well, damn. "He skipped?"

"Three weeks ago yesterday. Took his stuff and went. Left the trash, though. I had to clean that stinking mess. If you find him, tell him I'm looking for him. And I'm keeping his security deposit."

Brodey glanced at the door leading to Ed Long's now-vacant apartment and considered asking for a peek.

The landlord jerked his thumb toward Long's former living unit. "Why're you lookin' for him? I don't want no trouble here."

Brodey reached into his jacket pocket and unfolded the copy of the sketch Lexi had done, let the landlord have a look. "We go back a ways. My sister saw him a week or so ago. She's an artsy type and drew this sketch of him. I didn't recognize him with longer hair." He snatched the sketch back and shoved it into his pocket again. "Figured I'd track him down and see what he was up to."

"Your sister is pretty good. He had that long hair the whole time he lived here. Two years he made on-time rent payments. Then he skipped on me."

"Yeah, well, sorry 'bout that. I'll rip him one when I see him."

The landlord shivered against the frigid air. "Yeah. Thanks."

Brodey made his way back to Lexi and his Jeep SUV. As he approached, the door locks clunked. Lexi must have hit the button. He hopped back into the vehicle, plucked the skull cap off and tossed it over his shoulder. "No dice."

She cocked her head, studying him for a second before lifting her hand—*what's she doing?*—and mashing down one side of his hair. He would have liked to say something about that being nice or whatever, but she'd likely freak on him, so he'd keep those thoughts to himself. Wouldn't stop him from fantasizing about other things she could be doing with those hands.

She finished fiddling with his hair and sat back again, apparently unaffected. She may have been unmoved, but not his nervous system. Nope. That sucker couldn't have been more alert. He shook it off. "Thanks. For fixing my hair."

"Sure. It looked cute, but I didn't think you'd want to be walking around like that. You have great hair, by the way. It's wavy, but not curly."

"Yeah. Used to make me nuts. Then I gave up trying to control it. Wherever it lands, it lands."

"With the right cut, it doesn't matter."

"I've learned. And believe me, I take a ton of garbage from my brother because the only person I've found who can deal with it works in a swanky salon in the Loop. Sixty dollars to cut my damned hair. On my salary. My brother pays fifteen."

"Yes, but your brother's hair probably doesn't look—or act—like yours."

"My point exactly!"

Irritated over his trip to Long's being a bust—not to mention thinking about that damned sixty dollars—he slid the car into gear and hit the gas.

"I guess Mr. Long wasn't home? Or is the rental sign for his place?"

"He skipped three weeks ago. Landlord can't find him. And, just so you know—" Brodey cleared his throat, readying for his croaking impression of the landlord "—he's keeping the security deposit that no-good bum left."

Lexi laughed. “Did you show him the sketch? Is it him?”

At the traffic light, Brodey glanced at her, grinning like an idiot because he’d made her laugh. “Yeah. It’s him.”

As expected, her laughter died. Boom. Gone. “Lex, it’s okay. It’s part of the process. We’ll find him. Next stop is his lawyer. Somehow, their lawyers always know where to find these guys.”

Chapter Eight

Lexi's voice mail was full.

At least that was what the email from Nate, delivered via her phone, told her. Full. How many voice mails could that be? Scratch that. She didn't want to know. It would only stress her out. Spending the morning running around with Brodey, as easy as he was on the eyes, didn't do her business a bit of good.

He parked in a small lot adjacent to the three-story brick office building on the Far West Side of Chicago. "This is it. The lawyer is on the first floor. You coming in?"

Returning calls should have been her priority. But how many times did a girl get to ride shotgun with a hot detective about to question someone? Forget the calls. "Yes. I'm going in. I'm curious. Do you have the sketch? I have extra copies in my briefcase."

"Grab one. Mine is crumpled from being in my pocket." He grinned. "We don't want to appear unprofessional after you've coiffed my hair."

Seriously, she could jump him. "Heavens no."

An icy parking lot and sidewalk made for a life-threatening expedition, and Lexi decided a good detective shouldn't wear heels while on an assignment. They'd managed to enter the office, a first-floor unit badly in need of updating from its '90s decor, and a woman in her sixties, also in need of updating, greeted them.

Brodey plastered on another jump-worthy smile and Lexi's toes curled.

"Hello," he said. "Is Henry available?"

The woman eyed him, but shifted forward slightly, her body clearly submitting to the pressure of Brodey in full-on charm mode. "Did you have an appointment?"

An appointment. Lexi glanced at the three metal-framed and extremely empty chairs lining the outside wall. The faux leather had enough dirt to seal a bleeding wound. She would, without question, remain standing.

The good detective turned the wattage up on his smile and leaned in, meeting his new love slave halfway. "Do we need one?"

Wicked, wicked boy.

"Generally," the receptionist said. "But let me see if he's available. Who should I say is calling?"

"Brodey Hayward. Chicago PD Homicide."

All along he'd been insisting on keeping his identity quiet, and suddenly he was practically flashing a badge.

The receptionist hung up. "He'll see you now, Detective." The woman pointed to the door behind her. "Right through that door."

"Terrific. Thank you."

"Of course."

And, hey, Grandma just checked out *Brodey's* rear. Backsides were popular with these two. Boundaries, people. *Boundaries.*

Lexi shook her head as they stepped into the cramped office of Henry Blade, Esq. Surprisingly young, maybe mid-thirties, considering the man's office hadn't been renovated in twenty years, Henry stood to greet them. "Detective, nice to meet you. I'm Henry."

The two men shook hands and Henry turned to Lexi, hitting her with his own winning smile. His couldn't compete with Brodey's, but he was no slouch, either. "Hello," he said.

Lexi extended her hand. "Hello. I'm Alexis Vanderbilt."

"Are you a detective, also?"

"No." She couldn't help herself. "I'm an interior designer."

One your office needs.

"Oh," he said.

If he wondered why a homicide detective and an interior designer were in his office, he didn't show it. In his line of work, he probably met all kinds. She certainly did.

"Have a seat. What can I help you folks with?"

Lexi glanced at the two guest chairs, found the upholstered cushions infinitely cleaner than the ones in the waiting room and sat.

Brodey did the same, his big shoulders filling the chair, his gaze focused with such intense confidence that it would terrify mere mortals. God, this man. So hot in a truly annoying way that left Lexi ready to slap him *and* snuggle up all at the same time.

"We're looking for one of your clients," he said.

"I see. Obviously, I can't share any information about cases with you."

"I realize that. We're not interested in your cases. All we want is to locate Ed Long."

"Ed Long?"

"Yes, sir."

Henry propped one elbow on the armrest. "Hell, I haven't seen him in two years."

Two years. She was no detective, but with Jonathan Williams being dead for that long, the timing fit.

"Is he in trouble again?"

Brodey shrugged. "Not sure yet. He approached Ms. Vanderbilt at one of her job sites and there've been some thefts in the area."

A lie. But there could have been thefts. Who knew? Henry glanced at her, but didn't ask why a witness would be tagging along on this little jaunt. Whatever his concerns, he went back to Brodey. "And you think Ed did it?"

"I didn't say that. We'd like to talk to him about why he was in the area."

"What area was this?"

"Cartright," Brodey said.

A few seconds passed with Henry eyeballing Brodey and Brodey eyeballing right back.

Eventually, Henry lost the battle. "I, uh, once knew someone who lived in Cartright. Our kids went to preschool together."

"Let me guess. Jonathan Williams?"

Henry lurched back, his poker face disintegrating. "How'd you know that?"

Now, this was fascinating.

"Ms. Vanderbilt is doing work on Mr. Williams's home. His widow is trying to sell it."

Henry finally looked over at her. "And Ed was there?"

She pulled the sketch from her briefcase and set it on the desk. "A man pretending to be a neighbor stopped me in front of the house and asked questions. I drew this sketch of him."

"You recognize him?" Brodey asked.

After studying the sketch for a few seconds, Henry put his poker face back together. "Looks like him. He claimed he was a neighbor?"

"Yes, sir."

Back in lawyer mode, Henry sat back again. "I'm sorry. I can't help you. Not only would I be sanctioned by the bar, as I said, I haven't seen him in years."

"I understand." Brodey pushed out of his chair and extended his hand. "Thanks for your time."

"Of course."

That was it? All the way over here for that? Lexi opened her mouth, but Brodey had already stridden to the door and opened it. So confusing, this detective work. And she'd blown off clients for this. Sighing, she followed him to the outer office, where the love slave looked up from her paperwork and smiled. "You have a great day, now."

"Thanks," Brodey said. "You, too."

When they hit the sidewalk, Brodey latched on to Lexi's elbow, hanging on to her so she didn't slide across the ice. "They should salt this," he said. "Someone could get hurt."

On that, they agreed. "Why'd you give up so fast?"

"Give up? I'm just getting started. He's a lawyer clamming up. But he told us he knew Williams. That's damned intriguing." He unlocked the Jeep SUV and pulled her door open. "With him knowing Williams *and* Ed Long, we now have a connection. All we have to do is figure out where and when Ed made that connection."

"Okay. How do we do that?"

"We see if he ever visited the Williamses' home."

"Which means asking Brenda."

"Yep."

Please. He couldn't honestly believe Brenda Williams,

a woman who loved her children more than life, would be involved in their father's murder? "You're not thinking she's a suspect?"

"I'm not thinking anything. Just chasing down a lead."

BRODEY PARKED HIMSELF on Brenda Williams's sofa and scooted to the edge of the cushion, his back straighter than a solid-steel pipe, his face completely neutral. Alert, attentive and nonthreatening. He'd assumed this position many times when speaking with a witness. Or in really rotten situations, a devastated family member. In this case, he wasn't sure what the hell Brenda was.

Having a solid alibi, she'd been cleared early on, but how hard had the detectives looked at her on a conspiracy charge? With the mess her husband left—the lying, the millions he stole, the *humiliation*—it all added up to motive. Motive to collect life insurance by having her husband whacked.

Bam.

Beside him, Lexi leaned into the arm of the sofa. She'd been quiet since they'd left the lawyer's office, and it might have been the longest three hours of his life waiting for Brenda to get home. He hadn't wanted to leave Lexi alone and tagged along on her appointments to make sure she at least made it to and from her meetings without incident.

Chatter came from the kitchen, where the kids argued over a notebook. A minute later, the racket died down and Brenda entered the room, closing the French doors behind her. "Sorry. I wanted to get the kids squared away. It's always crazy around here right when they get home."

She dropped into the cushy chair across from Brodey,

glanced at him and then to a miserable Lexi, who'd lost her game face somewhere. Either that or she stunk at masking her feelings.

"Is everything all right?"

He nodded. "Yes, ma'am. I wanted to show you a sketch. See if you recognize the man."

"Of course."

He slid the sketch from the folder he'd set on the coffee table and handed it to Brenda. "Take your time."

Before looking down, she met Brodey's gaze and held it. "Is he a suspect?"

"I'm not sure."

"Who is he?"

Unwilling to speculate on what Ed Long's involvement in her husband's death might have been, Brodey gestured to the photo. "Do you recognize him?"

The not-so-subtle hint that he wouldn't pony up intel worked and Brenda peered down at the photo. She tilted her head one way, then the other, her expression blank. Total gamer. Lexi could take a lesson from Brenda Williams on hiding her feelings.

She slid the paper away. "I don't think so. At least he's not someone I interacted with."

"Could he be a friend of your husband's?"

"Maybe. I didn't know all of Jonathan's associates."

"Mrs. Williams, I know you're trying to keep the children out of this. I get it. Believe me."

"But?"

Smart lady. "But after you and your husband split up, the children spent time alone with him at his house. They may have seen people coming and going."

"You want me to ask the children to look at the sketch."

Statement. Not a question. "Yes, ma'am. I apologize, but they may have seen him."

And if they saw him in the house, Brodey's theory on Williams possibly knowing his attacker—assuming Ed Long was that attacker—might be more than a theory. Which would cancel out his *other* theory that Brenda hired an assassin.

She sat back, her torso rolling forward as her body closed in on itself. Sometimes this job sucked the life right out of him. Sometimes? He'd just asked a mother, a woman he half suspected of murder, to possibly expose her children to emotional trauma and he had no problem justifying it. He glanced at Lexi, who twisted her lips in a noncommittal "sorry, dude, can't help you" look. Terrific.

But then she sat forward, resting her elbows on her knees, loosely clasping her hands together. "I'm not a mother. I cannot imagine what this feels like for you, and I'm sorry he has to ask this, but I've spent time with Brodey. He's not reckless and he wouldn't put your children through this if he didn't have to. If there was another way, he'd do it. I'm sure of that."

Nice. Finally in sync on something. And the bonus was she'd given him a compliment.

Brenda flicked a glance at him, then went back to Lexi. "Thank you for that."

"Of course."

She stood. "I'll bring them in together. They'll each take a turn looking at the sketch and then I'll have them leave again."

"If you want," Lexi said, "we can tell them I drew the sketch. It might be more interesting to them if they know that."

That stopped Brenda. "You drew it?"

"Yes. I saw him outside the house yesterday."

Cripes. What was she doing? Until they knew, without question, Ed Long's role here, there'd be no sharing of information. If Brenda knew him, she'd call and warn him the second they left. Brodey reached over, squeezed Lexi's arm to shut her the hell up. "Let's bring the kids in."

Sharp woman that she was, Brenda shot a look between them, knowing full well she didn't have the whole story.

"I'll be right back."

Brodey spun to Lexi, stretching closer so he wouldn't be overheard. Her long hair tickled his nose, made him want to bury his face in her neck, and what an inappropriate thought that was right now. "The less she knows the better. If she'd recognized him, that'd be one thing. She didn't. All we know is this guy was in the neighborhood. He could be casing homes and have nothing to do with this murder."

"I'm sorry."

"It's all right. Let's play it close to the vest until we figure out what his involvement is."

Children following behind, Brenda came through the doors again. She set her hand on the boy's head. "This is Sam. This is Patrice and our little squirt there is Meghan."

"Mama, I'm not a squirt."

"I know, baby. I just like calling you that. It makes me smile."

"Hey, guys." Brodey stayed in his spot on the sofa, eye level with the kids. No sense freaking them out by hovering. "So, here's what we're gonna do. Miss Lexi here is a pretty good artist." He motioned them to the coffee table. "In fact, she drew this picture."

"Cool!" Sam said.

"It is cool. How about you guys take a look at the

picture and see if you recognize the person. Would that be okay?"

Sam shrugged. Meghan, all missing front teeth and pigtails, bobbed her head hard enough that the thing should have flown off. Patrice wandered closer, totally noncommittal, and Brodey's brain snapped.

What the snap meant, he'd find out soon enough, but generally that intensely visceral reaction meant someone knew something and in this bunch, eight-year-old Patrice might be the one.

Sam and Meghan flanked her while Brenda stood back, her shoulders dipped, body once again folding in. She glanced up, made solid eye contact and slowly pushed her shoulders back. For a woman in her thirties, she'd had her share of life's brutality. All Brodey needed to know was if she'd taken it upon herself to battle that brutality by killing her husband.

"I don't know him," Patrice said.

So much for instincts.

Meghan swung her head back and forth. "Me, neither."

Sam stayed silent. Interesting.

"Sam?" his mom said.

The kid shrugged. "I'm not sure."

Not. Sure. Brodey forced his body still. If he moved, the kid could get spooked. Even the smallest change of energy affected kids.

"That's okay," Brodey said, his voice somewhere between comforting and authoritative. "Do you think you've seen him?"

The kid's eyes bounced between Brodey and the sketch, but he backed up a step. "No."

From not being sure to no. This day was bringing all kinds of screwy surprises. As a cop, liars came in steady supply, including scared kids. What he had here might be both. The kid could be mentally reliving his father's murder in their home. No kid deserved to live with that mess.

Sam spun to his mom. "Can I go now?"

"Sam?" Brodey said.

"Yes, sir?"

"Are you sure you don't know him?"

"You know what," Brenda said, "they have homework to finish."

The kids left, their mother following them out, and the pressure behind Brodey's eyes exploded.

Brenda Williams, for whatever reason, suddenly didn't want her children asked any more questions.

BRODEY HELD LEXI'S briefcase while she unlocked her funky red front door. Only a decorator—scratch that, *interior designer*—painted the front door of a nine-hundred-square-foot bungalow glossy red. The place was begging to get knocked off. The bad outside lighting only added to the "rob me!" message.

"You know," he said, "the place could use better lightning. Especially if you do these late nights regularly."

"Seven-thirty is late?"

"It's dark, isn't it?"

She flipped the lock and pushed open the door. "You're funny, Brodey."

"I'm a cop who's seen women get mugged—or worse—because they didn't take their surroundings seriously."

"I do take them seriously." Inside, she hit a switch and flooded the cottage with light. "But it's winter and there's only so much daylight. I can't avoid coming home after dark. Particularly when a cute homicide detective runs me all over town and my work doesn't get done. As it is, I had to cancel my last two appointments."

"Sorry about that. And I'm not cute. Men don't like to be called cute. Puppies are cute."

She dumped her briefcase by the door. "Fine. You're not cute. Tomorrow, though, I have to get moving on the Williams house. Are you going to let me tear up that laundry room?"

"You can't work around it?"

"Brodey!"

He put his hands up. "Just for a day or two."

"You've been over that place a million times. What will happen in a day or two that will make a difference?"

Hell if he knew. He *had* been over it from top to bottom, and everything he'd thought might tell him something—the slug in the wall, the broken glass, the open window—turned out to be nothing. No wonder the case was colder than Lake Michigan. Not one damned piece of workable evidence. And Lexi was on a deadline she intended to make.

"You can't tear it up. Yet."

She folded her arms, tapping her fingers against her biceps. "Forty-five days, Brodey. That's how long I have. And that's not to finish the renovation. That's for the house to sell. And the real-estate agent is calling me three times a day."

"Are you serious?"

"Yes, I'm serious. My voice mail was full today. Full. All clients wondering why I'm not responding. And this real-estate agent handles some megalistings. If I blow the deadline, I lose my chance at an assistant and, worse, my reputation. So, yes, handsome man, I need to rip that floor up."

Damn, she was beautiful. *No distractions here.* "Call

me stupid, but I love when you get pushy like this. Makes me willing to give you just about anything."

"Great. Tomorrow the floor comes up."

"Except that."

Lexi burst out laughing. "I'm telling you straightaway, it will take a minor miracle to keep me from ripping up that floor."

She moved into the kitchen, grabbed two bottled waters from the fridge and set them on the counter separating the rooms. "Are you hungry? Earlier you promised me dinner and we haven't eaten since lunch."

Definitely, he could eat. Then again, he could always eat. "I'd love to buy you dinner."

"We can order something. All I have is chicken salad that might poison us. The Italian restaurant down the street delivers."

Her phone buzzed, rumbling against the countertop, where she'd set it. "Does that thing ever stop?"

"Only when I shut it off." She dug a menu out of the drawer and handed it to him. "Take a look. We'll order and then figure out what's next in your investigation."

He twisted his lips, perused the menu for all of two seconds. "Chicken parm. Spaghetti on the side."

"Good choice."

While she ordered, he scanned the stark-white counter, where a pitcher with splotches of color sat in one corner. Opposite that was a three-foot-high black vase with some kind of long-stemmed greenery poking out of it. Other than that, the counters were clear, no jumble of utensils, no appliances, no spice rack, nada. Everything in this kitchen had its place. Orderly.

Kind of like him, but he didn't want just order, he wanted control. Always.

Lexi set the phone down and immediately stored the

menu back in the drawer. “Okay, handsome. We need a game plan here or I’m not getting the Williams house done. You’ve got two minutes to come up with something while I ditch my shoes. Then you’ll tell me what we’re doing about finding Ed Long.”

She wandered to the other room. The bedroom. Unconcerned about her directive, he peeked around the column for a glimpse because, hey, the place wasn’t that big and he was curious.

“I need to dig around,” he said. “Figure out what the connection might be between Williams, Ed Long and Long’s defense attorney. If we’re going with Williams knowing his attacker, and Ed Long was that attacker, why was he in the Williams house the night of the murder? A guy like Williams wouldn’t be hanging with someone like Long. There’s a reason he was there. I may pay a visit to Henry again. Put a little pressure on him to see if he ever introduced them and why. He won’t talk but I’ll scare the hell out of him. He may be a defense lawyer, but he admitted he knew Williams. And Williams is definitely dead. Which doesn’t look good for old Henry.”

Lexi appeared in the bedroom doorway, her eyes huge, her mouth partially open. Every vibe coming off her screamed panic. What the hell?

“Lex?”

Eyes bugging out, she paddled her hands. Pure and potent adrenaline spewed, tearing up his veins, making his stomach churn, and he hauled butt to the bedroom, gently nudging her from the doorway. “What?”

“The mirror. There.”

She pointed to the stand-up mirror in the corner. Taped to it was one of the flyers she and Jenna had flooded Cartright with.

Another burst of adrenaline hit him and his vision blurred. He blinked it away and scanned the room, eyes sweeping left, right and back again. The top of the tall dresser held a few bottles of lotion and a couple of small glass bowls, all lined up like soldiers. Same thing with the long dresser, the two lamps and various decorative jars. Nothing out of place. "Did you tape that there?"

She'd damn well better say yes. If not, they had bigger problems than her needing more outside lighting.

"I DIDN'T PUT it there," Lexi said.

She stood in the doorway while Brodey studied the mirror, running the flashlight from his phone around the surface. Probably looking for fingerprints. A whirring noise drifted from the kitchen and Lexi glanced down the hall before moving closer to Brodey. She'd heard that refrigerator hundreds—thousands—of times and suddenly it terrified her?

Still, couldn't hurt to get closer to the trained police officer in the room. Yes. Good thought. "Do you see anything?"

"Maybe a print on the tape. You need to report it as a break-in. Is anything missing?"

Please, no. In her shock, she hadn't thought to check her belongings. Nothing looked out of place but…

She rushed to the dresser, riffled through the drawers where she'd strategically hid her quality jewelry—her grandmother's wedding ring, the diamond necklace she'd bought herself after her first big job, the heart earrings her father had given her. *Yes.* All items accounted for, she pushed the drawer closed and collapsed against the dresser, breathing in and out until her ears stopped their annoying whistling. "It's all here."

"You sure?"

"Yes. The important things are here."

Wedgwood vase. Would a petty thief know it was worth five thousand dollars? Another thing she hadn't paid for, but was given in exchange for the exposure offered from the design contest. She spun back, ran to the doorway and checked the side table in the tiny hallway. *Still there.* "That vase is the only other thing of value. Unless they wanted to carry the sofa out. Everything is here."

Except…she hadn't checked the top drawer. Her underwear drawer. She never kept anything important there, well, other than her underwear, but for the sake of completion, for the detail-oriented person in her who couldn't ignore the last drawer, she slid it open.

And oh no. Sitting in the middle, resting on top of her silk underwear, was another flyer. She focused on it, blinked away her blurry vision and read the words written in red ink across the top. Silently, she recited each word, letting her lips form them as they sunk in.

LEAVE.

THIS.

CASE.

ALONE.

In my house, in my house, in my house. "No," she moaned. "This is *not* happening."

Brodey leaped up, charged across the room and followed her gaze. He stared at the flyer a few seconds, then reached for his phone. "I'm calling it in. Don't touch that."

"You can bet I won't."

Not after some pig had put his hands on her things. Her extremely private things. Her stomach turned rock hard as Brodey spoke with a dispatcher and marched to the front door. Without touching it, he checked the lock, then went to the back door and did the same. She stood, half shivering, feet fused to the floor in the tiny hallway, watching him prowl around the house. All because she'd helped Jenna post those damned flyers. He'd warned her about this. Told her how dangerous it was. At the time, she'd considered him paranoid. A worrywart. Mr. Cynical.

Well, Mr. Cynical had nailed this one, and the caged panic inside her banged against her chest. Tears bubbled up—no crying—and she pressed her palms against her eyes.

Ending his call, Brodey reached for her, pulled her in for a hug and slid his hand over her hair. Mr. Touchy-Feely. Right now, she didn't mind. Not one bit.

"You're okay," he whispered, kissing the top of her head. "You're okay."

She gripped his shirt at his waist, drew in all his heat, praying it would douse the deep freeze that had settled inside her. "He was in my house."

"I know. I'm sorry. It doesn't look like he broke anything to get in. He probably picked the back-door lock. It's cheap. And useless."

"This had to be Ed Long. He was so creepy when he talked to me. It has to be him."

"You got someone's attention."

She tipped her head up to look at him. "Not any random person. Him. I know it. I can feel it."

"Or someone he knows. Could be someone he's working with."

In my house.

"They know where I live. They could be following me."

"Could be."

She shoved him back, flapped her arms. "You're not helping. You're supposed to make me feel better."

"By lying to you? By telling you not to worry when someone gets into your house and leaves you a threatening note? Not my style."

Mr. Cynical turning into Mr. Anti-Sensitivity. Killer combo, that one.

He latched on to her arms, gave them a squeeze. "I won't lie, but I promise—I swear to you—nothing will hurt you." He inched closer, still hanging on to her. "I'll make sure of it."

Of all the things men had told her over the years, for whatever reason, this might be the one she believed most. She imagined when Brodey Hayward, annoying as he was, made a promise, he kept it. She absorbed his words, took them in, once again silently repeating them over and over. After the third time, like a mantra, they settled the madness scouring her mind.

Relax. *You've got this.*

Brodey slid his hands to hers and grasped them. "Are you okay?"

Considering what had just happened and what *could* have happened had she walked in on the person? Yes. Absolutely okay. More than okay. Because her intruder wanted this, wanted her to give in to the fear. *Don't.* No. She lifted her head, imagined some stranger pawing through her possessions—her underwear—and suddenly her rock-hard stomach morphed into something else. Something loose and violent that tore up her insides in an angry, burning way.

She lifted his hand, kissed the back of it and held it to her cheek. "Thank you. For being here. Finding this alone would have been…"

"But you weren't alone, so don't go there."

Someone banged on the front door, devouring the silence and brief calm. Another surge of panic flooded her brain and she shot straight, her body in full alert.

"Relax," he said. "I've got it. It's probably a patrol car."

Chapter Nine

By the time the last police officer left, Lexi wanted nothing more than a hot bath, a full barrel of wine and to sleep for a month. When this mess began, she had dreams of an assistant. Her goals had been simple. Get the assistant, clean out the garage and make it an office. Now her privacy had been violated and her sense of safety right along with it. After putting so much energy into her home, endless hours of pouring herself into it, she wasn't sure she'd ever manage any sleep in it again.

All because she wanted an assistant.

She glanced around the living room, took in the red accents and the mint walls meant to bring tranquility. The camel chairs she'd spent so many nights sketching in, the sofa she'd prized to the point of worship. In a matter of hours, everything she felt about this home had changed.

She plopped onto one of the counter stools, considered what had gone on here and shook her head, letting her festering rage burn into her. No one should be allowed to steal another person's sense of safety.

Brodey swung through the front door after talking with one of the officers outside. Now he bolted the door behind him and double-checked it.

"You know what?" she said.

"What?"

"I'm angry."

"You should be."

"A couple of hours ago, this house was my safe haven. Everything I've worked for is here. When the world is rotten, this is my shelter. And someone changed that. It's not right. I had to be *fingerprinted*."

"It's only to rule out your prints."

"I know that, but the entire episode is unsettling."

"Well." He motioned one hand in circles. "Ah, hell. There's nothing to say. Yeah, it's unsettling. No two ways about it."

Finally, no lecture, no infinite wisdom on how to avoid something like this. *Thank you.*

He wandered to her, brushed a few stray strands of hair from her face, then set his big hand on her cheek. "You should feel violated. I'll make sure it doesn't happen again. But you need to make changes around here."

Should have known. The man simply couldn't help himself. "Like what? Bars on the windows?"

"For one thing, motion-sensor lights by the front and back doors. Better locks, too. And you need a security system. Any single woman living alone should have one."

A security system. That would set her budget back, but feeling the way she did, her safety and sense of comfort compromised, whatever the cost, she'd accept it.

"I'll do it. No argument. Do you know a good security company?"

"I'll call a guy I know in the morning. I'm getting you lights with motion sensors, too. They'll be in by lunchtime."

"You can do that?"

He grinned. "I happen to be handy. Remember that when you think I'm driving you batty."

Parked on the stool, her life a wreck around her, she laughed. Straight from her toes it shot up and felt so darned good that she grabbed Brodey by the shirt and smacked a kiss on him. Just plastered her lips against his because if she'd been here alone, this situation would have been so much worse. He deepened the kiss and it became more than the quick smack she'd intended. His hands closed over her lower back and dragged her closer, their tongues clashing as he pushed between her legs. Oh my, this man could kiss.

He broke away, moving his lips along her jaw, dotting kisses until he got to her ear.

"I like kissing you," he whispered.

"I like you kissing me," she said.

He laughed and dropped his head to her shoulder. "Damn, you're great."

"But you stopped."

"Because we should get you settled for tonight before I beg to do dirty things to you. Why don't we move this to my place? It's a frat house compared with this, but you'll be safe there."

She hugged him, held him close, once again drawing in all that protective warmth. With Brodey came a sense of calm that anchored her, helped her stay in control.

Kept her sane.

Relatively.

She knew she wouldn't—couldn't—be chased from her home. If she gave in, her intruder won. And she refused to live that way. "I can't leave."

"Lex—"

"I've loved this cottage from the second I saw it. It

has every piece of me I could give it. Whoever did this won't take that from me."

Brodey let out a breath, releasing the air through his lips in one long flow. "I want to argue with you."

"But?"

"I get it. You don't deserve this. And it stinks. But you can't be alone until we get this place secure."

"Well," she said, suddenly feeling hopeful but maybe not quite ready to share a bed with a man, "*you* could stay here with me. I'll even give you the bedroom. I'll take the couch. Which is a major thing since I barely let anyone sit on it, much less put their feet on it."

"Hell no. I'll take the couch. You sleep in your bed and maybe it'll halfway feel like a normal night."

A normal night that included a break-in and a man who kissed like a demon sleeping on her twenty-thousand-dollar couch.

Sure.

Normal.

STARING AT LEXI's living room ceiling at 2:00 a.m. stunk. Afraid to fall asleep, Brodey kept his mind sharp by doing math problems in his head. When that got old, he switched to the Williams case, methodically organizing a mental to-do list. He'd need to swing by Jenna's office and update her murder board. This thing was full of interesting angles, and laying it all out, seeing the flow, would help him build a solid theory. They had Ed Long pretending to live in Cartwright, possibly to get info out of Lexi. They had his number in the appointment book Lexi found buried in the wall. They had his lawyer knowing Jonathan Williams. How the hell did all this fit together?

"I need to check his financials," he said to no one.

Financials always told some sort of story. People were habitual with their spending. Whether a person was frugal or materialistic, a good detective could learn any number of things by simply studying bank records.

Moonlight filtered through a skylight in the kitchen, giving the place a terrific cozy feel. He could see why she loved it here. She'd built a home for herself, made it comfortable for anyone who walked in the door. When he'd told her his place looked like a frat house, he wasn't exaggerating. It came complete with milk crates as side tables. Maybe he'd have Lexi help him with it. Nothing crazy on his salary, but at least something that resembled an adult living there.

Footsteps in the hallway bolted him upright. He swung around and spotted Lexi in the hallway in a pair of silky-looking shorts and a V-neck top, her blond hair backlit by the moonlight. God, she looked great right out of bed. "You okay, Lex?"

In the darkness, her bare feet smacked lightly against the hardwood. "I'm fine. Restless. Did I wake you?"

He jammed his thumb and middle finger into his eyes for a good rub. "I was awake. Can't sleep."

"Me, neither. I hate it." She slid into the spot next to him and curled her legs under her. "Usually when I can't sleep, I come out here and work. Maybe do some sketches. It relaxes me."

"Work relaxes you?"

From his perspective, his job gave him nightmares.

"I guess with what you do, that sounds weird, but yes. I think it's more the quiet that comes with sketching rather than the actual activity. Although, there's something therapeutic in creating something with my own hands, watching it take shape."

"Uh, I can't draw a lick."

"So, don't draw. You said you're handy. Build model airplanes or something."

Brodey twisted his lips. That idea had possibilities. "Boats."

"What?"

He leaned back, bringing his bad arm up to rest it on the back of the couch. "I like boats. When I retire, I want to be on the water. Maybe do fishing charters or something."

"From homicide to fishing?"

"Yep. And I'm moving someplace warm in the winter. I can't take this cold. I've got another fourteen and a half years and I'm done. Then I'll do something else."

She spun sideways, propped her arm on the cushion and her fingertips brushed his elbow. "You'd leave Chicago?"

"Only in the winter. My family is here. Besides, I love it here."

"I love it here, too. Unfortunately, my business doesn't allow me to pick up and go. Unless it's an out-of-state job. And what about kids? Do you want kids?"

He shrugged. "Never thought about it. Maybe."

"If you have kids, they'll be in school."

That was a problem he hadn't considered. Most likely because he hadn't met a woman who'd motivated him to think that far ahead.

At least not until now.

He tried to picture Lexi with a bun in the oven. His bun. Hello? A couple of kisses and a few laughs weren't nearly enough to build a family on. "You want kids?"

Using two fingers, she pressed on his hair. Probably the cowlick that sprang up every morning. "I think so. I'm a little old-fashioned, though, so I don't want to be a single mom. I guess if the right guy doesn't come along, I'd consider doing it myself, but right now, I'm okay to wait."

"Single parenting is tough. I don't think I could do it."

"Brodey, you can do anything you put your mind to. You're stubborn that way."

He snorted. "My mom says that."

"She must be a smart woman."

She'd like you. Yep. Sure would. His mom would like her spunk. *He* liked her spunk. He liked a lot about her. Particularly the way the moonlight lit enough of her for him to see her top dipping low into her cleavage—a nice view if he ever saw one. *No bra.* And that sent his mind spinning to thoughts of lifting the pajama top, running that silky fabric through his fingers and getting a look at her. He already knew her breasts were enough to fill a man's hand—his hand—nicely, but he'd never seen them. And that was what he wanted.

For safekeeping, he brought his arm down and clasped his fingers on his stomach. Thoughts of his hands on Lexi's breasts were trouble. Big-time. His growing erection straining against his jeans proved it. Damn it.

"Did you fall asleep?"

Ha. "Hardly. In fact, I think it's safe to say I'm wide-awake."

"Why do I feel like I should apologize?"

He lifted his head, met her gaze, and that instant spark zapped him. So hot. "My mind wanders when I'm around you. Being here, in the dark, makes me think things. Seriously wicked things you'd slap me for."

A small intake of breath was her only response. He laid his head back again and sighed. *Moron.* What kind of man took advantage of a woman who'd had her safety, her sense of comfort in her own home, violated?

A horny one.

Sometimes, the truth stunk. He wanted to consider himself honorable, someone who wouldn't manipulate a situation to reach the conclusion he wanted. As a detective, he battled tunnel vision and that driving need to solve a case at all costs. A good detective worked with the evidence he had, made it fit, and sometimes, despite honest intentions, that evidence added up to convicting the wrong person.

She lowered her head to his shoulder. Definitely not slapping him. Maybe he wasn't such a lowlife.

"What kind of things?"

Man, oh, man. The living room was definitely warming up.

"Lex?"

She lifted her head, met his gaze. "Yes?"

"You're about to throw a match on leaking gas."

"I know. I've been alone a while and it's a little scary to me—this attraction to you."

He reached up, tucked his hand behind her head and pulled her closer. Even in the darkness, her hazel eyes were bright, charged with something resembling anticipation.

Waiting.

Damn, they weren't exactly perfect for each other. She viewed the world with a sense of innocence, wanting only to make it more beautiful. Him? All he saw was what could happen. The danger that existed the minute she stepped out of her house. The danger that now made its way *inside* her house.

But he wanted her.

Simple as that.

Then she made a humongous mistake by leaning in, enough that her breath skittered across his cheek and—

man down—any motivation he had to stop flew out the window. Right out. *Bye-bye.*

"There are a million reasons we're wrong for each other," he said.

She slid her hand over his chest, between his pecs, and the friction ripped right into him. He should give in now because it had been too long since he'd had a woman, and this wasn't just any woman. This amazing, beautiful, sassy woman he'd like to hear moaning underneath him. At least when his damned elbow healed since he couldn't put any weight on it. *Way to kill the mood.*

"I think you're wrong about that," she said. "Besides, do we care right now? Clearly, we're attracted to each other. I mean, I'm not great with men, but that smoking kiss was a good indication, don't you think?"

A good indication.

So much for honorable. Brodey gave his head a hard shake. He didn't know what the hell he wanted. No. That was a lie. He knew. He just didn't want to give in to it. And how dumb was that? They were adults, reasonable adults—mostly—who wanted to have some fun.

Fun. That was what they'd have.

And while he did all this thinking, the furnace clunked, driving even more heat into the already boiling room while she straddled him.

"I like to think I'm a fairly confident person, but this is starting to feel like a rejection. You've got ten seconds to kiss me before I give up on you. And, Brodey, when I give up on a man, it's over. No going back."

As proved by her walking away from the cheating ex.

Couldn't have that, could they?

He slid his hands around her waist, settled them on her hips where his fingers hit bare skin at the bottom edge of her top. His blood raced and he breathed in, enjoyed the sensation of his skin against hers. He curved his hands over her rear, inching along because why not? Putting his hands on her was the thing he'd been craving for days.

"I hope you're not tired," he said.

"Why?"

"Because you're about to have a long night."

LEXI SQUEEZED HER thighs against Brodey's and her legs tingled with each bit of contact. She'd missed that feeling. The anticipation. The *lust*. "Bring it on, fella."

She lowered her head to kiss him, but he was already in motion, pulling her in, and then her lips were on his, raking against them, nipping and sucking and...crazy good. A fierce buzz roared inside her, tearing straight up into her breasts and—wow—this kiss. Too much. Too. Much.

Never before had she thrown herself at a man. Never. They always came to her. With Brodey, she didn't need him to chase her. She simply knew what she wanted. Somewhere along the way, he'd given her reasons to trust him. The way he watched over her, protected her, listened to her. All of it brought safety. Emotionally and physically.

Even if the man drove her insane. Which he was about to do on her treasured sofa.

In a grand way.

He dug his hands under her shirt, slid the hem up, his roughened fingers scorching over her skin. "Get it off."

Together, eyes locked, they worked the fabric over her head and tossed it on the floor. Her own little striptease. She took a second to absorb the fact that she was almost fully naked—tap pants still firmly in place—and he hadn't removed a stitch of clothing.

She kissed him again, pressing against him and reveling in the light abrasion of his shirt against her bare skin. "You have too many clothes on."

Then she was airborne as he shifted her sideways. "I can fix that."

The two of them went to work on his clothes, him removing his shirt while she worked on his zipper. The shirt gone, he grabbed his wallet from the arm of the sofa. Before tonight, that wallet sitting there, disturbing the order, possibly leaving smudges on the fabric, would have grated her nerves. Now? Who cared? He pulled something from the wallet. Condom. Good thinking.

He boosted his hips and she glided his jeans down, hooking her fingers into his boxer briefs, bringing them along with the jeans. Multitasking at its best.

His erection sprang free and Lexi figured she'd just hit the lottery of male perfection. She skittered her fingers over his legs, good solid legs a woman could count on to hold her up. He stepped out of his jeans and she tossed them aside, then stood in front of him, running her hands along the ridges of his stomach, up his chest and—dear God, the man was all lean, sinewy muscle. This was a body toned and carved to perfection.

"Lex?"

"Yes?"

"Uh, there's one thing."

Of course there was. The man had a lecture for everything. Forget that. She dived into his neck, trailing kisses up and up and up, along his jaw, to his lips, and he set her back a step.

"Brodey, I love this protective streak in you and how you worry about every darned thing, but you can stop now. Please."

"I'm sorry, but..."

Enough. She lurched back. Might as well just let him say what he needed to say and they could get down to business. "What is it?"

He stuck his elbow out. "Bum arm."

She burst out laughing. "And that's a problem now?"

"Uh, yeah."

"I don't understand."

He grunted. "I can't believe you're gonna make me say it."

As the seconds ticked by, tension mounted and her brain hit overdrive—*what am I missing? What's he worried about?* No idea. Using her palm, she banged on her forehead. "I don't know what you're trying to say."

"Lex! I can't put any weight on my arm. You have to do the work."

Say what now?

Again, he held his elbow up and the look on his face, the pressed lips, the scrunched nose, all of it a cross of frustration, humiliation and sheer will. She grabbed his cheeks and dotted kisses over his face. "It's okay, it's okay. I get it now."

"It's not okay. I should be able to hold up my own damned weight."

More kisses. "You can. Just not right now. It's okay. Really." She shoved him backward until the backs of his legs hit the sofa and he dropped onto it. "Lucky for you, I like being on top."

He smiled at her joke. Mission complete. Gone was the frustration and embarrassment. The vulnerability. From a man who'd never shown her any sign of weakness. *I could love him.*

But she wouldn't go to that particular place. That meant risking heartbreak. For now, she'd focus on the lust that, after months and months without it, brought her alive again. She stood in front of Brodey, watching him tear the condom wrapper, anticipating that second when he'd be ready and she'd pounce—literally—on him.

She waggled her hand. "Seriously? How long does it take? Should I do it?"

He snorted. "*No.* Sheesh, someone's in a rush."

You know it, mister.

He held his arms wide. "Come and get me."

Then she was on him and a frenzy of kisses and licking and touching ensued. Neck, shoulders, jaw, everywhere. *Poof.* Total combustion. Insanity.

Loving the feel of his skin against hers, that rub of flesh against flesh, she inched closer, craving that first second when he'd be inside her, filling her. He gripped her hips and—*finally*—she gasped at the intrusion. So long she'd been without this.

He stopped. "You okay?"

"I'm great. Keep moving or I'll kill you. Right on my sofa."

The one she barely let anyone sit on.

She rolled her hips and he moaned, a low, guttural sound that melted her mind.

They moved together and her body became a tight coil, waiting, waiting, waiting. *Please.* So perfect. How was it possible he felt this perfect? This right.

Kidding herself.

Struck stupid by lust. Had to be.

Did she care? *No.*

He bucked his hips and her breath hitched. Something bright and sharp and beautiful flashed behind her eyes. *I could love him.* Her body exploded, just came apart bit by bit, and she cried out, hanging on as he moved inside her. She grabbed his cheeks and held on, wanting to see his face when he went over.

Gritting his teeth, he took a sharp breath as his orgasm hit him full force. He tightened his arms around her, bringing her with him as he slumped back against the sofa. So good together. Who knew? The cynical cop and the hopeful designer. What a team. Snuggling in, she rested her head against his chest, where his heartbeat thump-thumped in her ear. Slowly, she twirled her fingers in the smattering of dark hair, enjoying the silence and the odd familiarity, the comfort, that shouldn't come from a man she'd slept with only once.

Comfort and familiarity that she'd experienced only one other time, with someone who'd humiliated her with his intern.

Don't think about it. The hurt and anger and unwillingness to take a chance on someone.

Not now. Not when she'd finally found a man who wouldn't lie to her or keep secrets.

One she might trust.

FOR THE FIRST time in months, Brodey woke up thinking he'd not only hit the lottery, he'd also hit the sex-all-night *mega*lottery, and in his mind, that was one hell of a way to start the day.

Even if he was dog tired.

He pried his eyes open, blinked a few times and focused on the weird color of Lexi's bedroom ceiling. Why the hell would anyone paint a ceiling peach? Then again, why would anyone pay twenty grand for a couch?

He didn't get it.

Lexi's world was an enigma. An enigma he'd have to start understanding if he expected a woman like her to continue playing the megalottery with him.

But, damn, her world was all happy, calm colors, while his was dark crime. She saw light where he saw gloom. Eventually, his need to point out the obvious dangers and her need to ignore him would blow any relationship to bits.

Next to him, Lexi flopped to her stomach, her sandy-blond hair splaying over her pillow. Immediately, thoughts of nudging her awake and really giving this day a bang of a start filled his mind. He considered it. Sure did. But as tired as he was, she had to be just as tired and had clients to see today. At least he could nap.

He stared back up at the ceiling, tilted his head one way, then the other. Oddly, his already supremely under-control blood pressure dropped another notch. Huh. Maybe she had something with all this feng shui nonsense. He closed his eyes, thought about the day ahead. After last night's break-in and the subsequent call to the PD, he needed to come clean to his superiors about his involvement investigating this case. He was a cop and cops talked and before he knew it, the brass would want answers.

Plus, he needed help. After the warning left for Lexi, he couldn't investigate and keep her safe at the same time.

Hold up here, bud.

His superiors? Was that necessary? They didn't know the case, at least not the intricacies, the nuts and bolts. Not as well as the lead detective. And that guy was a friend of his father's. Brodey could head in there, turn over any evidence he and Lexi had found and tell the detective to help himself to the credit. Brodey's name wouldn't even have to come up.

This might be a plan.

Slowly, he folded the sheet and bedspread back and slid out of bed. The sudden chill bolted right into his feet. Damned winters. A hot shower would do him some good. Help run the morning kinks out of his elbow. He'd help himself to that, head for clean clothes and call his father to hang with Lexi while he went to the PD and confessed his sins.

Chapter Ten

Brodey stood in reception at Area North headquarters waiting for Detective Lawrence McCall to answer his page. A woman sat to his left, her head buried in some kind of needlepoint project, and a sudden punch of yearning blasted him, ate right through his core. Who would expect to see a woman doing needlepoint in a police station? A cop. That was who. Because cops saw oddball stuff every day and that part of the job kept him sane, gave him something to laugh about after seeing things no right-minded human should.

"Junior!" McCall's booming voice echoed against the walls.

The man stood at the door leading into the main area of the building, his big chest stretching his dress shirt to barely bursting, and Brodey thought maybe the guy had lost some weight. He also wore a snarky grin. Old-timers like Larry, guys who couldn't understand why female detectives didn't want to be referred to as *broads,* knew being called Junior broke Brodey's chops. In a bad way.

"Lawrence," Brodey said, loading him up on the sarcasm, "how's it going?"

McCall snorted. *Yeah, you're not the only one who can bust chops.* When Dad had arrived at Lexi's, he'd given Brodey inside information that as a child, McCall was often teased about being a nerd whose mother called him Lawrence instead of the shortened Larry. At times, the guys around the station liked to crawl under the man's skin by calling him Lawrence.

McCall whapped him on the back of the head and shoved him through the door with a laugh. "How you been? Everything okay? Your dad told me about the elbow."

"I'm good. Don't start with the elbow jokes. I'm out of my freaking mind with boredom."

McCall gestured down the long corridor. "Who'd have thought you'd miss this job, right?"

"Amen, brother."

"What are you doing here?"

"It's about one of your cases. You got somewhere we can talk?"

McCall flopped his bottom lip out. "Sure."

He led him down the corridor to an empty interview room where the ripe, stagnant smell of sweat and fear permeated the air. Thousands of people had sat through questioning in here, some guilty, some not. But one thing was for sure—when they entered this room, their central nervous systems reacted. And not in a good way.

Brodey dropped his messenger bag on the floor. The bag contained his notes, Lexi's flyer and a sketch of Long that he'd be turning over to McCall. He parked himself in one of the metal chairs bracketing the table and tension sped up his arms like swarming spiders, their tiny legs powering along. He cupped a hand over the back of his neck and rubbed. How the heck had he'd gotten himself into this mess? All he'd wanted to do was kill a day by helping his sister.

McCall scraped the chair against the linoleum, and

the sharp sound drove into Brodey's skull. Or maybe that was just his nerves.

"So, what's up?"

Making direct eye contact, Brodey eased his shoulders back. Command presence, the ability to look confident and in control, sometimes meant the difference between bleeding out in the street or making a bust.

"The Williams case."

"My nightmare. What about it?"

"I have information. All I ask is that you hear me out."

The detective dropped his chin to his chest and groaned. "Ah, Junior, what the hell's this, now?"

"Nothing horrible." Brodey waggled a hand. "It's good. But my butt could wind up in a sling."

"Start talking, kid."

"You know my sister is an investigator for Hennings & Solomon."

"You better believe I know. She's too damned good at her job and wrecks my cases."

Brodey smiled. "I hear you. She's been volunteered by her boss to help Brenda Williams figure out what happened to her husband."

"Damn it."

He didn't know the half of it. "She asked me to take a look at her evidence. Couldn't make sense of a few things."

McCall made hard eye contact. "Junior, are you gonna upset me?"

Probably, but Brodey blew that off, just kept right on talking. "I took a look at the crime scene."

He'd casually leave out that his father had gotten him copies of the reports without McCall's knowledge. The thing with old-timers was to dazzle them, not give them a chance to pound on you before you got to the good stuff.

"And?"

"There's a guy. Ed Long. You know him?"

Slowly, McCall moved his head back and forth, his cheeks tinting red, but so far, no major tantrum. Brodey reached into his messenger bag for Lexi's sketch and his file on Long. "This is him. He's got a sheet. Mostly robberies. No murders."

"How does he tie back to Williams?"

"Mrs. Williams wants to unload their house. She's broke and needs the cash. She hired a decorator to stage the house, you know, make it look good so it'll sell faster. The decorator was approached by this Ed Long outside the house, started asking her questions."

McCall screwed up his face. "And what? He introduced himself? Gave her his name?"

"Hell no. That's where it gets good."

Brodey spent the next ten minutes walking McCall through how he and Lexi learned Ed Long's identity. When he finished, McCall picked up the sketch, compared it with the photo of Long from his rap sheet.

"The link between Williams and this Long guy is the lawyer?"

"I think so. The lawyer's kid went to school with Williams's kid."

"So what? How does that tie Long to Williams?"

"I don't know. But someone broke into Lexi Vanderbilt's house last night and left one of the flyers with a note telling her to back off."

That got McCall's attention. "Hell no."

"Hell yes. I was there with her."

"Why?"

Why? Dummy him hadn't anticipated that question, and he should have. Any good detective would. "I had follow-up questions about her conversation with Long, so I went over there. She found the note while I was there." As recoveries went, that one wasn't half-bad. "Obviously, I called it in. The crime-scene guys took the note to check it for prints."

"And you're coming to me now because you're on disability and might get jammed up."

"For the record, this was supposed to be a one-day thing. I'd give Jenna my opinion. That's all. She's my baby sister and she was stuck."

Working McCall's soft spot as a family man, another inside tip from Dad, couldn't hurt.

The big man snorted. "Your father prepped you. So far, you've worked my nerves with the Lawrence crack and sucked up by mentioning your family. You're a kid after my own heart."

Brodey waggled his eyebrows. "I'm trying."

"But you're messing with my case." He mashed his finger into the table. "I want Jenna's evidence. Make that happen and I don't jam you up with the brass."

For Brodey, that worked. He'd have a not-so-happy Jenna to deal with, but his sister would agree if it kept Lexi out of danger. When it came to people's lives, the Haywards didn't mess around.

And, hey, if all else failed, guilt, in his family, was an intoxicating drug. If things went sideways, his involvement with the Williams case could wreck his career, and he'd damn sure use it to get his sister's cooperation.

"Fine," Brodey said. "I can take you to Hennings & Solomon. That's where her notes are. There's one thing."

"What?"

"We need to look at the Williamses' and Ed Long's bank statements. Ed Long is broke. He skipped out on his landlord last month. So, he's either run out of money or never had any in the first place."

McCall sat back, rested his hands on his belly and eyeballed Brodey. The man had been doing this job long enough to follow the trail of Brodey's thoughts. Whether he agreed with those thoughts would soon make itself evident.

"You got a set of stones, kid. You bust in on my case and now you're thinking the wife may have something to do with this—like we didn't already work that angle? Well, genius, we did. We cleared her."

"I know you did."

"But you're gonna break chops about it. Like I haven't been doing this thirty-five years? Like I'm some baby detective who can't find the john on his own?"

Guys like McCall, any detective really, didn't want to be second-guessed by younger, slicker detectives who went to college, who got their starts by studying criminal behavior in a classroom rather than on the street. Brodey met his gaze straight on. Showing any signs of intimidation would absolutely give McCall power. And Brodey didn't give away power. "All due respect, I'm coming to you. Telling you what we've found. And yes, confirming a few things. This is a cold case. An unsolved murder. I don't think kicking the tires a second time hurts. But that's up to you. It's your case skewing the city's unsolved violent crime stats."

Brodey stood. He'd said his piece. If McCall wanted to ignore what he'd found, that was his problem. It would eat Brodey alive, tear at him like acid in his gut, but he'd walk away. He had to. Now that he'd admitted working the case, he'd have to back off or be subject to sanctions when McCall went to the higher-ups.

But Brodey wouldn't leave this alone. Not completely. His sister was a skilled investigator. He'd stay in the background, advising her until they busted Ed Long and possibly Brenda Williams. Lexi he'd have to keep close, make sure she stayed safe. After last night, a damned fine option.

Right now, sitting in this interview room, despite a beefy, hardened detective—damn, he didn't want to be this guy in thirty years—trying to aggravate him, Brodey's life didn't stink.

"What's the matter, Junior? You gonna take your ball and go home?"

Thirty years.

A stream of mental curses he'd love to unleash banged around in his head. *Stay calm.* Once again, he set his shoulders. "That's the thing, McCall. It's not my ball. It's yours."

Bang. The detective flew out of his chair, his face hurtling beyond crimson and landing on blue.

"What?" Brodey said. "You're gonna take a swing at me? That'll be easy to explain."

The big man halted, literally skidding to a stop as his reality took hold. He had an unsolved case, new leads provided by a detective who shouldn't be anywhere near said case, and now he wanted to bust that detective up. Truth be told, the guy was big enough to pummel Brodey. He'd give him a go, make McCall work up a sweat and maybe get a few good licks in, but the bum elbow wouldn't help and he'd wind up with a whupping.

But McCall unclenched his fists, backed up three steps, and the redness in his face, all that surging blood, drained. Within seconds, his color reached the pasty white that came with a Chicago winter.

Or years as a homicide detective.

McCall leaned against the wall, crossed his arms and contemplated the floor. "You really boxed me in, didn't you, Hayward?"

Again, the hardened detective's ego had him veering toward the negative. *I don't want to be this guy.* If this was what thirty-five years on the job did to a man, Brodey would be taking Lexi's advice and finding a hobby. Fast.

"I don't see it that way, McCall. If Ed Long is a murderer, I helped you solve your case. Do you have the financial records?"

"Of course I do."

"Then let's start there. See if there's a money trail."

LEXI UNLOCKED THE front door on the Williamses' home and strode inside. Behind her, Brodey's father carried two sample books in each hand, saving her a second trip to her car. This would be life with an assistant. She couldn't wait. A helper and a fellow creative to bounce ideas off of, to sketch with, to plan with. They'd work side by side building her—their—business together. In a few years, Lexi wanted to see her name among the top five designers in Chicago—maybe in the *country.* Why not? Talent, hard work and the right assistant would get her there.

First, she needed to get this house done so the real-estate agent could sell it in time for her to get her bonus. Without the bonus, there'd still be an assistant—and an office—it just wouldn't happen for another six months. In which time, she might collapse from lack of sleep, fall into a lifelong coma and never have sex with Brodey Hayward again. And that might be the biggest tragedy of it all.

"Ew," she said.

Mr. Hayward swung the sample books onto the kitchen's center island. "What happened?"

"Nothing. I was thinking."

About comas. And world-class sex with your son. A burst of heat shot into her breasts because—thank you, thank you—Brodey Hayward was an ace in bed. He'd managed to light up every inch of her body, something she'd never experienced before and wanted plenty more of.

I need that assistant. Without the assistant, her Brodey time wouldn't happen. Particularly when he went back to work. Assuming he wanted to continue spending time with her. Maybe one night was all he'd wanted and now they were done.

Nah.

Sure didn't seem that way.

And wasn't this *exactly* what she didn't want in her life? When she'd walked out of her ex-fiancé's office, she vowed to never invest that much of herself in another person again. In the beginning with him, she thought she'd had it all. A rising superstar in the financial world, a caring, patient man who understood her and her business. Instead, she got a person who kept her up at night worrying over silly and not-so-silly things. A person she loved enough that it drove her to debilitating stomach issues when he'd betrayed her, a person so selfish that he'd left his damned office door unlocked while he had *sex* with his *intern* on his desk.

Moron.

Life this past year had been busy, and maybe a little lonely, but when she managed to sleep, she did it like a champ. Every night when she finally dropped into bed, whether from exhaustion or her solitary life where she didn't concern herself with a mate, she passed right out.

A voice—Mr. Hayward—pulled her from her stupor and she spun back to him, this man whose son had his emerald eyes and dark hair. The build was all wrong, though. Brodey was taller, leaner where his father had bulk. Oh, she needed to get Brodey out of her head and get some work done. "I'm sorry. I didn't hear you."

He pointed to the laundry room. "Is this the room?"

The murder room. "Yes. You know, your son is quite stubborn. He won't let me rip up the floor."

Mr. Hayward grinned. "That's my boy. Stubborn and conscientious."

"Which I think is wonderful. But I have work to do. If there's still evidence in there, we need to collect it so I can get to work."

"You want me to talk to him?"

Somehow she didn't think Brodey would appreciate his father running interference between them. An alpha through and through, he'd want to deal with her directly. "No. I'll talk to him. But thank you."

Leaving her standing at the center island, Mr. Hayward checked out the laundry room. He reached in, flipped on the light.

"What's this box?"

A box? When she'd left yesterday, the room had been empty. Nate. Could be he dropped supplies off. She wandered to the doorway. In the middle of the room sat a cardboard box, roughly fifteen inches all around. The top flaps where interlaced but unsealed.

Two things immediately registered. One, if these were supplies, the box was in awfully good shape for Nate's standards, and two, the amount of tile they needed for this room wouldn't fit inside a box that size.

"Lexi?"

"It's not mine. It could be supplies from my contractor."

"But you don't think so."

She met his gaze and a nasty, sour taste poured into her mouth. "No. I don't think so."

"I'll open it. See what's what."

"Wait. Should we call the police? What if it's..."

What? *A bomb.*

Was she turning into Brodey now with worry and paranoia ruling her life? Still, after finding the flyer in her house last night, anything would be possible.

As if she were some feebleminded civilian, Mr. Hayward tilted his head, his face a cross between pity and amusement. "And if it's supplies from the contractor?"

That would be her luck. The first time ever she suffered a bout of paranoia and it could be paintbrushes. "You're right. I'm sorry. A little jumpy I guess. I blame this on your son. Before I met him, I wasn't paranoid. He's a maniac, you know."

Mr. Hayward smiled that same lightning-quick and incredibly charming smile Brodey liked to hit her with. "Maybe. But he's also a cop. A damned good one. You want to wait outside while I check this box?"

She sure did. But no, as with the note left in her home the night before, she refused to give in and run from her life. "No. I'll stay."

Squatting next to the box, he checked it from different angles, not speaking a word. Listening maybe? She didn't know. Did bomb timers even tick anymore? Weren't they all digital? Again with the paranoia about ticking bombs.

It paid off, though. By the time she refocused on Mr. Hayward, he had the flaps of the box open. For a few seconds he remained silent and Lexi studied the back of his head, where wisps of gray mixed with his dark hair. "What is it?"

"A blanket."

Now, that was weird. Who would leave a blanket in the middle of the laundry room? And why? She wandered over and peered over Mr. Hayward's shoulder. A flash of faded red caught her eye and she studied the two-inch trim. The patchwork. The flashes of pink here and there.

She gasped, holding her breath until her chest ached, and Mr. Hayward spun back to her.

"What is it?"

"That quilt."

"You recognize it?"

"It's my grandmother's. It should be on the shelf in the back of my closet."

Chapter Eleven

"You got here at what time?"

Brodey stood in the Williamses' laundry room, hands on hips, mind absolutely disintegrating, while his dad explained to him and McCall how the quilt was discovered. Thirty minutes ago, he'd been in an interrogation room sorting through financials and now—boom—he had another problem.

And it was a big one.

"Around ten forty-five," Dad said. "I opened the box at ten-fifty. I checked the time."

McCall moved to the door leading outside. Hands on his knees, he bent low to inspect the lock. Lexi scooted beside Brodey, arms folded, fingers digging into her blazer with enough force to practically protrude through the material. From his vantage point, her entire body appeared stiff. As much as she tried to soften her facial features, the sucked-in cheeks were a dead giveaway of the tension paralyzing her body.

He set his hand on her shoulder only to have her flinch in return. "You okay?"

"All I did was hang a few flyers and call that damned phone number. Why is this person harassing me? I mean, he broke into my house, stole my quilt and brought it here for me to find? Why?"

Whoever this was—and Brodey was pretty damned sure it was Ed Long—was in panic mode. For whatever reason, he'd fixed on Lexi as the one reigniting this case and aimed to terrify her enough to get her to back off.

"Because he can," Brodey said.

"I didn't even realize the quilt was gone."

"Lex, it was only last night."

"Still. I should have checked the closet. I checked everything else."

"Give yourself a break. I didn't check the closet, either. And I'm a cop."

McCall finished inspecting the lock.

"Anything?" Brodey asked.

"Nah."

"So how'd they get in? All the windows locked?"

His father nodded. "Checked 'em all."

"Which leaves the possibility that someone had a key."

Lexi's mouth dropped open, her face stretching long. "Like Nate? Or Brenda? Stop it."

"Hey." He waved one hand. "You want to walk around in your the-world-is-beautiful utopia, knock yourself out. But my guess is it would take a helluva lock picker to handle these locks. Maybe that's the case, but I doubt it. If the locks weren't picked and the windows are intact, someone got in here using a key."

"Brodey, you can be a jerk sometimes."

Great. Name-calling. "Why? Because I can't drill it into your head that sometimes people you think are innocent aren't? That people you trust shouldn't be trusted? You, of all people, should know that."

The minute—no, the second—it came out of his mouth, he regretted it. And by the stunned look on her face, those big hazel eyes so wide, he knew the arrow had hit its mark. She'd confided in him, trusted him with the fact that her ex-fiancé had betrayed her, and Brodey had just used it against her. Yeah, he could be a jerk sometimes.

"Like I said, *Detective*, you can be a jerk sometimes."

Completely aware that his father and McCall were dialed in and waiting for the next round, he held up his hands. No sense giving them a show. His father he didn't mind. He told him everything anyway. McCall? He didn't necessarily know him. Didn't necessarily trust him, either. "I'm sorry. That was a cheap shot."

"Ya think?"

Venom—pure and deadly—glistened in Lexi's eyes. Ms. The-World-Is-a-Beautiful-Place had a temper. "Lex—"

"Oh, Brodey. Just shut up. You've said enough."

All at once, his father let out a low whistle and McCall cleared his throat. Brodey had to laugh. Yes, indeed, quite a show. Time to get this conversation back on track. Later, he'd talk to Lexi, find a way to apologize for being a world-class moron. He turned to McCall. "You need to take this quilt into evidence."

"I'll get the crime-scene people in here and do a supplement to the report from Lexi's place last night. Did you get the badge number of the cop who responded?"

"Yeah." Brodey dug into his pocket for his notepad. "683. Ericson."

"All right. I'll get a hold of him and add this." McCall shrugged. "Who knows, maybe we'll get some DNA or fibers."

Off to the side, Lexi shifted. "What happens then?"

"Then," Brodey said, "we hope like hell we get a hit on DNA from the night of the murder."

THE SECURITY SYSTEM was in.

Lexi curled her lip at the ugly keypad disrupting the flow of energy to the left of the doorway. All that time spent sampling paint colors and that eyesore had just wrecked her wall. She'd have to come up with a way to cover the nasty-looking thing. Make it more unobtrusive and perhaps use a hinged frame to hide it.

As if it sensed her negative opinion regarding its appearance, the keypad beeped. Actually, it was more of a shrill, earsplitting whine.

Dear.

God.

Brodey stopped pushing buttons and glanced at her. "Are you paying attention?"

To the sqwauking, yes. His activity, not so much. She shook it off. "I got distracted. Sorry. Can we change the tone of the beep?"

"I know you hate this. But it's important."

"Just keep reminding me of that."

"I said you could come to my place."

"No. This is my home. I'm not running from it." She gestured to the keypad. "Show me again how to use this beast."

Five minutes later, he'd reviewed all the buttons on the keypad and gave her a cheat sheet of the codes. One for motion detection, one for glass break, one for both. All of it was too much.

"I think I've got it. As loud as that beep is, I certainly won't forget to disarm the system when I come in."

What she needed now was food and a glass of wine. After this day, maybe she'd take the bottle. Seven o'clock and she'd just realized she'd skipped lunch. By the time they'd gotten through at the Williamses' home, she was dangerously close to running late for her afternoon appointments and gobbled a handful of cashews she'd found in a bag at the bottom of her purse. From the look of the tattered bag, they'd been there awhile. She'd eaten them with gusto, though. What a life.

And they still hadn't talked about their little tiff today.

Wow. That Brodey knew how to deliver a zinger. Between the overbearing protectiveness and the constant lecturing, he was far from perfect. But, unfortunately, part of her loved that about him and it made it hard for her to stay mad. After all, there were worse things than having a man worry about her. Considering the last man in her life never did—on any level.

Brodey's expertly delivered zinger had stunned and hurt her, but at least he'd recognized it and apologized. She looked over at him. "I want to talk about what happened today."

"Good. Me, too. I was wrong. Too wound up and I took it out on you."

"I didn't like it."

He nodded. "As soon as I said it, I knew I screwed up." He rubbed his hands over his face, held them there a second before dragging them away. "You scare the hell out of me. I don't think you sense danger when you should."

"And I think you sense danger when you shouldn't. Maybe that comes from being raised by someone in law enforcement and then seeing it firsthand, but I am who I am, Brodey. And I have no desire to change. If I wanted to see the world the way you do, I'd become a cop. Simple as that."

"I'm sorry. It won't happen again."

Easily, she could continue this conversation and pound on him more, but really…not her style. He'd apologized and admitted his mistake. That alone was worth something. A lot of men would have attempted to justify their actions. Make her question herself. Not Brodey. He owned it.

"Thank you," she said. "Are you hungry?"

He angled his head, squinted a little. "That's it?"

"I said what I needed to."

"Huh."

"This may shock you, but I have no interest in making this a world crisis. It happened, you apologized, we move on." She grinned in that tight way people did when sarcasm was needed. "I hardly think that transgression requires me to banish you from my life."

"Thank you. And, for the record, I think you're amazing. I'd have definitely made me suffer longer."

"Yeah, well, remember this moment when I do something you don't agree with." She swirled her hands. "Come to the dark side, Brodey, and see the world with rose-colored glasses. You might like it."

He laughed. So did she, and the misery of the day suddenly didn't seem so bad. Being mad at him took too much energy and zapped her creatively. All of her afternoon appointments had been a struggle. She'd managed a few good ideas, but not nearly her best work. She'd make it up to the clients. Without a doubt, her next ideas and sketches had to be spectacular.

Even if it killed her.

"So," she said, "I need food. You?"

"Starved."

"I'll order us a pizza. I like veggie."

"You're joking, right?"

She laughed. God, she loved how he made her laugh. "I wish you could see your face right now. No. I'm not joking. I like veggie pizzas. No meat. If you want meat I'll get two smalls."

"I don't mind the veggies, but you sure as hell need some meat on there. Get me a supreme."

"Ew. Hope you weren't planning on kissing me tonight."

"Honey, I'm planning on doing a whole lot more than kissing you."

And oh my, that sounded promising. "I guess we'll see about that."

He dropped onto her sofa and tossed his messenger bag on the coffee table. "After you order, wanna help me look at the Williamses' bank statements? You've got the eye for detail."

Lexi ordered their pizza, poured two glasses of wine and joined Brodey on the sofa. "You do drink wine, don't you?"

So much she needed to learn about this man.

"I'm more of a beer guy, but wine is good, too."

"Got it. I'll add it to the list."

The carefully arranged photography books were moved off the coffee table and set on the floor. A week ago, she'd have gutted him for disturbing the balance of her carefully crafted room. Now? After all he'd done, she'd suck it up and allow him these minor intrusions. As long as it didn't include breaking her heart. That, he was not allowed to do.

He spread the statements across the bare surface of the table and snap, snap, snapped his fingers in front of her face. "I'm losing you again."

"No. You're not." She nudged him with her elbow. "That time I heard you. We're looking for a break in the pattern. Anything that looks odd."

"Correct. I looked at these this morning, but didn't have time to study them. McCall told me Williams moved money a lot. He constantly played with his own portfolio. You'll see all the transfers."

Lexi scanned the rows of numbers on one statement then moved to the next...and the next. *Holy moneybags.* Page after page indicated tens of thousands of dollars randomly withdrawn from the accounts.

"Wow," she said.

"Yep. He kept a money-market account he parked cash in every month. If they ran low, he or Brenda—she was a cosigner—would move funds from the money market into their checking account. He liked to have a minimum of twenty grand liquid at all times."

"Nice slush fund."

Someday she'd have that slush fund. Unlike Jonathan Williams, she'd use it for security purposes. To make sure the mortgage and bills were paid.

"Sometimes," Brodey said, "the amounts varied from five hundred to thousands of dollars. We don't know how much of that money, considering the Feds were investigating him, was his own."

He pushed one of the reports away and slouched next to her, resting his head back. Eyes narrowed in concentration, he appeared focused and—well—male. Incredibly, beautifully male. She'd love to sketch him at this moment, capture the intensity, the curve of his jaw, his straight, sculpted nose, his lightly curling hair. Not in this lifetime would she call Brodey Hayward pretty. Some men were. Her ex for instance. Perfectly groomed, well dressed, all of it screaming privilege. Never Brodey. Brodey was a man's man, rugged and strong and comfortable in torn jeans because that was who he was and accepted it.

Touch him. Go ahead. Why not? If it ended the way it had last night, she didn't imagine he'd complain. Giving her the invitation she needed, he closed his eyes and she moved closer, trailing her fingers over that perfect nose. He flinched and nearly got his eye poked for his troubles.

"What?" He rubbed his nose. "A fuzz or something?"

"No. I wanted to touch you. Really, I want to sketch you, but I don't think you'll let that happen."

"Good guess there." He waggled his eyebrows. "I'll let you do other things to me."

Such a man. "I'm sure you would. As soon as we finish going through these reports and you tell me I can rip up that laundry room. Ticktock, handsome. With each day, I see my bonus—and my assistant—slipping away."

"You're saying if I let you rip up that floor, you'll have sex with me?"

She laughed. "This is what it has come to. I'm bargaining myself for a laundry room."

"You can rip up the floor."

What? She pulled back an inch, opened her mouth, closed it again. *Really?* "Are you teasing me?"

"No. I'm not. Whatever was in there is gone now. I have to accept that and let it go. Tear it up. Let's see what's under there."

LEXI'S HEAD DIPPED forward and Brodey bit the inside of his cheek to keep from laughing. "I know it's shocking, but try to control yourself."

Her face—that gorgeous face that kept him awake at night—lit up, all perky and relieved, as if he'd just handed her the assistant she'd otherwise kill for.

"Thank you, Brodey."

He leaned over, dropped a light kiss on her lips. "The crime-scene people went through it again today when they grabbed the quilt. There's nothing there that'll help us. But we've got the break-in at your place, the quilt and the link between Ed Long and the Williams family. Now we figure out if that link goes further than the defense attorney and how. There's a reason Long is checking you out. He's nervous."

And people who were nervous had something to be nervous about. Particularly criminals. But according to his rap sheet, Ed Long wasn't a violent guy. Unarmed robberies made up his sheet.

Hold up here. Brodey lurched forward, ran his hands over the financial statements on the coffee table, shuffling through them. *Pfft, pfft, pfft.* Nothing. He moved to the next stack.

"What are you looking for?"

"There are no SAR reports."

"SAR?"

"Suspicious activity report. *S-A-R.* They're reports on funky transactions. Filed by financial institutions—banks, brokers, you know—and sent to the Financial Crimes Enforcement Network. FinCEN. It's part of the Treasury Department and helps the Feds identify terrorists and money launderers. Law enforcement can get subpoenas for copies of reports from FinCEN. Helps us figure out if a suspect is moving money around."

"So if the banks think something is hinky, they fill out one of these SAR reports?"

"Yes."

"Can anything trigger the report?"

He shrugged. "Anything suspicious, yes. The banks watch for patterns. If someone suddenly deposits six grand every week after only depositing hundreds for a while, that could trigger it."

Lexi picked up one of the bank statements. "The dollar amounts are all over the place. There's no pattern."

"That could mean this is a dead end or it could mean

Williams knew—because he was a broker and would have been familiar with SARs—if he kept to his pattern it wouldn't look suspicious."

Lexi threw her shoulders back, smacked him on the arm. "Yes! The SAR would have jeopardized his Ponzi scheme if investigators checked his finances."

He touched her nose, grinning at her because—holy hell—he might be crazy about this woman. "I love intelligent women."

Obviously wanting to play, she tapped his nose. "*I* love intelligent men. Especially ones who offer to sleep on my sofa—instead of trying to get lucky—so I don't have to be alone."

"But I did get lucky."

"After you said you'd sleep on the sofa. See how this works?"

Brodey cracked up.

Again she reached over, ran the tips of her fingers along his jaw, and that feeling, that surge of power, ripped through him. If she sensed it she didn't care because that hand kept roaming over his face.

"Please let me sketch you."

Maybe he could work this sketching thing to his favor. "What do I get out of it?"

She hopped up and grabbed her sketch pad. "You'll get something. We can talk while I'm sketching. It helps me think."

"Right. Sure. Just don't spread it around. This gets out, I'll never live it down."

Lexi sat across from him, tucking her legs underneath her into her go-to sitting position. She glanced up at him, a tiny smile playing across her lips and—damn—he wanted to kiss her. He wanted to do way more than kiss her, which, if she lived up to her end of this sketching bargain, he'd be doing before the night ended.

While she kept busy, he leaned back, focused on the financials and possible next steps. All these random numbers could have been Williams trying to fly under the radar. But what about Brenda? She had to question their money being moved. He glanced at Lexi, whose hand flew across her sketch pad. "I wonder how involved Brenda was in maintaining their household accounts."

"Meaning, did she know about all these transactions? Lift your chin a bit. Not too much...perfect."

"According to Jenna's notes, Brenda didn't know about the Ponzi scheme. But if she even looked at their bank statements she'd have seen the constant movement."

Lexi shrugged. "If I married a broker, I don't know if I'd question it. And Jonathan Williams was slick. I mean he swindled people out of millions of dollars and they didn't know it. Convincing his wife of something would be simple. She loved him and trusted him. It's easy to be fooled by someone you love."

That, he knew, was her voice of experience, but this time, when she mentioned her ex, she didn't sound as... what? *Affected.* That was it. Score one for Team Brodey if she was ready to move on from her former idiot fiancé.

"And the bank wouldn't flag small transactions—small to Williams anyway."

Still sketching, she waggled her free hand. "Turn a little to the left."

Seriously? What was he? Some kind of art experiment? He rolled his eyes.

"Brodey, don't be a wuss."

He turned left. "Just warning you, I'm cashing in when this is over."

"As if that'll be horrible?"

He grinned, loving this casual banter between them. He could thank scumbag Ed Long for that at least. Had he not allegedly—God forbid a detective should accuse someone of something without adding *allegedly*—broken into Lexi's place, they probably wouldn't be sitting here cracking jokes about getting lucky.

"Ed Long," he said.

"What?"

"I missed something."

He sat up and riffled through the reports on the coffee table until he found one from the month before the murder.

"Hey! I wasn't done."

"Sorry, babe."

She set the sketch pad down. "What is it?"

"This guy isn't the brightest bulb. He's also, as we know from him skipping on his rent, strapped for cash."

"And?"

He held up the report. "And we need copies of his bank statements to see if any of the transactions on Williams's bank statements match Long's. My guess is if the bank suddenly sees Long depositing large amounts they're going to—"

Lexi smacked her sketch pad on her leg. "File a SAR."

"Yep."

"How do we get that information?"

"We tell McCall to get a subpoena."

Chapter Twelve

"Hayward," Brodey groaned into his phone.

He blinked a couple of times, working the morning fog from his brain while he focused on the fact that McCall was calling him at six in the morning. A morning that came after another night of shortened sleep thanks to the beautiful, if not sometimes annoying, Lexi Vanderbilt.

"Junior," McCall snarked, "you gettin' soft since you been on leave? Get the hell out of bed."

Beside him, Lexi rolled over, her arm flinging sideways and blasting him square on the beak. Yikes. It was like sleeping with a circus act. Slowly, trying not to wake her, he shifted sideways, got to his feet and went to the still-dark living room, where the Chicago dawn had yet to do its magic and light the place up. "What's happening?"

"Got your subpoena for the SARs. Sending it over now. Also got one for his bank records. Bank opens at seven. I'm heading over there."

"Okay. You going back to your office afterward? I'll swing by."

"Yeah. I'm out."

The line went dead. Apparently that was the end of

the conversation. Brodey tossed his phone onto the couch in the general vicinity where he'd left his clothes the night before. He'd never again be able to look at that couch without picturing Lexi sprawled across it. Naked.

Waiting.

Yes, sir. Helluva night.

She wandered into the room wearing only a tank top and a pair of skimpy underwear. Definitely no bra. *Good morning, sunshine.* She bumped the wall and dropped a few other choice words. "Stupid wall."

Brodey snorted. "I see you're cranky in the mornings. You kiss your mother with that mouth?"

"All the time. It takes me an hour to wake up. If I could mainline coffee I'd do it."

Good to know for future mornings. What a switch this was, concerning himself with her morning habits. Something to get used to for sure. He blew air through his lips. "I have good news for you."

She threw herself across the couch, landing on top of his clothes and phone, and curled into a fetal position. "What is it?"

"McCall got the subpoenas. We'll have financial reports on Ed Long this morning. What's your schedule? Besides letting me take you back to bed?"

That got a smile out of her. "Why?"

He smacked her on the rear and ran the backs of his fingers down her thigh, then back up again as he formed a to-do list for the day. "Because I'm meeting with McCall to go through these reports. I can get my dad to hang with you, but I know he's got an appointment at nine. I'd like to park you somewhere safe until he can get there."

"Brodey," she said, "you're not parking me anywhere. I have two potential clients today. Both on the North

Side. Big opportunities. And I'm not missing them. Bad enough I can't keep up with my voice mail. I'm not about to start blowing off new opportunities."

"Lexi," he said in that same don't-be-an-idiot tone she'd hit *him* with, "I'm not asking you to blow off clients. I'm figuring out how to keep you out of trouble while you meet with them."

She stretched her legs and rolled to her back and—*oh, mama*—could he figure out a way to marry this woman without having to wake up to her cranky moods each morning? Maybe he could leave for work before she got up. And since when did he want to marry anyone? Much less a crabby, sexy-as-hell interior designer.

She sat up, stretched her arms over her head and—yeah—that tank top didn't leave a lot to the imagination. "Sweetheart, as soon as we finish this conversation, I'm taking you back to bed and putting a smile on that crabby face."

"I thought you were in a hurry."

"I am. Sometimes being in a hurry is more fun. Now, what's your schedule?"

She stood, walked over to him and hooked her arm into his, leading him back to the bedroom. "My first appointment is at nine. It's a high-rise with a doorman. You can drop me off. The other one isn't until noon."

"My dad will take you. I'll call him."

"Can we not talk about your dad right now?"

"Honey, we don't need to talk at all."

MCCALL SLAPPED A manila folder, its edges perfect and untorn, on top of the scarred veneer table in the PD conference room. At least they'd moved from the interview room this time. In the battle of stale odors, the antiseptic smell in this room beat the hell out of sweat any day.

"Anyone asks," McCall said, "you were here for a visit. You get caught near this evidence, we'll be pulling answers from our rears. I'm not risking evidence getting thrown out because a defense lawyer got wind you saw it."

Brodey set his hand on the file and dragged it across the table. If McCall was anything like him, when he received new evidence, he stored it in a new folder. The folder McCall just unloaded? That sucker was too perfect—too new—to be old evidence. "Understood. Whatcha got?"

"Junior, your hunch paid off. These are your SARs on Ed Long."

Yeah, baby.

McCall tossed another folder—this one tattered and ripped. "I also found another set of financials. They were in the bottom of the box. Someone shoved them into a separate folder. Drives me crazy."

"More financials?"

"Yeah. A second money-market account. Brenda was a cosigner but he was the only one who signed the checks. We pulled copies of every one. No Brenda."

"Maybe that's the account he was moving all the Ponzi scheme money through."

"Could be. *Millions* moving through that account."

Inside the newer-looking folder Brodey found four separate SAR reports on Ed Long, each containing his address, Social Security and driver's license numbers. Farther down was the good stuff. The details of how and why a SAR had been triggered on one Edward G. Long. Brodey skipped over the second section to the bottom of the page and the three rows of check boxes. Beside each box were options on different forms of suspicious activity—bribery, identity theft, check fraud. The only box checked on this particular report indicated a significant transaction had occurred for no apparent purpose. Meaning, Ed Long deposited money—four times—in a manner completely out of his normal pattern.

And, lookie here, the date range of the suspicious activity occurred three weeks before Jonathan Williams, financial fraudster, met his maker.

"Now we're talking."

"What?"

From his messenger bag, Brodey grabbed the copies of the financial reports he and Lexi had reviewed the night before and spread them on the table. "These are Williams's bank statements. Tons of transactions, big and small. This guy was obsessed with moving money. I'm thinking if we can match any of his transactions to Ed Long's SARs, it's worth taking another look at the loving wife."

McCall scooped up the financials and dug a pen from the inside pocket of his sport coat. "I follow. Give me the dates on the SARs and the transaction amounts."

"First one is for nine grand. November 5."

McCall scanned the pages and let out a low whistle "Nothing."

"Damn. Nothing even close?"

"Well, there's a few in that range, but they're odd numbers. Eight thousand one hundred and twenty, nine thousand five hundred and fifty-five. Nothing in flat amounts. You didn't think we'd get that lucky, did you?"

Yeah, actually, he had. But this was detective work and why he loved it.

Performing the same exercise, they reviewed all four SAR reports. No matches. *Son of a gun.* He knew—knew—there had to be a connection here. Call it instinct, call it a hunch, call it whatever, but in that moment Brodey understood how detectives got tunnel vision.

How they sometimes followed a path that didn't necessarily add up, but still managed to make a case. All along, from the day he graduated from the academy, he'd sworn he wouldn't be one of those cops who didn't keep an open mind.

Until now.

He sat back, breathed in. *Get it together here.* The other folder, the beat-up one, sat untouched. Another account that apparently Brenda Williams had never signed checks on. Something itched the back of his neck and he slapped his hand over it. "We're sure Brenda Williams never did anything with that money market?"

McCall gestured to the folder. "Check it yourself."

Sure would. He sat forward, shoved the SARs aside and opened the other folder. "Give me that pen." McCall tossed him the pen and Brodey went to work, scanning the money-market account's statement. When he hit the dates for the end of November, just a few weeks prior to the murder, he slowed his scanning, read each date, then checked the dates on Ed Long's SARs. No exact matches. But they were close.

Check the amounts.

Quickly he scanned the amounts, sliding the tip of the pen down over the column of numbers.

Nine grand.

Holy hell. Two days before Long deposited nine thousand dollars into his bank account, someone withdrew the exact amount from Jonathan Williams's account. Boom. The itch at the back of Brodey's neck turned to a full-on burn that lit his entire body.

"I got something." He circled the amount and the date on the money-market statement and slid it across to McCall. "It's a match. Could Williams's wife have forged his signature?"

McCall's lower lip shot out. "I guess. Check the other SARs."

Brodey grabbed the reports, laid them out in front of him and matched the three additional amounts on the SARs—all totaling fifty thousand dollars—to funds taken from the Williamses' account. He slid them across the table to McCall, who studied them for a few seconds.

The seasoned detective banged his knuckles on the table. "Son of a—"

"We got her. Somehow she withdrew fifty K from their money market without her husband knowing it. She had him murdered."

McCall pushed back from the table. "Time to *chat* with the grieving widow."

"Yep."

McCall pulled a face and slouched back, shaking his head. "Junior, you gotta sit this one out. I'm sorry. You can't be anywhere near this."

As a general rule, competition ran hot between detectives. Who caught what case, who closed how many cases, who got what convictions, it never ended. Brodey wanted to believe he was innocent in the whole thing, but—nah—he could be a dope among dopes when it came to one-upping another guy.

In this instance, hard-nosed McCall, King of the Dopes, appeared genuine in his apology for drop-kicking Brodey. "I know," Brodey said. "Call me when you're done."

LEXI FINISHED HER morning appointment with the Baldwins just before ten-thirty and marveled at her luck. Not only that, but also the appointment went well—seemed to anyway. One could never tell. The extra good news in this trifecta of luck was she had time before Mr.

Hayward—her *bodyguard*—arrived to shuttle her to her noon appointment.

She stepped off the elevator at the lobby level in the Baldwins' high-rise and her heels tapped against the marble floor, echoing in the three-story entry. The doorman rushed to open the door, but Lexi pointed to the corner where three leather chairs—dark chocolate, simple, but elegant design—sat unoccupied. "My ride won't be here for a while. Do you mind if I wait in here?"

Because if she waited outside, aside from a solid case of frostbite, one Brodey Hayward would have a mental breakdown over the risks involved with standing on a street in Chicago. In daylight.

The doorman nodded. "Of course, ma'am."

"Thank you."

She set her briefcase and sample book on the floor next to her chosen chair, the one pointed away from streaming sunlight. A good dose of sunshine during a Chicago winter was nice, but not when she didn't have sunglasses to cut the glare. Sitting down may have been a mistake. Particularly since she'd slept only a few hours the night before—thank you very much, studly Brodey—and fatigue suddenly pressed in on her. With the extra time, she could close her eyes for a few minutes. Enjoy the quiet.

Phone calls, Lexi.

Endless phone calls that hopefully one day soon her assistant would be fielding. Between the potential bonus from the Williams project and possibly landing one of the two clients from this morning, she'd be able to afford the assistant and a small renovation on the garage.

And more than five hours of sleep a night.

Well, if Brodey let her sleep. She hummed to herself and the image of what they'd done on her now-not-sovirginal sofa heated her cheeks. God, the man's passions ran deep. He did everything—yes, everything—with intensity.

Phone calls, Lexi. Banishing thoughts of Brodey, she let out a long, satisfied sigh. Phone calls meant happy clients, happy clients meant more revenue, more revenue meant an assistant, an assistant meant free time to spend with Brodey and all his magical intensity.

Phone calls it is.

On cue, her cell rang. *Happy clients.* She dug in her coat pocket and checked the screen. Ah. "Hi, Brenda."

"You witch!" she spat, the word stabbing like a ten-inch knife.

Lexi lurched back, her shoulders slamming against the back of the chair. She checked the phone's screen again in case she'd seen the wrong name. Nope. Brenda Williams. "Brenda? Are you all right?"

"Do I sound all right? I was just visited by a detective. Someone named McCall. Apparently, that other detective you hired has stirred things up."

Uh, she hadn't *hired* him. Maybe her connection to Mrs. Hennings got the ball rolling, but Lexi wasn't the one who agreed to let them help with the investigation. Although, this didn't seem to be the time to argue that. "What happened?"

"He walked in here and asked me if I murdered my husband!"

Lexi gasped, but Brenda kept rolling.

"It's not bad enough that I'm dealing with the fallout from his crimes—the humiliation and betrayal alone—never mind trying to explain it to our children. And now this? You brought that Jenna and her brother into my life and now I have the police accusing me of murder."

Energy spewing, Lexi shot out of her chair and paced

in small circles, around and around, rubbing her head with her free hand. "Brenda, wait, please. This is obviously a mistake."

"You bet it's a mistake. And it's one that better get resolved before they arrest me. And what about my children? I trusted you and now I need a lawyer!"

"Okay. Hold on. Please. Let me talk to Brodey."

Brenda made a huffing noise. "Absolutely not. You've done enough. All I need from you are the keys to my house."

"I'm sorry?"

"You're fired. I want the keys to my house here by noon today. Or I call the police and tell them you refused to give them back. Then it's on to social media, letting this city know what you've done to me. Noon, Lexi. Don't think I won't do it."

A sharp *click* sounded. "Brenda?"

No response.

No, no, no.

Lexi stared at the phone in her hand, her blood racing and yet fierce cold turning her feet numb. *Call back.* As upset as Brenda was, even if she answered, there'd be no reasoning with her. The clock on the phone blinked: 10:58 a.m. One hour until her next appointment. One hour. In that time, she could cab it home, grab the keys and run them to Brenda's house. While there she'd talk to her. Get Brenda to calm down and understand that even if she had connected her to the investigators, she didn't control them.

One hour to do all that and get to her next appointment. "Who am I kidding?" she muttered.

Damn it. All she'd done was try to help. To give a grieving widow some answers. And this was what she got? She got *fired.*

Because of Brodey.

No. He wouldn't do that. He wouldn't blindside and *humiliate* her this way. If he knew about McCall, he'd have warned her.

Buried somewhere in this mess she'd find a logical explanation.

Please let there be an explanation.

"Ma'am," the doorman said, "are you unwell?"

Unwell. One way to put it.

This was not happening. She'd worked too hard to allow this fiasco to destroy her reputation.

There goes the assistant.

"I'm fine," she said, grabbing her things. "Thank you. Would you be able to get me a cab, please?"

While waiting on her cab, she called Brodey. The truth was always somewhere in the middle and she needed his version. Then she'd talk to Brenda again. No problem. Misunderstandings happened all the time.

That was all this was—a misunderstanding.

She hoped.

By the third ring, he hadn't picked up and her stomach did a vicious twist. She tipped forward, drawing deep, even breaths—*don't freak out*—until the pain leveled off.

Please answer your phone.

A slight *click* sounded—he'd picked up—and the pressure in her belly released. *Thank you, thank you, thank you.*

"It's Brodey. You know the drill."

Voice mail.

Refusing to panic, she focused on there being a logical explanation for him not picking up her call. He was a good man. He wouldn't ignore her. Any number of things could be occupying him.

The beep sounded and she straightened, determined to battle the hysterical female controlling her body. “It’s me,” she said, hating the pathetic tremble in her voice. “I need you to call me back. Brenda Williams just fired me.”

Ten minutes later and a block and a half from her house, the cab came to a halt in the middle of snarled traffic. *Can’t get a break today.*

She grabbed a twenty from her wallet and shoved it over the seat. “I’ll jump out here. I can walk the rest of the way. Keep the change.”

On her tight schedule, she wasn’t about to wrangle over change. She hauled her sample book and brief-case out of the car and did a quasi-run-walk down the block. Sample books were not made for carrying long distances, and halfway to her cottage, she stopped and swapped everything to the other side. A blast of frigid wind smacked her cheeks and she sucked tiny ice picks of air.

Her phone rang. Scooting sideways, she dumped her sample book on the ground and scrambled for her cell in her coat pocket. Brodey. Excellent. Now they’d straighten this thing out and she’d prove to herself she didn’t have rotten taste in men.

“Hi,” she said. “Where are you?”

“Where am I?” he snapped. “Where are you? My dad was early and the doorman at the address you gave him said you left.”

Just one second here. She’d gotten fired and he dared take an attitude with her? Really?

“I’m on my way to my house to retrieve the key to the Williams place. Brenda demanded I return it by noon. After she *fired* me.”

"You should have waited for my dad. You can't go there alone."

Oh, please. As if she had time for one of his annoying lectures. And had he even heard she'd been fired? He'd completely blown by that fact when he should be thanking her for not going ninja on him. For restraining herself when all she wanted was to demand answers and beg him to tell her he hadn't humiliated her.

"Well, Brodey, I don't have the luxury of waiting for an escort. I have clients to see. Considering I just lost one because your friend Detective McCall went to her house and accused her of killing her husband."

"Stop it. He didn't accuse her of killing him."

So he knew.

Fueled by her damned heart splitting in two, a burst of anger soared and she gritted her teeth, fought the rage shredding, absolutely dismantling her from inside out. God, how did she have such colossally bad judgment with men? Honesty shouldn't be a lot to ask for.

She stared at the cars moving through the intersection, focused on the movement, the various shades of blue and silver and red, and brought her mind to a place of detached calm. "You knew about this and didn't tell me?"

"Lex, it happened fast. When was I supposed to tell you?"

"Uh, maybe when you decided she was a suspect?"

"Come on. You knew I hadn't completely ruled her out. You *know* the wife always gets a look."

Now he wanted to weasel out of it on a technicality. And worse, manipulate her into thinking this was her fault because he hadn't shared information with her. He could have at least warned her this might happen. She'd trusted him to do the right thing, to not keep things from her, to not *betray* her. Instead, she'd been blindsided. She may not have walked in on Brodey with another woman, but he hid things from her, and a lie by omission was just as devastating.

Once again, she'd allowed a man to humiliate her.

And break her heart.

Foolish, foolish woman.

"Don't even, Brodey. You never told me things were moving forward on her. Or that McCall was going there today. Frankly, I can't blame her for firing me. I'd probably do it, too. You knew what I had riding on this project, and now she's blaming me because you and your detective buddies accused her of murder. You could have warned me!"

"Why is she blaming you?"

Ugh. Idiot man. "Because I brought you into this! She thinks if you weren't involved, the case would be stalled."

Still holding the phone, she slid her briefcase to her shoulder and scooped up her sample book. The left side of her body would be a war zone after hauling all that weight, but right now, that was the least of her issues.

"She'll calm down," he said. "I'll have Jenna talk to her."

"Oh, you'll have Jenna talk to her? Why, thank you. That makes me feel *so* much better."

A car flew by the intersection and beeped at a truck stopped at the corner. That would be the capper of the day; getting mashed between two vehicles. She'd just hook a right and cross at the other end. Away from this traffic.

"What's that honking?" Brodey asked.

"Cars. It's a city. We have them."

"Are you gonna knock it off with the sarcasm and let me explain?"

"What's to explain? You knew she was a suspect and didn't tell me."

"It's an investigation."

"Oh, oh, oh, it's an *investigation*. Funny. You weren't saying that last night when you had me stripped naked on my damned sofa! You lied to me. I trusted you to do the right thing. God help me, I always pick the liars."

"What?" he roared, his voice so loud she yanked the phone from her ear. "Do not lump me in with that scumbag."

Lexi sucked in a breath at the outburst. Brodey had a temper. Even if she'd never seen it in action, she'd sensed its swarming presence, waiting to be unleashed.

Well, she'd apparently set it free.

"Don't yell at me."

"And what? You want me to sit here and let you compare me to that cheating piece of garbage you almost married? *That's* what you think of me?"

No.

Yes.

So confused. Continuing her trek down the street, she shook her head, blinked back tears. "I don't know what I think."

"Then you need to figure it out. I didn't lie to you, Lexi. I'm not even supposed to be investigating this thing. I'm on leave. My involvement could seriously screw up this case. If they bring charges against her, I'm gonna have to answer for it. I could lose my damned job."

"Now that's my fault, too? I didn't tell you to get involved. Talk to your sister about that. In fact, I don't want to hear from you anymore."

"I'm a homicide detective. There are things related to cases I won't be able to share with you. It comes with the territory. You want full disclosure all the time, and as much as I'd like to do that, I can't. Simple fact."

And, wow, didn't that just sum up their biggest issue. Yes, she wanted honesty. More than that, she deserved it. Clearly, he didn't understand that. "I trusted you and you…you…you *disappointed* me. Brodey Hayward, you broke my heart. And that, I won't tolerate."

Chapter Thirteen

"Lexi!"

Brodey dragged the phone from his ear. Call Ended. Damn it. She'd hung up on him. And eee-doggies the woman was steamed. Well, hell, so was he. After all this damned work, she'd compared him to a lying, cheating scumbag. As much as he enjoyed her, *craved her*, that was a no-go and he really would be a liar if he didn't admit the whole scenario got him riled.

Temples throbbing, he stood on the sidewalk in front of the coffee shop where McCall had given him the what's-what on his talk with Brenda. A fight with Lexi, he didn't need today. Suddenly, his professional and personal lives were crumbling into a hot mess.

Take a breath. Yeah, a minute to regroup. Focus. Get organized.

He inhaled, drew in the filthy fumes from a city bus—just his luck—and released the poison from his body. *Regroup.*

From what McCall had told him, there were no accusations made, but Brenda Williams wasn't stupid. The minute the detective started asking about the suspicious transactions, she'd shut him down, which meant she had something to hide or she'd panicked.

Maybe both.

With the timing of Lexi's call, Brenda must have called her the minute McCall had left. Who else had Brenda called? *Think like a criminal.* Had it been him who'd hired Ed Long to kill his spouse, old Ed would be next on the call list. She'd want to alert him, close ranks and make sure they had their stories straight.

And Long had already tried terrorizing Lexi. Seemed both Brenda and Ed wanted to blame her for their screw-ups. A siren blared, bringing Brodey out of his mind and he turned to see a patrol car whipping around a cab and screaming through the intersection. Sometimes he missed patrolling and that shot of adrenaline that happened when the sirens wailed. Sometimes. Most times, he'd take a good, complex investigation.

Right now, he wanted to do a time reversal, go back to the day when his sister asked for his help and tell her to beat it, that he wasn't risking his career for something that would wind up being a pain in the chops.

Yeah. As if he'd ever do that with Jenna. He loved his baby sister too much for that. And she knew it.

Women.

He took two steps and froze. *Lexi's on her way home.* If Brenda had called Ed Long…

A stream of pavement-melting swearwords flew from his mouth. An older woman standing on the corner gasped and shot him a horrified look.

"Sorry, ma'am!" he hollered as he ran by.

His feet hammered against the sidewalk and the joint-shattering pounding shot straight up his legs to his bum elbow. Nothing but issues today.

He'd parked three blocks over. From there it'd take him fifteen minutes, if he got lucky, which wasn't typical lately, to get to Lexi's. She could call him paranoid all she wanted, but if Long had tried scaring her off before they'd had any solid evidence, what in the hell would he do if Brenda had broken the news about a paper trail?

At the second corner, a man pushed the button on the light pole and waited for the walk sign. Forget that. Brodey angled around him and jumped off the curb, where a cabbie screeched his brakes in an attempt to not tattoo Brodey to the pavement. Brodey held up his hand and kept running. "Sorry, dude!"

He stopped at the adjacent corner, his breaths coming in short, hard bursts from the sprint. *Ignore it.* He inched his way into the street, his elbow howling as traffic whizzed by. He'd be in that sling for a month after this. *Come on, come on.* Finally traffic cleared and he darted across the intersection. With only a block to go, he alternately scanned the sidewalk in front of him—no one blocking his way—and scrolled for his dad's number. There. He hit the button.

Voice mail. Of course. "Dad, get over to Lexi's. She's on her way there. So am I. I'll explain later, but bring your sidearm."

LEXI DUMPED HER briefcase and sample bag at her front door and dug out her key. Between the lack of sleep and the emotional onslaught of the past thirty minutes, a sob gurgled in her throat. Blasted man. After a night of pure sin, ecstasy to the highest level, he'd duped her. But, no, she would *not* cry. Damn him. He'd had her thinking maybe, just maybe, he could be trusted. That he wouldn't hurt her. Not intentionally anyway. And he'd done it. All he'd needed to do was be honest with her. Instead he'd lied. He knew what the Williams project meant to her, that she'd finally be able to afford an assistant and have some kind of life again, sleep a few extra hours a night and not die of a stress-induced heart attack anytime soon. And he'd disregarded that. Tossed it aside like last week's moldy bread.

And that might be worse than finding her fiancé with his intern.

She slapped her hand against the front door, and stinging pain rocketed into her palm up her forearm. *Brilliant, Lexi. Way to make it worse. The heck with it. I'm crying.* Why not? After the week she'd had, she deserved a good healthy cry. She flipped the lock and shoved the door open. Immediately, the annoying *beep, beep, beep* of the alarm filled the house, scraping against her eardrums like sharp nails. Thirty seconds. That was how much time she had to punch in the code. *Beep, beep, beep.* She grabbed her sample bag and briefcase, dragged them over the threshold, kicked the door shut—*beep, beep, beep*—and reached for the keypad. *Beep, beep, beep.* "I know, I know. Just shut up."

Before this week, life had been so simple. Busy but simple. No annoying beeps from the alarm, no ugly keypad marring her perfect walls, no man making love to her on her precious sofa.

No strangers invading her house.

The door. She hadn't locked it.

"Shoot."

Beep, beep, beep. She tapped in the code, silencing the alarm—*thank you.* Something squeaked. Oh no. An instant prickle skidded straight down her spine. She hadn't locked the damned door.

She turned toward the door, her body moving slower than her brain would like until finally… *Oh God.*

Ed Long stood in the entryway, his cold, dead eyes squinting at her. Fear stormed her, spreading everywhere at once, her heels, her legs, her arms. Then, as if taunting her, it slowed, prickling along, making her shiver until it reached her neck.

She stepped back, her body moving of its own accord, wedging her between the outside wall and the man blocking the front entry.

Back door.

The front door would be useless. She'd have to get through him to escape. Plus, she had heels on and he'd easily catch her. But she wouldn't stand here having a conversation. Whatever he wanted wasn't good. Not if he'd murdered Jonathan Williams.

Slowly, she slid out of her shoes and he smiled at her, his crooked top teeth flashing. She'd missed that the first time. Not this time. But that menacing look let her know that he knew she'd run.

Which she did.

She tore sideways, her socks slipping on the floor, but she'd gotten a decent jump and focused on the back door at the end of the short hallway.

Almost made it, too. Just past the kitchen, he grabbed hold of her coat, yanking hard and tugging her backward. Momentum knocked her off balance and she swayed left—*don't fall, don't fall, don't fall*—before toppling over.

Still he hung on. She scrambled, her feet sliding against the tile as she tried to get up.

"No, you don't," he said.

"Please. I haven't done anything. Just leave. I won't call the police."

"Too late for that, isn't it?"

He jerked her to her feet, pain blasting her shoulders. On the way up, her arms rubbed against his jean-clad legs, and the stench of his soap, something cheap and medicinal, burned her throat.

"I warned you." He shoved her, hard, and she flew against the sofa, the edge of the arm connecting with her ribs. Ow. Knifing pain sliced into her and the tears started again.

"Please," she screamed, praying someone outside, maybe Mrs. Jenkins, who heard every tiny thing, would hear her.

But he grabbed her again, scooping her up around the waist and tossing her onto the sofa as if she weighed nothing. For a skinny man, he was strong. *Too strong to fight.* Getting away would be her only chance.

"Get out!" she hollered again, still praying for the miracle of her nosy neighbor.

He smirked. "She's not home. I saw her go out half an hour ago. Lucky me, I got a parking spot two doors down. Been waiting on you, Lexi. And now we'll have some fun. And then your boyfriend is next. You two are causing way too much trouble."

Rolling sideways, she got to a sitting position and he leaped on her, straddling her in the exact spot where she and Brodey had made love last night. The image burned in her mind and she smacked at Long, flailing against him when he tried to grab her hands. She landed a punch, right in the chest, startling him for a few seconds. *Groin.* Fist still at the ready, she snapped her arm out.

And connected.

Yes. Her attacker reared back, teetering on the edge of her knees and howling enough that her ears should have bled. He covered his crotch and—*push*—she shoved. One good thrust that sent him tumbling backward, his arms pinwheeling as he tried to catch his balance the second before he landed—*fwap*—flat on his back on the floor.

One chance she had to run and to get out.

She bolted off the couch, made it as far as the hallway that led to the back door before he caught her again. To her right stood her beloved Wedgwood vase. The one she'd been so concerned about after the first break-in. The one that made her realize the intrusion wasn't about money. Ed Long gripped the waist of her slacks and she smacked at him. No good. Too strong. He yanked her to her knees and she hit the floor hard, every bit of that hit blasting through her legs. *God, help me.* She kicked out and her heel connected with his jaw, startling him enough to give her a few seconds. She reached up, grabbed the neck of the vase with her right hand and swung. Whoosh! It bounced off his shoulder. She kicked out again, followed it up with another swing of the vase and, *boom,* clocked him. Right on the head. The vase shattered and its delicate pieces flew, sprinkling over the floor and creating a path of broken glass she'd have to run on. Lexi clawed at the wood and a sharp shard pricked her skin. She winced but leaped to her feet.

And ran.

Back door. So close. Right there. Locked. Got it. Before she had even stopped running, she had her hand out, ready to flip the new dead bolt Brodey had installed. Short, heavy gasps filled her lungs and her head spun from the oxygen burst. She reached for the lock, flipped it and swung the door open.

Frigid air hit her cheeks, brought her mind to a hyperfocus. Just ahead, the side of her garage and the back alley came into view. Get there.

Oooff. A huge weight landed on her and something dug into her shoulders. She went down, crashing to the path leading to the garage, and pain exploded in her hip. "No!"

God, she couldn't get away. So close.

"I'm done messing with you. That boyfriend of yours is talking to the cops. He sent one of them to Brenda's."

And his voice, low and gravelly and angry, fired another burst of panic. Lexi smacked her hand against the pavement. "Help me!"

Now on his feet, he gripped her arm, powered her to her feet, and she finally got a look at him. Blood streamed from the side of his head where she'd clocked him with the vase and a red mark stretched over his jaw where she'd kicked. She'd done some damage. *Do it again.* She would not die on one of the coldest days of the year. Why that should matter, she had no idea, but no. She would not have it.

As tired as she was, she'd hit him again and again and again.

"Let's go." He yanked her toward the garage. "In here."

Not the garage. If he took her in there, she'd never come out. That she knew. And there were enough tools—hammers, axes, saws—from the previous owner to do some real damage.

Just a foot in front of them was the side door to the garage. He kicked out, his heavy boots decimating the hollow door. "Inside. Now."

Another shove sent her stumbling and she sprawled across the cement floor, her hands taking the brunt of it. A few scrapes wouldn't be the worst of it if she couldn't get out.

Once again, she pushed off the frozen floor and got to her feet. Pricks of icy cold shot into her sock-clad feet and up her calves. She screamed again, raging at her attacker, wanting to claw his eyes out. Beat him worse than she'd already done.

Suddenly the assistant she'd wanted so badly didn't

matter. Her growing business didn't matter. Brodey lying to her didn't matter. None of it mattered.

Not if she died.

"Why are you doing this? I didn't do anything."

"Yeah, you did. This case was dead. Cold as they come. For two years. And then you got nosy and put that damned flyer up. You stupid, stupid witch, you should have stayed out of it."

"Whatever Brenda told you—"

"Brenda didn't tell me anything. I don't even *know* her."

His gaze skittered around the garage to the assortment of tools hanging on the walls, sitting on metal shelves or in piles on the floor. Only a small open space remained where all the junk hadn't cluttered together. Closest to him was the workbench and he picked up a rusty screwdriver, ran his hand over the head.

"The plan was flawless," he said. "Flawless. He dies, she collects the money and everyone's out of hot water. No jail for him, no debt for her." He stroked the edge of the screwdriver, then switched hands, stroking it again and again. "Twisted as it was, the plan worked. Until you came along." He shook the screwdriver at her. "And I'm not going back to prison because of you."

SOMEONE SCREAMED.

Two houses down, Brodey heard it. *Outside.* Lexi. Rear of the house. Panic flooded his already bursting veins. Get there. He picked up the pace and again the pressure shot right to his bad elbow. He cut around the edge of the house, bumping the gutter hard enough that it crunched. The sound reverberated in the alley. Way to draw attention to himself.

He hauled down the narrow alley between Lexi's cottage and the neighboring house, easing his steps as he reached the end. He stopped, peeked around the side of the house and scanned the patch of yard. The single-car garage to the left faced the back alley where cars and garbage trucks had access. From his spot, he couldn't see a side door, but the path from the house dead-ended and most of these old garages had an alternate entry.

No Lexi.

Where was she? Inside? Down the alley? Where? He whipped back against the house and squeezed his eyes closed.

"Shut up!" a man shouted from inside the garage.

Gotcha. Brodey visualized the garage. Single car. One large cargo door. Possible side door with a paved path leading to it. Lexi had told him the space was stuffed with junk from the old owners.

"Please," Lexi pleaded.

A door slamming cracked the air and then all sound ceased, leaving an eerie quiet that punctured Brodey's skin. He glanced around. No one at the back door, which only confirmed there was a side door to the garage.

Time for reinforcements. He dialed 911, identified himself, gave the dispatcher Lexi's address and hung up. No time to talk.

He poked his head around the side again. More muffled voices. One deeper—Ed Long; one higher and in a quick, panicked staccato—Lexi. Only two voices. If luck was on his side and it was just the two of them in there, he and Lexi would outnumber Long. A definite plus considering his injured wing and lack of sidearm.

Time to go. He slipped around the side, staying low as he hustled the short distance to the garage. Pressing close to the wall, he moved to the edge of the dwelling and peeked around. Entry door. Lock? No way to tell.

Either way, he had to bust in there, go with the element of surprise and hopefully take Long down before he knew what the hell had hit him.

Still plastered against the house, Brodey inched around the edge, reached for the doorknob, wincing when it caught and clicked.

The door smacked open and he came face-to-face with—yep—Ed Long. Holding a screwdriver. Eyes darting, Long lurched backward, his face littered with that wide-eyed panic Brodey had seen on criminals a thousand times. With panic came irrational decisions. Time to go lights-out. Instincts roaring, Brodey swung, knowing it was going to hurt. The uppercut connected with Long's jaw and made a gut-twisting crunch. Long reeled backward, farther into the garage, arms flying. The screwdriver sailed through the air and he grabbed the edge of the workbench to break his fall. Lexi stood in the middle of the only clear space but hopped sideways and— damn it—went the wrong way. Now wedged into the far corner, her mistake must have hit her because she looked at Brodey, her perfect face drawn and pale and haunted.

"Run, Lex!"

Brodey went back to Long, still righting himself near the workbench, where strewn across the top was every form of weapon—pickax, screwdriver, hammer, a *vice*—Brodey could conjure. Great. A burst of sunlight filtered through the garage door windows, illuminating the interior. He scanned the junk-filled space. Shovels, rakes, extension cords were stored in every available spot. He shifted right, closer to the shovel. One good swing and any weapon Long chose would be knocked loose.

"Brodey?" Lexi said, still standing there.

"Run!"

Long lunged for her, his weapon of choice an ice pick he'd found in the rubble, and Brodey snapped. At that moment, he envisioned Lexi, that pick butchering her, and he knew, no doubt, he'd kill this man to save her.

Brodey dodged left, blocking Long's path to her as he swung the pick, his arm thrusting upward to run it through. Brodey raised his good arm, blocked the swing and kicked. *Boom.* His boot skittered across Long's knee. Brodey pounced, shoving him backward, away from Lexi. The pick came at him again, but the block was late and, oh, hell, the tip nicked him, drawing blood.

Long laughed. And it wasn't one of those sinister ones Brodey had seen in movies as a kid. This laugh was casual. Entertained. Somewhere along the way, Ed Long had gone seriously off his rails.

"Brodey! Back!"

Whoosh. Something flew in front of him and hit Long dead center in the forehead. A spade. Lexi had hurled a garden spade at him. Good for her. It bounced off his head, but drew blood before clattering against the cold cement floor. Long stared down at it with a dazed look that could have been surprise or unconsciousness calling him. He reached up, touched his head where blood trickled, then brought his eyes to Brodey's. Crazy eyes. *Desperate* eyes. And desperate eyes might be the most dangerous of all.

Any heat in Brodey's body disappeared, replaced by frigid chills. He stepped forward and Long came at him again. Brodey circled right, trying to pin his opponent to a corner as they squared off. His foot hit something. Big. He shot a look at it. Fire extinguisher. Compliments of Lexi, something else flew at Long. This time Long was ready and leaned right as a hand shovel arced by him.

He lunged for her.

Extinguisher. Brodey grabbed it with his good hand. If he could get the pin out…but his other arm hung limp at his side from that first crack at his opponent. He bit the end of the pin, yanked it out and hit the handle.

"Lex, move!"

Half a foot from Lexi, Long spun back and a spray of foam hit him square in the chest. Brodey aimed higher. Bingo. Long let out a howl that should have cracked the windows, a long, piercing sound that shredded the musty garage air.

Finally, Lexi darted past him, heading for the doorway.

But she stopped. "Seriously?" he hollered.

"What can I do?"

What could she do? If they lived through this, he'd kill her. "Get the hell out!"

Long rubbed at his eyes, trying to clear the stinging foam. *Go ahead, buddy, rub it all in there.* Brodey grabbed him by the shirt, hauled him the two feet to the workbench. And Lexi, once again ignoring his directive, moved beside him.

"I told you to get out."

"Shut up. Let me help."

Stubborn woman. Fine. "Stand over here. By the vice."

Long swung at her and Brodey, still hanging on with his good hand, kneed him in the thigh. Hard. Long howled. Quickly, Brodey let go, clamped on to his hand and shoved it into the vice attached to the table. "Close that," he yelled. "Fast."

She spun the lever and Brodey watched the sides squeeze against Long's hand. The man howled again. Not tight enough. He could see Long sliding his hand around, playing them, planning his counterattack.

"Shut up," Brodey said. "Keep going, Lex. Two more turns."

After the second spin, he checked the tension on the vice. Good enough. It would at least hold Long until they could tie him up. First, he'd have to get rid of the handle so their prisoner didn't get any ideas about reaching over and loosening the tension with his free hand. Brodey unscrewed the handle and held it in front of Long's face. "You're cooked."

"We'll see."

Ignoring the taunt, Brodey shoved the handle into his back pocket. Long kicked out. Apparently, that caused a whole lot of problems for his hand because he howled again. "Please, man. Let me outta here."

So much for his cocky posturing three seconds ago. "Forget it. But tell me what you did and I'll loosen it. Give you a few seconds to catch your breath."

Sirens filled the sudden silence and Brodey cocked his head to judge the distance. In this city, they could be going somewhere else. Who knew? But how about that, the sirens grew louder. Time to up the stakes on Long. "Dude, I couldn't care less if you talk. But the cops are gonna be here any second, and the way it looks to me is you and Brenda Williams murdered her husband. You're both going down."

"No!"

"Yeah!" Brodey mimicked his squealing voice.

Long swung his head back and forth so fast it should have flown off. Or at least paralyzed him. "She didn't have anything to do with it," he said.

"Right. Really heroic, but there's a money trail. The detectives didn't figure out the trail led to you until you came after Lexi. Now it's done."

"It wasn't…"

Brodey turned to the door, jerking his thumb at Lexi to get out. "Save it for your lawyer."

"She wasn't involved. She's a good mother."

Blah, blah, blah. He'd heard it a hundred times. "Yeah, I know. What was it? An affair? You and Brenda?"

"No."

"Police!"

Long's panic escalated. His gaze shot to the doorway, where Lexi stood, taking it all in, and then he came back to Brodey, again shaking his head hard enough to scramble what little brains he had.

"I swear. It wasn't her. It was him. Jonathan. He gave me a key and told me to kill him."

Chapter Fourteen

Lexi stood by the door, hands curled into fists at her sides, letting her attacker's words sink in. Not in this lifetime would she consider herself a good detective, but this was beyond reason. This insane man who'd terrorized her expected them to believe Jonathan Williams planned his own murder.

"Chicago Police!" a man yelled from outside the door.

Lexi spun sideways, holding up her hands "It's okay," she said.

"I'm Detective Brodey Hayward," Brodey called from behind her. "I'm with Area Central."

"Step outside," the cop closest to Lexi told Brodey. "Show me your hands."

Brodey did as he was told. Weapon drawn, one of the cops stepped into the garage, while the other covered them. If she never again saw the barrel of a gun pointing at her, she wouldn't mind. Right now, after the storm of emotional horror she'd just experienced, her body was too deflated, too spent to feel much of anything.

She slid her gaze to Brodey, whose eyes were on her with that same intensity she'd learned was so much a part of him.

"You're fine," he said. He addressed the officer. "This

man is Ed Long. He just attacked Ms. Vanderbilt. I arrived in the middle of it. Detective McCall from Area North is working the Jonathan Williams murder. Long claims he killed him. We need to get McCall here. Fast."

WHILE THE POLICE did their thing in her garage, Lexi went inside, searching for the comfort of her favorite chair. Sketch pad in hand, she worked with colored pencils, drawing random items for who knew what. Brodey sat across from her on the sofa, their sofa, and she dared not look at him. If she looked at him, he'd try to talk to her, and she couldn't do it. Couldn't form the right words to tell him what she needed to. That she'd been terrified and he'd saved her from Ed Long's torment and she would forever love him for it. But her emotions right now couldn't be trusted. Her *emotions* told her to walk over to that sofa, to Brodey, and curl into him. Cry it out. Take comfort from him and in him because he'd opened up a part of her that had been dead for almost a year.

And it would be easy to do. To just let go.

Only it wouldn't fix the fact that she needed—no—demanded honesty in a relationship and he, given what he did for a living, would never be able to truly open up to her. Some things would stay buried inside him and that, she knew, would terrorize her worse than Ed Long ever could.

So she remained rooted in her favorite chair doing her favorite thing, trying to pretend this was any other day. Sketching was about therapy. About keeping her mind and hands active while she worked through the stress of the situation unfolding before her. Even if her trembling fingers wouldn't allow for anything decent to be created, at least she'd be distracted from thoughts of what happened, and could have happened, in her garage.

The back door creaked and she looked up to see Detective McCall enter the house.

"Well," he said, "this one I haven't seen."

"Tell me," Brodey said.

McCall dropped onto the arm of the sofa, folded his arms over his chest. "This guy is unhinged. According to Long, he met Jonathan Williams through his lawyer. He was doing odd jobs at the lawyer's house and Williams came to pick up his kids at a playdate. Isn't that what it's called these days?"

Lexi nodded.

"Anyways, Williams hired him to do some work at his place. Nothing inside. Yard work, stuff like that. When the Feds closed in on Williams, he panicked. Guy like him? He can't do time. Doesn't have the spine for it. And if he went away, his wife, they were on the outs, would be left in one hell of a jackpot. Between the debt and what the scam victims got robbed of, even if they got divorced the wife would be busted."

"So, he wanted to what? Kill himself?"

McCall rolled out his bottom lip. "Not exactly. He wanted to take care of his kids. Give the mope credit for that. Suicide doesn't get an insurance payout, though. Turns out, our boy Long here is a family man. Believes a man should protect his family above all else." McCall snorted. "Gotta love that."

"And with no insurance money," Brodey said, "the wife and kids are stuck with the debt he'd racked up. She wouldn't even get the house. The government would seize everything."

"Unless he was murdered," Lexi added.

"Unless he was murdered." McCall circled his hand at Brodey. "Those withdrawals we thought Brenda made? Williams did it. He took the money out and paid his would-be assassin. Then Long deposited the money, and with amounts that high it triggered the SARs."

"And here we are," Brodey said.

Lexi was finally maxed out from trembling, and her pencil slipped from her hand and fell to the floor. "The man had himself murdered."

Brodey whistled. "Makes sense. Williams gives Long a key, tells him to sneak up on him in the house and kill him."

"Close," McCall said. "According to Long, he was supposed to show up the next day, but he's a career thief. Murder isn't his specialty. Williams paid him and he started to get cold feet. One night he gets banged up on a bottle of Jack whiskey and goes to the house a day early. Uses the key to go in the side door. Williams hears a noise and comes to check on it. Long startles him and—" McCall formed a gun with his fingers "—bang. Job done."

The man had actually done it. Absolutely horrifying. Lexi uncurled her legs and sat forward. "That explains the broken glass. He must have been carrying it when he went to the laundry room." She turned to Brodey. "Just like you said."

"What about the address book Lexi found?"

McCall shrugged. "Don't know. My guess is Jonathan hid it in the wall, but when Dr. Doom showed up early, he didn't have a chance to get rid of it. It's a helluva mess."

"We stirred things up again."

"Sure did. For the last two years, Long's been keeping an eye on Brenda and the kids. Heck of a guy, this one. He saw you coming and going and followed you to the house last week. If not for you, maybe he'd have gotten away with it."

Somehow, that didn't make Lexi feel better. Maybe they should have left it alone. Brenda Williams would have been debt-free if they had. But a murderer, albeit a murderer who wanted the kids to be cared for, would have gone free.

Later, after a month of sleep, Lexi would weigh the moral arguments. Hopefully, she'd decide they'd done the right thing by solving this case. Right now, Brenda and her kids and the emotional fallout they would again endure made her wonder.

Brodey turned to Lexi, waited for her to meet his gaze. Yes, she was mad at him and didn't think that would be even a remote possibility.

IN THE HOUR since McCall had left, Lexi moved to one of the counter stools, attempting to choke down a glass of water. Well, what was left of it after she'd sloshed it all over herself. No matter how hard she pressed her fingers against the glass, literally willing herself to relax, every little inch of her still trembled. She glanced up at her precious sofa that she'd taken such extreme care not to damage, where she'd finally allowed herself to be a little careless and made love to Brodey. Her precious sofa where she'd been pinned down, fighting for her life.

Forget it. She set the glass on the counter and pushed it away. Water wouldn't control this chaos.

The front door opened and Brodey stepped in, quickly shutting the door behind him and blocking the blast of cold overtaking the room. He took three steps, then stopped. In the short time they'd known each other, he'd learned her *stay back* signals.

"You okay?"

Was she? Hard to tell. Someone had tried to kill her. What were acceptable emotions after that? Fear, anger, panic? All of the above? At a loss for an answer, she remained silent.

"I know you're mad at me," he said.

Mad at him. Yes, she was that. She was also thankful and confused and...heartbroken. She'd fallen in love with a man who kept things from her. Unfortunately, she'd had enough of men like that in her life.

The door swung open again—her home might as well be Union Station at rush hour—and Jenna marched in wearing a long coat, boots and a knit cap and scarf. She looked as if she'd just hopped off a fashion magazine cover. Brodey, ever the gentleman—most of the time—shut the door for her.

"Hey, guys," she said. "Dad called me."

"Hi," Lexi said, suddenly feeling as if someone had opened a pressure valve and let some of the tension out. Being alone with Brodey brought more confusion and she was too hyped up, too *conflicted*, for that.

Jenna, at this moment, was Switzerland.

She may have been Brodey's sister, but she was a woman and understood a woman's emotions. Lexi patted the stool next to her. "Come sit."

Crossing the room, she took her coat off and set it on the arm of the sofa. That damned sofa. Lexi glanced back at Brodey, who had most certainly recognized his sister had been invited to sit, but not him. His eyes were on her, their gazes holding for a long moment, and the sadness rolling between them sawed right through, just tore into Lexi's flesh with agonizing speed. She blinked a couple of times, trapping tears she refused to let loose. Not now. Maybe later.

"I'll let you two talk," Brodey said, his gaze still locked with hers. "I'll call you later. Please answer your phone."

Oh, how he'd gotten to know her. It would be so much easier to walk away again. All this hurt and anger needed time to simmer. Eventually, maybe, they'd be friends. Now, she couldn't trust him. The ultimate death blow for any relationship.

She watched him turn away and open the door. "Jenna," he said, "lock this door."

Always so diligent. That was Brodey.

Jenna hopped off the stool and secured the door. Then she spun on Lexi and narrowed her eyes. "What was that about? I thought you two were, I don't know, dating or something."

Or something.

"We were."

"Past tense?"

"He lied to me."

Her eyebrows hit her hairline and she crossed her arms. "My brother is a nudge, but he's not a liar."

Little sister had gone into battle mode. Lexi reached back for her abandoned water and drained it. "Thank you."

"For what?"

"Before you walked in here I was shaking so hard I could barely hold this glass."

Jenna made her way back across the room, slid onto her stool and patted Lexi's leg. "I know what happened in the garage. My dad told me while you were talking with the cops. Now you're mad at Brodey. What happened? And don't tell me he lied. I don't believe that."

Being an only child, sibling loyalty was foreign to Lexi, and having never experienced it, she hadn't missed it. But the idea of it, that unconditional acceptance, she suddenly wouldn't mind having. "Let's say he lied by omission. He knew McCall talked to Brenda about her possible involvement in her husband's murder. He knew that and he didn't tell me. I was blindsided when Brenda fired me."

"She *fired* you?"

"Yes. If I hadn't talked to Mrs. Hennings about you helping on the case, none of this would have happened." She ran her palm up over her forehead. "Good God, what is wrong with these people that they blamed *me* for all of this? I didn't hire Ed Long to kill Jonathan Williams. How is it all my fault?"

"It's not. That's dumb. Ed Long is a criminal and Brenda is a single mother whose nerves took over. When she gets the full story, she'll hire you back."

Lexi shrugged. "I'm not even sure it matters."

There goes the assistant...

"Of course it matters. It's not right. As for Brodey—"

"Please don't defend him."

Jenna sighed, then scrubbed her hands over her thighs. "I won't. Well, maybe a little, but not in the way you think."

"Seriously?"

She held her hands out. "Just hear me out. I grew up surrounded by cops. I'm still surrounded by cops. Now it's worse because my boyfriend is a US marshal. You think Brodey won't talk about cases, try dating Brent. He's a vault."

"You poor thing," Lexi said.

"You have no idea. Anyway, my dad worked homicides as long as I can remember. Some nights he came home miserable and quiet. It took me years to understand he couldn't talk about his job. He kept his investigations to himself. Maybe he shared some things with my mom, I really don't know. But otherwise, he kept it all to himself. He always worried he'd somehow let something slip and it could blow his case. Brodey grew up with that, too."

"But he knew how important honesty was to me."

"So, it's not about you getting fired, but about him keeping it from you?"

"Yes! If he keeps something like that from me, what else will he keep from me? I walked in on my fiancé—a man I adored, a man I thought was honorable—getting busy with his intern."

Jenna's mouth opened wide enough to drive a truck through it. *"Really!"*

"Yes, really. Do you know how humiliating that is?"

"I'd have shot him."

"Wish I'd thought of that."

"Oh, honey. I'm so sorry."

"It's old news. Better I found out before I married the pig. But honesty is a hot button for me. Everything needs to be on the table. And your brother knew the Williams project was important to me and he let me be blindsided. Worse, he didn't trust me enough to believe I could keep quiet."

Jenna inched her head back and forth. "I don't think that's true."

"Well, what other option is there? And don't tell me it's his job. I understand that. This wasn't just any case. I had personal implications in this. I sat in Brenda's living room and vouched for him. And convinced her to trust him. I helped convince her to let her children look at a sketch of the man who murdered their father. He should have figured out a way to warn me. He didn't have my back, and I can't be with a man who doesn't protect me emotionally. As protective as your brother is, he is clueless when it comes to emotions. He doesn't get it, and for me that's a major thing not to get."

"You should talk to him."

"What good would it do? How do we get beyond him choosing what I should hear or not hear? If it involves me, I'm entitled to know. I'd do it for him. That's what I know."

They sat quietly for a few minutes. Lexi waited for an argument, but none came. At least one of the Hayward siblings understood her. Either that or Jenna simply didn't want to argue.

Lexi could budge on a lot of things. This was not one of them.

BRODEY PUSHED HIS dad's recliner back and settled in to watch the Bulls. Might as well. The fresh injury to his elbow had earned him another trip to the doctor and four more weeks of physical therapy, so he didn't have anywhere else to be tonight. Four more weeks of loafing around, doing nothing but thinking about Lexi's silent treatment.

In the next hour, his mom would remind him he was a single man sitting idle on a Saturday night and he should get a life. Then she'd throw his butt out. But for now, he'd delay venturing into another arctic night. Being here with his family meant avoiding going home to his empty apartment—and empty bed—to obsess about Lexi.

Three days had passed since they'd spoken. Outside of that first night when he'd called to check on her and she'd told him she was fine—he hated that word—she'd gone to radio silence. Their one conversation had been brief. Was she okay? Yes. Did she need anything? No, thank you. Was she still mad at him? Yes.

"Damn," he muttered to himself.

They had the Williams case all wrapped up and Ed Long would spend a good chunk of his life in prison.

Who knew what would happen with the Feds? They'd probably seize the home and auction it to make reparations to the fraud victims. Brenda Williams wouldn't get a dime. The insurance company might even go after her for the money it'd paid out on the life-insurance policy, but at least everyone had answers. Even if the answers stunk.

"Hey," Jenna said from the doorway leading to the kitchen. "Mom just set out pie. If you're interested, you'd better get in there before Brent and Dad destroy it."

"Nah. I'm good. Thanks. If there's any left, I'll take a piece home." He turned the volume up on the game.

"Nice try."

"What?"

"You want me to leave you alone." Jenna held her thumb and index finger up to her forehead. "*Loser.* Why would you even think that trick would work?"

Brodey sighed. "I'm tired. Go eat pie."

She sat in the other recliner and turned sideways to face him. *Yeah, she's not going away.*

"What's happening with Ed Long?"

"Lawyered up. He'll probably take a plea. He's still going away for a long time."

"Did you let Lexi know?"

"Tried."

"She's still mad at you, huh?"

"Don't know."

"Have you talked to her?"

He gave her a hard look. "See, that's the thing. Talking to someone requires that they return your calls, which she won't do. Short of stalking her at her house—not a banner idea—I'm out of options. You need to call her and make sure she's using the alarm. Every time she leaves, she needs to set it."

"And you wonder why she won't talk to you?"

What? His face suddenly got hot. He'd had a hell of a few days with women either telling him all the things he'd done wrong or, worse, not saying anything at all. "What does *that* mean?"

"All you do is nag about how she has to be careful. Not everyone thinks with a cop's mind. And apologize for keeping that Brenda Williams thing from her."

Here we go. Bad enough he had to explain himself to Lexi, who, as a matter of fact, wouldn't *let* him explain. Now he had to report to his sister. "It was an *investigation*. I was supposed to tell her and risk it getting back to Brenda? Come on. You know better."

"Yes, I do. I also know that maybe you could have figured out a way to warn her. Brodey, you're such a dope."

"Hey!"

"She's not mad because she got fired. She's mad because you didn't trust her. Right or wrong, she thinks you lied to her or that you kept things from her. With her history, it's a hot button. You need to apologize. Not because you didn't tell her. That's a tough call. Apologize because you didn't trust her enough to tell her there were certain things you couldn't share. That's what she needs to understand. To her, it looks like you betrayed her to solve this case."

He snorted. Women. "Wrong."

"Is it? What's she supposed to think? The first time you met Brenda, you tagged along with Lexi. Then you asked her to help sketch the crime scene and even review the financial reports. She convinced Brenda to trust you. She had faith in you, and when things broke loose you chose not to tell her what was happening. I know what I'd think."

"That's not what happened. And the Brenda thing wasn't my fault."

She slapped her hand on her thigh and stood. "Justify it however you like, but unless you figure out a way to get Lexi to understand, you're gonna be sitting in Dad's chair by yourself for a long time."

"Listen, Jenna, don't hold back."

Damn, he was tired of people accusing him of messing up. She bent over, kissed him on top of his head, shocking the hell out of him because she'd never done that before and he wasn't sure what to do with it. Although, after the rotten few days, not to mention his mother constantly bugging him to get a life, he didn't mind Jenna's sudden burst of compassion.

"You're a ding-a-ling, Brodey, but you mean well. Eventually, she'll see that. If you really care about her, and I think you do, don't give up."

Dishes clattered in the kitchen and Brodey glanced behind Jenna, where Brent and his dad waited for their pie to be rationed.

"Babe!" Brent hollered. "You want pie?"

She glanced over her shoulder, a small smile lifting her lips, and Brodey's heart slammed. His sister was in love. Knocked out, slam-dunked in love. And Brent was a good guy. Perfect for her in every way because he managed to not put up with her nonsense *and* take care of her at the same time. As happy as that made him, something pinged inside him. With Lexi, he'd had a taste of it. Not enough. Not the full-blown experience as his sister had. Suddenly, he wanted it. Hungered for it.

"Do you have any idea," Jenna said, "how much I love it when he calls me *babe*? I never cared for it before. Hated it, in fact. It always seemed so...I don't know...

sexist. Now? I can't go a day without hearing it. From him. Only from him."

"He loves you."

"Yeah, he does. And he makes me happy." She set her hand on Brodey's shoulder and squeezed. "I want this for you. I want you to know what it feels like to have someone love you that much. Don't give up."

DAY FIVE WITHOUT Brodey proved to be just as miserable as days one, two, three and four. At least he hadn't called today. Was that a good thing? Lexi didn't know. It hurt to see his name on her phone, to hear his voice when he left messages, and now it hurt worse to *not* hear his voice.

At the ugly core, thinking about Brodey simply hurt.

So, she'd gone back to doing what she did best. She worked. From dawn until evening, she reviewed samples, created sketches, caught up with clients and had even managed to land the client she'd seen on the day of Ed Long's arrest. Which meant, without a doubt, she could afford to hire an assistant.

She punched in the alarm code, silenced the annoying beep and set her briefcase in its usual spot next to the locked door. Thanks to automatic timers, the house was well lit. Never again would she walk into a dark house.

A murderer had taught her that.

Her phone whistled. A text. Before taking off her coat, she glanced at the screen. Brodey. So much for him not contacting her today. A text, though. Usually he called and left a voice mail. *Don't read it. Let it go.*

Would it hurt less if she ignored it? Probably not.

She tapped his name on the screen and the message popped up.

Can you come out back?

Out back? An eruption of excitement banged against her chest. Was he here? Putting her thumbs to work, she replied.

You're here?

Yes.

Oh, boy. How did she feel about this? She took a second and closed her eyes, then breathed in and out a few times before responding.

I don't want to fight.

If she knew nothing else, *that* she knew.

We won't. I want you to see something.

What was this man up to? She dropped the phone on the coffee table, went to the back door and peeped out. The darkening sky winked with a few scattered stars, but she could see him in front of the garage, hands shoved into his leather jacket, no hat. As cold as it was, he had to be freezing. She threw the door open. "What are you doing? It's freezing out here."

"I've only been out here a few minutes." He jerked his thumb. "I was in there."

"The garage?"

"Yeah." He waved her over. "I want to show you something."

"Brodey, what are you doing?"

"Just look. I promise I'll go after that."

Still in the doorway, she glanced back inside, down

the long hallway, where that blasted sofa she could no longer sit on, much less look at, taunted her. Whatever this was out in the garage, she needed to face it. And finally tell Brodey she couldn't stand hearing his voice every day. That he had to give her time. Time for what, she didn't know, but all the crying over the past few days destroyed her energy.

She clutched the top of her coat closed and stepped outside, where frigid air burned her lungs. "Brodey, it's so cold. You shouldn't be out here."

He led her down the path to the side entrance to the garage. Four days ago, this garage had been hell.

"Close your eyes," he said.

"What are you up to?"

"Close 'em. I'll guide you in. Don't worry."

After shutting her eyes, she held out one hand and he grabbed it, gave it a squeeze, and the connection, the boost, zipped up her arm. A ball of heartbreak jammed in her throat and she swallowed once, then again—no good—as he led her forward.

"One more step," he said.

But she knew that because the arctic air had been replaced by warmer air inside the garage. "Did you put a heater in here?"

"Yes. You can look now."

She opened her eyes, let them adjust to the interior light and, without moving her head, did a quick scan. Spotless. All the rusty tools were gone; the others, probably the salvageable ones, hung on hooks on the walls. The workbench sat in the far corner and shelves had been mounted above it. Nice shelves, too. Not the cheap ones She stood there, taking it all in. Even the floor had been cleaned. Sure, there were still stains, but the dirt, every bit, had been scrubbed away.

"Oh my…"

Brodey held his hand out. "What do you think? Are you mad?"

Was she *mad*? For two years she'd been wishing she had the time to clean out the garage. And after the torment they'd faced in there, she'd all but decided that damned garage would continue to be her own personal purgatory. "You did this all today?"

"Yeah. Well, I had help. Jenna and Brent took a day off and my mom and dad helped. With the bum wing, there's no way I could have gotten it done in one day. I wanted to start yesterday, but I didn't know if you'd be home. Today, I knew you'd be gone all day."

"Where's all the stuff?"

"Uh, in the trash. Most of it wasn't usable. We saved everything else and moved it to the storage place down the block. Figured you'd want to go through that yourself. At least now you can use the garage for something positive. Put the…uh…other stuff behind you. Did we overstep?"

She reached for him, squeezed his arm. "Of course you did. But I love it. It's amazing. Thank you. You didn't have to do this."

"Yeah, I did."

"Brodey—"

He faced her, grabbed her hand before she could pull away. "Wait. Please. Just one second. Let me talk and then if you want me to go, I'll go. Okay?"

She nodded.

"Great. Perfect. Just have a little patience. I pretty much stink at this."

"You don't stink at it."

"Yeah, I do. Anyway, here goes. I know I hurt you. I'm sorry for that. It was shortsighted. I should have thought it through and explained why I couldn't tell you about Brenda. Should have had that conversation early so you'd know certain things are off-limits. I could give you every reason I've come up with about why I couldn't tell you—and it's a long list." She smiled and it pushed him forward. "But it doesn't matter. All that matters is that I hurt you when I didn't mean to. I realize that now. I get it."

"Do you?"

"Yeah. I do. I didn't before. Shame on me. Now I know you need the communication. Whether it's what you want to hear or not, you need it."

Five days ago, she'd have dropped to her knees and thanked heaven above for this gift. She might still. Was she a fool for wanting to believe him? The old Lexi would say yes. This Lexi? The one who saw Brodey's face every time she looked at the sofa wasn't sure. "I need to know I can trust you with everything."

"You can. Look, I've never…I don't know…I guess I've never had someone who cared about my job. I've had relationships, sure, but none that, well, mattered. I came and went and that was it. This situation is new to me. And I screwed up." He waved his hand around the garage. "This is my way of showing you I'm sorry. Whether you give me a second shot or not, I wanted to show you I can take care of you in every way. I get it. It's about physical and emotional security. My keeping the Brenda Williams thing from you was about my job. I didn't put you first. If I could go back, I'd handle it differently. I'd tell you things were happening with the case that I couldn't share, but that you needed to be prepared. I'd warn you just like you asked. I'm hoping you'll tell me that's good enough. What I do is hard, I'll always have secrets, but…"

"I know."

"You know?"

"Jenna told me about life with a cop. I see it from the other side now. Before, I couldn't. I wanted you to understand why I was mad, though. It wasn't about the case. Not really. It was more that the case was the catalyst."

He nodded. "I get it now."

She grabbed his jacket and squeezed. "Thank you."

"For the garage?"

"For everything. I've missed you. Every time I looked at the sofa, I wanted to put the thing out for trash. All I could picture was you sitting on it, and it hurt even more." She inched closer. "Promise me I can trust you. Please. I need that."

"You can. Absolutely. No doubt. We're good together."

"Even when you're lecturing me?"

He smiled. "Yeah. Even then. Heck, maybe you can teach me to lighten up. See what's good in the world instead of what's not so good." He backed up. "Oh, gotta show you something else."

What now?

He dragged her to the workbench and the unopened box on top of it. The box was about fifteen inches long and had a picture of a ship on it. The *Titanic*. God help them if he wanted to compare their relationship to the *Titanic*. She glanced up at him. "I can't wait to hear this one."

"I bought that. It's a model-ship kit."

"And?"

"You told me to get a hobby. To take up something that relaxed me. Like you have with sketching. I took your advice. I'm going to build model boats. I may even get this one done before I go back to work. So now you have your sketches and I'll have model boats. We can do it together when it's quiet. What do you think?"

She picked up the box, read the contents. "It's a lot of pieces."

"Yeah, but I like putting pieces together. If I could do it with you next to me, even better. What do you say, Lex? Want to build boats with me and show me what things can be instead of what they are?"

"Oh, boy, Detective. That sounds like fun."

He waggled his eyebrows. "I hope so because, honey, I'm just getting started."

* * * * *